THE MOON'S EYE

THE MOON'S EYE

A.J. CALVIN

THE RELICS OF WAR
Book One

THE MOON'S EYE
Second Edition

ISBN 978-1-7379204-0-3

Cover illustration and design by Jamie Noble

Map illustration by Dewi Hargreaves

Chapter tile illustrations by A.J. Calvin

For Joshua

Without you, this book would not be.

AUTHOR'S NOTE

The Relics of War series is a project that has been on-going for more than twenty years. In its first iteration, The Moon's Eye and subsequent books were not marketed. They were published only for the enjoyment of a few close friends and family members.

Fast-forward two decades. I've decided the stories are worth sharing with a wider audience. All three books have undergone a complete rewrite, significant editing, and many updates. This is the version of the series that I have always envisioned, and this is the version I am sharing with the world.

The Relics of War is meant as a series of novels for adult readers. I want to stress the importance of this statement, as there are passages that depict violence, abuse, and torture within. There is also some language that may be offensive to some. Please be advised that I do not recommend these books for a younger and/or sensitive audience.

For those who don't mind reading about some of the uglier facets of humanity, I truly hope you enjoy the series that launched my aspirations to publish.

Thank you,
A.J. Calvin

THE FIVE KINGDOMS

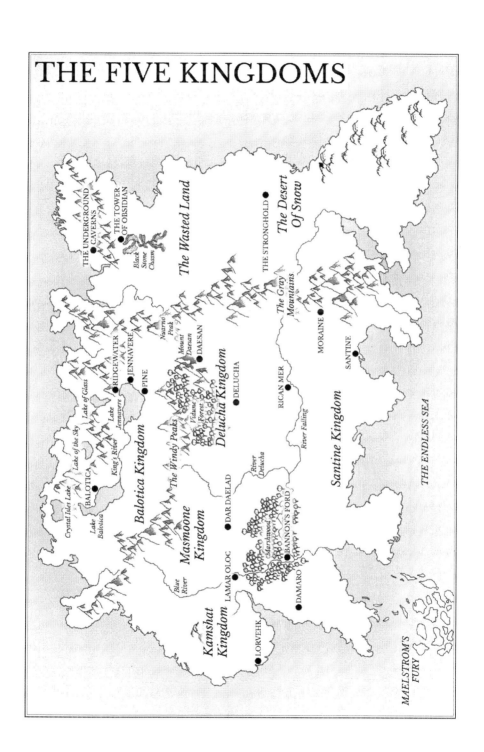

CHAPTER ONE

THE FIRE MAIDEN'S DAUGHTER

"Again," came the command.

Vardak braced himself, the wooden haft of his battle axe gripped tightly in both hands. Blademon charged toward him, a mace in his right hand, a shield strapped to his left forearm, and intensity in the god's otherworldly gaze. They'd been running the same scenario for an hour, and he still hadn't managed to avoid the Immortal's counterstrike. Blademon was convinced he could easily master the maneuver and would not allow Vardak rest until he did. Vardak wasn't certain.

Vardak swung the axe in a deadly arc, meeting Blademon's mace in mid-strike. The clash of steel reverberated loudly in the training hall. The sound momentarily deafened Vardak and caused a stir within the ring of spectators that always seemed to appear during his sparring sessions. He'd become something of a celebrity amongst his people after he was chosen as Blademon's apprentice, an honor given only once in a generation. More people had flocked to the hall than usual today, he noted. It was likely due to Blademon's announcement after his last session; the Immortal had deemed Vardak worthy of his legacy, though Vardak believed he still had much to learn.

Blademon brought his shield in for the counter strike Vardak had been attempting to block all afternoon. Frustrated, Vardak twisted the long haft of his axe toward the incoming blow and shoved with every ounce of force he could muster. It wasn't what Blademon meant for him to do, but it caused the Immortal to stumble backwards.

Blademon flashed a feral grin. "That move won't work well on someone with a lower center of gravity, though it will work well enough amongst your own kind. And me," he added with a laugh.

Blademon was the deity of war, and patron of the Scorpion Men. He had long ago assumed their form, though he towered over his mortal counterparts. They appeared human from the waist up, but below sported the body of the arachnid they were named for. Blademon wore a heavy set of plate armor over his torso and arms; it was black and shone like polished obsidian. Vardak's armor was boiled leather, light weight and sturdy, yet breathable when he ventured outside into the arid desert heat.

Though he was quick on his feet, Vardak knew he was at a disadvantage against the humans or the Murkor people when it came to agility. Two legs simply did not become as easily entangled as eight. It was for this reason that Blademon drilled him as he did; if Vardak hoped to live up to his chosen role and become the defender his people sought, his forms must be flawless.

"Show me again," Vardak said. He was tired, sore, and wanted nothing more than to be done with his latest session, but felt obligated to continue.

Blademon shook his head. "You've learned much and have grown strong. I have no illusions you'll figure it out, given time."

Vardak frowned and leaned his axe against the wall. He paused to study the dispersing crowd of spectators and wiped a trickle of sweat from his brow. A large number of young Scorpion Men, not yet of soldiering age, had come to observe, as he'd come to expect. There were clusters of others, too; sentries and scouts, and several dozen craftsmen, likely using the match as an excuse to take a break from their work. He spied his brothers amongst the crowd, but they made no move to leave with the others.

Patak was the eldest at twenty-seven, and like Vardak, a trained soldier. He was broad-shouldered and strong, and though the two were often mistaken for one another, Patak was slightly taller. Both had light blond hair and blue eyes, and resembled their father, or so Vardak had been told. Patak nodded once when he noticed Vardak's eyes upon him, then crossed his arms and turned to speak briefly with Travin.

Travin was the middle son, a scant year younger than Patak, but he sported the raven-dark hair from their mother's side. Travin was a head shorter than his brothers, but what he lacked in height, he made up for in muscle. Travin was an armor smith; years spent hammering steel had granted him a strength even Vardak's training with Blademon could not rival. Travin appeared nonplussed at Patak's words and quickly turned his attention elsewhere.

"There is a matter I must attend to," Blademon said abruptly. "I'll return when I'm able."

Vardak nodded his understanding. The Immortal was often forced to leave with little warning, though he rarely deigned to tell Vardak his reasons for doing so. Vardak may have been chosen by the war god, but he was not privy to the Immortal's other obligations.

Blademon vanished, and Vardak turned toward his brothers once more. Patak wore a mischievous grin, and Travin appeared exasperated as the pair made their way across the room. He wondered what had brought them to the training hall and what Patak was scheming. Patak liked to believe he could hide his intentions behind a stoic façade, but the truth was he made a poor liar, his emotions plain for all to see. There was no doubt in Vardak's mind that his eldest brother had some plot afoot.

"We have a surprise for you, little brother," Patak said once they were near.

Travin shot him an annoyed frown. "No, Vardak, *I* have a surprise for you. This fool wants to take credit when he's done naught but get in my way these past two weeks."

Vardak eyed the pair with curiosity. Travin scowled at Patak, who maintained his grin, unconcerned. "What is it?"

"I'd rather show you," Travin replied, giving a Patak a pointed look.

Patak laughed. "I promised I wouldn't tell him, and I'm a man of my word." He gestured to the battle axe leaning against the wall. "You may want to bring that along for effect."

Travin groaned and rolled his eyes. "Shut your damned mouth, Patak. You'll ruin the surprise."

Vardak nodded and hefted the weapon. Its leather sheath and the broad strap he used to carry the axe across his back was near the hall's exit, where he'd left it before his scheduled training with Blademon. He paused at the door to stow the weapon while his brothers waited. Travin was patient, but Patak was unable to remain still. His legs ticked upon the hard floor as he moved forward and back, eager for what Travin had in store.

"Gods, Patak, you'd think the surprise was meant for you," Travin complained as they began to walk once more. "It's little wonder the Warleader relegates you to patrol and watch duty. You've no patience to act the scout."

Patak's grin faltered briefly, then he shrugged. It was a sore spot with Patak, but he tried his best not to show it. "We only live once, Trav, and I mean to do more than sit about staring at the sand for days on end. I'll see battle one day, and the Warleader will be just as glad to have my blade as he will Vardak's."

"And he'll likely have you stationed in the second or third wave, if it comes to that," Travin replied dryly. "Unless you learn to rein in your enthusiasm, that is."

Vardak listened to his brothers' banter as he followed them into the broad, circular corridor beyond. Torches lined the walls at intervals, but they were otherwise unadorned. Their people had little use for trinkets and décor; they were a race of warriors and every resource they gathered was put to use in the defense of their home, the Stronghold. The desert surrounding their home was hostile, and it was not far from that of the Murkor. The Murkor were not always the peaceable neighbors they'd been during recent times.

Travin led the way toward the heart of the Stronghold, and Vardak knew his brother intended to escort him to the forges. The corridor opened into a vast, open space crammed with market stalls. Some of the merchants were Scorpion Men, though others were foreigners who had braved the treacherous journey across the Gray Mountains and through the Wasted Land on the promise of riches to be had as they sold or traded their goods. Most of the foreigners were human, though Vardak spied one hooded Murkor. The Murkor wore the vibrant green robes that marked him as an alchemist.

Before they reached the forges, Vardak had puzzled out what the surprise must be. Travin had been working on it for two weeks, he'd said, and combined with Patak's unconcealed excitement, it pointed to one thing: Travin had crafted something for him. He kept his thoughts to himself as they passed through the remainder of the marketplace and descended a long ramp.

The ramp led them into a large ring of smithies, each with their own set of forges. It was nearly evening, Vardak judged, given that most of the forges had fallen silent. A few burly smiths could be seen moving about their workspaces, but even they seemed to be finishing the last of their tasks.

Travin glanced over his shoulder at Vardak, the makings of a grin starting to spread across his face. He, too, was excited about the surprise, though he was slower to share his emotions than Patak.

Patak did not miss his brother's reaction. He placed a hand over his heart dramatically. "Gods! My dour brother knows how to smile. My poor heart cannot handle the shock!" He broke into a laugh at Travin's expense, only to receive a look of mock-annoyance in return.

Vardak ignored Patak's outburst, grateful his eldest brother had chosen this evening to mock Travin rather than he. He loved his brothers, but sometimes Patak took his jibes too far, and Travin tended to be much too serious. He'd learned from a young age that it was often easier to remain silent and observe their interactions without interruption, lest they both turn their attention upon him.

Travin led them toward his personal forge. He was quite proud of the space, having only acquired it a few months prior, after years spent honing his skills. Vardak took in the neat rows of tools set upon an anvil, the carefully stacked scraps of iron and steel on the workbench. Each item was precisely placed and ordered; it was Travin's way. On the far side of the workspace were several armor stands, most empty, though three displayed finely-crafted gear.

Travin gestured to the stand on his left. It held a steel breastplate, with pauldrons and matching bracers. He arched a dark eyebrow in Vardak's direction. "What do you think?"

Slowly, Vardak moved forward to examine the armor. To his eye, it was sturdy and well-made. He removed one of the gauntlets and was stunned by its light weight. He glanced at Travin briefly before he returned his attention to the gauntlet in his hands. He turned it over, noted the care that had gone into crafting each fitted plate. It was a masterpiece, but the lightness puzzled him.

"What is this metal?" he asked.

Travin moved to his side, grinning up at him. "It's steel, but I've found a way to forge it that makes it far stronger. That strength means I require less of it to achieve the same result. The armor may be light, but it is the best you'll ever have."

Patak skittered to his other side, beaming. "What are you waiting for?" he demanded. "Try it on. I've been kept in suspense long enough."

Ignoring Patak, Vardak said, "Thank you, Trav, but I don't understand why—"

Patak groaned dramatically. "Blademon announced two weeks ago that he deems you worthy of bearing his legacy, Vardak. *Everyone* understands what that means. You were his apprentice, but no longer. He comes to spar with you only to keep you in top form. It's entertainment for him—and for many of our people—but nothing more."

"He's right," Travin agreed, his tone contemplative. "When the announcement was made, I begged the Smith's Guild for the opportunity to make your first set of armor. I believe they only granted my request because you're my brother. By rights, the honor should have gone to Stanric or Velya."

Vardak grinned and wrapped Travin in a fierce embrace. "Thank you," he said again when they stepped apart.

Patak smirked. "I feel left out."

"Then you ought to go visit Shelri. Or was it Caruna this week?" Travin asked with a laugh.

"It's Loria." Patak's face flushed.

Vardak chuckled and slung the battle axe from his back to set it aside while he donned the new armor. Patak seemed to have a new woman in his life every few weeks. Each relationship was passionate for a short while, then Patak would claim incompatibility. Patak would never admit it, but he simply had not matured enough for most of the women his age, and they refused to tolerate his antics for long.

Travin crossed his arms and leveled his gaze at Patak. "One day, you'll need to settle down."

Patak snorted. "I'll settle down when I'm ready. Not everyone can find their way as easily as you, Trav."

Vardak focused on removing his leather to don the steel; he'd heard a similar version of the same conversation countless times. Since Travin had married the year before, he'd attempted to convince Patak to decide upon a woman to marry, as well. Patak simply wasn't ready for a steady relationship, let alone the prospect of a family.

The armor seemed as strong as Travin claimed, and it fit him like a second skin. He flexed his fingers in the gauntlets experimentally, pleased with the range of motion the armor afforded his hands. He grinned, pleased with the gift and grateful to Travin for the work he had done.

"I think he likes it," Patak said with a laugh. "Sometimes, I find myself wondering if our little brother knows how to speak."

Vardak chuckled. "Why do I need to speak when the pair of you are constantly chattering?"

Travin moved to stand before him. He inspected his work with a critical eye, a slight frown creasing his features. "It fits you well enough," he murmured as he adjusted the pauldrons slightly. "I wasn't certain, given I was using this lout as a guide for size." He gestured to Patak with a smirk. "How does it feel?"

"Trav, it's perfect." Vardak grinned.

"Good, I—"

Travin stopped abruptly as his gaze caught something behind Vardak. Vardak glanced over his shoulder, pleased once more with the range of motion the armor afforded him, and blinked with surprise. Blademon had returned; he stood with his arms crossed as he silently watched the trio, his expression unreadable.

Vardak and Travin bowed as the Immortal approached. Patak noted the god's reappearance more slowly. He, too, managed a frantic bow as he recognized their visitor. Blademon looked down upon them, his eyes fixed upon Vardak.

"Fine armor," he said with a nod to Travin. "You have skill."

"Thank you, sir," Travin managed.

"It's fortuitous that you've received this gift," Blademon continued, his strange eyes fixed upon Vardak's once more. "Your skills are needed, Vardak, and we have little time before the rendezvous."

Vardak frowned. "What do you mean?"

Blademon ignored his question and turned toward Patak. "Fetch the Warleader and bring him here. If I am to take your brother elsewhere, it is only proper that he is apprised of the situation."

Patak nodded eagerly. "Of course." He quickly skittered away on his errand.

"Your brother will require provisions," he informed Travin. "I must speak with him before the Warleader arrives, and I ask you to collect what he may need for a long journey, then return here. Move swiftly. We have little time."

Travin bowed again and departed without a word. Vardak met Blademon's eerie, incandescent gaze as he waited for the god's next words.

"Your brother is a skilled smith," Blademon remarked once they were alone. "Few others could craft such armor, and so quickly as he. It will be a boon to your journey."

Vardak frowned, tired of the vague insinuations Blademon had offered him thus far. "What journey?"

"My sister has given her daughter a quest," Blademon replied evenly. "That Flariel had a daughter was news to me, and that she insisted the girl go through with the business of countering the Shalin Stone seems folly. Her daughter was raised in the Shining Tower, but she is no wizard. She has no fighting skills and has seen nothing of the world beyond the gates of Dar Daelad. Flariel insisted I send my latest protégé to aid her." He frowned and his expression darkened. "I resisted her demands until she reminded me that I owe her a debt. If you help her daughter collect the object she has been tasked to acquire, the debt will be absolved."

"So, I am to act as protector for this girl?" Vardak asked, unhappy with the prospect.

"In part, yes." Blademon shook his head in frustration. "I'm afraid there is little I can do to spare you from the tedium, Vardak, but Flariel demands payment. Be wary of her. My sister is volatile like the element she embodies at the best of times."

"And her daughter?"

8

"Janna is young. Human. Today marked her twentieth birthday, and as I said, she knows little beyond the happenings in Dar Daelad. If she finds herself in danger, it is unlikely she will manage to defend herself." Blademon scowled. "Too many humans have grown soft and complacent during their long years of peace. It is fortunate for them your people remain vigilant. Though Flariel would not admit it, I believe Janna's task will prove dangerous. She would never have demanded your services otherwise."

Blademon paused to study him carefully. "There is one more matter to discuss before the others arrive. Your skills have been honed through our past five years of intense training, but there are still areas that you are less proficient in. I'd rather my students learn organically, but our time has come to an end, Vardak. I will grant you the knowledge you require in order to fill in the gaps your training could not." He placed one hand on either side of Vardak's skull. "This will not be pleasant for you, Vardak."

Vardak's mind was inundated with images, knowledge of battles from across the vast span of time, and the expertise to effectively use any weapon he found in his hands—not merely that of the battle axe he preferred. The deluge of information was passed to him in a matter of seconds, and the enormity of Blademon's final lesson left him reeling.

He gasped for breath as the Immortal dropped his hands to his sides, and Vardak felt his legs crumple beneath him. A throbbing headache suddenly raged into life behind his temples, and he squeezed his eyes tightly shut as he grappled with what had just occurred. He felt his scorpion's tail spasm as the venom glands near the sharp stinger began to produce in a biological response to the sudden stress. He wasn't certain, but he may have blacked out for a time.

When he became aware of himself once more, Blademon cupped his chin and peered intently into his eyes, as though peering into his very soul. Vardak blinked away the vestiges of the encounter, uncertain what he should feel beyond the remnants of pain.

"Fucking gods," he swore, then immediately realized whom he was speaking to. "Shit. I didn't mean…"

To his immense relief, Blademon chuckled and released him. "I've heard far worse epithets come from mortals, Vardak. It seems you've borne up well enough."

Vardak shook his head in disbelief and slowly regained his footing. "Please never do that again."

"I can make no promises, Vardak."

It was the response he'd expected. The Immortals rarely deigned to give their word to the lesser beings that inhabited their world, and Blademon was no exception.

"Collect your axe," Blademon instructed. "The others will return any moment."

He nodded absently and picked up his weapon from where it lay alongside Travin's workbench. He drew the strap diagonally across his body and marveled again at how well his new armor allowed movement. During the intense moments of forced learning he endured, he'd forgotten entirely about the others' imminent return. Slowly, he recalled his previous conversation with Blademon, and with it came a wave of frustration.

When he turned to face the Immortal once more, he noted Patak and their people's Warleader, Sevic, were walking down the ramp. Not far behind them he spied Travin with a satchel thrown over one of his burly shoulders, and alongside him, their mother. Blademon had not instructed Travin to inform her of the goings-on, but given that most of Vardak's necessities were kept in the family home, it came as no surprise she'd learned of the Immortals' demand of her youngest son.

Blademon drew Sevic aside and spoke to him quietly. It provided Vardak a few precious moments in which to say good-bye to his family. Travin handed him the satchel, and after a cursory examination, Vardak was satisfied. A change of clothes, his whetstone, a razor, dry rations enough to last at least a week, and the scant coin Vardak had managed to collect as payment for his periodic patrol duty.

"I suppose it was inevitable," his mother said after a moment, her lined face stoic.

He knew if their parting tore at her heart, she would not show it publicly, but wait until she was alone to shed her grief. It was her way and the way of their people. Zaria was one of the strongest women

10

Vardak knew, and amongst the Scorpion Men, that said much about her character. Women were trained in arms, just as their male counterparts were, and many continued to follow the path of the soldier even after they'd begun families. Zaria had been one such woman until the skirmish that had taken her husband's life, only weeks before Vardak's birth twenty-four years past. Upon learning of his death, she laid aside her arms and devoted her life to ensure the well-being of her three sons.

She smiled at him, and he noted, not for the first time, the amount of silver that shot through her dark tresses. "No matter what happens, Vardak, know that I am proud of what you've accomplished. That holds true for the pair of you, as well," she added before Patak could put voice to a retort.

"We'll be here when you return," Travin promised, "and I expect a full report on how your armor holds up."

He grinned. "Noted."

When he turned toward Patak, his eldest brother's eyes shone with emotion. "You'd best come back," he said gruffly. "That's an order, little brother."

"I will," Vardak replied.

"There's a reason our people rarely venture into human lands," Patak reminded him. "Be safe, Vardak."

Vardak turned from them as Blademon's shadow loomed over him. "It is time."

Vardak suddenly found himself within a circular room, much smaller than any he was accustomed to in the Stronghold. Candles lined the walls, though their light paled in comparison to the being who stood only paces away from him.

It was a bipedal woman with the strange, incandescent gaze that marked her as one of the Immortals, her body swathed in flame. Her skin was radiant, white-hot like iron superheated in a forge, though beneath the glow and behind the flames, Vardak could make out a few details of her figure. Flames cascaded from her scalp, swirling downward toward her waist in a semblance of hair.

He bowed, startled to find himself in the presence of Flariel.

She crossed her arms, her expression stern. "It seems you've learned some manners, at the very least. I wasn't certain what to expect from one of Blademon's lackeys." She sneered, daring him to speak. He did not.

After a moment she frowned and turned her attention to the other side of the room. Overwhelmed with her presence, Vardak had failed to notice the young woman who cowered near the wall, tears streaming from her eyes. Her loose red hair was disheveled, and it was clear from her expression that she was distraught.

"Blademon has fulfilled his promise to me," Flariel informed her coldly. "To that end, my work here is finished. You know what you must do. Succeed, and I will cherish you, always. Fail, and you will know nothing of your mother's love."

Flariel disappeared in a shower of sparks, a dusting of ash left in her wake. The woman across the room sobbed into her hands. Vardak was uncertain of how to react. He had little experience with such blatant displays of emotion, and her distress made him acutely uncomfortable. Should he go to her? Should he remain where he was? He had little experience with humans beyond the handful who ventured to the Stronghold for trade. Blademon's deluge of information had failed to include the proper etiquette for meeting with people of other races, particularly those in states of distress.

Finally, she seemed to gather herself and spared him from further uncertainty. She wiped at her eyes and rose to her feet, her green eyes fixed upon him. She attempted to smile, but the expression quickly faltered and she promptly looked away.

He decided he must say something to her and settled on giving his name. "I'm Vardak. Blademon told me something of what is expected of me, but I'm afraid he gave me few details. Are you Janna?"

She nodded forlornly. "Yes. Janna, without a surname, given to the wizards at birth by my mother who thinks I must become an adventurer of sorts to earn her love." She sniffed. "I'm sorry. Until an hour ago, I knew nothing of my connection to Flariel, nor of her quest. Why she believes I can accomplish this task is beyond my understanding. I'm not a wizard, I've never held a weapon in my life, and I haven't even been outside the walls of this city!" She was on the brink of tears once more.

12

Slowly, he edged closer. "This was sprung upon me rather abruptly, as well." Perhaps if he attempted to sympathize, she would find calm?

"And yet, you seem to be handling the situation far better than I." She closed her eyes as tears traced their way down her cheeks.

Vardak was uncertain of how to respond, so he remained silent and kept his distance. He was spared further awkwardness by the arrival of another woman, who strode into the room in a swish of white silk robes. She appeared to be quite old, though Vardak wasn't certain if humans aged at the same rate as his own people. Her hair was as snowy as her clothing, and her dark face was heavily lined.

She looked between the pair for a moment, then made her way to Janna and gathered the tearful young woman into her arms. "Hush, child. It is ever difficult when dealing with the Immortals, even those who claim you are their kin. They do not see the world as we do." She looked over Janna's shoulder to Vardak. "Has anyone informed you of your reason for coming here?"

"I was told only that I am to assist her." He gestured to Janna. "Blademon mentioned a stone, but I know nothing else."

The older woman's embrace seemed to have soothed Janna, for she grew quiet once more. "Tell him," she pleaded without looking at Vardak. The other woman nodded and withdrew her embrace. Janna turned toward him but refused to meet his gaze.

"Why don't we go somewhere a bit more comfortable, first?" she asked with a motion that implied they should follow her through the door. "My name is Daryla. I'm afraid we were not properly introduced."

"Vardak."

She smiled in welcome and led them into a wide corridor lined with smooth columns of alabaster. They came to another room furnished with cushioned chairs, and Daryla gestured they should enter. Janna immediately plopped onto one of the chairs. Vardak waited until Daryla had taken a seat before he folded his legs beneath him and settled onto the floor.

"There has been some trouble in the east," Daryla began. She cast a concerned glance in Janna's direction. "The Shining Tower has said little of what transpired, but the rumors state a wizard has fallen

13

to madness and is gathering a Murkor army with plans to attack Delucha."

Vardak arched an eyebrow. "If the Murkor are gathering in strength, my people would have taken notice of it."

She shrugged. "As I said, it is rumor. The news Flariel brought was far more concerning, however. The wizard has obtained a magical relic, the Shalin Stone, which prevents the Immortals from observing his movements. I do not know for certain, but Flariel insinuated the object has some connection to the Nameless. No matter what its true purpose, the Immortals fear this object and that it lies in the hands of a man driven by insanity."

"There is another relic that my mother said can counter the Shalin Stone," Janna said, her voice listless. "The Moon's Eye. She has ordered me to find it, but I don't know where to begin."

"I do not know where this relic can be found," Daryla said slowly, "but I know of someone who likely does."

Janna brightened at her words. "Who is it? Where can we find him?"

Daryla smiled patiently. "*She* lives deep within Vidune Forest. It has been decades since any of my order have made contact with her, though given her history, I know she still lives. I can provide you with a map for your journey and details of her last known location."

Vardak nodded to her. "Thank you. If we are where I believe we are—Dar Daelad—it will take several days to reach the forest, yes?" Blademon's knowledge was already proving useful. He could easily visualize the path they must follow in order to reach Vidune Forest. Likewise, he understood the landscape, as though he'd undertaken the journey himself countless times.

"I would plan on five days, at the least," Daryla confirmed. "You are in Dar Daelad, Vardak. This is Ukase's temple, and I am a priestess here."

He met her gaze uneasily. "Ukase is involved in this matter, as well?"

"All of the Immortals have a stake in this, Vardak," she replied evenly. "The Moon's Eye must be found, and the wizard I mentioned must be stopped. If what Flariel suggested is true…" She shook her head and trailed off, her face growing ashen in the candlelight.

"And what was that?" Janna demanded. "Mother didn't explain herself, and I'm no scholar."

Vardak frowned but kept his thoughts to himself. The little he'd learned of Janna caused him to question Flariel's true motive. Janna possessed no useful skills for survival, and no knowledge of their objective. Did the Fire Maiden wish to see her daughter killed?

"It is believed the Shalin Stone has some connection to the Nameless," Daryla repeated. "Flariel indicated the Immortals fear its use, and though I don't know what that is, I have a suspicion. The Immortals would only fear something with the power to break the Nameless free of his prison."

Janna gasped. "No. All twelve of the Immortals caged him *for eternity*," she said with emphasis. "The stories all say as much."

Daryla shook her head. "Janna, much of the lore my order teaches must be studied with caution. Some of those tales have been rewritten and revised many times. It is unlikely they resemble anything of their original character. The Immortals did indeed cage him, but as with all things of magic, it cannot last indefinitely."

CHAPTER TWO

THE AIRESS' PRICE

It took them six days to reach Vidune Forest. It was nestled in a broad valley between the rounded hillocks known as the Windy Peaks. Vardak could not refer to them as mountains; he'd traveled far enough across the Wasted Land to view the Gray Mountains from afar, tall craggy peaks that were snow-capped even at the height of summer. By comparison, the Windy Peaks were little more than overgrown hills.

They had traveled the Merchant Road from Dar Daelad in Masmoone Kingdom, and across the border into Delucha. Though their journey through Dar Daelad had been brief, Vardak had been relieved to be away from the city. It was filled to bursting with people, most of them human, though he'd spied a handful of scaly Drakkon amongst the crowds. No matter how quickly they moved, Vardak drew stares. The Scorpion Men rarely traveled to the lands west of the Gray Mountains, and it was clear the city folk were surprised by his presence. The attention was unwanted and uncomfortable.

Once they had departed the city and traveled several miles, there were far fewer people to stand agape at the stranger in their midst. Vardak preferred the open, rolling countryside to the confines of the sprawling city. Miles of farmland stretched before them, finally giving way to grasslands after they crossed the border into Delucha. Smaller cities and towns appeared at intervals along their route, and Janna insisted they stay at local inns when they were able. She preferred the comforts of a bed and a roof overhead to sleeping beneath the stars. He did not complain, though he would have liked to remain at a distance from the multitude of humans.

He learned quickly that Janna was prone to chatter, that she would talk endlessly for hours without pause when given the opportunity. He let her speak, often without interruption. He was not a man of many words, and there was much he learned from her, in spite of the seemingly superfluous nature of her conversations. She did not seem to mind his long bouts of silence, so long as he appeared to be listening.

It was mid-morning on the sixth day of their journey when Vardak recognized the subtle changes in the landscape that indicated they were nearing the area where they must part ways with the Merchant's Road. The information he'd gleaned from Blademon had provided him with this insight, and he had not yet felt the need to consult Daryla's map. As it was, Janna kept the map tucked in one of her pockets, though she rarely consulted it. She seemed content to follow his lead, though she never asked him how he knew the proper route.

"We turn here," he announced as they came upon a faint track that led into the hills to the north. He had been watching carefully for the path; it was almost indistinguishable from the grass, though he imagined it had once been carefully maintained.

Janna nodded and followed his direction. "This will lead us to the forest?" she asked.

"Yes."

"Good. I'm unused to travel. I've said as much before, but it's the truth. What do you suppose the forest is like? I've heard tales that people once lived there…"

She continued to prattle, and he nodded occasionally to indicate he listened. The woman they sought was the last of her kind, or so Daryla had told them. An Airess. Vardak had never heard the term, and Daryla explained that prior to the first Great War, the Airess people had been afflicted with a terrible plague. Only one of their number had survived through the intervention of the gods. That war had taken place nearly a thousand years ago. If anyone living had knowledge of the relic they sought, it would be this Airess.

By mid-day, the track had led them several miles into the rounded hills. The day was warm, but the wind that gusted around them held the cold promise of winter in its depths. Vardak frowned at the prospect. The spare shirts he carried in his satchel were light-weight, designed for travel in the desert or through the Wasted Land, where the sun scorched the earth relentlessly year-round. He doubted his armor would provide any lasting warmth.

As they crested another hill, a wide valley came into view, sprawling below them. Trees taller than any Vardak had encountered previously towered overhead, their leaves in shades of lustrous green, darkest crimson, and silvery-gray. He could hear birdsong from amongst the canopy, smell the green scent of the forest undergrowth, even from a distance. He gazed, awestruck, as he took in the forest in all its leafy splendor.

"You look as though you've never seen trees before, Vardak." Janna's teased.

He forced a grin. "The desert has no trees, and the Wasted Land is nearly as barren. The trees that do manage to survive are twisted, stunted things. This is a gods-damned wonder."

"There are no forests beyond the Gray Mountains?"

He shook his head. "I've never before seen so much...*green*."

By nightfall they were well within the confines of the forest. In spite of his previous wonder, Vardak had begun to think the closeness of the vegetation was oppressive. The tree branches interlaced so thickly overhead he could no longer see the sky, and the track they followed was overgrown with grasses, wildflowers, shrubs, and vines. Strange calls could be heard from within the trees, rustled movement came to them from within the undergrowth, but he rarely saw the source of either sound. Janna was unconcerned, but every strange noise left him on edge. He resisted the urge to unsheathe his axe.

They came upon a clearing, and Vardak decided the location was sufficient to make camp. At least he could see a portion of the darkening sky above, a small comfort after the hours spent beneath the thick canopy.

Vardak anticipated the noise from the surrounding forest would dissipate with the darkness, but he quickly discovered his error. The daylight tones faded away, only to be replaced by a different, more unsettling soundtrack as creatures of the night began to waken.

Janna settled into her cloak, prepared to sleep. He was unable to rest, concerned that just beyond the next tree may be a creature prepared to pounce upon them. He paced the perimeter of their tiny camp at intervals, before he settled down for an elusive sleep, his rest broken frequently by new, unusual sounds. He rose to pace again and hoped exhaustion would eventually force him into slumber. Janna, unconcerned with their surroundings, slept soundly.

The sky was lightening toward dawn when he finally drifted off. When he awakened later, the sun had climbed high enough into the sky he could see it above the treetops at the edge of the clearing. He sighed, disappointed in himself for wasting half their morning.

Janna giggled as he stood up and stretched. "I was beginning to wonder if you'd sleep the whole day away. It's no matter. I've been looking at the map Daryla gave us, and her instructions for finding the Airess. If we are where I believe, we don't have much farther to go." She held the map in her hands and waved it in his direction.

He made his way toward her and peered down at it. She was right; the clearing was mentioned in Daryla's notes, and if they continued to follow their current route, it would take little time for them to reach the location marked as "ruins". Other paths should twine with theirs at that point, and they would need to turn onto the branch leading due east. It would bring them directly to the Airess' home. As long as she hadn't relocated, he reminded himself. Daryla had cautioned them that there had been no contact with the Airess in decades, but they must start their search somewhere. Her last known location was as good as any.

"We traveled further than I realized," he said with a nod. "It's difficult to judge distances with so much vegetation about. I don't like it."

Janna laughed. "Oh, Vardak, forests are commonplace on this side of the mountains. You'll have to grow used to them eventually."

He shrugged and turned away to gather his axe and his satchel, and paused to rummage inside for a bit of his dwindling rations. He uncovered a few strips of jerky, shouldered his belongings, and glanced toward Janna. She appeared ready to depart.

As they exited the clearing and found themselves beneath the interlacing branches once more, the path they'd been following faded and nearly disappeared amongst the undergrowth. Vardak was forced to rely on more of Blademon's imparted knowledge in order to trace their intended path, and he began to wonder if the Immortal had known some of what lay in store for him. Vardak had always been a passable scout, but the landscape of his homeland was far more accommodating than the overgrown greenery of Vidune Forest. Without Blademon's final gift, they would have quickly become lost.

Silently, he thanked the war-mongering deity while Janna chattered beside him. He paid her little heed and focused on leading them toward their next destination. She explained the apprenticeship process of the Shining Tower and how she once longed to be chosen for it. She had no magical inclination, however, and the wizards had humored her so far as to allow her access to their library. What she knew of magic had come from years spent reading, though she admitted she'd known nothing of the relics they sought prior to Flariel's unexpected arrival.

After an hour spent within the dense confines of the forest, they came to another, partial clearing. Vardak surveyed the space carefully. He sensed something was different about this part of the forest, though he was uncertain what had changed. He edged forward slowly, and after a few steps his feet came into contact with a hard surface, in marked contrast to the surrounding loam. He peered down and noted that there were cracked tiles beneath his feet. They were encrusted with centuries of grime, and in some places, completely covered with mud. He followed the tiles with his eyes to a point where they abruptly ended along the remnants of a broken stone wall.

Janna had watched him closely, and after a moment she understood what had captured his attention. "The ruins," she breathed, green eyes alight with excitement.

He nodded and continued along the path to a point where several others joined it near the center of the space. There were many low ridges of what had once been walls interspersed with more trees and thick undergrowth. Blademon's knowledge told him a thriving city used to stand in this space millennia ago.

"Daryla never mentioned who lived here," Janna said as she followed him to the nexus. "Do you believe they were human? Or perhaps they were something else? I've heard the Drakkon tend to live in seclusion."

Vardak had met a few Drakkon merchants during his time and knew they preferred high, open places; cliffs, mountain peaks, plateaus. "This was no Drakkon city."

"I've only seen Drakkon from afar," she replied. "They seem fierce and temperamental…"

She continued, but he tuned out her words. Her chatter was inconsequential to their purpose, which was to find the Airess said to dwell within the woods. They would find no Drakkon here, no matter how fervently Janna wished to meet one.

He focused his attention upon locating the eastward path, and after a few minutes of searching through the undergrowth, he found what he'd been looking for. He motioned for Janna to follow him as he began to trace their new path away from the remnants of the lost city and into the deeper forest beyond.

"Do you think she'll still be here?" Janna asked in a whisper.

The deeper forest was hushed compared to the other areas they had traveled through, and the quietude seemed to have left an impression on her. Good, he thought. Perhaps a pause to her incessant chatter would allow him time to think.

He shrugged in response. "Even if she is not, it's our only clue."

"I hope she's here," Janna replied eagerly. "I wonder what an Airess is like? I don't recall reading anything about them in the library…"

He sighed quietly, resigned to the fact Janna's silences were temporary. Her whispered words were far easier to ignore than her speaking tone, he admitted, and wondered once again what he'd managed to become entangled in. The schemes of the Immortals were one matter, but Janna was becoming an irritation in her own right. He hoped if they encountered any true dangers, she'd be wise enough to stop speaking until it had passed.

Abruptly, a structure came into view between the trees ahead. It was a small hut, with dried moss atop its roof and ivy crawling up its sides. He could see what appeared to be a garden; neat rows of plants different than those of the surrounding forest protruded from the dark soil. Some bore flowers, others berries, but each was as unfamiliar to him as the next. The hut and its garden were too well-tended to be abandoned, and he was certain that someone must live there. Whether it was the Airess they sought, or someone else, was yet to be seen. He signaled for Janna to be silent and pointed ahead.

21

She blinked, then grinned. "Do you suppose it's—"

"Shh," he hissed.

He scowled ahead as she made an apology. Would she never understand that there were times when silence was called for, indeed, when it was necessary? If the hut was not inhabited by the Airess, there was a chance the person within may prove dangerous. It was possible, as well, that the Airess herself might prove hostile. He needed to assess their situation without Janna giving away their location prematurely.

They paused behind the next tree, and Vardak peered around its vast trunk. Janna had blessedly fallen silent, and he watched the hut and its surroundings for a time. There was movement within the structure; he could see a shadow beneath the door, as though someone walked inside.

He glanced at Janna and said in a low voice, "There is someone here. We will walk to the door, and I will knock. Stay behind me. We do not know if this is the Airess, or someone else who may prove unfriendly. And for gods' sake, please keep silent."

Janna bit her lower lip and nodded, her eyes wide.

He motioned that she should follow him, and they began to approach the hut. As they neared, he noted that much of the forest's undergrowth had been cleared away some distance from the garden. He knew little of plants, only that they were green and some were edible. The array of strange flora within the garden was a mystery to him. He glanced over his shoulder as he neared the door and saw that Janna stood a few steps away, hands clasped before her expectantly. Satisfied, he turned around and rapped swiftly on the door.

"Just a moment," a feminine voice called from within, followed by a series of muttered words in a language Vardak did not recognize. The voice was friendly and mildly surprised.

"Do you believe it's her?" Janna whispered. She had moved to stand just behind him.

He shrugged. They would learn who inhabited the hut in a matter of moments. It was useless to speculate.

The door swung open to reveal a tall, willowy woman with porcelain skin and ash-blond hair. She wore a stained white apron over her other clothing, which appeared to be sewn of soft leather. What struck Vardak foremost were the pair of pale pink wings that protruded from her back, reminiscent of a butterfly's in form.

"You're the Airess!" Janna blurted, but immediately fell silent at Vardak's glower.

To his relief, the woman smiled patiently. "I am, at that, though I have a name. Coreyaless. It is no easy task finding me here, so I must assume you've come upon a matter of great importance." She moved aside. "Please, come in. I will prepare tea, and we shall talk."

Once introductions had been made, Vardak found himself seated between the two women at a small wooden table, a steaming mug of tea before him. He was unused to heated drinks, and found himself waiting for the liquid to cool before he tasted it. The others sipped at their own mugs in spite of the steam billowing off the surface; he found the practice strange.

Across the room he could see another, larger table covered with an array of vials, bunches of dried herbs, jars, a mortar and pestle, and a thick leather-bound tome, which had been left open. Coreyaless had told them as she prepared the tea that she was a healer and apothecary by trade and was at work when they unexpectedly arrived. The garden outside was an extension of her trade, and the plants were herbs, spices, or aromatics used in her various concoctions and antidotes.

"Why have you come?" Coreyaless asked as she took another sip of tea.

Vardak glanced at Janna to indicate she ought to answer the question. Her mother had initiated this business, after all. Janna explained their situation in her typical, long-winded fashion, and when she was finished, she looked expectantly at Coreyaless.

The Airess stared at the mug between her hands, a deep sadness in her expression. "I know something of the relic you seek," she said slowly, "but I cannot help you."

Janna gaped at her, and anger flashed through her eyes. "Then we've come here for nothing?"

Coreyaless did not look up from her tea. "I will not be used by the Immortals a second time. You are Flariel's daughter, by your own admission, and you," she glanced at Vardak, "are Blademon's chosen.

The gods have wronged me, have caused me centuries of suffering, simply to further their own schemes. I will not be ensnared by them again."

Janna crossed her arms, frustrated and unwilling to let the matter lie. "We didn't seek you out because *they* asked it of us. We came because the priestess of Ukase's temple said you may be of some help. Clearly, she was wrong, but that's a matter for later. What have the Immortals done that causes you to hate them so?"

Coreyaless' expression became pained. "What do you know of the time before the first Great War, Janna? Do the humans still deign to teach their youngsters proper history?"

"The first Great War was initiated by the Nameless One's minion, the first of the Soulless," Janna recited.

"Yes, and of the time *before* that war began?" Coreyaless pressed.

Janna shrugged. "What of it? I was taught the basics of the wars, not the events that came earlier."

Coreyaless sighed and turned her attention upon Vardak. "Surely your people teach proper history, particularly when it comes to that era."

Vardak nodded uneasily. It was a subject they learned from a young age, meant to instill proper fear and hatred for those who resided within the black tower in the northern reaches of the Wasted Land.

"There was a plague," he said.

"Yes. The Nameless created the plague to destroy my people and those who allied with us—the Felenes. No doubt you saw the ruins on your journey here."

Vardak nodded. "It looked as though it was once a great city."

"If this plague were so terrible, why is it that you've survived?" Janna asked with a frown.

Coreyaless sipped her tea and took a moment to gather her thoughts. "I, and one other, did not succumb. We were promised to one another, he and I, but I have not laid eyes upon him in these many years. Karmada learned of our plight, but as is her way, she intervened without considering how it might affect those involved. She exacted a steep price from us in return for her 'favor'. She spared Danness and

24

I, but condemned us to eternal separation. We are the last of the Airess people, but she took him to the lands beyond the southern sea. By the time I learned of her involvement, he was already gone."

"We will help you find him," Janna replied without hesitation, and Vardak stared at her, stunned.

"You are not the first to make such a promise, Janna." Coreyaless shook her head, bemused. "There is but one way I know of to reach the lands where Danness now resides, and it is not by ship. Believe me—I have tried that method numerous times, and it has always ended in failure. Maelstrom and Hydralene make certain no ship can cross the ocean safely."

Janna shrugged. "How do we reach the southern lands, then? You said there was a way."

Coreyaless fixed her with a pointed gaze. "That way is dangerous, and I suspect *you* are not equipped for such a journey." She turned to Vardak while Janna gaped in outrage. "Given your training, you might be the only person alive who could lead me through the paths I must trod, if you mean to uphold your friend's promise to me."

Vardak sensed he was being manipulated, and he scowled at Janna for her hasty words. "Tell me, and I will consider it."

"Very well. I will help you in finding this relic you seek, *if* you help me locate Danness. I will understand if you decline, for the only means of reaching the southern continent lies deep within Stonewall Hall."

Vardak groaned internally and he looked down at the untouched cup before him, now cooled enough that it no longer steamed. Stonewall Hall was not merely dangerous, it was almost certain death for anyone foolhardy enough to venture inside.

"We can't travel there!" Janna exclaimed, horrified. "Even the wizards fear to enter that place. The Undead, and those giant flying insects, and *ghosts*, and—"

"There are no ghosts," Vardak replied, cutting her off, "but the insects and the Undead are a real threat. The latter, in particular."

Janna sighed heavily and crossed her arms. "We have to find The Moon's Eye if we are to stop the threat in the east. You know something of its whereabouts," she said heatedly to Coreyaless, "yet you won't help us with this matter, unless we help you find Danness."

"Those are my terms," the Airess replied evenly.

Janna shook her head in frustration. "What would my mother think of this? Surely, Stonewall Hall was never in her plans for me. Vardak, what are we going to do?"

"I need time to think," he replied. "I don't like this gods-forsaken business with Stonewall Hall."

Janna released an aggravated groan. "I've already promised her, Vardak. What more is there to consider?"

He glowered at her. "You spoke when you should have remained silent. You do not understand what you demand of me."

"Vardak is right to ask for time, Janna. You may stay here tonight," Coreyaless said, "but I will require an answer on the morrow. I have waited too long for this opportunity, and the centuries have ground my patience to dust."

CHAPTER THREE

THE SOULLESS

Aran'daj crossed his arms and frowned beneath his hood as he surveyed the soldiers sparring before him. Raj'im could scarcely hold his ground against the physically smaller Tarj'ah. Aran'daj pushed his anxiety aside; the wizard was present to observe. Their match was meant to impress the wizard, not call the Murkors' competence into question.

The last pair with the misfortune of displeasing the man who now called himself Shan'tar—dreadful, in the Murkor tongue—now lay broken at the bottom of Blackstone Chasm. Shan'tar, living up to his name, had thrown the pair over the precipice in a violent display of magical dominance. Aran'daj could still hear the echo of their terrified screams as they plummeted toward the chasm's depths.

Beside him, Shan'tar growled and muttered angrily, a dangerous light in his dark eyes. If the soldiers continued to falter in the presence of the Murkor's new benefactor, Aran'daj was certain he would quickly run out of trained warriors, casualties of the wizard's wrath.

He returned his attention to the sparring pair and called a halt to their activities. He rounded on the rows of black-clad soldiers, hoods drawn up to shield their sensitive eyes from the sun's infernal glare. "Is this the best our people can muster?" he demanded angrily in their tongue. "You disgrace your people. You disgrace your commander. You disgrace the mighty Shan'tar!"

"Peace, Commander," the wizard's low baritone ordered. He spoke the common tongue, though it quickly became clear he understood the Murkor language well enough. "They fear me, as they should. Fear breeds anxiety, which in turn manifests in mistakes."

27

Aran'daj met Shan'tar's gaze warily. Leniency was not something he'd come to expect from the wizard, nor was this moment of strange lucidity.

"Continue with the drills, Commander. Speak with me again at nightfall, and we will discuss the next phase of my plan." Shan'tar turned on his heel and strode away toward the tents a half-mile away.

Aran'daj glared at his retreating form. The Murkor people dwelt underground for good reason; the Wasted Land provided little shelter from the relentless burning of the sun. The hoods they wore served the dual purpose of providing them with cover and concealing their identities. Their pale, sensitive eyes were protected from the glare, but their garb did nothing to alleviate the heat radiating from the barren sky or reflecting from the hard-baked ground. The soldiers were miserable, Aran'daj was miserable, and the madman they followed could not be reasoned with.

Reluctantly, he turned to face the unit whose unfortunate luck had placed them in Shan'tar's crosshairs that day. "The wizard has ordered further drills," he barked at the gathered Murkor in their own tongue once more. Aran'daj did not agree with the demand, but he was no fool; he would not directly disobey the wizard. His predecessor had disappeared for a lesser offense.

The Murkor soldiers did not argue as they began to carry out the order. Aran'daj observed them, taking time to stride through the ranks and inspect as many of them as he was able. He would forge them into a proper army, or perish in the attempt, but the soldiers would be better for it no matter the outcome.

Hours later, as the sun began to sink below the Gray Mountains in the west, Aran'daj dismissed the unit. Conversation sprang up amongst the soldiers as they trudged toward the camp, and he heard many grumble about the heat, the light, and above all, the wizard. The Murkor could tolerate the sun, but the day-long drills were beginning to take their toll. Aran'daj knew he must do something to alleviate the soldiers' discomfort, but the prospect of posing the idea to Shan'tar left him cold with dread.

He pondered his options as he strode toward the camp in the wake of the others. He recalled Shan'tar had ordered him to meet with him at nightfall and knew the wizard would likely be within his tent at the center of the camp. It puzzled Aran'daj that the wizard continued to refer to himself as such; by his own admission he'd cut his ties with the Shining Tower the moment he acquired the strange relic he kept on his person. Shan'tar seemed content to follow his own path, his actions fueled more often by the madness that slowly consumed his mind than by rational thought.

Aran'daj arrived at the wizard's tent more quickly than he'd intended and paused for a moment to brace himself for what might ensue. The encounter could range anywhere from brief conversation, to threats, to Shan'tar wielding his magic and smiting Aran'daj where he stood. It was dependent upon Shan'tar's temperament in that moment, what else may have transpired during the course of the day, and how much control the wizard currently maintained over his ravaged psyche. He drew a breath, squared his shoulders, and entered the tent.

Shan'tar stood hunched over a table littered with maps, scrolls, and books, his back to the entrance. In the center was a lacquered box with ornate carvings swirling across its surface; it was this object that captured Shan'tar's attention. Aran'daj paused for a moment, uncertain if the wizard had heard him enter. When Shan'tar failed to acknowledge him, Aran'daj knew he must initiate the conversation.

"You wished to see me, sir?"

Shan'tar straightened slowly and turned. "Yes. Come here, Commander."

Aran'daj swallowed his fear and stepped forward. With a swift movement, Shan'tar grasped the black hood that covered his commander's face and jerked it back to expose the Murkor beneath. Aran'daj stiffened with unspoken outrage, but feared to voice his complaint lest Shan'tar kill him for insubordination. The Murkor did not show their faces to anyone unless they were with immediate family or intimate partners. Shan'tar's act was a violation.

Aran'daj fixed his pale blue eyes on the wizard's dark ones and clenched his fists furiously. Every fiber of his being screamed for retaliation, to strike at Shan'tar for exposing what was to Aran'daj one of his most closely guarded secrets. Shan'tar's hand touched the side of his commander's midnight-blue face, tracing the contours of his jaw, then the patterns of the silvery tattoos that marked nearly every inch of his exposed skin. Some of the markings were familial, while others indicated his profession, his position and rank, his life's achievements.

"The Murkor are stunning," Shan'tar whispered. His face drew near, and Aran'daj could smell the stale odor of the wizard's breath as the examination continued. "These markings you bear," he said, tracing a pattern along the side of Aran'daj's neck, "do you bear them everywhere?"

"Yes," Aran'daj growled through clenched teeth. He silently prayed to any god that was willing to listen that they prevent Shan'tar from demanding he disrobe. It was a line he would not cross, even if it meant his life was forfeit. The wizard had caused him enough humiliation as it was.

To his relief, Shan'tar dropped his hand and stepped back. "Truly stunning," he said to himself before he abruptly turned toward the table once more. "Allow me to show you something, Commander."

Aran'daj replaced his hood and glowered at the wizard's back as he made his way to the table. Shan'tar drew the lacquered box toward him and flipped the ornate latch open with his thumb. The lid sprang open to reveal a pale, green-white stone, glowing softly within.

"This relic is the Shalin Stone," Shan'tar informed him. "I found it within Stonewall Hall, where it lay for centuries. Millennia, perhaps. It called to me then, and I desired it. It speaks to me, even now."

Aran'daj had been briefed on the relic before departing from the Underground Caverns he called home. Kal Aran'jandah, the spiritual leader of the Murkor and the commander's grandfather, had drawn him aside to inform him of his new role as commander of the armies, of the terms the Murkor had agreed to with the purpose of furthering themselves—as well as Shan'tar's goals—and of the relic the wizard possessed. The Shalin Stone had once belonged to the Council of Enlightened before it was stolen during the first Great War. Nearly a thousand years had passed before Shan'tar rediscovered it.

Its purpose was twofold, the Kal had told him. It created a vast aura around its location that prevented the Immortals from appearing within its radius, which Shan'tar was fond of reminding them. Without their interference, Shan'tar believed he could achieve anything, and his goals were lofty. The stone's other use was far darker, and the very thought of it being used for such a purpose struck fear into Aran'daj's heart. The Shalin Stone was tied to the Soulless, and the Kal believed if used properly, it would resurrect all of the fallen leaders of the Enlightened.

The Soulless were creatures of legend, magic wielders of the utmost power, ruthless, savage, their purpose to free the Nameless god of death from his prison. As each Soulless had come into power, war had broken out across the land, spilling across the Gray Mountains and into the Five Kingdoms. Death followed in the Soulless' wake, and the Murkor had always been terrorized into submission, or slaughtered by the thousands as the Soulless sought to further their single-minded goals. If the Kal was correct, and the stone was capable of summoning all five Soulless, it could bring devastation of an unimaginable scale.

The Shalin Stone was currently in the possession of a madman.

Aran'daj found his voice after a moment. "The stone speaks to you, sir?"

"Oh, yes. I can hear *them* inside. They long to be freed." He grimaced. "I can do it if I wish. And perhaps I do wish it. Perhaps, I do." A wild light shone in his dark eyes as he gazed upon the stone, and Aran'daj feared he would use the stone then and there, effectively condemning the world to another age of chaos and death.

Reluctantly, Shan'tar closed the box and snapped the latch closed. He caressed the lid, much as he might a lover, and shook his head. "It is not time. Not time!" He shouted, his voice raw with sudden rage.

Aran'daj took a step backward, his hand finding its way to the hilt of the saber he carried at his belt. "Sir?"

"Oh, Commander, yes. I asked to see you, did I not?" Shan'tar glanced at him furtively. "When will the soldiers be ready to strike? I've made plans for Delucha."

Aran'daj nodded slowly, grateful for the hood he wore and its ability to hide his stunned expression from the wizard. "The men are well-trained, sir. I know the demonstration earlier was not up to par, and I will speak to the pair involved—"

Shan'tar waved his hand dismissively. "That won't be necessary. They will do better next time." He reached down and tapped

31

upon a map that lay across the table's surface. "Delucha. I wish to march upon Delucha."

"Of course, sir. Arrangements can be made within the week." Aran'daj swallowed, relieved the wizard seemed focused on something other than the stone. "I will need to send word to the caverns, sir. We'll need provisions, craftspeople, alchemists…"

"Yes, yes. Do as you require. You are dismissed, Commander."

Aran'daj began making the necessary arrangements that evening, under the blessed darkness of night that his eyes preferred. At odds with the heat of the day, the Wasted Land became almost frigid at night, and his breath puffed in the air before him as he strode through the Murkor camp. The land was a simulacrum of extremes; blistering heat and icy cold, jagged mountains and deepest chasms, the hard, cracked ground seemingly inhospitable until one came upon a grove of twisted, stunted trees. Life struggled to survive in the Wasted Land, yet his people had endured, against the cruel odds Karmada had thrown their way.

Aran'daj sought out Shen'jem, one of their quickest scouts, where he was on patrol duty along the camp's perimeter. He had a written request of the Kal and the Matriarch for the people and supplies the army would require, as well as the sparse details Shan'tar had provided him. It would take several days of hard marching to reach the Gray Mountains, and at least another week, perhaps two, to cover the distance through those craggy peaks. The journey would be grueling, but at least it was late summer and the likelihood of encountering storms in the mountains would be small.

Shen'jem saluted as Aran'daj approached. Though most Murkor soldiers were indistinguishable in their black garb and hoods, Aran'daj stood taller than the majority, and bore the curved, black saber at his belt that marked him as commander. All Murkor weapons were forged of the inky metal and imbued with deadly poison by the alchemists, but most carried axes or spears, crossbows or maces. Sabers were reserved for those in positions of command.

Aran'daj handed his message to Shen'jem and instructed him to depart as quickly as he was able for the caverns. The message was to be delivered directly to Kal Aran'jandah, and he imparted the veiled threat of Shan'tar's wrath should it fall into the hands of anyone else.

Shen'jem, obedient soldier that he was, nodded briskly and assured the commander it would be done.

Glad to be done with his final task for the evening, Aran'daj trudged back to his tent. The Murkor were nocturnal by nature, and the long day spent in the sun had proven draining. He removed his boots and the dark ring mail he wore over his black soldier's garb, leaving both neatly beside the entrance. He unfastened his belt and set it aside after withdrawing his saber from its scabbard. Seeking the whetstone he kept with his belongings, he sat down and began the process of honing the blade's curved edge.

The repetition of the task provided his mind with the opportunity to process the day's events, unencumbered by distraction. He still hadn't gathered the courage to approach Shan'tar regarding the soldiers' needs and the wizard's unreasonable daylight schedule, but he knew it must be done soon. His people came first, and the wizard's aspirations be damned.

The Murkor had been used—for good or ill—by forces beyond their control for centuries, and Shan'tar was but the latest in that long succession. Aran'daj had been schooled in history from a young age, given that he was descended from the present Kal. Not all Murkor were expected to learn such things, nor were they held to the same standards as he.

First, there had been the god now referred to as the Nameless. Under threat of annihilation, he forced the Murkor people to fight his bloody wars millennia ago. The Nameless had ultimately been defeated and cast into the prison where he now resided. Then had come the Soulless, magic wielders of terrible ferocity, bound to the Nameless for eternity. Four wars had been fought with the Soulless at the helm, and each time, the Murkor had been compelled to fight for them, though the histories could not explain how it came to be. Aran'daj suspected the Soulless, like their master before them, and threatened his people with the prospect of destruction if they failed to cooperate. Now, there was Shan'tar. Aran'daj did not know the details of his arrangement with the Kal or the Matriarch, but he knew both feared the wizard and his tainted relic.

Something must be done to prevent Shan'tar from summoning the Soulless, but Aran'daj was uncertain of how to proceed. The

Murkor did not possess magic as the humans and Drakkon did, which made Aran'daj uneasy as he considered his options. He did not fully understand what Shan'tar was capable of, beyond what he'd witnessed weeks ago at the edge of the chasm. Two soldiers had displeased the wizard, and with a wave of his pale hand, the pair had been flung through the air to tumble into the depths. Aran'daj grimaced once more at the memory of their terrified screams.

He tested the edge of his blade with his thumb, satisfied it was sufficiently sharp. He sheathed it and lay back against the blanket he'd been sitting upon. He must do something to stop Shan'tar, but what could he do when faced with such an adversary? Was his life worth risking on the chance Shan'tar might use the relic in his possession?

He closed his eyes, but no answers came to him. He was exhausted and short on ideas. Shan'tar and his relic could wait for morning.

Aran'daj was awakened from a heavy slumber by a pair of rough hands shaking his shoulders. He caught a glimpse of pale eyes from beneath the hood of the Murkor that knelt beside him, panic in the soldier's gaze. He sat up and shrugged away.

"I've had little sleep for days," he growled ominously in their own tongue. "This had better be important."

"Commander, sir," the soldier replied, his tone wavering on the edge of terror, "it is. The wizard is at the chasm's edge, sir. He's performing a ritual, or so Sal'zar claims. He's an alchemist, sir. He would know."

Aran'daj tugged on his boots and grabbed his belt, buckling it over his rumpled clothing as he stepped outside in the soldier's wake. If it came to a fight with Shan'tar, his mail would do him little good; he left it within and followed the soldier to a place near the edge of the camp. The other Murkor milled about in confusion that bordered on panic. He strode past them, shoving those in his path brusquely out of the way. Most who took notice of his presence began to calm, though all remained fearful.

As he broke through the last of the crowd, Aran'daj was greeted by the sight of several large fires burning brightly along the chasm's edge. The flames danced and swirled in intricate patterns

34

unlike any he'd witnessed previously, and he knew immediately it was the work of the wizard's magic. Shan'tar's figure moved between each mound of burning tinder, a silhouette amongst the midnight shadows. He danced at times and gesticulated at others.

"What does he do, Commander?" one of the nearby soldiers asked.

Aran'daj shook his head and continued to observe the wizard's strange performance. "I'm not certain I want to find out."

"He calls powerful magic," a low voice said from beside him.

Aran'daj turned to find a Murkor hooded and garbed in vibrant green standing beside him. The color marked him as an alchemist; there were only two presently within the camp, but he suspected this must be Sal'zar. He was nearly as tall as Aran'daj, with a thin, wiry frame.

Alchemists specialized in creating weapons and tools, salves, potions, and elixirs using the ingredients they encountered in the land. Some of their concoctions were used with devastating effect, while others were meant for healing or simply to improve fortune. Murkor could not use magic, but the alchemists' creations were a close proxy.

In that moment, Aran'daj wished Sal'zar had brought with him one of the exploding stones the alchemists had been perfecting, if only to distract the wizard from his task. Shan'tar's blatant use of magic made him uneasy.

"Can we stop him?" he asked of Sal'zar.

Sal'zar shook his head. "He is nearly finished, I believe. What he does feels...*wrong*."

Aran'daj did not question him further, though he wondered how Sal'zar could seem so certain of Shan'tar's actions. Perhaps the alchemists had learned a means of detecting magic, but had not yet perfected it enough to share their knowledge. Alchemists were known for experimentation, which often spanned years before they unveiled their creations.

Aran'daj focused his attention upon the strange human in the distance as he gyrated and spun toward the central fire. He caught a gleam of light in Shan'tar's right hand, a green-white glow that outshone the flames for a moment before the wizard changed direction and his hand was hidden from view.

"What was that?" he asked of Sal'zar.

The alchemist shrugged. "It was a part of his magic, but separate, somehow. I do not know."

Shan'tar fell to his knees at a point equidistant between the three pyres he'd built; his arms stretched upward toward the midnight sky. His voice soared in volume until it thundered across the barren landscape between them, a veritable shockwave of sudden noise. The words he uttered were in a language the Murkor could not decipher, neither their tongue, nor the common, but to Aran'daj, it sounded as though it had come from a time long past, ancient and mysterious.

The green-white light shone brilliantly. It enveloped the wizard and the three bonfires surrounding him. Instinctively, Aran'daj shielded his eyes and turned away from the sight, unwilling to risk blindness from the terrible, searing glare. Most of the other Murkor did the same, though given the sudden bout of swearing he heard from behind, some must have failed to avert their gaze in time.

When the light receded, Aran'daj gaped at the spectacle unfolding near the chasm's edge. The pyres had been extinguished, and Shan'tar remained kneeling between them, but five figures now encircled him. Even from a distance, Aran'daj knew something was terribly wrong with the newcomers. They seemed human, but their skin appeared grayish, as though rife with decay, while their movements were too fluid and quick to be natural. He could see one of the newcomers' eyes, and they glowed dimly in the night, crimson and filled with rage. Each wore antiquated garb that Aran'daj recognized as human-made.

"Gods preserve us," Sal'zar murmured, his tone stunned and horrified.

"Who are they?" Aran'daj asked quietly, though he suspected he already knew. His stomach churned and flipped as bile rose into his throat.

Before Sal'zar could respond, one of the newcomers, shorter than the rest, with a figure that appeared female, strode forward to meet Shan'tar. She raised her hand toward him, but her fingers never met his flesh. At the last moment, she drew her hand into a fist, and Shan'tar's neck snapped sideways at an unnatural angle. She waved her hand dismissively at his corpse. It rose into the air and tumbled over the edge of the chasm behind her.

"Gods," Aran'daj breathed, unable to tear his eyes from the sight, terror rooting him in place even as the figures began to march toward him.

"They are the Soulless, Commander," Sal'zar replied, his tone faltering. "The wizard has doomed us all."

CHAPTER FOUR

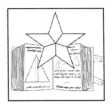

AETHEREAL MAGIC

Tavesin Drondes found himself in a strange place, one unlike any he'd encountered in his fourteen years. He stood upon the precipice of a vast chasm; its black sides were sheer and glittered where the light hit them as they plummeted to unfathomable depths. The light was eerily blue, with a harsh, flat cast to it that caused his shadow to fall like a pool of ink upon the hard, cracked ground. The surreal lighting and the unfamiliar, barren landscape that surrounded him felt much like a dreamscape, though he was certain it would prove an unpleasant one.

Slowly, he turned away from the chasm's edge. Some distance away, hundreds of tents sprawled across the land, though he could see no people amongst them. Another curiosity. He frowned, puzzled, and decided to investigate further. Perhaps the people of the camp were merely asleep? It was impossible to determine the time of day or night it was in this strange land.

The ground appeared dry enough to be dusty, but as his feet passed over it, not so much as a mote was kicked into the air. He was mystified by his interaction with the landscape, its otherworldly illumination, and the lack of people, though the chasm and the tent he approached both appeared much as he expected. He could not make sense of where he was or how he had come to be there.

After a few moments he passed the perimeter of the camp and began walking between the tents. They were small, perhaps built for one person apiece, and constructed of a pale hide that he could not identify. He quickly came to the conclusion the people who had built the camp were not present; it was too still, too eerily silent. He ducked his head into one of the nearest tents to find it held a blanket, a pair of sturdy leather boots, and a set of darkly glittering ring mail. He frowned and returned outside.

As he did, he noticed a figure near the center of the camp that he had failed to take note of previously. He wondered if the person would be able to tell him where he was or how he might return to the Shining Tower. The landscape around the empty camp was like nothing he'd encountered before, and he was certain he was leagues from Dar Daelad.

Hesitantly, he approached the figure. Its body shifted and blurred rapidly, making it impossible to discern any details. As he drew near, the figure tilted its head to one side as though contemplating his presence.

"H-hello?" Tavesin asked uncertainly.

The voice that greeted him was masculine and low enough to issue from an adult's throat, though Tavesin noted with some surprise he stood nearly as tall as the shifting form. He was not tall by any standards, and at fourteen, he still had much growing to do.

"How did you come to be here, little rat?"

Tavesin blinked, affronted. "I...I don't know. The last thing I remember was falling asleep in my bed. What is this place?"

His question was met with a dry chuckle. "What do they teach youth these days? This is a realm you ought not venture into, if you value your life." The figure reached toward him, faster than Tavesin could follow, and gripped his shoulders painfully. "You don't belong here, rat. It's best you go."

The man shoved him with more force than Tavesin believed possible for one with such a small stature, and suddenly he felt himself flying through the air at an impossible speed. He knew he would quickly find himself above the chasm, and was certain if he flew over the edge, it would result in his death. Helpless to stop his flight or alter his trajectory, he began to scream.

Tavesin bolted upright in his bed, his breaths coming in rapid gasps. He stared around the darkened room, comforted that he was within the apprentice quarters of the Shining Tower, as he should have been. Across the room in the other bunk, Rostin Ver'an, another apprentice of approximately the same age, snored softly. It had been nothing more than a nightmare, and yet...

Something about the place triggered his memory. The illumination, the way the landscape failed to react to his movements, even the strange absence of people—it felt familiar, somehow. He racked his brain, trying to recall what he knew of the place. He'd only been an apprentice in the Shining Tower for two months, and during that time he'd learned vast amounts of information about magic, its uses, and its history. But this dream, if that is what it was, had felt as though it were tied to magic, to the celestial ability contained within him.

He frowned, unable to recall anything from his lessons that related to his dream. It was not yet dawn, but he knew the wizard assigned to oversee his training would be awake. Hasnin was a habitually early riser. Quietly, Tavesin climbed from his bed and began to dress in the darkness so as not to awaken Rostin.

He slipped through the door and closed it softly behind him. The corridor beyond was lined with colorful sconces in shades of blue, green, yellow, gray, and white, each lit from within by a steady, magical light. The colors signified the five Sects of the Council of Auras, of which he was learning to become a part. The walls were unadorned between each sconce, and the floor was bare stone. The apprentice quarters were largely unfurnished; the newest members of the magical community were not allowed many luxuries to encourage their focus remain on their studies.

Tavesin hurried along the empty corridor, unsurprised it was empty at the early hour. The corridor ended in a large, rectangular room where a pair of staircases flanked either side. One led upwards, toward the library and the restricted areas farther above, while the other led down, to the first of several levels that housed the wizards' private quarters. He took the latter stairs to descend two levels to the White Sect's floor.

The sconces that lined the walls were colored according to the Sect in residence on each level; he was bathed in yellow light as he passed the first landing of his journey, then was greeted by white light as he arrived on the second. Hasnin's quarters were not far from the landing, and Tavesin was relieved to find his door was propped open.

Hasnin Veransehk was aged; his back stooped as he bent over the thick tome on his writing table. Hasnin's hair—what little there was left—was snow white, in stark contrast to his mahogany skin. In spite of his advanced age, his dark eyes remained bright and observant. As Tavesin raised his fist to rap on the door frame, Hasnin looked up sharply from his work.

"Taven? What brings you here at this early hour?"

"Sir, I—"

"Come inside, boy, and sit down."

Hasnin ushered him into the cluttered room. He waved absently at one of the sturdy wooden chairs that faced the writing table, while he closed the door to the hall beyond. Tavesin did as the wizard ordered and perched upon the chair, waiting for Hasnin to seat himself once more. The wizard steepled his fingers and peered at Tavesin closely.

"You are troubled, Taven. Tell me why."

Tavesin nodded nervously and began to describe his nightmare. Hasnin quickly held up one gnarled hand before his apprentice began to describe more than the landscape and its eerie lighting.

"You speak of the Aethereum," Hasnin explained. "I've heard accounts of the place, but most humans cannot summon the magic required to venture there themselves. I knew you were talented, boy, but I did not know you possessed aethereal magic."

"What is it, though?" Tavesin inquired. "I didn't mean to go there, sir. It just…happened."

Hasnin chuckled genially. "As I understand it, that is how many begin their journeys within the Aethereum. If you wish to learn more about the place, we may need to contact the Drakkon—their kind harbor aethereal magic more frequently than we humans."

Tavesin blinked with surprise. The Drakkon tended to keep to themselves, though he had spied one or two in the marketplace after traveling to Dar Daelad. He knew they possessed magic, but they did not affiliate themselves with the Council of Auras, nor did they follow the darker path of the other human guild, rumored to reside somewhere in the Wasted Land.

"The…The lizard-people, sir?" he stammered.

41

Hasnin's sharp gaze bored into him. "I would advise you not to call them such, Taven. They may resemble lizards in many ways, but they find such terms offensive. *If* you possess enough talent in aethereal magic to pursue that path, you will need guidance, and you will need to set aside any preconceptions you might have of the Drakkon. They are fierce, proud, and can be rather prickly when it comes to their dealings with humans. You'll need to use the utmost respect when working with them."

"I'm sorry, sir." Chastised, he looked down at his hands and began to fidget.

"Now, as I was saying, I believe you found your way into the Aethereum." Hasnin rummaged beneath the writing table for a moment and when he sat up, he held a thick, dusty tome in his hands. "This book describes the place in detail. I borrowed it from the library some time ago and forgot to return it, but perhaps that is fortuitous. You'll have need of its words, I believe."

He smiled knowingly and placed the heavy book upon the table, opening it to a seemingly random page. "The stories state the Aethereum was created by the Immortal Solsticia, keeper of the stars, the heavens, and all things celestial. Magic is considered celestial, as you ought to recall from your lessons." He arched a bushy eyebrow in Tavesin's direction.

"Yes, sir." It had been one of the first lessons he'd been given upon entering his apprenticeship in the Shining Tower.

Hasnin nodded, satisfied. "Good. It is said that she created the Aethereum for her only child, a mortal human with the Ability. The stories are unclear on her reasons for doing so, though it was not long before the first Great War. Few blessed with magic are capable of entering the Aethereum, and most of those are Drakkon. Your description is identical to the one written here," Hasnin stated. He pointed to a passage in the book as he turned the tome around for Tavesin to read. "The light, your interaction with the landscape—it is all described here."

Tavesin skimmed the indicated paragraph with growing wonder. It was as Hasnin said; he had somehow managed to find himself within the Aethereum.

"Sir, I didn't tell you the whole of my story," he said haltingly after a moment, and his elation began to wane.

"What more did you see, Taven?"

He drew a breath and described the strange encounter with the man, whose features had blurred and become distorted time and again, making identification impossible. He related their brief conversation and how the man had violently ended it.

Hasnin was silent for several long seconds after Tavesin finished speaking. His expression was contemplative, yet apprehensive. "This is a grave matter," he said finally. "There are tales… No, it's best I don't speculate. I must speak with the Radiant, and you must go about your lessons for the day."

An hour later, Tavesin found himself seated amongst a dozen other apprentices in a semi-circle on the floor of Carylla A'dan's study. Carylla was another member of the White Sect and taught magical history. She was as much a fount of knowledge as Hasnin had proven to be, though Tavesin often found his mind wandering during her lectures. She was a kindly woman, but her delivery was often dry and relatively boring. Today proved no exception.

"For well over two thousand years, the Council has consisted of five Sects," she informed them as she paced across the small space. "Each Sect, as you know, is defined by a color and by its purpose within the Council. For example, my Sect, the White, are the Council's historians and seekers of knowledge. Some of our number remain here in the tower, to assist with the scholars and to teach the new recruits like yourselves. Others go into the world in search of lost relics and artifacts imbued with magic."

Beside him, Rostin raised his hand into the air. When Carylla nodded to him, he said, "Do you mean like Varasin? They say he went into Stonewall Hall and returned mad!"

Tavesin cringed at his friend's question, but it was typical of Rostin. He craved excitement and was unafraid of disrupting a planned lecture in order to achieve it. Three days past, Rostin had caused a stir during one of their shielding lessons, which had landed both he and Tavesin with a days' work in the kitchens, scrubbing pots and pans.

Tavesin hadn't been a part of Rostin's ploy, but because it was known they were friends, he'd suffered the same punishment.

Carylla fixed Rostin with a cool gaze. "Yes, Varasin did venture into Stonewall Hall in search of relics. And yes, he sadly lost his sanity in the process. Hunting for relics is *not* a safe profession, particularly if you choose to set foot into a place such as Stonewall Hall." She crossed her arms and resumed pacing, the matter closed.

"The Green Sect specialize in healing magic, and often know much about herbs and remedies," she continued. "They rarely remain in the tower, as their skills are needed in the wider world. During their travels, many take the time to seek out others with the spark—the Ability—and recruit them for training. Certainly, most of you sitting here today were sent here by a Green."

Tavesin reflected on his own recruitment. A pair of wizards had ventured to the tiny village of Rican Mer, near the southern border of Delucha Kingdom, though Tavesin could not recall if either had mentioned their Sect affiliation to him. They had sensed the Ability within him and swiftly negotiated his journey to the Shining Tower. His mother had beamed proudly at the news her only son was gifted with magic, while his father had seemed despondent. There would be no one to carry on the family's farm, with Tavesin gone to become a wizard, but after long hours of persuasion, his mother had won out. Two days later, Tavesin had left Rican Mer behind in the company of the wizards.

"The Gray Sect are the warriors of the Council. They hone their bodies and their minds for combat and specialize in offensive magic. There are few Grays within the Council at present, for we have been at peace for many generations. Similarly, the Blue Sect are the defenders of the Council. Blues are known for shielding techniques and are most often credited in the histories with saving many lives during battle. Again, there are few Blues in the Council, simply because there is little need for them."

Rostin raised his hand again, and Carylla frowned. "Yes, Rostin?"

"What about Shan'tar?" he asked. "Larsen said—"

"Larsen may have been with the Council longer than you have, Rostin, but you must learn not to listen to everything he tells you," she chided. "He is still an apprentice and is not privy to the details of what is presently occurring in the east. Rumors serve no purpose but to rouse suspicion and ire, and it's best that you ignore them."

Rostin nodded and looked down, crestfallen. "Very well."

"Good. Now, the final Sect within the Council is Yellow. The Yellows are the inventors of new magical devices and experiment with their powers to find new methods and uses for magic. It is not uncommon to hear strange noises or experience unusual phenomena when passing through their level of the tower. There are—"

There was a loud rap on the doorframe of Carylla's study, and she paused in her lecture to acknowledge their visitor. Tavesin turned in his seat to find Hasnin in the doorway, his face unusually grim.

"My apologies for the interruption, Carylla," he said, "but I must borrow Tavesin for a time. There is an urgent matter he must attend to."

"Of course," she replied, as Tavesin rose from his seat. Rostin shot him an envious look, which he ignored as he made his way toward Hasnin and the door.

Hasnin ushered him into the corridor and did not speak until the door to Carylla's study was firmly closed. "The Radiant has asked to see you, boy."

Tavesin blanched. "Am I in trouble, sir?"

Hasnin chuckled and clapped him roughly on the shoulder. "No, Taven, you're in no trouble, and nothing is amiss with your family, so far as I know. This is in regards to your visit to the Aethereum."

"Oh." Relieved, he followed in Hasnin's wake as they made their way to the stairs leading to the lower levels of the tower.

They traveled below the White Sect's level, through the landings of the Blue, Gray, and finally, Green. One level below that found them in a curving corridor that encircled the vast Council Chamber, where the Council of Auras could meet in its entirety. Hasnin led him quickly past several sets of ornately carved doors that would lead into the Council Chamber, to a room that, to Tavesin's mind, lay behind the chamber and directly opposite the stairs. The door was carved with the five-pointed star insignia of the Council; the star was divided into five equal pieces, and each had been carefully painted to correspond to the five Sects that made up the Council.

"No doubt you haven't been to this part of the tower," Hasnin said quietly. "This door leads to the Radiant's private study. He is expecting us, but do not make a habit of coming here unannounced. He is a busy man, Tavesin."

Tavesin nodded and clasped his hands to keep himself from fidgeting. This would be his first meeting with the Council's appointed leader. The Radiant was a strong wizard, but he was also one of the most influential people in the known world. Tavesin had little experience with dignitaries, which Rostin was quick to point out at every opportunity. Though Tavesin had learned to avoid gaping when he met new people or witnessed something for the first time, the encounters still made him terribly nervous.

Hasnin rapped his knuckle against the door, and they waited in silence for several seconds before it was pulled open from within. Tavesin was startled to see a man half of Hasnin's age appear. He smiled at them and motioned for them to follow him inside. He was not a tall man, but of stout build and had the dark hair and pale skin common to those of Deluchan heritage. As the Radiant turned to lead them inside, Tavesin was presented with the five-toned cloak bearing the Council's insignia that was unique to the Council's leader. He paused to close the door at Hasnin's wordless instruction before following the aged wizard across the room to a cluster of chairs.

The Radiant had already seated himself and gestured they should do so as well. He leaned forward, elbows on his knees, to study Tavesin for a time. "You're the apprentice gifted with aethereal magic, then? Hasnin told me your tale, but I should like to hear it from you."

Tavesin found his mouth had gone suddenly dry, and he swallowed hard before speaking. He related his encounter for the second time that morning, but on this occasion, he was not interrupted. The Radiant gazed at him thoughtfully, his blue eyes never straying from Tavesin's.

When Tavesin fell silent, the Radiant sat back in his chair with a troubled frown. "There are accounts of the Soulless entering the Aethereum, Tavesin. Because they have given their souls over to the Nameless, they were granted great power, but they are not truly human

46

any longer. When one of the Soulless appears in the Aethereum, they are incapable of maintaining a recognizable form, and will appear distorted, blurred, faceless."

Tavesin felt a chill permeate his core. "The Soulless, sir?" His voice cracked upon the words and he was unable to mask his sudden fear.

The Radiant nodded. "Yes. We have known for some time that the madness inflicting Varasin had driven him into the Wasted Land, and that he is working with the Murkor. We received troubling news nearly a week ago, and I have good reason to believe he…He may have resurrected the Soulless. The man you encountered was one of them."

Tavesin looked down at his hands as a wave of panic washed over him. Hasnin spoke quietly to him, but he could not hear his mentor's words over the cacophony of his own thoughts. After a moment, a pair of hands gripped his shoulders and he forced himself to look up. The Radiant knelt in front of him, his eyes wide with concern.

"You've done nothing wrong, Tavesin," he stated evenly. "In any other circumstance, we would be celebrating your newfound ability. Indeed, we ought to, even now, but there are greater forces at work that must be attended to first. The wider Council must know of your encounter, Tavesin. I am calling a full meeting of the Council for tomorrow evening, and I require your attendance. You must tell the Council what you've just told me. Can you do that?"

Reluctantly, Tavesin nodded. "Yes, sir."

CHAPTER FIVE

ENLIGHTENED ROYALTY

Ages had been spent, trapped within the confines of the gray netherworld, but in one blinding, glorious instant, she'd been reawakened, resurrected to her former power. The man responsible had been wrestling with insanity's dark hold, and she'd done him a mercy by ending his miserable existence. Certainly, she could have ignited his clothing and watched him burn alive, a more entertaining end, but the soft-hearted, weak-willed Alyra had been present. Dranamir ended him quickly. She'd broken his neck, then discarded the remains into the depths of Blackstone Chasm.

Afterwards, she'd returned to the tower, appalled at its present state. It had been empty for far too long. Dust coated every surface, strands of cobweb hung from doors and window ledges, once-fine wooden furniture lay broken and riddled with dry rot, and the air itself smelled stale and stagnant. The tower must be restored to its former glory, and with it, the Council of Enlightened.

She had traveled through several floors of the tower before growing tired of the long, winding stair and the puffs of dust that rose into the air with each footfall. She created a portal into the Aethereum and transported herself to the tower's topmost floor, where she knew the others would gather. She didn't care if they'd been waiting long. She was the first and the most powerful of their master's chosen; the others were meant to bask in her shadow.

The topmost floor was ringed with windows, and along the outer walls were an array of glass cases. This part of the tower was under protective enchantment; only those with the master's touch upon them were allowed physical entry, and not even the ravages of time had been able to leave its mark on the space. The cases held more relics and artifacts than they had in her time, a testament to their Council's determination and prowess in years past. Where had they gone? She wondered. It was an affront to their master to leave the tower abandoned and in such a state of disrepair.

Slowly, she turned her attention to the four figures gathered at the far end of the room. Three men, none of whom she recognized, and another woman, Alyra. How had the bitch finagled her way into the master's graces enough to become his second chosen? Alyra was of mediocre Ability, and was too soft to prove effective as a leader. Yet, there she was, still recognizable in spite of the changes their master's touch had wrought upon her fair features. Dranamir scowled and crossed her arms as she strode toward them.

"Gods, it's about time you arrived," Alyra snarled. "Not only have you already made a mess of things, but you kept us waiting as well!"

Dranamir leveled an icy stare at the other woman, noting how her once perfect mocha complexion had lost its luster and become a shade of sickly gray-brown. Her once lustrous black hair was thin and matted; the eyes that had once been a captivating chocolate-brown were now a baleful crimson. Alyra had retained her hourglass figure and some of her former beauty, to Dranamir's chagrin.

"The man needed to die," she replied coldly.

"That was always your solution," Alyra sneered. "If someone no longer serves a purpose, they are disposed of. There are better ways of achieving our goals."

The tallest of the men spoke up then; he had the distinct, clipped accent that marked him as being of Kamshati descent, though his skin appeared nearly as gray as Alyra's. He may have once been quite handsome, Dranamir thought, but as with the others, the master's touch had taken it from him.

"She is right," he told Alyra. "The man was insane. A liability, no matter whose side he appeared to be on. Death was the best course of action."

Alyra scowled at him. "And who might *you* be, that you know what the best course of action should have been?"

"Only the most successful of us since her," he replied gesturing toward Dranamir. "I am Kama."

Dranamir smiled coldly; perhaps Kama would prove to be an ally in her machinations. "I do not care what your weeping heart felt for that man," she informed Alyra, "and as you well know, I do not waste my time nor my breath if the path forward is clear. I acted as I always have, and I suppose it is little wonder that you balk at it. You've never had the spine to carry out the master's true work."

Alyra lifted her chin, outraged. "I became Soulless after you fell, Dranamir. He saw in me the potential for greatness."

"And the war was ended by the Fireblade only months later," the smallest of the men countered. "The histories we were taught in the years following your defeat stated quite clearly you were not as adept as your predecessor."

Dranamir studied him with interest; another potential ally. He was small, almost to the point of frailty, but she could sense the magic within him, a power that radiated and outshone the other three. It was no match to her own, but he was not the weakling he appeared to be at first glance. His skin had likely been pale before his transformation, for now it was white as new-fallen snow, tinged with a strange greenish hue. Of the four who stood facing her, his eyes shone the brightest, with a lurid, bloody glow even in the daylight.

She nodded to him with approval. "You seem to be a historian."

He shrugged indifferently. "I learned much during my time leading the Enlightened. If I wished to succeed in the master's plan and not repeat the failures of my predecessors, I knew I must learn the history of the previous conflicts." He gestured at the third man, who still remained silent. "Jannyn, for instance, lost his war and his life within weeks of its onset."

Jannyn bristled. "I failed to detect the spies within the tower until it was too late. You cannot count that as a strike against me!"

The small man shrugged again. "I only state what I know from the histories. Yours was a sad tale, as was hers." He pointed to Alyra. "My own command outlasted both of yours, though not so long as Dranamir's. Nor of Kama's, it seems, but he came after I."

Kama appraised him. "You must be the one called Garin."

"I am."

"Enough with the bloody introductions," Jannyn growled. "What are we to do about that man's death? Should we not have discussed such an action before it was carried out?"

Dranamir snorted. She knew she would like him about as much as she did the act of stepping on a sewing needle barefoot, which was on par with how she felt regarding Alyra. "Discussions are useless if the path is clear. And his path was, indeed, clear."

"You'll never change, will you, Dranamir?" Alyra was seething.

"As we have established, mine was the most successful out of all our campaigns. I am the most powerful, as well, or do I need to demonstrate that for you again, Alyra?" She smiled grimly, envisioning what she might do to the other woman, given the chance. "In your newfound state, I could prolong your torture for weeks before you succumbed, and I would savor every moment."

"You threaten her?" Jannyn demanded. He stepped in front of Alyra as though to shield her from Dranamir's perceived threat.

Dranamir frowned, unimpressed. She seized her power, and with a simple gesture of her arm, sent Jannyn hurtling through the room to crash into the nearest window. She simultaneously shielded herself from the others' retaliation. Jannyn slid toward the floor, a dazed expression upon his face, and she stormed toward him in a fury.

She heard Alyra shouting behind her, but she pointedly ignored the other woman, her focus solely upon Jannyn. A magical attack ricocheted from her protective shield, likely from Alyra; she was not strong enough to penetrate the barrier alone. One of the other two men may have been, but they remained silent, content to observe the confrontation.

"Listen to me well, for I dislike repeating myself," she informed Jannyn as his eyes met hers. "I take orders from no one but the master, and I will threaten whomever I please."

She gestured with her right hand, peeling his gray flesh away from the glistening muscles beneath his left forearm. He writhed and screamed in sudden agony.

"I will not tolerate your defiance. Have I made myself clear?"

He nodded and choked back another scream, his eyes riveted upon the arm. Blood had begun to ooze from the exposed tissue to fall in fat droplets upon the black, tiled floor.

She frowned and peeled the flesh back further, exposing more muscle and the knobby, yellowed bones of his elbow. Another attack bounced off her shield, more feeble than the last. She kept her gaze upon Jannyn and waited for his howls to subside before she spoke again.

"I don't believe I heard your answer."

"Y-yes," he stammered through clenched teeth. "You've made...yourself very...fucking...clear."

She nodded once and released him, then flicked her wrist to mend the damage she'd inflicted. She maintained her shield, knowing well that Alyra—or possibly Jannyn—would attempt another attack at any moment. It seemed the pretty bitch had made at least one ally that morning, though Dranamir was confident Kama would remain on her side. Garin was an unknown. She suspected with enough time and torture, he too, could be convinced to join her.

The room was silent for several long moments as Dranamir rejoined the others near the center, and Jannyn regained his composure. The Soulless may be powerful and difficult to kill, but they could feel pain just as any other mortal. And Dranamir excelled at inflicting pain. Kama eyed her with interest, Garin appeared indifferent to the display, and Alyra simply sulked.

"Are you finished?" Garin asked, his tone bored.

She arched an eyebrow in his direction, her lips twisted into a frown. Perhaps she should have prolonged Jannyn's torture, if only to impress upon the deceptively frail man that she was not to be trifled with. She crossed her arms and leveled a flat gaze in his direction.

"For now."

"As Kama likely knows, I was chosen by our master because I have a unique aptitude with magic that allows me to make direct contact with him," Garin continued. He picked at his chipped fingernails rather than looking at any of the others. "He has issued us several commands since our reawakening."

"What does he wish of us?" Alyra asked eagerly, her eyes suddenly aglow with desire. Dranamir felt her stomach churn at the sickening display of subservience; the Soulless bowed to no one, not even the imprisoned god they referred to as their master.

"Foremost, we are to recruit others of like mind, to reform the ranks of the Enlightened," Garin replied. "He has given me a list of potential candidates. Secondly, we are to prepare a diversionary strike upon the Stronghold. It is not our master's primary objective, but he means to test the defenses of the Scorpion Men. I assume the Murkor will need some…convincing." He flicked his gaze toward Kama. "The master has chosen you to head the armies. The rest of us shall focus on recruitment and then upon the training of those who join."

They dispersed a short time later; Alyra and Jannyn left together via portal, and Garin departed by the tower stairs. Kama lingered, while Dranamir studied the brief list of names Garin had given her. Next to each name was written a location, and one drew her immediate interest: Tamarin Serales, Deluchan Royal Palace. The recruit could have proven to be anyone from a mere servant to the Queen herself, and the prospect of royalty amongst their ranks was tantalizing.

"Your power is impressive," Kama said into the silence, drawing her attention away from the list in her hand.

"Of course, it is. The master chose me as his first for good reason."

"Based upon what I've sensed from the others, he did not choose you for your power alone," Kama continued as he came nearer, "though you outshine even Garin. No, he chose you for your ruthlessness. A trait I rather admire."

Dranamir fixed him with her coldest glare. "Admire all you wish, but from a distance. I will flay you alive and roast your entrails if you so much as lay a finger upon me without my express desire that it be so."

Kama chuckled, unfazed. "I have no doubt you will make good upon that threat, and so I will do as you ask. I simply want you to know that should you ever need anything, I am available." He stood very near, towering over her, but he bent to speak directly into her ear. "*Anything*, Dranamir."

"I will not forget your vow," she replied, "and you'd best not, either. I have no tolerance for those who cross me."

He chuckled again and straightened. "I never forget, Dranamir, and I wouldn't dream of crossing you."

She watched as he created a portal for himself and disappeared to leave her alone at the top of the tower. Kama was not what she had expected, though she was pleased with his promise to her. She would exploit his lust in order to achieve her own goals, and perhaps if he proved valuable enough, she would allow him to satisfy his unconcealed craving. She'd always hoped to meet a man that was more interested in her than he was in Alyra, if only to flaunt the fact to her long-time nemesis. As with everyone she met, Kama was but another tool to be used and discarded once he'd served his purpose.

With a brief smile that failed to touch her cold, crimson eyes, she returned her attention to the list. She would pay this Tamarin a visit and learn what she could of her talents and personality.

She went to the end of the room opposite the stairs, where a large, oval mirror hung upon the wall. The glass within the twisted black frame was smoky, her reflection within it a mere shadow of her true self. A cursory glance told her she looked much as she had before her final moments during the war, centuries ago. The master's power had not failed her; she was restored to life, just as he'd promised. Her skin was a sickly gray-green, akin to that of Jannyn's, and her hair had managed to maintain much of its dark luster, unlike Alyra's. The eyes that gazed back at her from the depths of the mirror were a livid red, glowing with an inner fire.

If she were to successfully recruit anyone to their cause, particularly someone residing within the Deluchan royal palace, she would require a disguise. Anyone who looked upon her face would know her for what she was—Soulless. It was best they kept themselves hidden, their resurrection a secret, until the time arrived to announce their return to the world.

She glanced around the room with a frown. The rows of glass cases along its walls were filled with magical relics and tools, not one of which would prove useful as a disguise. She doubted there would be anything of use within the tower's lower levels, after witnessing its decrepit state first-hand. If any items of clothing had been left behind when the last of the Enlightened fled, they would have rotted away long ago.

She closed her eyes briefly and called a minor summoning magic; she wove strands of power together deftly until a thick, hooded cloak had formed between her hands. The crimson fabric felt luxurious as she drew the newly-formed garment around her shoulders and pulled up the hood. Her face was hidden, but her eyes glimmered balefully from within the shadows.

She frowned again. The master's touch was proving difficult to hide. Previously, she had no reason to disguise herself; she was the chosen leader of the Enlightened, proud of her position, and if her altered appearance struck fear into her subordinates, all the better. Now, she was considered an equal amongst four others bearing the same blessing from their master, and she had no subordinates—yet. In order to succeed at her appointed task, she must find a way to hide what she was. Dranamir worked best unencumbered, but necessity dictated she don this ridiculous mask, however ineffectual it proved to be.

She opened a portal into the Aethereum and stepped through. The flat, bluish illumination failed to touch the surface of the mirror in front of her. In this plane, the glass seemed to absorb the light, leaving a dark smudge against the tower's wall. The mirror had been part of the tower long before she joined the ranks of Enlightened, and though she did not know its true purpose, she understood it was tied to their master in a profound way.

She turned her back on the mirror; it was a puzzle for another day. She visualized what she recalled of the Deluchan royal palace in her mind, and instantly the scenery around her blurred in a rush of motion that she sensed rather than felt. A moment later, she stood in a courtyard brimming with vegetation in various states of bloom. Surrounding the courtyard were the high, inner walls of a castle, constructed of age-darkened gray stones. Though the courtyard of her memory had been a stark, barren place, its plants reduced to ash during her conquest, she recognized the space for what it was.

She closed her eyes briefly, sensing the environment around her and seeking the aura of the woman named Tamarin Serales. It took little time for her to pinpoint the woman's location; she was presently in a chamber on the topmost floor of the main castle, a space typically reserved for the royal family or high-ranking nobility. Dranamir smirked at her good fortune, and willed herself into the room.

She found herself in a large bedchamber. Centrally positioned against a wall was an enormous, canopied bed, adorned with frilly sheets and far too much velvet for Dranamir's taste. On one of the adjoining walls was a large, picture window with heavy drapery matching the owner's bed, while across the room from the window was a partitioned area ensconcing a wardrobe, and beside it a full-length oval mirror. This mirror appeared normal in the Aethereum, unchanged as the other had been by magic.

Dranamir decided the best place to learn of her quarry was from behind the partition. It was almost noon, and the chance that the room's owner was currently within and changing garments should be small. She stepped into position, then created another portal and exited the Aethereum.

Once in the physical realm, her ears were immediately assaulted by anguished wails. Given that the room belonged to someone of rank, she assumed either a great tragedy had occurred, or the diamond had fallen out of a favorite piece of jewelry and could not be located. One was just as plausible as the other. She pulled her hood lower and crouched behind the partition. She surveyed the swaths of silk and satin, lace and velvet spilling from within the wardrobe, while she listened to the sounds in the room beyond.

"Princess, I know this has been a difficult morning," a strained male voice stated as the wailing abated. "You have my deepest condolences for what has transpired, particularly since the horrible deed was carried out by Lukin. No one could have foreseen this tragedy."

A loud sniffle could be heard, then a woman's voice, shaken and on the verge of hysteria. "I told father Lukin was plotting something! And now he's dead, along with mother!" Her voice dissolved into a howl of despair.

Dranamir nodded to herself. She did not know who Lukin was, but she was certain the woman outside was Tamarin, and a princess, no less. Her last statement made it clear that both the king and queen were dead, and at this Lukin's hands. If Dranamir's luck continued to hold, the Enlightened would not only acquire a new member, but potentially Delucha's future queen.

"I am sorry, princess," the male voice stated. "I will ensure the proper arrangements are made for your parents. A state funeral must be held, of course. Lukin has been apprehended and is currently in the dungeon. There is no doubt about his guilt. He will hang for this, crown prince, or not."

There was a pause, then the man continued. "Send for me should you need anything, princess. You require time alone with your grief."

Dranamir considered her options. A woman in the clutches of despair could be manipulated, but she must tread carefully. Tamarin's emotions might cause her to be irrational and erratic.

The door closed with a heavy thud and the room quickly fell silent. After a moment, Dranamir heard rustling, then footsteps crossed from the bed to the door. The heavy bolt slid into place, and then surprisingly, the woman began to laugh softly to herself. Dranamir listened carefully, but detected no indication the laughter was spawned from hysteria; it had a grim undertone, one Dranamir understood well.

She stepped into the room and found the woman facing away from her while she chuckled darkly to herself. At a glance, she was younger than Dranamir had anticipated, perhaps no more than a teenager. She possessed the porcelain-pale skin, lustrous dark hair, and short stature of those native to Delucha. The gown she wore was sewn of heavy blue and gold velvets, adorned with lace at the neck and sleeves. Clearly, the bedclothes had been made to suit her taste, and Dranamir sneered.

"How did you do it?" she asked, startling the princess.

Tamarin spun around, green eyes wide with surprise. "How did you—?" The words died upon her lips and what little color her skin naturally possessed drained away as she took a good look at her visitor. "Who *are* you?"

Dranamir had wasted enough time in her game of eavesdropping and was no longer in the mood to delay. She seized her power and lifted the girl into the air while simultaneously sealing her mouth closed.

"Answer my question—and do not scream, for it will be the last thing you ever do," Dranamir replied coldly. "I will lift the suppression so that you may speak, but if you attempt to call anyone to your aid from outside, I will kill you."

Tamarin nodded emphatically, and Dranamir allowed her to speak once more.

"I snuck into my mother's chamber first," she said slowly. "Mother often had difficulty sleeping, and had taken to using an apothecary's remedy at night. Once she fell asleep, she heard nothing until the morning. I had stolen my brother's hunting knife and used it to kill her."

Dranamir crossed her arms and began to pace in front of the princess, suspended in the air. "And your father?"

"He did not return to his chambers until very late. By then, mother was already dead." She swallowed and blinked away the beginnings of tears—genuine tears, this time. "Please, don't kill me."

Dranamir smirked; she would not make a promise she could not keep. "Answer my question."

"I hid in his wardrobe until I heard him return, and I remained there until I was certain he was both alone and asleep," Tamarin continued, her voice quavering with fear. "I used Lukin's knife on him, and left it beside father's bed. I took some of mother's sleeping draught when I returned, and the servants were forced to awaken me with the...news."

"Committing murder is a bloody business," Dranamir replied indifferently. "What did you do with the clothing you wore?"

Tamarin gaped and a tear spilled from her right eye. "I...I hid them in...the bottom of my wardrobe. No one should look there..."

Dranamir snorted. "Foolish girl."

She strode toward the wardrobe and pulled the heavy door open fully. She found the pile of blood-soaked silks easily enough, and brought them into the center of the room where the suspended princess could look upon them.

"I do this as a favor to you, princess," Dranamir sneered as she set the clothing ablaze with a flick of her wrist, "but like Karmada, I expect something from you in return."

Tamarin, unable to look away from her captor, managed a brief nod.

"You will tell no one of my visit, and when I return, you will obey my every command. You will become a member of the Enlightened, and you will serve me."

Tamarin blinked. "E-enlightened? I don't understand."

"You possess the Ability, my dear princess. Have you not been assessed by the wizards?"

Tamarin's expression became guarded. "No. My mother didn't trust the Council of Auras, and dismissed our magical advisor when I was very young. Are you one of them?"

Dranamir laughed. "No, princess, I am something else entirely. The Enlightened were once a powerful force in opposition to the Council of Auras. Perhaps you've heard them called by another name, such as the Shadow Council?"

She smiled to herself as Tamarin blanched further. It was not every day she could instill such fear into a potential recruit, and even rarer that she could do so to royalty.

"You're one of them..." Tamarin managed in a strangled tone. "Your eyes..."

"You're a quick study," Dranamir replied with another smirk. "I have devoted my very soul to the Enlightened cause. Now that you understand my position, you must also understand that my offer cannot be declined. If you refuse me, you will die."

"I understand."

Dranamir's nostrils were hit with the tang of urine as the princess lost control of her bladder. She crossed her arms, unimpressed by the display of weakness in a woman who aspired to be queen.

Tamarin squeezed her eyes closed and grimaced. "I accept, Great One."

Dranamir nodded in approval and set the princess down upon the soiled carpet before releasing her restraints. "I do not require an honorific, but 'Great One' has a certain ring to it. You will address me as such—and any of the others who may partake in your training. I will return in the night. Ensure you are alone."

"Of course, Great One."

Dranamir smiled beneath her hood, pleased that she had forced the princess to grovel. "Good. Clean yourself up, and make certain you haven't left any further incriminating evidence in your wake. I'd hate to see you share your brother's fate."

CHAPTER SIX

A DANGEROUS PATH

Vardak sat alone just beyond Coreyaless' garden, his arms crossed as he contemplated their options. He knew there was but one choice left to them if they were to fulfill the mission Flariel had set upon them, and he was obligated to do so at Blademon's behest. When he'd agreed to train with the warrior god, he'd been elated—so much so that he never considered his apprenticeship might come with hidden costs. Now, as he mulled over how they might survive a journey through Stonewall Hall, he wished he would have questioned the Immortal's motives.

Janna had already expressed her blatant fear of pursuing such a path, but it could not be helped. No matter how long he sifted through their limited options, nor how many times he tried to come up with a different solution, he was forced to circle back to the path the Airess had laid before them. They must venture into Stonewall Hall, find the shrine at its heart, and travel to the southern continent while somehow eluding the Undead that roamed within.

He scowled at the nearby forest as though it were at fault for his present predicament. It was the only sure path to gain the relic they sought, but it was the most dangerous.

He heard footsteps approach from the direction of the hut, but he did not turn around to acknowledge them. Instead, he glanced skyward. It was nearing noon, and he'd promised Coreyaless he would have a decision for her this morning. His scowl deepened; she'd left him with no true choice, and he suspected she knew it.

"It's almost noon." Coreyaless came to stand beside him. Her grey eyes studied the forest beyond.

He glanced at her from the corner of his eye and frowned. "I know."

"Have you come to a decision?"

"Have you spoken to Janna?" he countered. "I'm unused to her overt displays of emotion and I'm no use when it comes to calming her. She knows the only path that will bring her to the Moon's Eye lies within Stonewall Hall, and it's clear to me she isn't prepared for the journey."

"I have, and she has deferred to your judgment."

Vardak suppressed the urge to roll his eyes, and instead clenched his jaw in momentary frustration. "Then you know my decision."

Coreyaless turned to face him then, a faint smile crossing her lips. "I will be in your debt, Vardak. If it is any consolation, I am the best healer you will ever meet outside the Shining Tower."

He did not return her smile. "I don't like being manipulated."

"I hardly think trading favors is manipulation, Vardak," she replied evenly. "Besides, I prefer to stay far away from the machinations of the Immortals, and entangling myself with the pair of you goes against my better judgment. It is only fair that I obtain something from this arrangement that is to my benefit."

"By risking all of our lives," he growled.

"If anyone has the proper skills to help me reach Danness, it is you," she stated. "Until you have waited over one thousand years to be reunited with someone you love, you will never fully understand my desperation. Your appearance here was an opportunity I was not about to pass over."

In spite of himself, he understood her plight and her disdain for the gods. He wanted to help her, and he possessed the skills to do so, which ultimately led him to this decision. With a sea voyage south impossible for more than reasons of weather, he'd known since their first conversation what his answer would be. He'd delayed in giving it to postpone the inevitable emotional thunderstorm it would spark within Janna.

He sighed and relented. "I suppose I'd best tell Janna our plan. She won't be happy."

"For a daughter of Flariel, she has led a sheltered life." Coreyaless followed him as he made his way through the garden toward the hut.

He shrugged. "It's for that reason I was recruited. She cannot defend herself, and her mother has unrealistic expectations. I've worked with Blademon for some time, but my brief encounter with Flariel left me...unimpressed."

Coreyaless laughed softly. "Flariel is fickle as the flame she commands." She studied him for a moment as they approached the door. "Perhaps you feel more kinship with the war god simply because he is the patron of your people."

Janna looked up from the book she was reading as they entered, and her face fell when she met Vardak's gaze. Perhaps she was more perceptive than he'd given her credit for.

"We're going, aren't we?" she asked despondently.

"Yes." He made his way toward her and sat down a handspan away, folding his legs carefully beneath him. "We won't leave today, but tomorrow, with the dawn."

"Vardak, I'm not made for this type of journey." She looked down and carefully closed the book in her hands. "My mother must wish me dead, if she thinks I can win her favor by traversing Stonewall Hall—and the gods only know where else."

"Janna, I don't believe your mother factored your mortality into her scheme," Coreyaless replied gently. "The Immortals rarely do. Do not lose heart. I've concocted a few potions in my time that have proven helpful against the creatures within Stonewall Hall, and Vardak is likely the finest warrior you will ever encounter. We will prevail, Janna. I'm certain of it."

Vardak remained silent, surprised by the Airess' fervent conviction of their success. She had not mentioned her potions previously, and though he was pleased to hear they would have more than just his battle axe for defense, her admission irritated him. She'd withheld her own contributions to the coming journey for the sake of forcing him down the path of her choosing. No matter how she saw the situation, he believed she'd manipulated him. He crossed his arms and glowered at the floor.

"How long will it take us to reach Stonewall Hall?" Janna asked after a moment's tense silence.

"Five days, perhaps six," Vardak replied, relying on the knowledge he'd been granted by Blademon.

Coreyaless looked at him sharply, as though she hadn't expected him to answer. "Yes, what Vardak says is correct. I've been to the entrance on the slopes of Nuarno Peak, but I did not venture inside. That was…many years ago."

"What brought you to that place?" Janna asked. "What was it like?"

"I traveled there with the last of the Fireblade's bearers— before she acquired the weapon," Coreyaless replied. "It had long been considered lost when rumor spread that her predecessor had fallen in Stonewall Hall. It was at that time I devised the potion I spoke of, and I traveled with her to Nuarno Peak. I did not go inside, though I was sorely tempted to. The time was not right, and Arianna had larger matters to concern herself with than my desire to find Danness."

Vardak frowned at her, but kept his thoughts to himself. If the Immortals were correct, their present concern was just as great as the legendary Arianna's had been, if not more so. He found himself liking the Airess less the more he learned of her.

"You knew Arianna Janis?" Janna gasped, eyes wide with wonder.

Coreyaless nodded. "She came to me for help only weeks before Kama's War began. The Shining Tower was compromised— the Shadow Council had spies amongst the wizards, and she believed she could not trust any of them. She knew what she was, but she did not know how to locate the sword. I agreed to act as her guide as far as Nuarno Peak."

Vardak knew the history Coreyaless spoke of; nearly everyone of a certain age, no matter their upbringing, race, or profession knew the legend of the Fireblade and its wielders. It was said the wielder's soul would be reborn time and again, when the need was greatest. According to the legends, each appearance of a wielder coincided with the appearance of the Soulless. The wielders were users of magic and tied to a relic of immense power that only they had the capability to use. Vardak had little interest in the magic or the relic, but he wondered if Coreyaless had also known Arianna's commander, a man reputed to be one of the greatest strategists the world had ever known.

"I loved hearing the Fireblade legends when I was younger," Janna gushed before Vardak had the opportunity to frame his question. "What was she like?"

"She was driven and fearless," Coreyaless replied. "That the sword was within Stonewall Hall did not deter her—she knew what she was destined to become and believed she must face the Soulless of that era without the backing of the Shining Tower. I have met few people of stronger character."

"Ah, if only I could be like her," Janna replied dreamily. "The prospect of going into that place wouldn't be half as terrifying."

"Do not mistake my words, Janna," Coreyaless countered. "She feared what might happen when she ventured inside. Where she differed from most was that she did not allow her fear to hinder her."

A shadow seemed to pass over Janna's features, but she nodded thoughtfully after a moment. "I believe I understand."

Coreyaless glanced at Vardak, amusement in her eyes. Vardak understood she'd maneuvered the conversation specifically for Janna's benefit. He nodded a silent thanks to her; without her intervention, he would likely have upset Janna further and quickly lost his patience. He simply was not adept at managing the emotions of others.

"I would like to spend some time this afternoon preparing for our departure," Coreyaless added after a time. "There are a number of herbs I need to harvest, and I must ensure I have the proper ingredients for the potion I spoke of. It deters the Undead from entering an area—for a time. It is the best I can do."

"That is more than I'd accounted for," Vardak replied quietly.

"You didn't know, Vardak?" Janna asked, surprised. "You didn't know, and you still believed Stonewall Hall was our best option?"

"She didn't tell me." He wanted to add that he suspected she'd withheld the information by design, but kept silent on the matter.

"Perhaps we'll have no trouble, then." Janna smiled to herself, a glimmer of hope in her green eyes.

Vardak did not reply. It was foolish to underestimate the Undead, and he would remain vigilant from the moment Nuarno Peak came into sight, until they reached their destination somewhere deep within. Blademon's memories gave him some insight into their nature, and he knew a single lapse of concentration could prove deadly for them all. Though they could not be killed, they could be maimed enough to give up their fight for a time.

He prayed that his training, and Blademon's memories, would suffice to see them through unscathed.

CHAPTER SEVEN

THE COUNCIL MEETING

Tavesin found himself in the great market square of Dar Daelad, but immediately knew he was within the Aethereum. The stark, bluish lighting was but the first indication, the lack of other people the second, and more obvious. He frowned, at once both elated and terrified. He wished he knew how he'd managed to magic himself into the realm twice, and hoped this venture into the other realm would end better than his first had.

He examined the merchant stalls that lined the square. Some were empty, while others seemed filled to bursting with wares. Many objects appeared blurry and unfocused, but he didn't understand why. Puzzled, he peered down at the nearest such object. If he squinted, he could make out brief details; it seemed to be a map of the Five Kingdoms and the lands to the east beyond their borders. As soon as he opened his eyes fully, the image dissolved and he could no longer discern the words and markings drawn upon it.

He turned away from the stall, and as he did so, the silhouette of the royal palace caught his gaze. He'd always wanted to visit a proper palace and wondered if—

As soon as the thought entered his mind, he found himself standing within the palace's gates. He blinked in surprise and stared in wonder at what he'd just accomplished. It seemed if he desired to *be* somewhere strongly enough, he was immediately transported to that location. Pleased with his newfound knowledge and the prospect of swiftly traveling from place to place, he began to explore the palace's courtyard.

To his right were a row of stables, though in the Aethereum there were no grooms or horses present. To his left was a paved walkway lined with trees that led to the castle proper. It ended before a set of broad stone steps. Atop the steps was a wide double-door. Tavesin had little interest in exploring the empty stables and quickly opted for the pathway to his left. As he approached the steps, one of the palace doors swung silently open.

The small, distorted man he'd encountered previously stepped outside, and Tavesin felt his breath freeze in his throat. This man—*Soulless*, he told himself—was far more powerful than he was, and Tavesin didn't fully understand the rules of the Aethereum. He scurried behind the trunk of the nearest tree, hoping the man hadn't noticed him.

"How is it we keep running into one another, little rat?"

Tavesin shuddered and flattened himself against the tree, praying to any god that might listen to save him from the monster that approached. He heard the man's footfalls upon the stone walkway as they slowly neared his location.

"I cannot have you continually interfering in my business," he stated, his voice only paces away. "I'm certain you know what that means."

Tavesin squeezed his eyes closed while he trembled in fear. He wished he knew how to wake himself up, but try as he might, he remained rooted within the Aethereum.

"Peek-a-boo," the voice said beside his ear.

Tavesin was unable to hold back a shriek of terror. His eyes flew open to meet the shifting, distorted features of the Soulless only inches away from him.

The Soulless laughed. "You've no inkling of how you came to be here, do you? And you don't know how to leave." He stepped back, and Tavesin thought he may have grinned, though it was impossible to discern his expression. "Let's have some fun, shall we, little rat?"

"N-no," Tavesin managed. He quaked like a leaf caught in a gale.

"Oh, come now. I'm not so bad." A flicker of a smirk flitted across the Soulless' features.

"I know what you are," Tavesin whispered.

"Then you know I could have killed you the instant I became aware of your presence," the Soulless countered, "but I did not. You are young, but also quite powerful—or rather, you will be, one day. The fact that you've come here untrained fascinates me." He tilted his head thoughtfully. "I can teach you of this place."

Tavesin shuddered as he realized the Soulless was attempting to lure him into what was certainly a trap. He shook his head adamantly.

"No? That's a shame. I doubt any of the wizards will be of help. Only a handful of humans are graced with aethereal magic in a generation." He leaned toward Tavesin. "If you join me, I can help you."

Tavesin looked down, unable to watch the shifting of the man's features any longer. Hasnin and the Radiant both had alluded to the rarity of Tavesin's ability, and he sensed the Soulless in front of him spoke the truth. What frightened him more than the Soulless' presence was the temptation to accept the offer. He wanted to learn more, *needed* to learn more, but what price was he willing to pay? There must be another means to learn of the Aethereum.

He found himself shaking his head again. "I won't."

The Soulless stepped back, and Tavesin could sense the displeasure radiating from his being. "You've made a grave mistake, little rat. You will—"

His words were cut short by a blinding shaft of white light that cut across the courtyard and struck him in the chest. He stumbled backward as his form seemed to shift and distort even more. As the light faded, the Soulless growled a curse under his breath and abruptly vanished.

Tavesin frantically searched the courtyard for the source of the light, and his eyes widened in surprise as they landed upon a figure near the stables. She stood upright, taller than most humans, and was covered in polished, garnet-colored scales. She wore leather armor and an axe hung at her hip. Behind her a pair of leathery wings were spread wide, as though she prepared to leap into the sky at any moment. Her golden, reptilian eyes met his, and she beckoned to him.

Tavesin swallowed nervously. He recognized her as one of the Drakkon, but he'd never interacted with one of her people before. He recalled Hasnin's warning to him; he must be respectful. He stepped forward tentatively and made his way toward her. She studied him with interest as he approached.

He stopped several paces away, gazing up at her as he began to fidget. He did not know what he ought to say or how he was expected to act.

"What is your name?" she asked in a voice like velvet.

"T-Tavesin," he stammered.

He hadn't expected her voice to sound so normal, so *human*. Her face was clearly reptilian, not unlike those of the small lizards he knew from the forest near Rican Mer. Her hands, though covered in scales, sported four fingers and a thumb. She had two arms, two legs, and wore her armor in the same manner he'd seen human warriors wear theirs. Beyond the scales, the wings, and the long tail she possessed, he supposed the Drakkon wasn't terribly different than he was.

"Well, Tavesin," she replied, "I've been tracking that man for several hours, and you led me straight to him. I would have stepped in sooner, but I needed to understand what his interest was in you." She folded her arms across her narrow torso. "A lesser human would have agreed to his offer, yet you resisted. That was admirable, but foolish. He meant to torture you into submission."

Tavesin shuddered. "I know."

"Luckily for you, I was here." She flashed a grin, and he noted her teeth were small and sharp. "Do you study with the wizards, Tavesin?"

When he nodded, she continued. "Perhaps we can come to an accord. You clearly need to learn the workings of the Aethereum, and I doubt there are many within the Shining Tower who can properly teach you. I will make arrangements."

"Arrangements?" he asked, bewildered.

She laughed. "I cannot merely take you under my wing without your Council's approval, can I? No, there are proper channels that must be followed, and I will do so."

She smiled at him, and in spite of himself, Tavesin began to relax. "Thank you."

"Do not thank me yet," she replied with another grin. "I've gained a reputation amongst my own people as being a difficult task-mistress, but you'll be safer with me than on your own. Or with one of the Soulless."

"Yes."

"Now, it's best you return to your body and perhaps speak with your mentor. Do you know how to return?"

When he shook his head, she chuckled. "I suspected as much. Listen carefully, Tavesin."

It was only after he was in Hasnin's study that he realized he'd failed to learn the Drakkon's name. Hasnin did not seem overly concerned by it, though he cautioned Tavesin to refrain from returning to the Aethereum until the proper arrangements had been made.

"But, sir, I don't know how I entered to begin with," he replied helplessly.

"I will learn what I can, Taven," his mentor promised. "We will solve this predicament for you, if we are able. Now, focus on your lessons today, and visit me again before the Council meeting begins tonight. We can discuss what I've learned then."

Dismissed, he went about his day as though it were any other, but he found it difficult to focus. His thoughts spiraled around the Aethereum, the Soulless, the Drakkon, and the upcoming Council meeting. He was expected to speak to a hall filled with wizards about his encounters, and he wasn't certain he would maintain his composure without faltering. It was too much, too soon, and he began to despair.

By the time he met with Hasnin again, late in the afternoon, Tavesin could scarcely remember any of his lessons from the day. Each minute had passed in a blur of anxiety that even Rostin had failed to shake him from, although his friend had made several valiant attempts.

Hasnin greeted him in a rush, and quickly bustled him away from the study and toward the steps that would lead them down the tower to the Council Chamber. "I looked into what I could of the Aethereum today," he told Tavesin over his shoulder as they walked. "As I told you previously, the Drakkon are the experts of that realm. It was perhaps fortunate you met with one of their number during your latest venture. You at least know how to exit the plane without being forcefully ejected."

Tavesin shuddered at his words and recalled his first encounter with the Soulless. "Yes, sir."

"There was little information that I could glean about how one enters the Aethereum," he continued. "It seems most humans with that ability find themselves there unintentionally, much like you have. The skill to enter at will can be taught, however, but only by one who can also enter that plane."

"The Drakkon said—" Tavesin began.

"I know what you told me, boy," Hasnin interjected, "and she followed through on her promise to you. She made contact with the Radiant this afternoon, and arrangements for your training are being made." Hasnin paused to glance over his shoulder, his dark eyes probing. "She is no mere Drakkon, Taven. Her name is Aziarah, and she is the leader of their magical order."

Tavesin gaped at his mentor. "What?"

Hasnin chuckled. "You heard me, boy. She is their leader, and has requested to train you personally. It is a high honor. The Drakkon rarely descend from the heights to interact with humans, but she seemed quite impressed with your character."

Tavesin shook his head, bewildered. "She found me cowering behind a tree while I tried to hide from the Soulless."

They had reached the landing outside the Council Chamber amidst a whirlwind of activity. Wizards representing every Sect could be seen in the corridor, some in small clusters where they spoke amongst themselves, while others strode purposefully to their destination. Hasnin motioned for Tavesin to stay near, and he lowered his voice.

"Aziarah can sense your potential, just as any fully trained wizard can," Hasnin stated. "Our arrangement with her is not yet known to the wider Council, and it must remain that way until the Radiant announces it. Do you understand?"

Tavesin nodded warily. "Yes, sir."

"Good. Now, let's head inside and find our seats."

The Council Chamber was a vast, circular room with a raised platform at its heart. The floor sloped gently downward toward the platform so that each row of carefully arranged chairs was slightly lower in elevation than the preceding row. The arrangement allowed for every seat to sport an unobstructed view of the room's center. Six empty chairs were arranged in an arc upon the stage. Many of the chairs beyond were occupied by wizards representing every Sect, accompanied by their apprentices.

Hasnin led him toward a pair of open chairs near the platform; Tavesin remembered with a sinking feeling that he was expected to speak at this gathering. There were more wizards than he could easily count, and many of the apprentices were his peers. His mouth became suddenly dry, and he clasped his hands in order to hide their shaking.

"Sir," he said in a breathless whisper as he sat down, "how many people will attend?"

Hasnin studied him carefully for a moment before making his reply. "As many who are able. The Radiant and the Sect Masters will have questions for you, but all you must do is answer them truthfully. Focus on them when you are called to the stage, Tavesin, and ignore these others. I have every confidence in you, boy."

Tavesin shifted uneasily in his seat. "I hope so, sir."

Hasnin chuckled, amused by his response. "If I did not believe you were capable of speaking for yourself at this gathering, I would have asked you to prepare a statement ahead of time. The Radiant would have read your words verbatim, and that would be the end of it. However," he continued, with a knowing smile, "you'll never grow into a proper, respectable wizard if your limits aren't pushed a bit now and again. Think of this as one of your evaluations—you've impressed your teachers thus far with your performance, so don't allow your nerves to overwhelm you now."

Tavesin swallowed and looked down. He understood Hasnin's desire to see him succeed, but a part of him wished his mentor had given him the option of writing a statement. Certainly, it was the easier path, but the room was rapidly filling and he wasn't sure he'd manage to speak coherently once he was called. His nerves were a jangling cacophony, drowning out the surrounding sea of conversation.

It was only when Hasnin nudged him sharply that Tavesin realized the Sect Masters and the Radiant had entered the room. He scrambled to his feet to stand with the others in attendance, as protocol dictated.

The five Sect Masters strode in single-file down the aisle opposite his seat. Each was garbed in their ceremonial colored robe and accompanying cloak of their respective Sect. Behind them was the Radiant in robes of white, marking his former Sect, and the multi-hued cloak of shimmering fabric reserved for his position.

Tavesin studied the ensemble as they approached the stage, only steps away from where he stood. Though he knew their names from his lessons, it was the first time he'd set eyes upon the Sect Masters. All but the Green Sect Master appeared as old as Hasnin; the Green Sect Master appeared to be just shy of middle-age, though he sported a broad scar along the left side of his face that twisted his features strangely. Tavesin wondered what sort of injury he must have sustained that even the leader of the Green Sect, the healers of the Council, could not fully repair.

The Council's leaders ascended to the platform, and the five Sect Masters moved to stand in front of their respective chairs. The Radiant remained in the center of the platform, and Tavesin watched as he twitched his fingers nimbly at his sides and muttered an incantation beneath his breath. When he spoke to address the hundreds gathered within the chamber his voice was magically amplified. Even those in the farthest reaches of the room would have no difficulty discerning his words.

"Good evening everyone, and thank you for attending this meeting of our Council on such short notice. Several important matters have come to our collective attention," he gestured toward the Sect Masters, "which must be addressed promptly. Please, be seated."

Shuffling erupted throughout the chamber as the masses returned to their seats. The Radiant stood patiently upon the platform for the sound to diminish before he continued.

"We will begin with the first matter that was brought to our attention yesterday morning." He scanned the crowd as though seeking someone specific, and after a moment he nodded briefly. "David Shearwall, please come forward."

Tavesin heard footsteps behind him and twisted in his seat for a better look at the man the Radiant had summoned. A tall man with sharp features and steely eyes strode down the nearest aisle, his dark hair flecked with streaks of silver. The sword at his hip and the poised manner in which he held himself marked him as a Gray. He ascended to the platform and stood rigidly alongside the Radiant, his chin held high.

"I've had a Viewing," he stated, his voice amplified by the Radiant's magic. "As most of the Council is aware, the former White wizard, Varasin, recently ventured into Stonewall Hall. When he returned, he was no longer himself, mired in the grip of insanity."

Tavesin noted the Radiant looked down and a shadow seemed to pass over him at David's words. In that moment, his aged face appeared profoundly saddened, but he quickly regained his previous composure. "For the benefit of our newest apprentices, I will remind the Council that Viewings are glimpses of events granted the viewer as they transpire. It is a rare aptitude, and David Shearwall is one of our most gifted wizards in that respect." He gestured to David. "Please, continue."

"My Viewing showed me a terrible scene as it unfolded at the edge of Blackstone Chasm." He glanced briefly toward the Radiant, who nodded once. "Varasin, who was calling himself Shan'tar, held a strange relic in his hands and performed a summoning ritual that I can only describe as profane. After some research, with the aid of several White wizards, we have determined that relic was none other than the Shalin Stone."

His words were met with audible gasps from dozens of wizards, but Tavesin did not understand the significance. He glanced questioningly at Hasnin, who shook his head and indicated he continue to listen.

"Shan'tar's ritual served a singular purpose," David continued after a moment. "My Viewing showed its finale, and the five terrible creatures Shan'tar resurrected. As a show of thanks for his involvement, one of their number murdered him."

"They are the Soulless," the Radiant stated, his tone grave.

The chamber was silent for several heartbeats, and then a volley of questions began to pepper the stage from the audience. There were so many voices atop one another that Tavesin could scarcely determine who spoke, let alone what they had asked. The Radiant held up his hands in a plea for silence, and after a long moment, the chamber fell quiet once more.

"This is but the beginning of what must be discussed tonight," he informed the Council, turning to face each column of seats in turn. "There will be time for questions after the other matters have been brought forth."

Tavesin swallowed his fear and tried to still the quaking of his knees, but to his relief the Yellow Sect Master, Lilyna El'Vero was summoned next. She was a petite woman who stood only half as tall as the Radiant, but her fierce gaze and steady, measured gait commanded respect. Her coffee-brown skin was in stark contrast to her bright, yellow garments, and though her face was lined by age, her dark hair retained its natural coloration.

"As many from my Sect know, one of our apprentices went missing during the night," she stated. "A young man, only recently arrived from Balotica Kingdom. Jasom Riversend." She surveyed the audience briefly before she continued. "While it is not unusual for one or two apprentices to go missing, we are usually able to track them within a few hours, and most of those are still within the walls of Dar Daelad. It was not so with Jasom. His quarters within the tower gave no indication that he meant to leave, and the area reeked with aethereal residue. Aethereal magic is a rarity amongst humans, and Jasom did not possess such a talent. One of my fellow Yellow wizards created a device to track the movements of specific individuals through the Aethereum, though he cannot venture into the realm himself. We discovered Jasom's current whereabouts only an hour before this meeting began. He was taken to the Tower of Obsidian."

Her words were greeted with more gasps, muttered words and curses, but the gathered wizards refrained from bombarding the platform with further questions. The Radiant turned slowly toward Tavesin's direction as the room quieted once more, and Tavesin felt his heart begin to thunder in his chest. He knew he would be summoned next, and he clenched his fists tightly to mask how terribly his hands shook.

"The final matter has come to us from an unlikely source," the Radiant said evenly as his eyes met Tavesin's. "One of our apprentices has been granted the rare gift Lilyna was speaking of only moments ago, and though his training in that aspect is currently being arranged, he has encountered an individual within the Aethereum that can only be one of the Soulless. Tavesin Drondes, please come forward."

Tavesin drew a shaky breath and stumbled to his feet. His legs felt like rubber, and he feared they would fail him as he made his way toward the platform to stand amongst the Council's leaders. He tried to recall Hasnin's previous words to him, but all he could focus on were the thousands of eyes staring down at him from every angle. He trembled visibly and felt his throat grow tight.

Lilyna's stern countenance softened as he stood between her and the Radiant. "Focus on his words, child," she whispered in encouragement. "Keep your eyes on his alone and do not look beyond the stage. Hasnin believed you were up to this task, and we want to share his confidence in you."

Tavesin managed a nod and fixed his gaze upon the Radiant, who smiled patiently. He hoped he could find his voice when it was his turn to speak.

"Tell us of your encounters," the Radiant said. "Take your time, Tavesin."

Tavesin found his voice after a moment. His words came haltingly at first, but as he continued, they flew from his lips. He described his encounters with the Soulless, but left out his meeting with the Drakkon mage, recalling Hasnin's cautionary words to him. An immense wave of relief washed over him as he finished speaking; he'd done it, in spite of his anxiety.

"We will now open the floor for questions," the Radiant stated, and indicated that Tavesin and the others may return to their seats.

Gratefully, Tavesin fled the stage as dozens of wizards rose to their feet throughout the chamber. As he collapsed into his chair beside Hasnin, his mentor leaned toward him to whisper, "You did well, boy. Very well, as I knew you would."

He managed an uncertain grin. "I did my best, sir."

Hasnin chuckled softly. "That is all we ask of our students, Taven. You'll go far within the Council, at this rate."

Tavesin sat back, pleased with himself for mustering the courage to speak in front of the Council. As the Radiant began to field questions from the wizards in the crowd, he wore a faint smile in spite of the tense and fearful atmosphere that surrounded him.

CHAPTER EIGHT

MURKOR ALLEGIANCE

Aran'daj paced outside of his tent, riddled with anxiety as he watched the last of the day's light fade behind the Gray Mountains. Shen'jem had yet to return from his errand to the caverns, though Aran'daj believed the task was now futile. It had been two days since Shan'tar's final, bizarre spectacle and the reemergence of the Soulless. Two days since his world had been tipped on its side, his life threatened if he so much as considered leaving the camp or attempted to send word of his predicament to the Kal.

The Soulless had been uncompromising. He knew until one of their number returned, or he received instructions from the Kal, he could do nothing but wait and pray to the gods the monsters Shan'tar had released would not decide to kill him on a whim. His people, the soldiers within the camp, looked to him for guidance. Their survival teetered precariously on his actions. He could not fail them, but he had yet to formulate a plan. He had too little information regarding the Soulless, or how they meant to fit the Murkor into their schemes.

With the rise of each Soulless, the Murkor had been forced into fighting long, bloody wars that were not of their choosing. The ancestral home of the Murkor people and its proximity to the Tower of Obsidian made them easy targets. Coupled with the fact that the Murkor did not possess the ability to use magic, his people had succumbed to their threats time and again. The Murkor leaders throughout history had believed their survival could only be achieved by following the demands of the Soulless and their Nameless god.

Aran'daj knew this time would be no different. The Murkor would likely debase themselves even sooner than in previous eras, for they were faced with not one, but five of the demons. He would do all he could to ensure the safety of those under his command. Until he received further instruction, he could not formulate a plan to do so, and if there was one thing Aran'daj truly hated, it was finding himself without a plan.

His frustration propelled him forward; his fear pulled him back. He paced relentlessly in the growing darkness as his thoughts continued to spiral. What could be done? The Soulless were incredibly powerful, and if the woman's display with Shan'tar was any indication, they were without empathy, without remorse. They had instructed him to remain where he was, to await their next orders. If he disobeyed, his life would be forfeit. He took their threat to heart; if he were killed, there would be no one to ensure the safety of the soldiers and craftsmen within his camp. He would comply until he devised a means to escape the Soulless' trap. There was nothing more he could do but wait and pray, a state he despised.

It was fully dark when a faint bluish glow began to emanate from between a pair of nearby tents. The Murkor may not be capable of magic themselves, but he knew its workings when presented with it. He stopped pacing and watched as an oval space opened seemingly from within the air; it was the oval that produced the glow. A tall man emerged moments later, and Aran'daj felt his heart sink as he recognized the angular features, sickly gray skin, and crimson eyes of the visitor.

The Soulless glanced at his new surroundings briefly before his eyes landed upon Aran'daj. He waved one hand dismissively behind him, and the magical opening he'd come through vanished. He strode purposefully toward the Murkor commander.

Aran'daj held himself erect and forced an air of calm assurance. Thankful that his hood served to hide the panic in his eyes, he kept his gaze focused on the Soulless as he approached.

"Good evening, Commander."

Aran'daj nodded briefly in order to mask his surprise at the cordiality he heard in the Soulless' tone. "Good evening."

"If you prefer it, we can speak in your native tongue," the Soulless replied flawlessly in the Murkor language.

Alarmed at the Soulless' attempt at niceties, Aran'daj hesitated before making his response. He knew there would be more to the

80

man's visit than mere small talk, but why was the Soulless, a creature who by all accounts was a ruthless murderer, attempting to gain his favor? A dozen reasons quickly presented themselves to him, but he would not know the true purpose unless he continued to play along.

"Yes, thank you," Aran'daj replied briskly. He hoped the Soulless could not sense his growing unease.

"I have paid a visit to your Kal," the Soulless continued. He reached into one of his pockets to withdraw a sealed message. "He wrote this for you, and seeing as I've been planning to pay you a visit as well, I offered to act as messenger."

Aran'daj accepted the proffered message gingerly but did not open it. "Why would you do this for me? Forgive me, sir, but from the tales I've heard of your kind, this goes against your nature."

The Soulless chuckled mirthlessly. "We are not above granting favors when the need arises," he replied. "I know the contents of your note, and it is of no concern to me or to our greater plans. Read it now, or later, as you wish."

Disconcerted, Aran'daj slid the note carefully into his belt pouch. He would read its contents later, once the Soulless was gone.

"Walk with me, Commander."

Aran'daj nodded at the command and fell in beside the Soulless, who stood only slightly taller than he. The Soulless did not speak until they had covered some distance toward the camp's perimeter, and their path led them through the most populous areas— the sparring rings, the cookfires, the craftsmen's temporary workspaces. Aran'daj understood the Soulless meant for them to be seen together by as many of the Murkor as possible. He scowled beneath his hood, furious that the Soulless sought to undermine him, but helpless to do anything to prevent it.

"You keep order well in your camp," the Soulless remarked, breaking the long silence.

"I do my best," he replied.

"The Kal sang your praises quite effusively, as did the Matriarch. They claimed the army has not seen a better commander since the days of Kama's War." He paused, a knowing smirk upon his ghastly lips. "*My* war."

Though Aran'daj knew the Soulless before him must be one of those referred to in legend, to know he spoke with Kama sent a chill through him. With the exception of the first Soulless, Kama had been the most successful in his campaigns. It was said he knew not only battle, but strategy as well. It was a small mercy, perhaps, but when compared to the many horrific deeds the legends also attributed to his name, it left Aran'daj's mouth dry with fear.

He struggled to keep his voice steady. "The stories claim you are a great strategist."

Kama shrugged indifferently. "That's true. It is why the Nameless has chosen me to oversee our armies. You will retain command over the soldiers, as the Kal has requested, but you will report to me. Dranamir wanted you dead, but I believe you are more useful to us alive."

Stunned, Aran'daj managed a strangled, "Thank you."

"Relax, Commander. Dranamir may be bloodthirsty, but she has been assigned to oversee other aspects of our operations. So long as you don't displease *me*, your life is in no danger."

Aran'daj nodded his assent and swallowed his unease. The threat had been stated plainly, and given Kama's reputation, there was little he could hope to accomplish that would circumvent the Soulless' grasp on his people. He would comply but observe Kama's actions carefully. He would seize an opportunity to free his people if one presented itself, though at present he was relegated to waiting and acting his part.

"What would you have me do, sir?" he asked, adding the honorific to his question as a means to assure Kama he would follow the Soulless' orders.

A twitch of his lips conveyed a brief, albeit chilling, smile. "Your first order of business is to move this camp to the base of the tower to the north. It will be far easier for me to oversee the army when you're at my doorstep. I will leave you to your preparations soon enough, but there is another, more pressing matter to be discussed first."

"Of course, sir."

"There is an alchemist in your camp that I wish to speak with," Kama continued. "His name is Sal'zar, and it seems he is of some importance. Where might I find him?"

Perplexed, Aran'daj turned to point toward the craftsmen's area. "Both alchemists are often there. If he is not, he'll be within his tent."

"Take me to him, Commander."

Their circuitous route through the camp had taken them through the craftsmen's area minutes earlier, and Aran'daj had not seen the green-clad alchemist then. He suppressed a sigh and began to thread his way through the camp toward the area where Sal'zar's tent was pitched. He'd spent little time with the alchemists and did not know Sal'zar well. He hoped for Sal'zar's sake that he recognized the danger that trod in the commander's wake this evening.

They encountered Sal'zar not far from his tent. When Aran'daj hailed him, the alchemist stood stiffly as Kama appraised him. Kama's malevolent gaze raked the alchemist from head to toe, his expression oscillating between displeasure and curiosity. Aran'daj remained silent during Sal'zar's inspection, though he pitied the alchemist his misfortune. He wondered what had drawn the Soulless' attention— Sal'zar was a talented alchemist, but he was not experienced enough to have risen far within his guild.

After an interminable amount of time, Kama stepped back and crossed his arms. "So, Garin spoke true. A Murkor with the Ability."

Aran'daj did not understand the significance present in Kama's words. "He is a gifted alchemist, sir—"

Kama smirked. "I suspect half of his 'giftedness' is due to his untrained use of magic, not because he has any remarkable talent others in his profession lack."

Sal'zar seemed to deflate at his words. "No, sir. Our people cannot—"

Kama held one gray hand up for silence. "It seems we've been wrong, Sal'zar. Perhaps most of your people cannot use magic, but *you* can. The Nameless who we serve gave your name to us as a potential candidate. I cannot say I'm pleased with the prospect. A Murkor has never set foot inside the Tower of Obsidian. You'll be the first. Make certain you don't disappoint."

Sal'zar looked down, and Aran'daj imagined the despair that must have been written upon his face. "I will gather my belongings, sir. I don't have much."

"Very well." Kama turned to face Aran'daj as Sal'zar scurried away. "You have your orders, Commander. I expect to see your soldiers in place at the base of the tower within three days. You are dismissed."

Aran'daj forced himself to nod, though the dismissal stung. It was unwise to make his displeasure known to the Soulless. He turned away and hurried toward the center of the camp, where he would announce their new orders. As he walked, he remembered the Kal's letter and withdrew it from his pouch.

He scanned it quickly and frowned, disheartened by the words within. The Kal and the Matriarch had been visited by Kama and another of the Soulless. It had been agreed upon that the Murkor would support their efforts in the coming war. Aran'daj suspected that, like him, the Soulless had given them little choice.

Four wars had been fought in the same manner, his people subjugated and forced into service under the Soulless. Four wars, with hundreds of years marking peace between them, and they still had not found a means to free themselves from the clutches of the Nameless god and his followers. History continued to repeat its vicious cycle, the gods continued to ignore the Murkor pleas, and Aran'daj found himself at the forefront of a conflict that was not of his choosing.

He resolved he would find a means to break the cycle, to free his people, even if it resulted in his death. He simply needed time and information to formulate a plan.

CHAPTER NINE

ANCIENT RIVALRY

Dranamir's gaze flitted between the objects carefully ensconced in the glass case. She studied each briefly before moving on to the next, paying careful attention to form and function. The Enlightened had obtained a sizeable collection of relics and artifacts in the nearly one thousand years that spanned between her death and recent resurrection. Some of the objects were clearly meant for destruction, while others served more subtle uses. She desired to know what tools were at her disposal and their exact location for easy retrieval. War was on the horizon, and she meant to be prepared.

She sensed a tingle of magic behind her as a portal opened. It would be one of the others, though she hoped Alyra hadn't appeared to sour her mood. She ignored the newcomer and continued to peruse the case. She paused above a pair of glowing orbs the size of large melons that emitted an oily light, tainted as they were from their original design. They were Oldara's Orbs, one green, the other gray. She smiled; their corruption had been her work, and the magic she'd unleashed afterward was one of her finest achievements. The gods were not the only beings capable of creating new forms of life.

"Dranamir? I wasn't expecting anyone to be here." Garin's voice drew her out of her reverie.

She turned around and fixed a scowl upon her face. "I wasn't aware I required anyone's permission to inventory our wares, least of all yours."

Annoyance flickered in his eyes. "That was not my intent," he replied evenly. "I have need to speak with our master, and the only means I have of doing so is through the mirror." He gestured toward the crimson oval in its twisted, black frame that hung from the adjacent wall. "I suppose I must grow used to having four others about when I conduct my business."

She crossed her arms and studied him carefully. Garin remained a puzzle to her. He refused to take sides in her continued battle with Alyra, though the other men had clearly aligned themselves. He rarely displayed emotion, seemingly content to observe and bide his time. She wished she could unravel his motives and discover his true purpose. Garin was second in power only to her, and she knew she could not make an enemy of him. A battle between the pair would prove catastrophic to their plans and likely draw their master's wrath.

"And what need drives you directly to our master?" she asked, feigning innocence. "Surely one of us might have the means to assist you."

Garin raised an eyebrow; he'd seen through her façade. "I'll not be taking sides between you and Alyra, but I applaud your attempt at recruitment."

She smirked. She liked the man in spite of herself. "Very well, but I do believe my point was valid. I may be of help, Garin. From what I've uncovered during the past few days, it seems much of our knowledge was lost to the ravages of time. No matter your power, I know many things that you do not."

His expression was unreadable, but after a moment he conceded. "Fine. I'll tell you what happened, and if you have advice, I'll consider it."

"I knew you were reasonable," she replied.

"It seems the wizards have a young recruit gifted with aethereal magic," Garin said slowly. "I've encountered him twice now. He hasn't learned to physically enter the realm, so I cannot exterminate him as I'd like. I sent him away once, but during our second meeting, *I* was forced away. He had the help of a Drakkon mage."

Dranamir glowered; the Drakkon had long been an obstacle to their master's plans. They were often far more powerful than their human counterparts when it came to matters of magic, a lesson Dranamir had learned at the cost of her own life during the first Great War. She had a score to settle with the Drakkon.

"There are methods of drawing the conscious mind far enough into the Aethereum that it can never return to its host." She would focus on the portion of Garin's problem she could solve. "I can show you how it's done, but I'd advise you only attempt it if you find the boy alone. The Drakkon mage will prove problematic."

"I'm aware," Garin replied dryly. "I suppose it was fortunate that I did not encounter any of their kind during my own campaign. I was not prepared to be sent away as I was."

"You're fortunate that the Drakkon did not kill you," Dranamir stated without sympathy. "You cannot travel the Aethereum without drawing their notice, Garin. Their aptitude for the realm far exceeds our own. I'd advise you to prepare yourself more thoroughly before your next foray."

He crossed his arms. "This is why I meant to speak with our master directly. I know how you died, Dranamir, and your condescension grows wearisome."

"Grow used to it, Garin. I have no intention of changing my ways."

He rolled his eyes and turned away, his focus on the mirror. She smirked at his back before her gaze was drawn to the windows across the room. Evening was falling; it was time to pay a visit to the princess in Delucha.

Tamarin was pacing the length of the balcony adjoining her private quarters when Dranamir stepped from the aethereal portal. Impatience and displeasure were written across her features as she whirled to face her visitor in a flurry of velvet and lace. Dranamir smirked, certain she knew what would come next.

"How dare you keep me waiting!" The princess seethed.

Dranamir was not one to pass up an opportunity to bring a member of the royal family to her dainty knees, and the princess had clearly forgotten what had transpired during their first encounter. She had come to Delucha to teach the girl, after all, and some lessons were best learned alongside misery.

She made a subtle gesture, calling forth magic that would stimulate every pain receptor in Tamarin's body. The princess shrieked and stumbled against the balcony's railing. She gripped the balustrade until her fingers were white from the exertion required to maintain her footing. Tears began to stream from her eyes.

"You have forgotten whom you speak to."

Dranamir strode toward her and pulled back her hood so the girl could take her first glimpse of the corrupted features beneath. Tamarin's eyes widened with horror and she quickly averted her gaze.

"Forgive me…Great One." Tamarin's breathing was shallow, her voice strained.

Dranamir did not relent but instead increased the magnitude of the princess' pain. She took hold of Tamarin's chin and forced her to meet her crimson-eyed gaze while Tamarin moaned in agony.

"Let this be a lesson to you, Tamarin. I am not one of your subjects, and I do not answer to the Deluchan crown. You agreed to obey me, and if you cannot remember your vow, mere pain will be the least of your concerns." She sneered contemptuously. "Have I made myself clear?"

When Tamarin hesitated, she intensified the magic inflaming the princess' body. Tamarin fell to her knees with a scream.

"I'm afraid I didn't hear you, princess."

"I…I u-understand, Great One," she blubbered. "P-please…Please, forgive m-me."

"In preparation for our next meeting, be sure to remember your place." Dranamir released her hold on the princess' chin, stepped back, and relinquished her magic.

Tamarin remained panting against the balustrade for several seconds as she recovered from her ordeal. Dranamir studied her with a frown, certain this would not be the last time she'd be forced to make a spectacle of the entitled princess. Such was the way of those born into power.

When Tamarin gathered herself enough to stand upright without the aid of the railing, she risked a fearful glance in Dranamir's direction, but wisely kept her thoughts to herself. Dranamir's lips quirked into a smug smile; perhaps the princess would learn her position within the hierarchy after all.

"We shall begin," Dranamir stated. "Listen carefully. I have limited capacity for patience, and you will rue your failure if I am forced to repeat myself."

Tamarin nodded eagerly, her green eyes wide. "I am at your command, Great One." A tremor of fear laced the princess' words.

"Close your eyes."

Tamarin drew an unsteady breath but did as ordered.

"Empty your mind of all conscious thought. Focus on my words and nothing else." Dranamir watched as Tamarin's expression shifted from one of unease to puzzlement and finally to a confused frown.

"I don't understand the purpose of this exercise." Tamarin opened one eye to peer at her.

"If you wish to harness your innate power, you'll do as I command." Dranamir folded her arms and began to pace from the balustrade to the stone wall, her cold gaze fixed on the princess. "Close your eyes, or I'll do it for you."

Tamarin's face paled and she squeezed her eyes shut.

"It may take several sessions before you learn to tap into your power," Dranamir continued. "Focus on my words, and allow your thoughts to melt away. There is darkness within everyone, princess, and yours is more profound than most, given what I know of your parents. Focus—"

"How dare you?" Tamarin snarled as her eyes snapped open. "You come into my home, threaten me—" Her words dissolved into a pained yelp as Dranamir inflamed her pain receptors once more.

"The purpose of this lesson is to teach you how to utilize the darkness I spoke of, to bend it to your will, and manifest it in the form of magic," Dranamir replied evenly. "That you continue to lash out, to *disobey*, is becoming problematic."

Tamarin whimpered as Dranamir moved toward her. She glared at the princess with open disdain.

"This is your final warning, princess. My patience has worn thin."

She released her magic, and Tamarin collapsed into an ungraceful heap, sobbing uncontrollably. She was about to order the princess onto her feet so they might continue the lesson when she sensed the tingle of magic in the air behind her. Her glare deepened as she turned to find Alyra exiting a portal.

"There you are," Alyra said, flicking a glance toward the princess. She arched one slender eyebrow but said nothing in regard to Tamarin's current state. "Garin has spoken to the master," she continued in a hushed tone. "It seems he has news for us."

"I'll be there presently. I cannot leave this mess unfinished." She waved one hand idly toward Tamarin.

"You shouldn't be so harsh," Alyra chided. "She's only a novice, and hardly more than a girl, at that."

Dranamir snorted. "Her age is irrelevant, Alyra. If she's capable of committing murder, she's capable of learning the ways of magic from me."

Alyra's eyes widened slightly in momentary surprise. "It's no wonder the master assigned her to you. Two of a kind." She glanced at the open portal behind her, then said, "I'll tell Garin you won't be long."

Dranamir nodded stiffly, glad the other woman was finished. She was done maintaining the pretense of civility for Alyra's benefit. When Alyra was gone, she refocused her attention upon Tamarin, who had managed to regain her feet.

"Fortunately for you, I have more important business to attend to this evening," she informed the princess. "When I return, I expect you to be properly respectful. As I said, my patience is all but gone, and when it vanishes, so will you."

"I am eternally sorry, Great One," Tamarin whispered without meeting her gaze. "I will make an effort to do better."

"See that you do."

Dranamir opened a portal with a dismissive gesture and entered the Aethereum, leaving the whimpering princess behind. She knew Alyra disapproved of her methods, but at least they garnered results; Alyra was unable to say the same. She prepared herself for a confrontation as she thought herself into the tower's highest floor. She expected nothing less from the other woman and wove a shield around her person before exiting the Aethereum.

She was greeted with an image of Garin's glowering countenance as he paced in front of the mirror. Alyra stood alongside Jannyn, while Kama leaned against one of the glass cases, feigning boredom. Garin was animated in a way Dranamir had not believed the

90

small man capable of; he gesticulated angrily and shouted as he continued to pace.

"…does not matter what excuses you have concocted, Alyra. The master is not pleased!"

Alyra crossed her arms and huffed. As she turned away from Garin, her gaze fell upon Dranamir and her expression darkened. "It seems our master's pet has arrived."

Dranamir tipped her head back and laughed at the statement. "It's hardly my fault you're proving inept in your duties. I'm still recovering from the shock that our master saw fit to name you as my successor."

Alyra's eyes narrowed dangerously, but Dranamir knew she was of no threat; her shield would withstand any magical attack the other woman attempted. She smirked an unspoken challenge.

"I worked my way into this position," Alyra spat. "Unlike you. You were gifted it due to your power, once Ravin no longer stood in your path."

Dranamir ignored the reference to the man who had once stood to gain all of their master's favor, the only man who had ever managed to best her in a duel. He was long dead; Alyra's words no longer held any sway over her.

"I'm certain you did 'work' your way to your position," Dranamir replied mercilessly. "It's too bad the beauty that landed you here no longer serves you."

"Ohhh," Alyra snarled through clenched teeth. She raised her hand as though to strike, but before she could unleash any of her magic, Garin's voice thundered through the room.

"*Enough!*"

Dranamir sensed he'd amplified his voice to overpower theirs, but the sheer power in his tone stunned her. For such a small, seemingly frail man, Garin continued to surprise her with his strength.

Alyra dropped her hand and sulked, while Dranamir continued to smirk knowingly in her direction. It was a small victory, but it had sparked a plan, one which would lead to the eventual removal of Alyra from amongst their ranks.

"I've called this meeting to relay some additional information from our master, not to listen to the pair of you bicker." Garin pinched the bridge of his nose as though the brief argument had left him with a headache.

"And what does our master have to say?" Dranamir inquired lightly.

"Our progress has been too slow thus far," Garin replied tartly. "He demands we work more diligently on recruitment and stated rather forcefully that those who have agreed to train beneath us must learn our ways faster. Something has him perturbed, and it leaves him in a foul temper." He fixed his gaze upon Alyra. "As I was saying when Dranamir arrived, your performance has enraged him. You were tasked with teaching the Murkor, and though you feel he is beneath us, he *does* have the Ability."

"A Murkor with the Ability is an abomination," Alyra muttered, affronted by the mere prospect.

"Be that as it may," Garin replied evenly, "the duty was given to you. I'll not stand alone to face his wrath upon our next meeting."

Alyra crossed her arms, her expression wrinkled by displeasure. "Very well. I'll see the Murkor is trained."

"Jannyn, you and Dranamir are to continue as you are. It seems our master, though impatient, is content enough with your progress that he said very little. And Kama, it seems he has a plan of attack that does not focus on Delucha. He is considering other options but asks that you ensure the Murkor army is compliant and prepared to march at his command." Garin stopped pacing for a moment to make eye-contact with the tall Kamshati. "You, he is pleased with so far."

Kama nodded in acknowledgment but made no reply.

Alyra looked as though she'd bitten into something sour. "Am I the only one to be reprimanded?" she asked, seething. "I've done as much as anyone else—"

"If you'd like to argue your point further, I'll contact the master again," Garin interrupted, his tone venomous. "Believe me when I say he'll be less than pleased with a second disruption this evening."

Dranamir pounced on the opportunity that suddenly presented itself. "Perhaps you need to see how proper training of one's pupils is done. I'd be happy to let you observe my work." She smiled coldly.

"Aeon take you, Dranamir." Alyra summoned a gout of flame and aimed it unerringly in Dranamir's direction.

92

Dranamir laughed as the magic was deflected by her shield to scorch the nearby tiles.

"Goading her into an argument is not productive," Garin stated dryly, unimpressed.

"I merely offered my assistance. She can choose to take it, or not, but I do agree with you, Garin. Her response was not helpful."

"You manipulative bitch!" Alyra shrieked.

"Do you see?" Dranamir continued in a bored tone. "Nothing I say or do will be good enough for her. She'll seek a fight where there is none."

Garin's expression indicated he could see through her façade, though she doubted he had any true idea of what she planned for Alyra. Kama's attention was once more riveted on her, while Jannyn looked decidedly uncomfortable. She relished the tension that permeated the room and decided it was time to make her next move.

"This is my offer, Alyra. When I return to Delucha next, you may observe the proceedings and learn what you can of my methods. You may watch but not interfere." Dranamir smiled smugly and crossed her arms. "Take my offer, or leave it."

Alyra glowered. If she accepted, she would appear weak before the others, but if she refused, she would concede defeat. Dranamir knew what her answer would be well before she uttered the words.

"It seems you leave me no choice, Dranamir. I'll take note of how deftly you handle the dear princess."

CHAPTER TEN

STONEWALL HALL

Vardak sat in silence and watched the sun slowly crest the ridge of mountains to the east. It was a rare moment of solitude in which he could reflect and prepare his mind for the challenges he knew the day would bring. Janna's constant chatter had been the backdrop to their journey from Vidune Forest, and he found himself enjoying the brief respite as she continued to doze in her tent.

They'd made camp in the valley beneath Nuarno Peak the afternoon before, setting their tents along the shore of a deep, cold pond that had formed in the mountain's shadow. His gaze drifted across the still water and came to rest on the rocky path that wound its way to the dark opening rent in the mountain's broad flank. It was square, its edges chiseled with precision, the first indication that he was not looking at a natural cavern. It was the entrance to the maze of tunnels known as Stonewall Hall.

Blademon's gift included some knowledge of the area. The location Coreyaless sought was a shrine that was built in honor of Flariel, deep within the mountain. The builders of Stonewall Hall were a mystery to him, but he knew they had adorned the carefully carved walls with an array of symbols meant to guide a traveler through its depths. With this knowledge to guide them, he was confident they would find their way. That the shrine belonged to Flariel was an irony he'd come to expect from his dealings with the Immortals.

He heard movement behind him. Turning to peer over his armor-clad shoulder, he saw Coreyaless emerge from her tent and stretch her arms skyward, her wings spread wide. He stood and gathered the water skins he'd filled before taking those few, precious moments for reflection. It was time to begin breaking camp; the sooner they entered the treacherous mountain, the sooner their errand would be complete, and the danger past.

"Janna may sleep well into the morning unless I wake her," Coreyaless said quietly as Vardak joined her.

He set the water skins down once more and paused to give her an inquiring look.

"I heard her pacing outside her tent well into the night," Coreyaless explained without further prompting. "I brewed a tea for her, one which would calm her nerves. She's terrified of what we may find within the mountain."

"As she should be," he replied. "I have often wondered over the past five days if I made the right decision when I agreed to help you. I'm not certain you fully grasp the danger we're about to walk into."

She raised her eyebrows in momentary outrage. "And you do?"

"Yes."

She shook her head, exasperated. "Unbelievable."

He shrugged and picked up his axe from where it leaned against the canvas side of his small tent. "I also understand how to navigate Stonewall Hall. Do you?"

He focused his attention on the weapon, carefully removing the leather sheath to inspect the cutting edges gingerly with his thumb. Coreyaless was silent for several moments as he worked, then she sighed heavily.

"No, I don't."

He nodded in acknowledgment. "The final portion of my training with Blademon granted me knowledge beyond what my own experiences could have taught me. You were right when you said I may be the only person alive who could successfully lead you through the mountain. I doubt any other mortal knows what I do."

His tone was matter-of-fact, and he did not look up at her for some time. He hoped by confiding in her, he would begin to gain her trust, and that she would better understand his frustration with the journey. Stonewall Hall had claimed countless lives throughout history, and even with his extensive understanding of what lay before them, he could not guarantee their safety. Coreyaless, for all her years, had rushed into the opportunity his arrival presented without pausing to contemplate the potential consequences of her actions. Though he was not particularly fond of Janna, he didn't wish to see her meet a gruesome end at the hands of the Undead or harmed by the other denizens of the mountain. The Airess' request had been borne of desperation, but he sensed a selfishness within her as well.

When he lifted his gaze, she stared into the distance, her expression contemplative. "Why didn't you mention this to me, Vardak?"

"I haven't told anyone. It wasn't necessary until now."

Her brow furrowed as she considered his answer. "Are all of your people so reserved, Vardak?"

Immediately, he thought of his brothers, which caused him to chuckle. "No."

"Somehow, I am not surprised." She smiled ruefully. "I suppose this means you'll be taking the lead once we're inside since it's clear you know how to reach our destination?"

He nodded. "I would have, regardless. Your potion may help deter the Undead, but there are other creatures that may need to be dealt with. You're no warrior, and neither is Janna."

"Perhaps I've misjudged you, Vardak."

He shrugged. "You would not have been the first. It's no matter."

He understood that many people mistook his frequent silences for brooding or disdain, but he simply chose not to speak unless he had something relevant to say. It often took time before he began to open up to new acquaintances, and because of that, he had few true friends. That fact didn't bother him; those he became close to remained so indefinitely.

"I'm pleased we've come to an understanding," Coreyaless continued and paused to offer him a smile. "I'd begun to fear the outcome of my decision to come here, but it seems I was wrong. Perhaps we can start anew."

He smiled faintly in return. "Yes."

"Good. I'll wake Janna. We should not waste any more time today."

The entrance of Stonewall Hall opened into a vast, circular gallery. Twisted columns of carefully chiseled stone rose from the smooth floor to ascend to the ceiling several spans above, forming precise rows within the room. The stone itself glowed with a soft, white light, eliminating the need for torches as they traversed the mountain's extensive interior. The air was stale, with an undercurrent of something faintly unsavory, a scent Vardak did not recognize.

"For a place of such ill repute, it's beautiful, in its own way," Janna breathed. She craned her neck to scrutinize the nearest column.

Vardak frowned in her direction. He'd been explicit in his instructions to her before they'd entered. Silence was imperative if they were to avoid attracting the attention of the mountain's more deadly denizens. Janna failed to see his silent response to her words, captivated as she was by their surroundings.

He focused his attention on what lay ahead, and hoped Janna would remember the inherent danger present within Stonewall Hall before he was forced to remind her. Silently he moved forward; he heard the soft footfalls of the others as they followed closely behind. He recognized that his physiology gave him a distinct advantage when it came to moving stealthily and that the two women were making an effort to mask the sound of their steps. There was little more he could ask of them.

On the far side of the gallery, there were a series of corridors that led deeper into the mountain. At each junction, a series of symbols were carved into the stone, markers that indicated where each would lead. He studied them carefully, seeking the one that signified Flariel's long-lost shrine. He found it at the fourth juncture and pointed it out to the others. There were a series of vertical, waving lines bisected with a downward-pointing triangle.

"This is the marker we must follow," he whispered.

Coreyaless nodded after taking a moment to inspect the symbol.

"How do you know this?" Janna asked quietly.

"My story can wait for another time. It's not safe to talk."

She nodded her understanding, and they pressed on. The marked corridor was wide enough to allow the trio to walk abreast, with room to spare. Intricate carvings of animals adorned the walls, so lifelike that Vardak expected them to spring into motion at any moment. Some of the creatures he recognized from his desert homeland; lizards, wide-eared foxes, small birds, snakes, and trap-door spiders. Intermingled with those he recognized were far more that he did not, some so fanciful he was certain they could not have been real. Blademon's knowledge extended to creatures relevant to combat situations or those that may pose a threat to his safety. He was reliant upon his own limited experience to identify anything else sculpted on the walls.

As the corridor opened into another large room, Vardak tensed and motioned for the others to remain behind him. Figures lined the adjacent walls, and he was at first uncertain whether they were more intricate statuary or something far more sinister. He gripped his axe firmly and slowly crossed the distance to the nearest, his feet moving almost silently across the stone floor.

To his relief, the figures remained still and he quickly determined they were mere stone. Each was subtly different than its neighbors, though all depicted a race of beings long since lost to the world. They were tall, bipedal creatures with large, sharply pointed ears, and bat-like wings where arms should have been. At the end of each wing were an array of spindly appendages that resembled long fingers. The carved face that stared back at him was elongated to resemble a snout, giving its features a lupine appearance. He peered at the statue, transfixed by the alien creature it depicted.

"The builders," Coreyaless whispered behind him. He startled and glanced over his shoulder at the Airess, noting with surprise Janna stood alongside her. He had failed to hear their approach.

"Builders?" Janna echoed.

She nodded. "I do not know what they called themselves, but it was their people who built this place. They were the first victims to fall to the Nameless god's misplaced ire. They were cursed by him, and upon physical death, they became the Undead. It was his curse that drew the wrath of the other gods. They stripped him of his name and bound him deep within the earth."

Vardak was familiar with the legend of the Nameless god's imprisonment, but he'd never heard the rendition that included the builders of Stonewall Hall. It was only then that he understood the

98

connection between the statues and the image of the Undead he'd recognized from Blademon's imparted knowledge.

"They will look much the same, even now," he said, troubled by the revelation. "As the Undead, they hold no memory of the people they once were. They are mindless and seek only the destruction of those they deem trespassers within their halls."

Coreyaless nodded her agreement. "Yes. I fear to linger in this place."

With a nod, Vardak led them toward the far end of the room. The rows of exquisite statuary provided the perfect place for one of the Undead to hide, undetected, until ready to ambush the unwary traveler.

Though his axe would do little true damage against such foes, its heft was reassuring. He knew if they were confronted with those cursed beings, their only chance of survival would be to flee and pray they did not run headlong into more of them. The legends of Stonewall Hall indicated the Undead continued their pitiful existence by feeding off the souls of the living, though even Blademon's extensive knowledge was unable to confirm the tales. He knew only that the creatures could not be harmed with conventional weapons, nor could they be killed. They occupied a level of existence beyond death but had been denied their eternal rest. He would take no unnecessary risks if they encountered any of the creatures.

He located the symbol that would lead them to Flariel's shrine, carved into the wall beside the entrance to the next corridor. Like the hall before it, the walls were adorned with more intricate sculptures. They depicted life-sized figures from every race that inhabited their world, with the exception of his own. The Scorpion Men had not existed during the time of the builders, but had been created using corrupted magic during the first Great War. His ancestors had been human prisoners of war, transformed against their will and forced to serve the Soulless by means of mind-controlling magic.

The stone figures peered at them from either side of the corridor, a myriad of expressions frozen in place, as though the builders had striven to bring them to life through their carving. Humans stood alongside Airess, Felene, Drakkon, and Murkor. He was surprised to see the Murkor depicted hoodless, their fine, hairless features adorned with intricate tattoos.

"Who are they?" Janna asked of the first Murkor they passed.

It was little wonder she did not recognize them, Vardak thought to himself as Coreyaless whispered a brief explanation to her. Most humans knew the Murkor only as "the hooded ones". Their customs forbade them from showing their faces even amongst their own kind. To look upon a Murkor face was to know that Murkor intimately; only immediate family and lovers were granted such privilege. Vardak knew almost as much about the Murkor as he did his own people, given their long, shared history of both peaceable trade and extensive conflict.

"I never imagined the Murkor would be so *beautiful*," Janna whispered in a reverent tone.

"They are a secretive people," Vardak replied quietly.

"They appear almost human," she continued, marveling at the nearest statue.

"The stone does not reveal their coloration," he replied. "But yes, their form is much like your own."

"If the builders had been themselves when the Scorpion Men came to be, do you think they'd be carved here, too?" Janna asked.

Vardak scowled into the corridor ahead and took a few moments to rein in his temper. Janna did not understand the topic was anathema amongst his people, a fact learned at a young age but loathed for the duration of one's life. A lifetime of ingrained anger at his ancestors' misfortune was better spent on the battlefield; lashing out at Janna's ignorance would serve no purpose.

"I don't know," he replied briskly.

"But—"

"There will be time enough for questions later," Coreyaless interjected sharply. "This place is not safe, Janna."

Chastised, Janna nodded and followed his lead. She continued to pause at intervals to peer at one statue or another, but mercifully, she remained silent. They pressed on, following the symbol engraved in the stone at each junction as the corridors drew them ever deeper into the mountain. Each large room they came to was different than the last, but all were adorned with intricate carvings and statuary, the artistry unlike anything Vardak had encountered. Viewing the work of the builders firsthand saddened him; he was certain they had not deserved their cursed fate.

After several hours, they came upon the largest room yet. It was a vast ovoid, ringed by decorative, fluted columns. Numerous corridors emptied into the room from both long sides of the oval. At the room's heart, a waterfall cascaded from somewhere far above, falling in a steady curtain of crystalline water to form a large lake. The light emanating from the stone allowed him to see that a single, arcing bridge spanned the water. Given the size of the waterfall and the apparent height from which it plummeted, Vardak knew the lake must have been fathoms deep.

He shuddered involuntarily. He was unused to seeing water in such quantities, and the idea of crossing the lake—even with the aid of the bridge—unnerved him. He could not swim.

The roar of the falling water drowned out all other sound as they approached the lakeshore, adding to his anxiety. It was an ideal location to stage an attack, particularly once they found themselves on the narrow bridge. If he were planning an ambush, he would have soldiers staged in a corridor on either side of the lake, making it a simple task to trap the unwary enemy at the center of the span, where they would be unable to flee.

He stopped at the base of the bridge to study it further. The stone was solid, but slick with spray from the waterfall. The film of water would not affect his footing, but he feared it might be treacherous to the others. The span was only wide enough to allow them passage singly, and though it sported an ornate railing, it was only waist-high. His eyes scanned the dark surface of the water uneasily.

"Vardak?" Coreyaless was forced to shout in order to be heard over the rush of water.

He drew a breath and turned away from the bridge to scan the openings of the corridors behind them. All appeared quiet, but he knew that could change in an instant. He did not like their present location, yet there was nothing to be done but press forward. Their destination lay on the far side of the lake.

"We must cross quickly," he told her. "I don't like the feel of this gods-forsaken place."

She nodded, understanding, and motioned for Janna to move ahead of her. "You take the lead," she said to Vardak. "I'll follow Janna, and call to you if I see anything from the rear."

He faced the bridge once more and drew a breath to steady himself. He could not allow the others to sense his fear, for it would only serve to heighten their own.

"Let's go," he said over his shoulder, "and tread carefully."

They crossed the span without incident. Relieved that they had not encountered any of the mountain's residents, and doubly so to be away from the water's edge, he began to inspect the entrances of the next set of corridors for the shrine's mark. He motioned for the others to follow him once he located it, but they paused only steps beyond the corridor's threshold.

A low, droning hum vibrated through the air toward them, the sound akin to that of a large beehive. He pushed ahead of the women, widening his stance to block the corridor from the creature he knew was approaching their location. He adjusted his grip on his axe and tensed his scorpion's tail in preparation to strike.

"What is that?" Janna whispered in a quavering tone as the drone steadily increased in volume.

Vardak ignored her question, his focus on the bend in the corridor ahead. He believed he knew what creature approached them, though whether it would attack or flee was yet to be seen. The stone sciarids were a large breed of flying insect, equipped with a pair of serrated pincers they used largely for defense. Blademon's knowledge told him the creatures were usually harmless but were known to attack the unwary traveler on occasion.

Vardak would take no risks with their safety, and prepared to combat the insect as the sound of its wings continued to increase in volume. It was rapidly nearing their location, the hum of its approach drowning out the echoes from the waterfall in the previous chamber.

The stone sciarid stopped to hover in the corridor moments after it rounded the bend. It had small, compound eyes, and seemed to study them for several seconds before it quickly turned around and flew away. Vardak remained in position as he listened to the sound of its wings fade into the distance, and only when the corridor fell silent once more did he relax.

"What *was* that?" Janna asked again, her voice small and unsteady.

"A stone sciarid," he replied quietly. "They rarely pose a threat here, but where there is one, there will ultimately be more."

He began to walk forward while Coreyaless continued the explanation. "The builders once used them as a means of rapid transportation through these halls, or so the stories claim. Some of the old legends even state they were used in battle. I suppose for a winged race, a winged steed of some manner is feasible."

"What will happen if we encounter more of them?"

"I will fight, if need be," Vardak stated, "but I pray I won't be forced to. The Undead are drawn to sounds of combat."

Janna fell silent then, her face drawn and pale in the unnatural illumination provided by the stone. He did not wish to scare her, but he felt it was important she know what trouble may lie ahead. It was best she was prepared.

They moved on with little more than the soft echoes of the women's boots to break the silence. Vardak was disturbed by the quietude; their brief encounter with the stone sciarid left him on edge. He was certain they would encounter more of the creatures deeper within the mountain.

Another span of time passed, though he was uncertain if it was an hour or an afternoon. Time did not seem to touch Stonewall Hall, and without the passage of the sun through the sky, he did not know how long they'd been traveling. When he became aware of a low hum permeating the stone around them, it took him a moment to realize they'd been hearing the sound for some time. He recognized it as belonging to the rapid wingbeats of the stone sciarids, but the magnitude of the perceived noise gave him pause. To his ear, there seemed to be dozens, perhaps hundreds, of the insects, and each step drew them nearer to the source of the sound.

He glanced over his shoulder and caught Coreyaless' eye. "Be prepared for anything."

Not far ahead, the corridor bent at a right angle. He edged toward the curve, uncertain of what he'd find once he rounded the bend. The growing drone of the stone sciarids beyond told him much, but he needed to see for himself what potential dangers lay before them.

He gestured to the others to remain where they were as he sidled up to the corner. Peering around it, he was met with the sight of another expansive chamber rivaling the waterfall room in size. On the far side he could make out a broad staircase that led to a long row of ornate columns, carved to resemble gouts of flame. Between the columns at the center was a wide, arched doorway. He recognized the place from Blademon's imparted memories—it was Flariel's shrine.

Between their present location and the steps leading to the shrine, however, scores of stone sciarids hovered in place. Their attention was drawn toward the wall to his left, but he could not make out the source from his present location. Some of the sciarids snapped their serrated pincers in a display meant to threaten. The clacks they produced were loud enough to be heard clearly over the drone from their wings.

Slowly, he crept toward the corridor's threshold, hoping he would not draw the notice of the nearest sciarids. From his perspective, the insects were agitated, and the cacophony of their snapped threats rippled through the air.

As the rest of the room came into view before him, he gripped the haft of his axe more tightly in response. The sciarids were disturbed with good reason; the three halls that adjoined the chamber were packed with the ethereal, winged visages of the creatures he recognized as the Undead. He ducked his head back into the corridor and surveyed the rest of the room ahead.

If they made a run for Flariel's shrine, they would be immediately noticed by both the sciarids and the Undead, but he saw no other option. He hoped the insects would prove enough of a distraction for the long-dead builders that they could reach the shrine before the Undead were upon them. They had but one opportunity to reach it and pray that Coreyaless' information would prove true. If their means for escape was not within, their lives would quickly be forfeit.

He returned to Janna and Coreyaless, but could not force the grim expression from his features. He told them what he had seen and their only means of escape. "I pray to the gods that your path to the southlands remains after so many years."

Coreyaless frowned and began digging in her satchel while she pointedly ignored his final remark. After a moment, she retrieved a trio of small stoppered flasks and handed one to both Vardak and Janna. "It is the potion I spoke of," she stated. "Drink it quickly, and then we must go."

Vardak did so, grimacing at the bitter aftertaste. He handed the flask back to Coreyaless and gripped his axe, prepared to use the weapon if it meant he must sacrifice himself to ensure one of them would reach the shrine on the other side. He motioned for them to follow him, then set a rapid pace.

When they came to the opening, he paused to reassess the room. The sciarids were engaging the Undead, who had remained near the corridors where he'd last spotted them. More sciarids hovered throughout the room, and it seemed their number had increased. He fixed his gaze upon the shrine and pointed toward its steps.

"Go. Run as quickly as you can. I'll cover the rear."

Coreyaless gripped Janna's elbow and the pair began a frantic dash toward the shrine. Vardak followed them quickly and found himself dodging and ducking the sciarids within. Some of the insects clacked their pincers in warning but he ignored them, keeping one eye on the rapidly advancing Undead. The sciarids, for all their numbers, were falling in droves before their former masters. Mounds of chitinous bodies were forming, though they proved no obstacle against the spectral forms of the builders. The Undead passed through them, as if they were no more substantial than the surrounding musty air.

He suppressed the urge to shout a warning to the women ahead of him, fearing any sound he made would force the Undead to shift their focus away from their sciarid victims. Even if he did not survive the crossing, he believed Janna must.

As they reached the staircase, Janna stumbled and found herself sprawled upon the steps. Coreyaless pulled her to her feet, but Janna limped and could not put her full weight on her right leg. With a grimace, Vardak slung his axe onto his back and scooped her up as he raced toward the top of the stairs. He set her on her feet once more and turned around to survey the chamber behind them a final time, while Coreyaless helped Janna inside.

Dozens of Undead had swarmed into the room, and countless sciarid lay dead amongst them. A number of the specters had reached the base of the stairs and Vardak drew his axe, prepared to defend the shrine's entrance with all he could muster. His tail drew tense, and though he knew his venom would prove useless against such a foe, his body's reaction to the adrenaline coursing through his veins caused the glands at the base of his stinger to begin producing. He widened his stance, blocking the entrance from within.

"Vardak!"

He ignored Coreyaless' call, focused on the enemy ascending the steps before him.

"Vardak!" she shouted again, more urgently.

He risked a glance over his shoulder to find the Airess beckoned to him insistently from an interior doorway. His options were limited: trust her or die fighting an unconquerable foe. He opted for the former and skittered across the shrine's anteroom toward her location. He prayed he was not making a mistake that would cost all of their lives.

Within the next room a large mirror hung upon the far wall, its surface discolored with age. Janna stood before it but where her reflection should have been was the image of Flariel, her molten figure ensconced in flame. The Fire Maiden's luminous eyes fell upon him, and she nodded to herself thoughtfully.

"I will grant you passage to the southlands," she stated coldly, "but my services do not come without cost."

"Mother, please!" Janna cried out in frustration. "The Undead are—"

"They are within my shrine. Yes, I know." She crossed her arms and fixed Janna with a contemptuous glare. "Your goal was to retrieve the Moon's Eye, daughter, not chase some madwoman's folly."

"Mother—"

Janna's voice was cut off as a blinding flash illuminated the area, followed by absolute darkness. Disoriented, Vardak found himself falling forward. He wondered fleetingly if he'd been overtaken

106

by the Undead. Unable to break his strange and sudden descent, he flailed, only to be stopped by an abrupt, bone-jarring impact. Another, more forceful blow struck him across his shoulders, and a third met the base of his skull. He closed his eyes with a groan and succumbed to the enveloping darkness.

CHAPTER ELEVEN

A DESERT SKIRMISH

"You will engage them. Assess their defenses." Kama looked down his long, hooked nose at Aran'daj. "Take prisoners if you wish. I care not."

Aran'daj averted his gaze from the Soulless' callous crimson eyes, and focused on the long, low structure in the distance. The metallic outer shell glimmered softly in the fading evening light, encircled by pristine white sand. The Murkor could see well enough in total darkness, but the light would be enough for their adversaries to see nearly as well. Aran'daj frowned in displeasure; he disliked the illumination of the landscape and the prospect of making enemies of the Scorpion Men.

He swallowed his misgivings and nodded once in acknowledgment. "Of course, sir."

"I've brought you here with your chosen battalion, in order to better understand what threat, if any, these people pose to our plans," Kama continued. "You are to engage them, Commander, but do not hesitate to retreat if things begin to deteriorate. I require *every* fighting man your people can produce, and casualties must be kept to a minimum. The master has plans beyond the mountains."

Aran'daj suppressed a shudder at the zealous light that had entered the Soulless' eyes.

"This is also a test of your skill, Commander. If I deem you have failed me, you will die." Kama's tone was uncompromising.

"Yes, sir." There was nothing to be done but agree, as the Soulless expected him to.

"Good. I intend to watch your actions from there." Kama jabbed one long finger in the direction of a tall dune, perhaps a half-mile away. "You've trained many years for this moment, Commander. Do not disappoint me."

Kama opened a portal in the air beside him and stepped through to leave Aran'daj alone with his bitter thoughts at the head of the battalion. Kama had come to him not long after dawn that day and ordered him to gather his best soldiers in preparation for a skirmish. Kama had leveled several threats to ensure his compliance, but said nothing more of his plans until he returned in the late afternoon to inspect the Murkor soldiers Aran'daj had selected.

Kama had not returned alone. Two of the other Soulless accompanied him; a small, frail man, and a tall woman with a buxom figure that belied the horror etched into her face. Together, the three had called forth a powerful magic, and moments later, Aran'daj and his battalion found themselves hundreds of miles south, a stone's throw from the Stronghold of the Scorpion Men.

Now, he was expected to draw them into a fight. An uneasy peace had existed between the Murkor and the Scorpion Men for many years, and both sides thrived on the trade of goods and services they'd developed. His next move would shatter that tenuous alliance, but if he did nothing, he knew the Soulless would inevitably slaughter his people. He would merely be the first in a long string of casualties.

He studied the shifting white sands before him, taking note of the sentries that patrolled the perimeter. They hadn't yet taken notice of him, a lone Murkor standing atop a high dune. From their vantage point, the battalion spread on the slopes of the dune behind him would be invisible.

He sighed heavily as the gravity of his next action weighed upon him. He unsheathed his curved, black saber and held it aloft, a signal to his soldiers to march forward to his location. If Kama wished for a fight, he would deliver, though his heart was not in the maneuver. He was choosing his people's continued existence over that of the Scorpion Men.

Drums sounded at the rear of the unit, beating a cadence through the night air in time with the marching of the soldiers. The sound drew the attention of the patrolling sentries below. Aran'daj watched as the handful of Scorpion Men shouted to one another. A pair broke from their position to race across the sands nimbly toward the low, metallic structure they called home. It would only be minutes before a fighting force was assembled to face the Murkor threat looming in the dunes above—minutes that Aran'daj wished would not pass. He held the Scorpion Men in high esteem and loathed the thought of bringing war to both of their peoples.

He glanced toward Kama's location as the first of his soldiers formed ranks around him. The Soulless stood motionless upon his chosen dune, and in spite of the distance between them, Aran'daj was certain his fierce, crimson eyes were locked upon his own. He shuddered and averted his gaze, focusing once more on the task at hand.

"Commander, we await your signal."

Aran'daj recognized the confident tones of the young Murkor now standing on his left as belonging to Jal'den. Due to his unusual training, Jal'den had been elevated to the status of Arms Master, a position only marginally below his own. He wore a curved saber at his belt much like the commander's, though Aran'daj knew he preferred to use the larger, two-handed broadsword strapped to his back. The broadsword had been given to him at the completion of his training and was the only weapon amongst the Murkor forged of traditional steel, rather than the black, poison-infused *gulob'arscon*.

Jal'den had proven himself fierce in the sparring ring, and since his recent return from Blademon's side, he was undefeated amongst the Murkor. Jal'den was no strategist, but he commanded respect from much of the army due to his prowess in the ring alone.

"The Soulless has ordered we engage merely to assess the Scorpion Men's strength," Aran'daj replied. "We will do as ordered and retreat when necessary. The Soulless are merely testing them—and us. They do not wish to waste men on this cause."

Jal'den snorted derisively beneath his hood. "This seems a damned waste of time, Commander."

Aran'daj agreed with his sentiment, but there was little he could do to reverse their course. "My words alone were insufficient to sway them. They have insisted on this demonstration of our power and fortitude. As you are undoubtedly aware, I am in no position to defy the gods-forsaken creatures."

THE RELICS OF WAR: THE MOON'S EYE

Jal'den was silent for several moments, and Aran'daj imagined he was scowling. "What are your orders, Commander?"

"We will wait until they've gathered a small force below," Aran'daj replied. "On my signal, you'll lead the charge. If the Soulless want a show, we'll fucking give them one." His last words came out in a snarl; he was unable to contain his frustration any longer.

Jal'den snickered. "As you say, Commander."

They waited; the precise lines of Murkor soldiers stood in clear view of the entrance to the Stronghold. Aran'daj detected movement within the torchlit opening and understood the Scorpion Men were mustering their defenses. It had taken them far less time than he'd anticipated, though it did not surprise him. They were a people borne of war, trained in the use of weapons as soon as they could walk, and the favored people of Blademon himself. Battle was their calling.

"I assume you'll remain here," Jal'den stated after a time. "After all, we'll need you visible—and alive—in order to judge when it is time to retreat."

Aran'daj nodded, a nearly imperceptible bob of his hooded head. As he had risen through the ranks of their army, he'd found himself farther away from the physical fighting each time. He'd been a passable fighter, but it was his mind for strategy that won him true victories.

"Good." Jal'den signaled the others to ready themselves for their commander's next order.

It was then the Scorpion Men began to spill from within the Stronghold, long lines that quickly formed rank and file across the sand. Aran'daj noted with dismay their numbers quickly surpassed his own. Retreat would not simply be desirable; it would be imperative.

Aran'daj spied no obvious weakness within the growing ranks, but he held Jal'den and the others within his hand-picked battalion in high regard. He knew they could hold their own for a time, even against such odds, but he must time the signal for retreat carefully in order to avoid a massacre. When he glanced at the eager Arms Master at his side, he caught a glint of mischief in the other's pale eyes.

"Meet them head-on," he told Jal'den. "Listen for my call to retreat, and for the love of the gods, do not delay."

"Yes, sir." He could hear the amusement in Jal'den's tone as he began to signal their plan to the rest of the soldiers. Wordless communication was paramount when facing the Scorpion Men; most understood the Murkor tongue.

Aran'daj steeled himself and hoped Jal'den's skill in the sparring ring would yield similar results in his first skirmish with an enemy force. He held his saber aloft once more and brought the blade down in a sweeping motion meant to signal the attack. The drums increased their tempo as black-clad Murkor soldiers in ring mail surged toward the Scorpion Men awaiting them below. He found himself within an eddy in the stream of soldiers moving forward.

A single shout came from within the midst of the foe, followed by several rapid clangs as weapon hilt met steel shield. Aran'daj knew it was their own version of wordless communication, that it was undoubtedly the Warleader himself issuing commands. Aran'daj had met Sevic years ago during one of his rare visits to the Stronghold. Sevic was uncompromising in his loyalty to the Scorpion Men and had a keen mind for battle. Aran'daj was facing an opponent he considered an equal.

The Scorpion Men below raised their shields in unison, weapons at the ready as the Murkor rushed toward them. Another series of loud clangs were issued, and Aran'daj watched as a volley of arrows arced skyward to land among his soldiers. A dozen or more fell, but the Murkor pushed on as they'd been trained to do. They closed the gap before a second volley of arrows could be fired and began to engage their newfound enemies.

The last of the Murkor soldiers raced past him, leaving him alone on the dune with the pair of drummers for company. He would rely on their cadence to sound a retreat when the time came.

Below, the Murkor clashed with the men and women of the Stronghold and casualties began to mount on both sides. He was able to pick out Jal'den amongst the fray easily enough; the young Arms Master whirled in a deadly dance with his broadsword, multiple fallen enemies left in his wake. It seemed he lived up to his reputation.

He averted his attention to the distant dune where Kama stood, motionless against the backdrop of the night sky. He was uncertain how long the Soulless wished to watch the farce below them play out, but Aran'daj was loath to lose any more of his best soldiers due to the man's whims. He scowled in the direction of the Soulless, wishing he knew a means to free himself and his people from their grasp.

"Sound the retreat," he ordered the drummers, unable to conceal the misery in his tone.

Without a word, the pair of drummers adjusted their rhythm. It took several moments before the soldiers took notice of the change, but once they did, they began to flee the field rapidly. Some of the Scorpion Men began to pursue the Murkor, but another set of metallic strikes issued forth from the rear of their formation, and they halted. Sevic was allowing his men to quit the field, though Aran'daj suspected their recent quarrel with the Scorpion Men would not be the last time he'd find himself facing off against the Warleader. The fight had lasted less than an hour.

Aran'daj signaled the soldiers to regroup at the base of the dune where they'd begun their evening. As the ranks reformed, he noted with some satisfaction that more than a dozen of the Scorpion Men's warriors had been captured. They would be taken to the Underground Caverns, where the alchemists would harvest their venom. His thoughts flickered briefly to Sal'zar, and he wondered how he fared in his magical training.

"Commander." Jal'den was breathless, but Aran'daj heard glee in his tone.

"Arms Master."

"That was a glorious first battle, even if it was cut a bit short." He chuckled. "We could have lasted a few more minutes, but I understand—"

He stopped abruptly as a faint blue oval opened in the air before them. Kama stepped out and surveyed the pair silently, his expression unreadable. Aran'daj forced himself to stand erect, to swallow his fear, and meet the man's fiendish red gaze.

"Your men have proven themselves, Commander," Kama said after several tense moments. "For that, I will allow you to live. Garin and Alyra should arrive momentarily to assist in the transportation of you and your men back to the tower." Kama turned slowly, taking note of the captives in the Murkor's midst. "I assume you will have them taken to the caverns."

"Yes, sir."

"Good. No doubt your people will need more weapons forged for the coming war. A ready supply of venom will help."

"Yes, sir."

Kama turned to face them once more, his arms crossed. He focused his attention on Jal'den. "I know your history, Arms Master. It seems Blademon's favor serves you well."

Jal'den hesitated, and when he spoke his voice was hoarse. "It has, sir."

"Where there is one, there is always another," Kama replied cryptically, a faint frown twisting his ghastly features. "It is no matter. You've proven yourself and allowed me insight into the Scorpion Men's preparedness. It is enough for one day."

CHAPTER TWELVE

BLADEMON'S MESSAGE

Vardak was first aware of the tremendous pounding in his head, then slowly realized much of his body ached as well. He opened his eyes to find the area around him illuminated in flickering firelight. There were hundreds of trees towering overhead, many more than he'd encountered in Vidune Forest, but these were markedly different. Their leaves were much broader and larger, and their trunks were entangled with vines. Dense undergrowth filled every conceivable space between the trees. The air was thick and moist, and an earthy, green scent filled his nostrils.

Slowly, he pushed himself upright, and stifled a groan as he did so. His ribs protested the movement poignantly, and he wondered if some were broken. It would not have been the first time he'd sustained such an injury, but he was uncertain what had transpired to cause his pain. The last clear memory he had was standing before Flariel in her shrine, as a bright light enveloped him.

To his left, he heard movement. He turned to find Coreyaless striding toward him from the direction of a small campfire. Janna lay beside it, soundly asleep. Their makeshift camp had been set up on what appeared to be a narrow dirt track that wound its way through the thick vegetation.

The Airess looked him over with a critical eye, her mouth drawn into a troubled frown. "You've been unconscious for some time, Vardak. I'm afraid when Flariel sent us here—wherever *here* is— both Janna and I landed atop you rather forcefully. We are unhurt, but I noticed bruising along your jaw. Are you well?"

He shook his head as though to clear it and immediately regretted the action. A sudden and violent wave of nausea passed through him. He managed to turn aside in time to avoid spilling the contents of his stomach on the Airess. He grimaced and spat, then drew a shaky breath. His face flushed with shame; he hadn't meant her to witness his moment of weakness.

"I'll assume your answer is 'no'," she replied after a moment, concern in her tone.

He remained still but began to tell her of his ailments. As he spoke, she peered into his eyes as though seeking an answer in their blue depths. Had he not been tended to by his people's healers on occasion, he would have found her attention disconcerting, but the familiarity of her expression set him strangely at ease.

"A concussion, I suspect," she informed him when he finished. "And perhaps a cracked rib or two. I can set the ribs and give you something to ease your headache and promote healing."

He began to nod, then thought better of it. "Thank you."

He followed her toward the campfire, where she began rummaging in one of her satchels for herbs and bandages. He settled himself nearby and took another few moments to study their surroundings. The forest canopy above was so dense he could see only a few swatches of sky between the interlacing branches. Strange calls carried through the night from animals he was certain he'd never encountered previously. The air was pleasantly warm, but heavy and cloying. He quickly decided he preferred the drier warmth of his homeland to the sticky humidity present in this forest.

"I'll need you to remove your armor." Coreyaless' no-nonsense tone drew him back to the task at hand.

He made no reply but began by removing his gauntlets. He remained impressed with Travin's work; the lightweight steel had served its purpose so far. He wondered how forcefully the two women had fallen onto him, that he'd managed to sustain injury simply from their impact. Belatedly, he realized his axe was not strapped to his back as he began to work loose the armor's straps. He glanced around the campfire and spotted it leaning against the trunk of a tree not far away.

"The undershirt, too," she said as he finished with the armor. "I need to have a clear look at your ribs."

He chuckled wearily. "All healers seem to share the same bedside manner."

116

"When you've dealt with your share of stubborn, irrational, and cantankerous patients, you develop a certain mindset."

She smiled ruefully as she waited for him to remove the undergarment. He winced at the movement as his muscles stretched and pulled at the injury. She examined his ribs, pressing her fingers into his flesh along each one. Her prodding did not cause him further pain, and he began to wonder if it was the least of his injuries. After a few moments, she stepped back, seemingly satisfied.

"I believe they're only bruised. Your head, however, is a more serious matter. Be still while I brew some tea."

"Might I at least put my shirt back on?"

She laughed quietly. "Yes, but make no sudden movements, or you'll likely be sick again."

He pulled on his shirt, then said, "I believe this is the first injury I've taken in many years that was not the result of sparring."

"I don't know what Flariel intended when she dropped us here, but I would have liked a softer landing. I suppose I ought to thank you for cushioning my own fall, and Janna's, though you had little choice in the matter."

Coreyaless carefully measured herbs into her hands, then dumped them unceremoniously into a small kettle she'd produced from her belongings. He watched her work, noting the meticulous nature she employed while plying her craft.

"How did Janna fare after coming here?"

Coreyaless shrugged but did not look up from her work. "She was concerned about you, foremost, since we could not manage to awaken you. She was quite frustrated by her mother's actions, though there is little even she can do to sway Flariel."

She set the kettle over the fire and peered up at him. "Janna also has many questions for you. I think she deserves to know how you came to navigate Stonewall Hall as efficiently as you did. If we are to work together, there ought not be secrets between us."

"I'm surprised you didn't tell her."

"It wasn't my place."

He sighed and cast a glance toward Janna's sleeping form. He feared if he allowed her to begin asking questions, she would never

117

cease. She meant well, but her chatter was wearisome and he was not one for words.

"I'll consider it." His reply was reluctant.

"You have some time before she wakes in order to prepare yourself," Coreyaless said dryly. "I gave her some herbs to help her rest again. Now," she said as she took the kettle from the fire and poured a measure of steaming tea into a metal cup, "you must drink this. I'm afraid it's bitter, but it will alleviate your headache and reduce your bruising."

She thrust the cup toward him, and he grimaced at the astringent aroma wafting from the dark liquid within. Another glance at her face told him if he didn't drink the brew of his own volition, the Airess was likely to force it upon him. Centuries of tending the ailments of others had left her with little patience for those who would resist her ministrations. He took a tentative sip, and decided it wasn't as bad as some of the remedies he'd been forced to ingest previously.

"You'll need to drink the entire cup, and it grows more unpleasant as it cools." When he frowned, she laughed. "I believe it only fair to warn you of the consequences of procrastination, Vardak."

By morning, his headache had abated, and his ribs no longer protested with each movement. He donned his armor and collected his axe from where it rested against the tree, while Coreyaless set about the task of waking Janna from her elixir-induced slumber.

With the light of day, he determined that the forest around them was far denser than he'd believed. Plants of every shape and size crowded the small spaces between the massive trees. Flowers in a myriad of colors adorned some, while others sported strangely-shaped contraptions that he learned were a means of trapping insects.

Dozens of different bird calls trilled from the branches, while other piercing cries with a more animalistic quality reverberated through the undergrowth. The hum of insects quickly joined the other sounds, and with it, clouds of small gnats and biting flies seemed to erupt from the earth itself. The biting insects seemed to favor Janna and Coreyaless, but left him largely alone.

"Where do you suppose we must go?" Janna asked as they gathered their belongings and took a small breakfast of jerky and dried fruits.

Vardak had relied upon Blademon's knowledge to see them through Stonewall Hall, but the war god's gift did not extend beyond the reaches of the Five Kingdoms and the Wasted Land. He did not know where they were, nor which direction they should travel. That Flariel had dropped them on what seemed to be a path was encouraging, but he had little else to go on.

"It seems we have two choices," Coreyaless replied, putting voice to his thoughts. "Do you have any insight we do not, Vardak?"

He withheld the urge to glower at her. "No."

"Then I suppose one way is as good as the other. It's a path, which means there must be a destination at either end." Coreyaless peered first in one direction, then the other, and arbitrarily settled on the track that would lead them east. "We'll follow the path this way."

Vardak shook his head, mildly amused.

"What's so funny, Vardak?" Janna asked as she waved away a cloud of gnats that had flown in front of her.

Before he could answer, Coreyaless said, "My choice of direction, apparently. Though I will point out you contributed nothing to the conversation, Vardak."

He sighed, exasperated. She meant to goad him into divulging his secrets to Janna, whether he wished to or not. "Blademon did not see fit to give me understanding of the lands beyond the Five Kingdoms."

Janna swatted at a fly that had landed on her arm. "Of course! That's how you knew to navigate Stonewall Hall, and how you knew the way to Coreyaless' home before that." She scowled as another insect alighted on her shoulder. "Don't you have anything to drive off the bugs? They're intolerable."

"I'm afraid I don't have anything prepared," Coreyaless replied. "I wasn't expecting to be assaulted by this variety of flying vermin."

As the sun climbed higher in the sky, the temperature increased to sweltering levels. Vardak was accustomed to the heat, but not so for humidity. It was a miserable slog, and even Janna fell silent after a time, succumbing to her discomfort. Their journey was punctuated by slaps as the two women continued to be assailed by biting flies.

"It's not fair," Janna complained at one point. "The bugs don't seem to bother you at all, Vardak."

"I suspect his venom keeps them at bay," Coreyaless replied.

"I wish I were so fortunate," Janna pouted.

When Vardak didn't respond, she huffed and fell silent once more. He was puzzled that she seemed upset with him. There was little he could do for her; his venom would kill her in a matter of minutes if she was exposed to it. He looked to Coreyaless for help, but the Airess merely smirked and turned away. Their behavior was a mystery, and he found himself missing the company of his brothers.

It was almost midday when a settlement appeared through the forest ahead. A wooden palisade surrounded dozens of small, square dwellings. A rickety gate blocked their path, and Vardak could see two figures standing on either side. As they neared and the details of the pair coalesced, he blinked with surprise. They were bipedal, though with distinctly feline features and covered in thick fur. He recognized them as Felene, but the stories he'd learned as a child spoke of the race as extinct.

Coreyaless gasped. "Flariel has brought us to the southern continent and what remains of the Felene people. She kept her word."

One of the Felene at the gate strode toward them purposefully. He wore leather armor, carried a bow and quiver of arrows upon his back, and a trio of daggers were tucked into his broad belt. The fur he sported was yellow-orange with intermittent white stripes. Large green eyes regarded them with open curiosity. He stood only shoulder-high to Janna, but Vardak sensed he was proficient with his weapons and not a person to be regarded lightly. His eyes flicked between each of them in turn but were drawn to Coreyaless at each pass.

"You recognize me," Coreyaless stated after a moment, one eyebrow arched in amusement.

"Not you, specifically," the Felene guard replied warily, "but we have heard stories of you. There is another of your kind who comes to Cynda Village on occasion."

Vardak watched as Coreyaless' expression filled with hope. "Danness? He is here?"

"No. He *comes* here, but is not in the village at present." The Felene extended one of his furry mitts toward her, and Coreyaless clasped it. "I am Maryn. I can allow you inside the village and show you to our hostel, if you wish to stay."

Coreyaless introduced herself, and Janna, who had mercifully remained silent during the exchange. When she came to Vardak, he spoke for himself.

"You are one of Blademon's people," Maryn stated with an approving nod. "I've not had the pleasure of meeting one of your kind before."

They shook in greeting and Maryn motioned for them to follow him to the gate. "Most of the village will be asleep at this time," he said over his shoulder. "We prefer to spend our nights in activity, though I suspect someone will be awake at the hostel to receive you. Not all of us take professions that allow us to nap through the day."

Vardak and the others were made to wait while Maryn communicated with another guard inside the village. After a moment, the gate swung open and they were allowed passage. The square dwellings he'd spied from outside were constructed of mud bricks, with windows and doors open to the outside air. Few Felenes stirred within the village.

Maryn led them to a slightly larger building on the far side of the village. Vardak was forced to duck once they entered; the ceiling was built for the smaller Felene people, not for someone of his stature. Even Coreyaless was forced to tilt her head to one side.

A Felene woman greeted them, blinking the vestiges of sleep from her wide, blue eyes. She offered them two rooms for accommodation and seemed pleased visitors had come to the village. Maryn quickly took his leave and promised to return at the end of his shift to see that they were properly settled in.

Vardak was given a small room furnished with a bed, which he would not use. There was just enough space on the floor alongside it to allow him to lay down if he chose, and that would suit him well enough. He set most of his scant belongings atop the bed, took his whetstone and axe, and made his way outside. His blade was sufficiently sharp, but the act of honing its edges provided him with an excuse to leave the cramped confines of the hostel.

He could hear Coreyaless and Janna conversing in their own room as he passed through the corridor but paid them no mind. Janna's usual prattle had been diminished that morning, but given the opportunity, she would begin again. Coreyaless wore on his nerves simply because, like his older brothers, she felt compelled to speak for him on numerous occasions. A break from their presence, however brief, was welcome.

He found a place not far from the hostel that was shaded by a small grove of trees. He settled himself and began to work, taking simple pleasure in the repetitive motion and the rasp of the metal upon the stone. The task enabled him to clear his mind, to forget for a time where he was and what had brought him there.

His solace was broken some minutes later with the arrival of Blademon. He did not see or hear the war god arrive, but Vardak recognized his voice when he began to speak.

"Vardak, I have news."

Blademon's tone was somber and Vardak understood immediately that something was amiss. He set his axe aside and turned around to face the patron god of his people while he braced himself for Blademon's next words.

"The Murkor were coerced into attacking the Stronghold during the night. There were few casualties amongst your people, but it is only the beginning of the conflict." Blademon scowled. "Had I not pledged your service to Flariel's daughter, fewer would have been lost."

"How were the Murkor 'coerced'?" he asked, troubled by the implication. "Does this relate to the mad wizard?"

Blademon shook his head. "Shan'tar, as he was called, is dead. The Soulless have returned, Vardak, and it is their influence that forced the Murkor into action. That is not why I've come, however. You must know of your brothers."

A cold dread settled within his gut as he stared up at the war god. When he spoke, his voice was rough. "What happened?"

"Patak was injured. He will recover but will likely retain the scars for the remainder of his life." Blademon's expression became grim. "Travin was captured and is being taken to the Underground Caverns as we speak. I will try to keep you apprised of his fate, but we both know what the Murkor seek from their prisoners."

Vardak looked down, furious. "I should have been there."

"Yes," Blademon agreed, "but it may be to our benefit that you were not. The Soulless are aware of my other protégé, who has been conscripted by them. As you know, we do not take sides in mortal conflict and it has always been my role to train two during each cycle. I have no doubt you will face him in battle one day."

Vardak shook his head angrily. His priorities had always been to place his people first, and without his consent, he'd been denied this opportunity to defend them. The wizard was dead, which meant the threat he'd presented was gone with him. Was Flariel's mission to obtain the Moon's Eye now futile? The Soulless had returned, and he understood the magnitude of their threat. He needed to return home to his people, and he required answers from Blademon.

"Tell me this damned business of Flariel's will not be in vain. Tell me there is meaning behind this fucking search we've undertaken. We narrowly avoided the Undead yesterday, only to be dropped here. I've no gods-damned knowledge of this jungle, nor of its people, and the Airess refused to lend her support to Flariel's mission unless we aided her first. I am beyond frustrated! I fucking want answers!"

Vardak knew his tirade would test the limits of Blademon's patience. Rage suffused him, propelling him ever further toward achieving disfavor with the Immortal. He no longer cared for propriety; his brothers had paid for his forced absence in blood.

"The Moon's Eye will be an asset in the fight against the Soulless," Blademon replied evenly after he was certain Vardak was finished. "I understand your position, but I believe you must continue on this quest."

Vardak scowled and was unable to mask the bitter resentment that flooded his tone. "If Travin is killed, the blame lies with you."

Blademon's expression became steely. "Your place is here until you've secured the relic. I will not argue the point further."

The war god disappeared before Vardak could form a reply, leaving him to brood over the recent events alone.

CHAPTER THIRTEEN

A SCHEME, INTERRUPTED

When Dranamir stepped out of the portal and onto the balcony adjoining Tamarin's private chambers, she was unsurprised to find Alyra was not present. She may have driven the other woman into a corner, but Alyra would prove defiant to the last. It was no matter; Dranamir had prepared for such an eventuality and would see to it the former beauty was excised from the ranks of the Soulless. Her refusal to appear this evening would only prolong the suffering Dranamir had planned.

Dranamir peered over the balcony's railing toward the courtyard below. It was well after sundown, and the carefully manicured lawns, trimmed hedges, and lushly cultivated flowers within appeared devoid of human life. The princess had done her part to facilitate the evening's training, ensuring they had the privacy necessary to carry out her illicit schooling. She shifted her gaze skyward to note the moon was half way to its zenith; Tamarin would be arriving any moment. Dranamir hoped the girl was late. She felt particularly cruel, and an excuse to torture the princess would prove a welcome diversion from the mundane routine they'd fallen into.

To her dismay, Tamarin arrived precisely on time, and even greeted Dranamir with a deep curtsey and words of subservience. It should have been sufficient to placate Dranamir's desire for obeisance, but on this night, she hungered for blood.

"Are you prepared to properly begin your training?" Dranamir demanded. "I will suffer no insubordination." She took hold of the princess' chin with a fierce grip and forced the girl to meet her fiery gaze. "*None.*"

"I will obey, Great One." Her voice trembled, but her expression belied nothing of her fear.

Dranamir released her and stepped back. It was progress, though Tamarin's willingness to abide by her own words was yet to be seen.

"We will begin where we left off." When Tamarin's face paled, Dranamir smiled mercilessly. "I believe we were attempting to harness your inner darkness when you chose to have a rather unfortunate outburst."

Tamarin nodded emphatically. "Yes, Great One. I assure you I will not repeat my previous transgression."

Dranamir studied the groveling princess and wondered how long the girl's compliance would truly last. Years of experience told her it was unlikely to hold for long. She swallowed the urge to lash out preemptively, though the prospect of watching the princess whimper in agony was tantalizing.

"In order to harness the darkness you possess, you must learn to come to terms with who you have become." Dranamir folded her arms and regarded Tamarin with an icy stare. "We were unable to progress on our last meeting—due to your failure. You must understand this fundamental principle."

"I am sorry, Great One. It will not happen again." Tamarin cowered, unable to mask her fear any longer.

A cold smile crossed Dranamir's lips. She preferred the princess remain in the grip of fear, subservient, obedient, and malleable. "See that it doesn't."

Tamarin was as good as her word and followed Dranamir's instruction unerringly. Within two hours, the princess had mastered the ability to tap into her power and stated she was eager to learn more. Dranamir was silently pleased with her enthusiasm, though she knew Tamarin must pace herself or risk irrevocable injury to her mind. Magic was not a force to be toyed with, nor underestimated.

Dranamir was preparing to conclude their session when a portal opened alongside Tamarin. Alyra stepped onto the balcony, a deep hood pulled over her face, though the baleful gleam of her eyes was visible from within. Dranamir scowled at the other woman, irritated with the interruption and infuriated by her tardiness.

"You're late, Alyra."

"I had other, more important, matters to attend to this evening," Alyra replied with an air of exasperation. "I am quite aware of your methods, Dranamir, and had no wish to see them on display." She pointedly fixed her attention upon Tamarin. "Has she harmed you, child?"

Tamarin took a step back from Alyra, even as the other woman reached one hand toward her. The princess eluded the intended contact, her expression wary. "I am well, thank you."

Alyra shook her head in disbelief. "Do not feel obligated to cover for that monster. Has she harmed you?"

"No," Tamarin replied as she took another step backward.

"You were to come here in order to observe my work," Dranamir seethed. "I will not allow you to subvert the progress we've made."

Alyra turned her hooded face toward Dranamir. "I simply wish to ensure the princess has been treated properly. Given your history, Dranamir, I doubt you've accomplished that."

She'd heard enough. She would not be undermined, her authority subverted, by the once-beautiful whore that cowered beneath the shelter of her hood. Dranamir drew on her power and flung Alyra forcefully into the nearest wall. She held Alyra against the rough stone so rigidly that the other woman was unable to blink.

"Dranamir—" Alyra began in a warning tone, which she promptly ignored.

Dranamir closed the distance between them rapidly, her eyes boring into Alyra's unflinchingly. She tore Alyra's hooded cloak away and ignited it in a ball of flame. It fell to the floor, exposing Alyra's ruined features for the princess' viewing pleasure.

"Dranamir, you must stop!" Alyra managed in a strangled tone.

"No."

She summoned another burst of fire. She directed it toward the garments Alyra still wore, and her magic quickly incinerated the fabric. The other woman screeched in agony as the flames coursed across her body, while the scent of charred flesh began to waft across the balcony.

Tamarin backed into the nearest corner, dry-heaving at the stench. Her eyes were fixed on the spectacle that unfolded before her, though it was clear the princess wished she could avert her gaze.

Dranamir ignored the princess, her focus on Alyra alone. She released the flames, and Alyra gasped, choking back sobs. Angry red burns marred her gray flesh, from shoulder to ankle, the edges of her wounds charred and blackened. The fire was extinguished, but the pain of her resulting injuries would remain for some time.

"I can do worse," Dranamir sneered. She cast a glance toward Tamarin's horrified countenance. "Would you like a further demonstration, princess? Perhaps, a reminder of what I am capable of, so that you never cross me as this wench has done."

Tamarin opened her mouth as though to speak, but she produced no sound. Her eyes darted between the marred and naked form of Alyra, pinned against the wall, and Dranamir's unyielding gaze. Dranamir was certain the princess would continue to obey after she finished making this example of Alyra.

Dranamir raised her arm to strike again when a powerful voice ricocheted through her skull. The sound reverberated through her very core and caused her to stagger. Her focus shattered, her magic interrupted; she wavered at the internal assault, then succumbed to the force and fell to her knees. Alyra collapsed onto the floor, her breathing ragged.

I will not permit this foolishness.

The words were felt more than heard. Dranamir recognized the furious tones of their master. She was stunned to realize he'd grown in power enough to communicate directly with them.

Alyra moaned and opened her eyes into slits, pain coupled with malice glimmering in their crimson depths. "I tried…to warn you…"

Tamarin, untethered to the Nameless god, could not hear the words, nor fathom the disruption that had stayed Dranamir's hand. Her wide, green eyes continued to dart wildly between the two women, but wisely, she remained silent.

"As you wish," Dranamir replied bitterly.

I do not request the pair of you cooperate. I demand it.

Alyra scowled and attempted to sit up, then cried out in anguish. Dranamir eyed her coldly as she fell ungracefully to the floor.

What say you?

The Nameless god's voice betrayed his growing impatience. As much as she resented his interference, Dranamir knew she must appease him or risk incurring his wrath further.

"I will do as you deem necessary, as I always have, master."

"As will I," Alyra managed between gasps.

I am displeased by your behavior, though it comes as no surprise. The child you fight over is beneath you. Return to the tower. Garin has further assignments for you. Do not disappoint me a second time.

Dranamir glowered at Alyra as she felt the Nameless' connection to them fade. Her plot was foiled, and Alyra would continue to antagonize her at every turn. Their tie to the Nameless god compelled them to obey his command. She was sworn to work *with* the fallen beauty, much to her distaste.

She glared balefully at the cowering princess. "Think of this as providence, to spare your delicate soul the indignity of watching this lecherous woman perish. Our master has spoken and deemed her unfit for death."

Tamarin whimpered in response and attempted to retreat further from the two Soulless, but her back was already pressed firmly against the wall.

"You'll receive no punishment tonight," Dranamir continued. "We shall meet again, princess."

She opened a portal and strode toward Alyra. She yanked the other woman roughly to her feet, aware her rough treatment would cause the other woman significant pain. Alyra shrieked in response but allowed Dranamir to assist her. She was in no condition to stand on her own.

"I'll deliver you to the tower," she hissed at Alyra, "but do not expect my generosity to continue once there. Perhaps Garin will take pity on you and tend your wounds."

She grasped Alyra's wrist viciously and stepped through the portal into the Aethereum beyond. Alyra drew a sharp breath but stubbornly refused to cry out again, much to Dranamir's disappointment. She shoved her displeasure aside and brought them both to the top floor of the obsidian tower, where they exited to the physical realm once more.

Garin appeared to have been awaiting them. He paced before the red-paned mirror, arms crossed, jaw clenched. He pivoted swiftly to face the pair, and Dranamir watched with some satisfaction at the disgusted downturn his mouth took as he assessed Alyra's condition.

"You look as though you failed a seduction attempt with Flariel," he said to Alyra.

Dranamir released the other woman's wrist and laughed mirthlessly. "Flariel's wrath would have been kinder."

"Bitch," Alyra hissed through clenched teeth.

Garin studied them, then sighed with a shake of his head. "I don't care what has transpired between you, as I'm certain from our master's words it won't happen again. You are both ordered to abandon the training of the Deluchan princess. The mantle will be taken up by someone else."

Dranamir snorted derisively. "You?"

Garin shook his head again. "No. The master has other work for me to perform. As punishment for displeasing him, he has tasked you with the recovery of lost relics. Dranamir is to go to the Moraine Mines. Alyra will scour the sea caves."

Dranamir scowled at him. There would be little to uncover in the mines, and she was certain to earn further disfavor if sent there. "And we are to trust you implicitly, Garin? The master may have ordered us to come here, to speak with you, but were the punishments of his design or yours?"

"They were his, but if you don't believe me, it is your life at risk, not mine." Garin shifted his gaze to Alyra. "I suppose you'll need healing before you go. Your injuries must be painful." There was no compassion in his tone, only disgust and apathy.

"I'll leave you to your work," Dranamir replied. "I'm certain you don't need my assistance with such a menial task."

"Don't mistake me, Dranamir," he said. "I will not continue to clean up your rubbish heaps, no matter how many you deign to light on fire."

Dranamir cackled at his response and Alyra's resultant, indignant expression. "I'll be certain to rein in my incendiary tendencies from now on, Garin."

CHAPTER FOURTEEN

ARRA SHANNIN

Tavesin was dismayed to find himself within the Aetherium. It had been nearly a week since his last accidental visit, the encounter with the Soulless, and his meeting with the Drakkon mage, Aziarah. The wizards had no means to prevent him from entering the realm while he slept, and he was still uncertain of how he came to be there. Aziarah had taught him how to exit, and he took comfort in the knowledge that if he found himself in danger again, he could safely escape.

He stood within the Shining Tower's large garden, though in the Aetherium the myriad plants sported few blooms. Some shifted strangely as he looked upon them, while others seemed to flicker and dissolve before his startled eyes. If he encountered Aziarah again, he meant to ask her what the source of such instability was and why it affected some objects, yet not others. Tavesin found himself further enchanted upon each subsequent visit. The Aetherium was a mystery, and he longed to learn more of it.

Since he'd found himself there, he decided to make the most of his time and explore. He would avoid the palace and the memory of his encounter with the Soulless. There were hundreds of locations in the world he wished to visit, but he could not settle upon a destination. His thoughts flitted between the many tales he used to hear from his father and uncles, telling of places exotic and new. Thoughts of his family brought a wave of homesickness, and suddenly, he knew where he wished to go.

He closed his eyes briefly and pictured the farming village of Rican Mer, near the banks of the River Falling. There was a particular grove of trees that overshadowed a slow, deep pool, where he'd spent many afternoons swimming, catching frogs, or on occasion, fishing. When he opened his eyes once more, he stood near the riverbank. The water seemed to be frozen in place; it glinted strangely in the harsh, bluish light. He could not visit his family in this realm, but he could return to this place to prompt his memories.

He sat down on the bank and allowed his legs to dangle over the edge. The water was some distance below his feet, but he was wary of touching it in its state of suspended animation. The thought of doing so left him anxious.

"What is this place?" a voice demanded from behind him.

He stiffened with apprehension. The voice was feminine, but it did not belong to the Drakkon he'd met previously. He feared to turn, to face the owner of the voice, feared to learn he'd managed to draw the attention of another Soulless. He steeled himself and slowly peered over his shoulder at the speaker.

A young woman, only slightly older than himself, stood not far away. She stared at him, her expression puzzled as she placed her hands on slender hips. She had long reddish hair, pulled back from her face in a thick braid, and fierce, green eyes. Her fair skin marked her as being of Balotican or Masmooni descent. She was pretty, in spite of the frown she leveled in his direction.

"Well?" she demanded. "Are you going to explain where we are, or are you going to stare at me like a dolt all day?"

He blinked and scrambled to his feet. "This 'place'," he said slowly, "is Rican Mer. My hometown."

She rolled her eyes in exasperation. "I didn't mean this village." She gestured vaguely at their surroundings. "I mean, what is *this* place? The light is strange, and I've seen no one for hours. Until I found you."

"It's called the Aethereum," he replied slowly.

Her frown deepened. "That does me little good. Explain."

Tavesin shifted uncomfortably under her piercing gaze. He was unused to being quizzed by anyone outside the tower, and certainly not by a girl of his own age that he found himself inexplicably attracted to.

"I am learning about the place, myself," he said carefully. "I do not know how I come here, but the wizards—"

"Wizards! You're an apprentice, are you?" Her frown quickly morphed into an excited grin.

"Ah…Yes." He looked down, feeling his face flush.

"That must mean this place has something to do with magic." She peered around them again, surveying each detail carefully, before she fixed her gaze on his once more. "I'm right, aren't I? This place is magic."

"Yes."

"By that logic, it means I must be able to use magic, too. I'm here, so it must be true." She nodded to herself.

"I suppose—"

"You *suppose*? If anyone could come here, don't you think the place would be teeming with people? As I said, you're the first I've come across, and I've been wandering for hours."

"The wizards will need to be sure," he replied defensively. "I don't know how to determine if you possess magic or not. I haven't learned the trick yet."

"Well, a fat lot of good you are," she replied teasingly.

"I—"

She sighed. "It was a jest. You are too serious. What is your name?"

He blinked at the verbal onslaught, flustered that he could scarcely get a word in. In spite of himself, he was unable to form a reply.

"You have one, don't you?" she pressed. "Fine, I'll begin. I'm Arra Shannin."

"Tavesin."

"See, that wasn't so hard." She smiled in satisfaction. "So, Tavesin, how might I contact the wizards about having come here? Do any of them venture here?"

"No. The tower seems to think I'm unusual," he admitted, as an idea struck him. "I can tell them about you, Arra."

She flashed another grin. "Yes, that will do! They'll need to know how to find me, yes?" When he nodded, she launched into a rapid description of her home and how the wizards might locate her. He learned she was from southern Masmoone Kingdom, in an area known as the Marshwood.

"You've no inkling how wonderful this is," she continued breathlessly. "I've been wishing for a means to leave Bannon's Ford. I have no interest in being married off to a farm boy and raising a brood of children. There's much more to the world, and I mean to see as much of it as I'm able."

He nodded uncertainly but did not know what to say in response.

"Now, Tavesin, I think you and I will become friends. I plan to see you at the tower one day." She grinned broadly. "How do I leave this...what did you call it?"

"Aethereum." He waited a moment to see if she'd allow him to explain without further prompting. When she merely stared at him pointedly, he related what Aziarah had told him on his previous adventure. "Focus on your body, and will your mind to return to it."

She gaped at him. "Do you mean to tell me that my body isn't here?"

He nodded. "Your consciousness is here, but your body is where you laid down to sleep."

She shook her head in disbelief. "I knew this place was odd, but this is difficult to comprehend."

"It's the only way," he replied. "Try it."

"You will speak to the wizards for me?" she asked hopefully. When he nodded, she smiled again. After a moment, she closed her eyes and suddenly winked out of existence.

It was late afternoon before Tavesin managed to speak with Hasnin about his nighttime encounter with the girl named Arra Shannin. He'd attempted to meet with his mentor before the call to breakfast had rung through the apprentice quarters, but Hasnin was busy and quickly ushered him from his study. Tavesin had fidgeted through his lessons; the anticipation of delivering his news gnawed at him ferociously.

He arrived in Hasnin's study promptly after his final lesson concluded to find his mentor deep in conversation with another wizard. He loitered in the doorway after Hasnin motioned for him to wait, though he could scarcely stand still. It was several minutes before the two finished their business. As the other wizard departed, Hasnin peered at Tavesin with a mixture of amusement and annoyance on his aged face.

"Alright, boy, what has you so riled that you cannot wait any longer?"

His words tumbled out in a cascade of excitement as he related his latest adventure in the Aethereum to Hasnin. His mentor leaned back in his seat and listened carefully but said nothing, even as Tavesin stumbled over portions of his tale. He was the epitome of patience in the face of Tavesin's unabashed enthusiasm. Hasnin remained silent for several long moments after he finished speaking, while Tavesin began to fidget anxiously.

"I suppose we must find this girl you've encountered." Hasnin leaned forward across his desk, his gnarled fingers steepled before him. "And it seems it grows ever more imperative that we finalize our negotiations with the Drakkon. You are in need of training, and I fear for your safety."

In his excitement, Tavesin heard only the first portion of Hasnin's statement. "Then you will find her?"

Hasnin chuckled. "Several Green wizards will likely be dispatched to her village, but I will make certain they are aware of your encounter. She will be escorted here, much as you were, and will begin training in the proper use of magic."

Tavesin beamed. "Thank you, sir. I promised her—"

"I know, boy," Hasnin replied with an amused smile. "You've followed through. Allow the Council to take over her placement from here."

CHAPTER FIFTEEN

THROUGH THE JUNGLE

Vardak was only marginally comfortable when seated in the confines of the hostel, but Coreyaless and Maryn had insisted they speak inside rather than outdoors where others might overhear. He strove to bury his frustration with his current situation, to focus on Maryn's words and the burgeoning plan the Felene laid before them. His thoughts continued to drift, to circle back to his conversation with Blademon the previous day, and he found himself paying less attention to the Felene guard than he ought.

Vardak resented that he'd been reduced to no more than a pawn in the Immortals' schemes. He had no option but to press onward, to assist Janna with the retrieval of the Moon's Eye, and pray that Blademon would grant him a measure of reprieve once the task was complete. He feared for Travin's safety, and for the first time since he'd been chosen as Blademon's protégé, he wished the honor had befallen someone else.

"As you requested, I've made some inquiries, Coreyaless," Maryn said. He sat cross-legged on the floor while his tail swished lightly behind him. "When I told you yesterday it had been some time since Danness was last here, that was the truth. I dispatched a message to Veran Township in the east to ask of his whereabouts. He was there only weeks ago. I suggest we begin our search for him there."

"We?" Coreyaless prompted, eyebrows raised.

"Yes. You'll need a guide to navigate the jungle, and as your sponsor in this village, I have requested to take on the role." Maryn smiled, pleased with himself. "Besides, guard duty grows tedious, and I'd like a change of pace."

Vardak nodded his assent, glad to have the company of another trained soldier on the journey, even for a short time. That Maryn also knew the land, its creatures, its people, and its dangers was a boon. He loathed moving blindly through unknown territory.

Maryn leapt to his feet nimbly and flashed a grin. "I must prepare for our departure. It's safest to move during the daylight hours, so I hope to set off not long after sunrise. If we are not delayed, we'll reach Veran before nightfall tomorrow."

As Maryn left them, Janna stifled an expansive yawn with the back of her hand. "All this talk of leaving, and the thought of traipsing through the forest again makes me weary. I think I'll turn in."

Vardak watched her silently and wondered if Coreyaless would follow in her wake. He'd spent much of his day outside the hostel, taking shade beneath the broad-leafed trees during the warmest parts of the day. His axe had been sharpened several times, his armor cleaned and polished, yet he sought another means to distract himself and keep a measure of distance from the women. He could not afford Janna to learn of his predicament; she was already far too excitable and prone to bouts of anxiety.

He rose carefully to his feet, tilting his head to one side to avoid cracking his skull on the low ceiling. He meant to return outside, but Coreyaless frowned knowingly in his direction.

"Vardak, I believe we need to talk."

He met her gaze with a neutral expression and remained standing as he awaited her next words.

"Something has occurred to put you in a dour mood, and I mean to learn what that is."

"I'll not burden you with my troubles." He turned toward the exit, but she rose swiftly and stayed him with a light touch on his elbow. He glowered at her.

"I believe I understand much of your concern," she continued. "Janna is abed, and we can speak freely."

His frown deepened, but after a moment he relented. "It concerns my homeland, and there is nothing I can do to remedy the situation. I spoke with Blademon yesterday."

"When were you planning to tell us you'd spoken with him?" Coreyaless demanded.

137

Vardak sighed and sat back down. "I wasn't. As I said, it concerns my homeland."

"What news did Blademon bring?" she pressed. "Talking over recent events may impart relief. It is unhealthy that you bottle your emotions as you do."

He wanted to contradict her, but he knew she was right. She was not the first healer to chide him for his reserved nature, and she would not be the last. Reluctantly, he relayed his conversation with the war god and the disappointment his parting words had wrought.

"By the gods, it's little wonder you've been irritable," she remarked when he finished.

He scowled. His attempts at masking his despair were a glaring failure if the Airess was to be believed.

"We will return to the Five Kingdoms, and I will accompany you to the Stronghold," Coreyaless promised, startling him with her words. "Maryn can guide us to the temple where the Moon's Eye is kept. It's here in the jungle."

"You've sought Danness for centuries, and now that he's close you would turn away and help me. Why?" He demanded gruffly. He did not understand her motives, but in order to ascertain them, he was compelled to learn more.

"Surely, your people know better than most what the Soulless are capable of."

When he acknowledged her statement with a terse nod, she continued. "This business of an attack on the Stronghold does not merely affect the Scorpion Men, Vardak. It will grow to consume the whole of the Five Kingdoms, as it has every time the Nameless seeks his freedom. I may only be a humble herbalist, but I mean to help where I can. If my search for Danness must be put aside yet again, then so be it."

"Calling yourself humble may be a stretch," he replied dryly. "I was under the impression you sought to further your own ends, nothing more."

Coreyaless' gaze was unreadable. "That may be so, but your news has forced me to change perspective. My desire to reunite with Danness is irrelevant when faced with the prospect of another war. What occurred at the Stronghold was little more than a skirmish, but it is the opening volley in the salvo to come. Securing the relic is paramount if the gods can be trusted."

"Perhaps I've been too harsh in my criticism of you, but you've dragged us into danger since the start. Your sudden change of heart leaves me skeptical."

"You forget that I have witnessed the aftermath of the previous wars, Vardak," she replied, sorrow creeping into her tone. "If we can prevent the death and suffering the Soulless will inevitably inflict, we must do so. Karmada's curse will ensure my survival. Danness must wait."

He released a long sigh. He believed her, though he still suspected her apparent altruism would not last. "Very well. You mentioned a temple, here, on the southern continent."

"I did. It is only fitting that an object called the Moon's Eye would be housed within the Star Keeper's temple." Coreyaless looked down at her hands. "I learned of its location long ago, but at the time, the relic was of no consequence to me. I led you to believe we came here solely to pursue Danness, but in truth, your mission coincided with my own desire. Both our goals lie within the jungle." She waved one hand toward the exit door.

"Do you believe Maryn will be amenable to this change in plans?" he asked.

"You heard his words, Vardak. He asked to guide us as a diversion from his typical duties." She shrugged, as though their new destination and Maryn's opinion were irrelevant.

"In my experience, changing plans on a whim rarely goes smoothly." He crossed his arms. "And I still question your motive."

"Question all you like," she replied indifferently. "It does not change the fact that without me, you and Janna would never have come this close to achieving your goal."

Maryn received the news of their change in plans with reticence. Coreyaless waited until they'd departed Cynda Village to inform him of the new destination, and the Felene guard fell abruptly silent. His ears drooped with dismay as he considered his options. Vardak studied his reaction carefully, certain Coreyaless' chosen path was not a route Maryn wished to tread.

139

"Veran Township remains today's destination," he said with an agitated swish of his tail.

"Then you'll take us to the temple?" Coreyaless pressed.

He regarded her coldly. "I will consider it. You know not what you ask of me, Airess."

"I don't understand," Janna broke in. "You were excited to guide us last night, Maryn. Is there something amiss with our new path?"

"Clearly." Maryn grimaced and fixed his attention on the overgrown path ahead, quickening his pace.

As with their previous trek through the jungle, the morning grew oppressively warm, and their passage was followed eagerly by the swarming, biting insects. The two women spoke quietly amongst themselves, their conversation punctuated by slaps and hisses of annoyance spat toward the throngs of flies. Maryn walked some distance ahead of them. He paused at intervals to slash at vegetation that had grown into the footpath. Vardak found himself acting as rear guard, which suited his dour mood. It gave him an excuse to avoid the women and to consider his options.

Given Maryn's reaction to Coreyaless' proposed final destination, he anticipated the route would prove dangerous. The Felene seemed to regard the change as eagerly as he had the prospect of navigating Stonewall Hall. If Maryn agreed to continue as their guide, Vardak believed they could overcome any threat that presented itself along the way. If he did not, however, they would be forced to seek another's guidance to reach Solsticia's temple. He would rather face whatever danger Maryn wished to avoid than attempt to recruit another Felene.

A short time after noon, Maryn called a halt. Vardak took the opportunity to drink deeply of his waterskin while Janna began to distribute portions of dried fruit. Maryn refused her offer and withdrew a snack of his own from within his pack. It appeared to be a small lizard, desiccated into a crisp. It crunched loudly as he ate.

"Do you not like fruit, Maryn?" Janna asked after a time. She seemed at once fascinated and appalled by the Felene's midday meal.

Maryn shook his head. "We are a carnivorous people, Janna. We do not subsist on plant matter of any sort. Your fruit would cause me physical illness. Thank you for the offer, but I must decline."

"And you eat lizards?" she pressed.

"Lizards, insects, fish, birds…" He trailed off and took another bite.

"I didn't know people ate lizards." Janna frowned and shook her head.

"It's not uncommon in the desert, either," Vardak replied. "We take meat when and where we can acquire it, just as we do water."

She gaped at him. "I thought your people weren't so different from mine."

"In many ways, perhaps we're not," he agreed. "I've known human merchants to dine with us on occasion. Not many of your people venture as far as the Stronghold, but those that do seem grateful for any morsel we might offer them. The crossing between the Gray Mountains and the Wasted Land provides little opportunity for game, and water is scarce. They've eaten lizards at our tables when necessity demands it."

"Ugh." She made a face and looked away. "I cannot imagine eating such…*scaly* things."

Vardak glanced toward Maryn, who appeared disgruntled by her words. "I suppose I prefer tarantulas to lizards, particularly when they're roasted and seasoned with hot peppers."

She glanced up at him with horror in her green eyes. "You eat *spiders*?"

He shrugged, enjoying her reaction. "As I said, meat is scarce in the desert. We eat what we find."

Behind Janna, Maryn met his eyes with the beginning of a sly smile. "Our people enjoy spiders, as well. I don't believe the variety found here are as large as those you seem to describe, but they are quite tasty."

Helplessly, Janna turned toward Coreyaless. "Surely you are more sensible than this pair?"

"The Airess do not partake in insects or spiders," she replied evenly, "and rarely, meat. Though I've broken that tenet more than I'd care to admit during the past week with you. I prefer fruits and vegetables."

Janna nodded triumphantly. "I knew you'd have more sense than they do. Lizards and spiders! Ugh!"

Vardak laughed to himself and caught Maryn's eye again. The Felene smiled, amused, and seemed grateful to have found an ally amongst their strange company. Vardak was merely thankful he'd managed to mend Janna's missteps. Whether the women understood or not, they required Maryn's help.

The afternoon passed much as the morning had, though Maryn appeared to be in better spirits. The path they followed gradually widened, and presently, Vardak could hear the sound of water rushing somewhere beyond the trees. The air grew marginally cooler as they neared the river's banks, though the density of biting insects increased accordingly. Vardak was grateful they left him be; angry, red welts and discolored blotches appeared on every exposed surface of Janna's skin, and Coreyaless fared little better.

Their path followed the course of the river for more than an hour before the trees suddenly opened into a vast clearing, crammed with an array of low, square buildings. Veran Township was easily thrice the size of Cynda Village, and as it was late in the afternoon, its residents were beginning to stir. Their party drew curious gazes and open stares. A few pointed discreetly in their direction and whispered excitedly amongst themselves.

Vardak forced a smile at the onlookers. He'd endured much the same when traversing Dar Daelad's stone streets, but at least in this instance, the Felene were equally curious about Janna and Coreyaless. He was no longer alone in his otherness.

Maryn led them to another hostel, though this one sported a common room with several proper tables and matching chairs, an improvement over their previous dwelling. Vardak was once again forced to duck once they entered, but he'd come to expect it. He was easily twice the height of the tallest Felene they'd encountered.

Maryn introduced them to a gray-haired Felene man with wide, blue eyes, who managed the hostel. Their host was deferential to Coreyaless, but was openly wary of Janna, and gaped as his eyes met Vardak's. Vardak understood he cut an imposing figure particularly when clad in armor as he was, but he did not know what to say that might set the man at ease.

Maryn saved him the trouble. "We're here just for the night and will set off again come morning. If you provide us with rooms and allow us to settle in, I can give you news from Cynda Village."

At that, their host perked up and managed to tear his fearful gaze away from the strangers in his foyer. They learned the hostel had but two rooms available, and Vardak found himself sharing a space with Maryn. They set their packs down and Vardak began unbuckling his armor, while Maryn left to find their host once more.

"I promised him news, after all," the Felene commented as he disappeared through the door. "There will be food in the common room when you arrive."

The prospect of a proper meal was appealing, and Vardak wasted no time in returning to the common room. Maryn was perched at a table with Coreyaless, but Janna was nowhere to be seen. He pushed a chair aside in order to join them, settling down with his legs folded beneath him.

"Janna suffers from a headache," Coreyaless informed him. "She won't be joining us tonight, but I've promised to take her portion to our room after we've finished."

Before they could delve further into conversation, the gray-furred host returned bearing a platter heaped with various Felene delicacies. There were more of the small, dried lizards Maryn had dined on previously, as well as whole, steamed fish, and an array of fried insects; beetles, large green grasshoppers, and the small spiders Maryn had mentioned. He placed a separate, smaller dish before Coreyaless that contained slices of a golden fruit.

"Danness claims to prefer this," he told her. "Perhaps you will find it enjoyable, as well."

She smiled in gratitude. "Thank you. Has Danness been here recently?"

Vardak focused his attention on the food before them but listened carefully to Coreyaless' conversation. It seemed she was reluctant to abandon her quest despite her earlier words to him. He decided he couldn't fault her; after nearly a millennium of separation he would have been loath to abandon it, too.

"Yes, perhaps three days ago," the host answered. "He was pursuing a path through the deepest jungle. I attempted to persuade him otherwise, but he would not listen. I understand your people are long-lived, but where he travels will be his death."

Vardak understood that it was not a quality of the Airess race that had imparted Coreyaless with her longevity, but it was a consequence of Karmada's interference in their lives. She'd insinuated several times that until she reunited with Danness, she could not be killed. How she knew this fact with such certainty he did not know, but he felt it was not his place to pry.

Across the table, Maryn muttered darkly under his breath. Vardak arched his eyebrows in silent question. The Felene merely shook his head in consternation. He suspected Danness had taken the path Maryn had attempted to dissuade them from pursuing themselves, based on the guard's reaction.

"What lies in the deepest jungle?" Coreyaless asked.

"The Living Forest," came the host's reply. "The paths between Veran and the old cities are no longer passable. It is death to venture there," he reiterated with emphasis.

"Thank you," she said again.

Once they were alone, Coreyaless fixed Maryn with a pointed gaze. "I assume the path he spoke of leads to Solsticia's temple."

Maryn frowned and bit viciously into the dried lizard he held in response.

Coreyaless sighed in exasperation. "Avoiding my question does nothing for progress."

Vardak shook his head, irritated by her perceived superiority. "If that portion of the jungle is as dangerous as the Felene claim, perhaps it would be wise to seek another route."

She crossed her arms and glared at him. "There is no other route, Vardak. You'd know as much if you had been paying attention to our discussion this morning rather than wallowing in your own self-pity."

He clenched his jaw in momentary anger and swallowed a number of choice words he would have liked to brand her with. "As I suspected last night, your altruism has failed to last."

"His path coincides with the temple's," she replied defensively. "And as I said, *there is no other route.*"

"Much to my dismay, she is right," Maryn cut in. "The gods must favor you, Coreyaless, because despite my best efforts, both of your objectives now lie within the deepest jungle." He sighed heavily and peered up at Vardak. "I pray you know how to use that axe you carry. We'll have need of it."

CHAPTER SIXTEEN

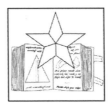

THE STAR-SHAPED BOX

"Sit down, boy, and stop fidgeting." Hasnin indicated the open chair across from his desk.

Tavesin sat, but was unable to remain still. He bounced on the hard seat in anticipation of his mentor's news. Hasnin had made good on his promise to speak with the Radiant, and he was eager to learn if the Council meant to send wizards south to the Marshwood. His chance meeting with Arra Shannin continued to replay through his mind. She was pretty, and—

"*Tavesin*," Hasnin stated forcefully, drawing his attention back to the present. "I understand your excitement, but you must focus. Did you hear any of what I just told you?"

Tavesin flushed and looked down, chastised. "No, sir. I'm sorry, sir."

Hasnin chuckled. "Listen closely. I will not repeat myself a second time. This is important, Taven."

"Yes, sir."

He met Hasnin's gaze and forced himself to remain still. It was a struggle, but one he was determined to win.

"We have spoken to the Drakkon, Taven. Aziarah and several others are preparing to make the journey here, to the Shining Tower." Hasnin peered at him closely as he let his words sink in. "They will be here within the week, and *you* must be ready for them."

Tavesin gaped, his mind reeling with possibilities. "She…Sir, I…What…What must I do?"

Flustered, he looked down once more. He found himself tongue-tied and unable to piece together a simple sentence. Excited, terrified, nervous, and thrilled were only a handful of the emotions that swirled within him.

"You must continue your lessons as you normally would." Hasnin's words were laced with amusement. "The Radiant has spoken with the Sect Masters today, and you may tell the other apprentices of your coming appointment if you wish. They'll learn of it within a day, regardless."

Tavesin grinned and looked up. He'd been itching to tell his secret to Rostin since his first encounter with Aziarah.

"We will determine how your lessons will change once the Drakkon mages arrive," Hasnin continued. "Until then, focus on your other studies. You'll wish to make a solid first impression upon Aziarah."

"Yes, sir."

Hasnin smiled. "I suggest you head downstairs to supper before the kitchens close."

Tavesin nodded eagerly and flashed another grin. "Thank you, sir."

He was halfway down the tower's main staircase before he realized he'd forgotten to ask after Arra. The enormity of Hasnin's news had overshadowed his natural inquisitiveness, and the ensuing thrill of excitement had left him giddy.

He resolved to ask Hasnin when next they spoke, but his attention was quickly diverted again when he arrived in the tower's sprawling kitchen complex. A dwindling line of apprentices stood along one wall, awaiting their portions of the evening's meal. He hurried to join the queue behind several older students whom he did not know.

"You're the one from the Council meeting," a small voice said from behind him.

He turned and shrugged uncomfortably. It wasn't the first time he'd been recognized for speaking at the recent meeting, but the notoriety he continued to experience left him feeling awkward.

The speaker was a boy, several years younger than Tavesin, with an open, friendly face, and the darker complexion that marked him as Kamshati. He offered Tavesin a smile that revealed two missing teeth.

"I'm Tavesin. Or Taven. Most of my friends call me Taven." He stumbled over his words, flustered for a second time that evening.

The boy grinned, his brown eyes gleaming with excitement. "I'm Badolo. I came to the tower only a week ago. Were you scared when you spoke at the meeting?"

Tavesin recalled that a Badolo had been given a room not far from his own, but it was the first time the pair had properly met. He nodded in response to the younger boy's question.

"I suppose standing before the Council was not so terrifying as meeting that Soulless," Tavesin added.

Badolo's eyes widened with unconcealed excitement. "What was it like?" he asked, bouncing on the balls of his feet. "I asked Beldra the next day if every wizard can travel to the Aethereum, but she told me it's rare. She said you were special. Did the Soulless hurt you with his magic? And how did you escape?"

Tavesin blinked, overwhelmed by the rapid onslaught of questions, but began to answer them as they awaited their turn at the serving counter. By the time the two received their portions of watery chicken soup and slices of dark bread, Tavesin had come to consider the younger apprentice a friend. He invited Badolo to join him as he sought the table he and Rostin frequented. Rostin was there, bowl half-empty, when they arrived.

Rostin offered Tavesin a guilty half-smile. "I wasn't sure you'd make it tonight, Taven. What did Hasnin have to say?"

Tavesin grinned broadly as he sat down across from Rostin and began to relate the story of his meeting with the Drakkon. To his delight, both boys were not only fascinated, but envious, too.

"A Drakkon mage is going to train you?" Rostin gaped, the remnants of his soup long-forgotten.

Tavesin nodded. "That's what Hasnin said. They'll be here in a week."

"Taven, wait... *They?*" Rostin asked, dumbfounded.

"There are several traveling here. I'm to train with the one I met in the Aetherum, but I don't know anything about the others."

"Gods, you're lucky. First the Council meeting, now the Drakkon! Soon you'll feel too important to call me your friend," Rostin teased.

"That's not true," Tavesin protested and shot a worried glance toward Badolo. To his relief, the younger boy seemed to be enjoying the banter.

"Well, I expect you to introduce me to your Drakkon friends once they arrive," Rostin continued. "I mean to benefit somehow from your fame."

That night, Tavesin found himself once more immersed in the Aethereum. When he became aware of his surroundings, he panicked and nearly fled the premises.

He stood upon the ledge of the vast, black chasm he'd stumbled upon during his first visit to the realm. He was in a different location along its gaping perimeter, though a similar camp was arrayed nearby. Beyond the camp, a square-sided, black tower loomed ominously over the parched landscape, its sides glittering darkly in the harsh light. He recognized the place from his studies: The Tower of Obsidian.

Dread suffused his being and his pulse quickened to a frantic pace as he looked upon it. The black tower, as it was more readily called, was home to the Shadow Council. The wizards referred to them only as "users of magic" and refused to acknowledge them with a proper label. Tavesin understood they were equal in power to the Council of Auras. Perhaps they were presently more powerful, he reflected; the Soulless were their leaders.

He stood rigidly, his back to the chasm, unable to tear his gaze from the menacing tower that dominated the skyline. Fear rooted him in place, curiosity urged him onward, and reason demanded he flee. The realization that he was perhaps the first member of his Council to approach the place in hundreds of years served to make up his mind.

He pushed his fear aside and ignored reason. Curiosity drove him forward, and in an instant, he found himself standing before a large, double door at the tower's base. The doors were open to the elements, a gaping maw without teeth. He stepped inside.

The foyer was devoid of people, and he breathed a sigh of relief. On his right was a broad staircase that appeared to have been carved of the same black stone as the tower's exterior. On his left were a series of doorways, each sealed tight against intrusion. He opted for the stairs.

When he reached the first landing, he gazed upward to find the zig-zag of steps ascended to the topmost reaches of the tower, high above. The black tower was easily as large as the Shining Tower in Dar Daelad. He smirked, pleased he would not be forced to traverse the entirety of the stairs unless he wished to. Reason began to gnaw at his resolve, and he knew his time within the tower must be kept to a minimum.

He willed himself to the top of the steps and paused to gather his courage as he was confronted with a single, arched door. He reasoned that whatever the Shadow Council stored within must be of great importance. There would be no reason for it to be placed at the tower's apex otherwise.

He forced himself to step forward before fear renewed its grasp. He gripped the door's ornate handle, noted that it felt cold and metallic as it would have in the physical realm, and pulled the door open. He peered inside, relieved to find the vast room before him was empty.

Long glass cases lined the walls, an array of peculiar objects nestled within. Some emitted light of their own, while others seemed to absorb it. He trailed along one of the cases slowly, taking a moment to examine each object as he passed. He was certain all were creations of magic. Near the center of the case, he came upon a pair of orbs that glowed and pulsated in a wild fashion. One was green in color, the other a drab gray. He stared at them, transfixed for a time, and watched as whorls and flares of light cascaded and burst across each surface. He shook his head in wonder before curiosity urged him forward.

As he neared the end of the case, he noted the adjacent wall was adorned with a large oval of darkness contained within a twisted, black frame. The oval was not encased in glass as the remainder of the objects were, but he sensed it was unwise to draw too near its shadowy surface. Inky tendrils of mist stretched from the oval's center toward the room beyond, writhing in the air as though they were alive and searching for unwary prey.

Fear threatened to immobilize him again, and he quickly averted his gaze. The darkness on the wall was far more dangerous than anything else he'd encountered within the tower. He did not understand its purpose, and he did not wish to discover it.

He crossed the room to examine the other glass case and the items it housed. He stopped abruptly as he noticed a small, star-shaped item sitting atop the case. It shimmered brightly in shades of pale blue and white, a mimicry of the Aethereum's innate illumination. He sensed no threat from the object, and without thinking, picked it up. He turned it over in his hands to find a small latch along its vertical side. He flicked the latch open and frowned. The box was empty.

He sighed in disappointment, then immediately froze. He glanced around the room, fearful someone had heard his exhalation. Reason took hold of him then, once more urging him to return to the safety of his bed within the apprentice's quarters of the Shining Tower. He willed himself to return to the physical realm, and moments later he bolted upright in his bed.

The star-shaped box was in his hand. It no longer glowed as it had in the Aethereum, but he gaped at it in the darkness. He hadn't realized it was possible to take objects from within the Aethereum, but its presence in the physical realm was testament to what he'd done.

Cold panic flooded through him as he tumbled from his bed to stumble through the darkness toward the door. Rostin turned over in his sleep on the far side of the room and muttered incomprehensibly. Tavesin ignored his roommate and raced into the corridor, clad only in his nightclothes.

He must speak to Hasnin, no matter the time. He'd taken the star-shaped box from the black tower, and the wizard needed to know. If the Soulless had not already made him a target, his theft of this object might ensure they did so.

Hasnin's door was closed for the night when he arrived, but Tavesin was not deterred. He rapped loudly, his terror overriding any sense of propriety. He'd stolen from the Soulless.

Hasnin drew the door open with a scowl, his eyes bleary from sleep. When they focused on Tavesin's harried appearance, his expression softened and waved him inside.

"Given we're in the late watches of the night, I do not have to ask where you've been," Hasnin stated as he sat down behind his writing table. "You are frantic, Taven. What's happened?"

151

Tavesin placed the star-shaped box on Hasnin's table and launched into his tale. His fear caused him to stammer, and it became a struggle to continue when he noted the disappointment in the wizard's gaze. He understood his actions had been foolish, that he should have fled the scene as soon as he'd realized where he was.

"Sir, I didn't mean to take it. It was in my hand, and I fled—"

Hasnin held up one gnarled hand for silence. "What you have done was incredibly unwise, Tavesin. The Shadow Council tracks its artifacts carefully, as do we. I suppose we should both be grateful that you've brought this matter to my immediate attention." He sighed heavily. "I will take the relic and your story to the Radiant. Do not be surprised if you are meted out punishment for your folly tonight."

Tavesin looked down and nodded his assent. It was no less than he deserved.

"I know you still do not fully understand how you enter the Aethereum, but I encourage you to make an attempt to keep your psyche firmly in the physical realm," Hasnin continued. "If the Shadow Council learns of this theft and traces the relic here, I have no doubt they will seek retribution. You have put us in a bind, boy."

"I'm sorry, sir." His voice was a feeble whisper.

"Gods help me, Tavesin, but I've rarely had a pupil that was at once so capable and yet, so damned foolish at the same time." He shook his head. "I will send for you on the morrow. The Drakkon cannot arrive soon enough."

CHAPTER SEVENTEEN

THE CORONATION

Dranamir exited the Aethereum near the entrance to the ancient mines she'd been assigned to scour, only to find she was not alone. A merchant caravan was stationed near the mine entrance, a temporary camp pitched between a trio of wagons laden with goods. She surveyed the surrounding area for signs of other occupants, but the valley below was empty of human habitation.

She smiled grimly, a wicked light in the depths of her crimson eyes. Since the master's reprimand and Garin's subsequent reassignment of her duties, she'd been seeking an outlet for her rage.

The camp was occupied by at least four men. They sat around a small fire between the wagons and tents, and failed to notice her approach until she was nearly upon them. One of the men stood as he saw her and offered a welcoming smile. As he took note of her features, however, his smile faltered and was replaced by a look of dread. The color quickly drained from his face and he began to stammer something incomprehensible to his companions.

Dranamir grinned wickedly. She rather enjoyed when her victims recognized the monster she'd become.

She seized her power as the others began to shout. The first man's body exploded in a shower of blood, entrails, and tissue that spattered the others with gore. One of the men acquired a hand axe from amongst his possessions, but as he moved to hurl it toward her, she tore his body raggedly in two. He fell to the ground; gouts of blood spewed from severed arteries while the weapon tumbled from his hand.

She fixed her glare on the remaining two just as a woman emerged from one of the wagons, drawn by the commotion outside. The woman took in the scene with horror written upon her features and promptly began to retch. Dranamir shook her head, unimpressed by the woman's weakness.

"We've done nothing to warrant this," one of the men said in an attempt to avert her wrath. "By the gods, please—"

She'd heard enough, and her rage continued to demand an outlet. "The gods won't save you from me."

She motioned dismissively, and the fallen axe hurtled across the campfire to embed itself in the speaker's skull. He collapsed and began to convulse as his life quickly ebbed. The woman had fallen to her knees. She sobbed and pleaded with Dranamir to put an end to the madness, to stop her unwarranted violence. The remaining man seemed frozen in place, unable to comprehend the savagery he'd borne witness to. She sneered at the pair, making a swift decision to end their miserable existences.

She channeled her remaining energy into the camp's fire, causing it to burst outward in a shockwave of fire and debris. The merchant camp fell silent as the tents and wagons were reduced to ash, their former occupants charred beyond recognition.

She drew a breath and smiled with satisfaction. Her bloodlust was sated, her rage diminished, and though she felt weak from the outpouring of magical energy, she was pleased with the results. She faced the entrance to the mines, prepared to do her master's work at last.

The mines were a maze of passages, though few were still used. It was said they'd been constructed by the same builders responsible for the creation of Stonewall Hall far to the north, and Dranamir believed there was some truth to that legend. Carefully carved symbols adorned the walls which served as markers and guideposts for those who traveled beneath the mountains. In some areas, intricate statues with life-like features stood sentinel in the corridors.

When the builders had displeased the Nameless god and suffered his wrath, their creations had remained behind. She did not know the true name of the mines. The locals had taken to calling them the Mines of Moraine, named after the city some miles down the slope. The city itself was named for a mass of rocky detritus left behind by an ancient glacier, which had formed a large mound near its outskirts. It was an unimaginative name, but the Santinian people lacked creativity. Alyra was proof of that.

She made her way through the lesser-used passages, ignoring the symbols that would lead her toward the mine's exit in the Wasted Land. If she were to find anything of value within, the passages used by merchants and the like would be of no use to her. The treasures they once contained had been picked clean millennia ago.

She spent several hours wandering the dusty corridors, ensconced in a magical glow just strong enough to provide her light to see by. She could manage little more until she was sufficiently rested. She'd overextended herself with the vicious destruction of the merchant camp, but the pleasure she received from the act was worth the resultant fatigue.

Her search turned up nothing useful that day. The Nameless understood her hatred of menial tasks, particularly those which bore no fruit; it was a suitable punishment for her. That Alyra had received a similar task was little consolation. Seeking power on the premise of hope alone had defined the other woman's role within the Shadow Council. Dranamir harbored no illusions that Alyra was secretly pleased with her task.

Thoughts of Alyra soured her mood, and she considered the events that led up to their latest spat carefully. Alyra had provoked the argument, and though she'd attempted to sway Dranamir from striking her down, she never mentioned how she'd known their master would intervene. And she *had* known.

Dranamir felt as though she'd been played the fool. Her preferred method of revenge had been taken from her, but she was nothing if not adaptable. She would find another means to eliminate the insufferable wench.

Her thoughts returned to the palace that night, the horror in the princess' eyes. Garin had stated another would take up the mantle of her training but indicated he was not the one to do so. He had other, more important, tasks to complete for their master. If not Garin, then who had been named? She doubted it was Kama; his duties were focused solely upon expanding their military might.

Which left Jannyn.

She scowled at the notion. Her first impression of him was one of a weak-willed, subservient man who seemed more interested in fawning over Alyra than being of any true use to their master. His magical power was meager, and he'd yet to prove his usefulness in the coming war.

She supposed there was only one way to know for certain who had been assigned to the princess. She would go to the palace and observe from afar, utilizing the last scraps of her magic to disguise herself. It was nearing sundown, she believed; the princess' training session would soon be upon her. Her efforts in the Moraine Mines had been wasted, in any case. It was time to seek another diversion and perhaps learn who their master had tasked with the princess' tutelage.

She opened a portal into the Aethereum and stepped through, then transported herself to the courtyard below Tamarin's quarters. She conjured a hooded cloak to hide her features before opening a second portal into the physical realm. The courtyard was empty, as was the balcony above.

A blare of trumpets sounded from somewhere within the palace, which gave her pause. Perhaps the princess had other matters to attend to this evening. Dranamir frowned; the girl was supposed to be in mourning after the untimely deaths of her parents and her brother's subsequent execution.

Following the sound of the brassy notes, she exited the courtyard to find herself in a wide corridor lined with tapestries. It was unusually empty. She'd expected to encounter a servant or two, perhaps a messenger or a noble lady. Instead, she was met with nothing. The trumpets heralded something of importance, it seemed.

The fanfare sounded again, and Dranamir quickly turned, seeking its source. She hurried down the corridor, turned along another, and found herself on the fringes of a vast crowd. Judging by their manner of dress, most were nobility, though she spied numerous others in servant garb. She peered through the press of bodies to see the princess walking unaccompanied down a carpeted aisle near the center of the room.

Tamarin was dressed in shades of gold trimmed in black, the colors of her royal house. Dranamir followed her progress to the front of the room, where two men stood awaiting her. One bore a long roll of parchment, the other, a velvet cushion with the heavy, bejeweled crown of Delucha upon it.

Dranamir observed the proceedings silently from the rear of the crowd, watched as the men bowed to the princess, and Tamarin knelt before them. The man with the parchment unfurled it with a flourish and began to read, his low baritone carrying easily through the room. The onlookers fell silent.

"It is hereby declared, on this, the seventeenth day of the eighth month, in the four-hundred-sixty-third year of the Serales reign, that the princess, Tamarin Serales, assumes the throne of Delucha."

He paused and took a step backward as Tamarin rose to her feet. The second man stepped forward to kneel before her. He offered the crown on its cushion to his new sovereign with his head bowed low in supplication.

"Princess, please take up your crown," the first man stated.

Dranamir watched as Tamarin lifted the crown and placed it securely atop her head. The cords in her neck stood out as she did so, the weight of the heavy, jeweled circlet a struggle to maintain. She turned away from the men to face those gathered before her, a cool, regal expression on her young face.

Dranamir itched to strike, to watch the new queen fall to the ground and writhe in agony, but she suppressed the urge. She could not risk revealing herself, and she lacked the energy reserves to manage the feat.

"Deluchans, I present your new queen!" The man with the scroll called out triumphantly. He said more, but his words were drowned out by the thunderous applause and boisterous cheers of the audience.

Dranamir turned away and discreetly exited the room while the others were preoccupied with their celebration. She returned to the courtyard, but saw nothing of Jannyn, if he was in fact her replacement. She glowered at the palace walls a final time before disappearing into the Aethereum. She would be forced to seek her information another day.

157

CHAPTER EIGHTEEN

BATTLE PLANS

"Commander, Sal'zar is here to see you."

Aran'daj recognized the black-hooded soldier that stood in the entrance of his tent as one of the pair assigned to act as his personal guard. Until the Soulless had become involved in his army's movements, Aran'daj believed there was no need for such guards. Since Kama had arrived, however, he was unable to relax as he once had. If the Soulless meant to cause him or his people harm, he wanted to know in advance, to save those he could from their wrath. The guards acted as a conduit of information as much as they served to protect him.

Sal'zar's visit came as a surprise. Since the young alchemist had been snatched away from the camp and pressed into service within the tower, Aran'daj had received no word from him. That he arrived unannounced told Aran'daj one of two things: Either Sal'zar came under duress, or he'd come of his own volition but at great risk to himself.

"Send him in."

Aran'daj looked down at the table before him, littered with documents and maps. There was little for Sal'zar to see that the Soulless were not already party to. If the alchemist came as an unwilling spy, he would find nothing out of the ordinary.

When Sal'zar entered, he glanced around the tent nervously before turning to face Aran'daj.

"We're alone, Sal'zar," he said in the Murkor tongue.

The alchemist's shoulders sagged visibly with relief. "It's taken me too long to make my way here, Commander, and for that I apologize. They keep a very close eye on those of us conscripted into service."

He did not have to elaborate on who "they" were. Aran'daj felt guilty for automatically assuming the worst of Sal'zar, but it was difficult to know whom he could trust when it came to his dealings with the Soulless.

"And how does your training progress?"

Sal'zar visibly flinched. "It's why I've come, Commander. I hoped you might send word to the Kal on my behalf. I cannot do so. It was a great risk coming here." There was sorrow in his tone, laced with the memory of pain.

"Sal'zar, what have they done?"

Sal'zar shook his head, unwilling to answer. "Please tell the Kal that the Soulless confirmed his suspicion of me. Tell him..." His voice broke and he looked down as he tried to gather his composure.

Aran'daj crossed the distance between them and placed a hand on the alchemist's shoulder, providing what little comfort he could. "I know the Kal is the leader of your guild, but he is also my grandfather. He will understand your situation, Sal'zar, and better than you may believe."

Sal'zar drew an uneven breath and nodded. "Thank you, Commander. I pray you are right."

"What do you wish me to tell him?"

"Tell him that I cannot bear the brand. He will know the meaning of my words." Sal'zar stifled a sob, and Aran'daj knew there was more behind the alchemist's words than he could comprehend.

"I will tell him, Sal'zar," he promised, his tone gently.

Sal'zar nodded again and peered up at the commander, a glint of pale blue eyes visible within the depths of his green hood. "Thank you, Commander. I dared not risk speaking to anyone else."

"I know." Aran'daj sighed and dropped his hand to his side. "They've placed us in a difficult position, Sal'zar. I will help you if I can."

"That is more than I'd hoped for, Commander." Sal'zar cleared his throat and forced himself to stand up straighter. "I must return to the tower before they realize I've gone." He hesitated, then said, "Please tell Jal'den that I'm well."

Aran'daj watched him go, a deep melancholy suffusing his being. He wished there was more he could do for Sal'zar, to ease the suffering he seemed to have endured while in the tower. He did not know the alchemist well, but he'd seemed a strong, capable sort before the Soulless had escorted him to the black tower. Sal'zar now seemed uncertain, despairing, on the verge of becoming a broken soul.

"Remain strong, Sal'zar," he whispered to the empty tent.

He turned back to his table, seeking ink and parchment. He would send Sal'zar's cryptic message to the Kal, pray his grandfather would indeed understand its meaning, and hope some good came of it for the alchemist's sake. He strode to the tent flap and peered outside at his guards.

"Find Shen'jem," he instructed. "I know he only just returned from the caverns, but I have urgent need of him."

He retreated inside as one of the pair departed on the errand. He must focus, and Sal'zar's unscheduled visit had shattered his concentration. Kama had promised to return by dawn and expected an outline of his commander's strategy for the assault on Delucha. He forced himself to study the maps he'd laid out, but his mind refused to cease its worry over the alchemist's condition.

He knew little of Sal'zar, beyond their recent interactions. He liked to believe he cared for all Murkor under his command, but Sal'zar was different, somehow. Perhaps it was the fact the alchemist possessed the Ability and would one day wield magic as readily as the Soulless, or the wizards beyond the mountains. He shook his head, frowning in thought. Perhaps...

"Commander?"

He looked up from the maps to find Shen'jem saluting him. He plucked his message to the Kal from the table and folded it carefully several times.

"Take this directly to the Kal," he ordered the scout. "It is for his eyes alone, Shen'jem. Do you understand?"

Shen'jem nodded once in understanding. "Of course, sir. To the Kal. Is there anything else I should say to him?"

"Ask him to pray, Shen'jem. Our people suffer."

160

Shen'jem looked down at the folded note in his hands, silent for a time. Finally, he tucked it into his belt pouch and straightened. "Yes, sir. I will tell him."

Aran'daj spent another few hours poring over the maps Kama had provided him with. He determined the best route to take through the mountains, the first city he planned to strike, and the number of soldiers required for the journey. He added a few notes regarding supplies, the craftsmen and alchemists needed to bolster the army, and the number of soldiers he wished to leave behind to defend the caverns.

Kama believed the Scorpion Men would not dare retaliate against the Murkor for the recent skirmish, but Aran'daj was not as certain. Blademon had chosen to become their patron for good reason, and the Murkor had taken prisoners. The Scorpion Men would seek retribution. He would not leave the caverns undefended, no matter Kama's beliefs.

The sky beyond his tent was lightening toward dawn before word came to him that Kama would arrive any moment. Aran'daj acknowledged the warning with a tired nod. The night's planning had left him drained.

The Soulless arrived without ceremony, striding boldly into the commander's tent without greeting. He made his way to the table, studied the maps upon it, and picked up the detailed list Aran'daj had painstakingly completed through the night. He crumpled it in his fist, his expression unreadable, as Aran'daj felt his stomach turn a somersault.

"Commander." Kama began to pace across the tent, his gestures agitated.

"Sir?"

"I'm afraid there has been a change of plans. The work I ordered you to undertake is now useless." He scowled, and Aran'daj stiffened, fearing the Soulless' wrath.

"What do you require, sir?" He kept his voice steady, though his insides were quaking.

"Dranamir informed me the Deluchan queen is undergoing training to become Enlightened." He shook his head. "Garin has known of this matter for days, as have the women, it seems. I've laid plans to attack Delucha, and for what? They tell me our focus is better spent elsewhere."

"Yes, sir." Aran'daj breathed a silent sigh of relief. Kama was not angry with his performance.

Kama stopped mid-stride and faced Aran'daj directly. His crimson eyes gleamed maliciously. "Balotica. Draw up plans to assault Balotica." Without waiting for the commander's response, he strode from the tent and was gone.

Aran'daj sat down heavily on the floor, his head in his hands. The Soulless had spared him yet again, a thing to be celebrated, but his night's work was wasted. Futile.

Balotica Kingdom was his new focus. He would need to chart a different course through the mountains and pray the vicious winter storms that raged in the north would be delayed as the summer dwindled. He had studied enough maps of the northernmost kingdom to understand the terrain would be problematic. Balotica was a land of many lakes and was more mountainous than Delucha. Its people were proud and strong, renowned warriors acclaimed as some of the best in the Five Kingdoms. Taking Balotica would prove no easy task.

CHAPTER NINETEEN

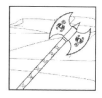

THE LIVING FOREST

Vardak was privately pleased to be leaving Veran Township behind. After learning Danness had taken the same path Coreyaless sought, Maryn had wrangled with the hostel's owner to allow them another two days' stay. He and Vardak had spent that time bartering with the locals for additional supplies. Maryn negotiated while the Felenes tasked Vardak with numerous jobs in exchange. Several had involved patching roofs, though some had simply asked him to reach items stowed in high places; all tasks took advantage of his stature. It was a small price to pay in exchange for the merchants' wares, but he'd grown weary of the menial labor.

He estimated they had enough supplies to last a week in the jungle, but Maryn assured him it was merely a precaution. Their Felene guide believed they would reach the Star Keeper's temple in the old city within two days. He'd informed Vardak of the dangers inherent on their new path the previous evening, but it wasn't until they were leaving Veran that he broached the subject with the two women.

"I've alluded to my dislike for our chosen path through the jungle," Maryn said from the head of the group. "There's good reason my people avoid this route, and it's best you understand why before we travel much farther."

"Vardak led us through Stonewall Hall without difficulty," Janna replied breezily. "This can't be worse."

Vardak heard Maryn snort in exasperation. He understood the Felene's irritation with Janna; she was naïve to the danger and placed her faith blindly in those who might protect her. They'd spoken at length the previous evening about both women and had come to an understanding through their commiseration. Vardak believed he could trust Maryn, not only as their guide, but as a fellow soldier.

"Listen to him, Janna," Vardak said gruffly.

She glanced over her shoulder, waving away the cloud of gnats that swarmed before her face. "Do you believe it's worse than what we've already been through?" Her tone was incredulous. "Surely nothing can be as terrifying as the Undead!"

Vardak gave her his stoniest expression. "The jungle poses a different sort of danger, Janna, but it may prove just as perilous. Listen to him."

She pouted at him and looked away, clearly unhappy with his words. An awkward silence descended over the group, and Vardak contented himself with listening to the unfamiliar birdcalls in the canopy overhead. Maryn had cautioned him they would be near the worst of the jungle's creatures if the birds fell silent.

"As I was trying to say, the path we'll be taking is dangerous, and my people avoid it." Maryn paused as he considered his next words. "Tomyn, our host in Veran, called the deepest jungle the Living Forest. We did not name it such because it is teeming with life, though in a matter of speaking, it is."

"Every inch of your jungle teems with life," Coreyaless retorted. "What makes this portion different?"

Maryn shrugged uncomfortably. "I do not have any direct experience in dealing with the...things that inhabit the area between Veran and the ruins you seek. I have gone as far as the Fringe Zone, where the birds cease to call. The jungle creatures do not venture beyond that point."

"Why?" Janna pressed.

"The plants themselves are predatory."

Janna's steps slowed to a halt. She peered at the trees around them, the dense undergrowth, the vines snaking up trunks and along branches. "The...plants?"

"We are safe here," Maryn replied. "The plants around us pose no threat. They are ordinary plants, no different than those you are used to in the north. When we reach the Fringe Zone, I will point out signs of the other variety. The jungle will fall silent around us as we approach the Living Forest, and it will not take you long to understand why."

Vardak was forced to stop in order to maintain his station as rear guard while Janna gaped at the vegetation surrounding them. He swallowed his mounting frustration and crossed his arms. "As he said, there is no threat here," he told her quietly.

She startled as he spoke. "I'm sorry, Vardak. I didn't know you were so near."

He gestured at Maryn, paused some distance ahead near a bend in the road, Coreyaless not far behind him. "We ought to catch up."

"Of course." She hurried forward but cast a nervous glance at the trees she passed.

Nonplussed, he shook his head and followed in her wake. She was proving flightier than the sand quail he used to hunt before his duties took him away from the desert. She'd shown less fear and more curiosity traipsing through Stonewall Hall than she displayed now.

He caught Maryn's eye as they neared, and the Felene nodded once, seeming to understand Vardak's unspoken concern. Janna's terror could prove as dangerous as the flora they had yet to encounter. Panic, and the confusion it sowed, was problematic in any situation where weapons must be drawn.

Coreyaless took note of their silent exchange and spoke quietly to Janna as they began to move forward once more. "You must trust Maryn to lead us through safely. I have every confidence that he will."

"And if he doesn't?"

"Then you must trust in his skills, and Vardak's."

Janna sighed heavily. "My mother must wish me dead, Coreyaless. I don't have the knowledge to carry out this mission. If not for Vardak, we would have become lost in Stonewall Hall. If not for Maryn, we would be lost. At least you can mend their hurts, Coreyaless, but I don't even possess that ability." Her tone was forlorn.

Vardak frowned to himself, a twinge of guilt gnawing at him for his previous impatience with her. She was overwhelmed with their task, and he could not hold her accountable for Flariel's erratic decisions. She was coping with the situation the best she knew how.

"Janna," Coreyaless said firmly, "you must not give up. Your mother gave this mission to you not because she wishes you harm, but because she desires to see you grow and flourish. We cannot learn to become more than we are without challenge, without hardship."

"Do you truly believe that, Coreyaless?" Janna's tone was filled with hope.

"Yes, I do."

Vardak was once again impressed with the Airess' deft ability to change Janna's outlook. Perhaps if Janna believed her words, she would not pose a risk to the rest of the group when they ventured beyond the Fringe Zone. He prayed that would prove the case. Maryn had revealed much to the women, but he'd withheld even more.

They stopped to make camp before nightfall. Maryn did not wish to continue any further and risk stumbling into the Fringe Zone as the light began to fail. Vardak went about setting up a tent for Janna and Coreyaless, while Maryn scouted ahead, and the others worked at making a fire and preparing supper.

He could hear birdsong above, the buzzing of insects, and numerous calls from other creatures he could not identify. If Maryn was correct, however, the danger was not far off. He would remain wary.

He sat down near the fire after finishing with the tent. Janna sat across from him, carefully slicing some root vegetables Coreyaless had produced. She paused in her work to look up at him.

"Coreyaless told me some things about your people, Vardak."

He arched an eyebrow and glanced at the Airess inquiringly. Coreyaless shrugged and continued stirring the cookpot she'd set over the flames.

"When I asked you, in Stonewall Hall, if you believed the builders would have carved statues of your people, you seemed angry," Janna continued. "I'm sorry, Vardak. I didn't understand what I asked or how it might affect you."

"You didn't know, but it was also not the place to ask such a question." He sighed, then went on in a gentler tone. "My brothers tell me I am far too serious. I know it's worse when I'm tense. Stonewall Hall set me on edge, and where we travel tomorrow will do the same."

"Your brothers?" she asked, curious.

He grimaced and looked down. He had spoken little of his family to Janna. She was unaware of the situation in his homeland, and he'd hoped to avoid telling her. She would blame herself for his predicament, but she was not at fault.

"Vardak?"

When he looked up once more, Coreyaless shot him a pointed look. If he didn't tell Janna the story, he was certain she would.

"Blademon paid me a visit while we were staying in Cynda Village," he said slowly. "He brought news, but I didn't want to burden you with it."

"What did he say?" Janna pressed.

"There was an attack on the Stronghold. One of my brothers was injured, the other taken prisoner." His words came reluctantly, and to his dismay, Janna's face crumpled.

"This is—"

"No," he said sternly. He would not allow her to continue along that dark path. "It is not your fault, Janna. If anyone is to blame, it's Flariel. She covets this relic we chase, she coerced Blademon into sending me along, and she's the one that has failed to help you, time and again. I do not blame you, and I never will."

She stared at him for several long moments while she blinked tears from her eyes. "You...You truly mean that, don't you?"

He nodded once. He had nothing more to say, and for once, she'd seemed to truly listen. He was not forced to elaborate.

She managed a strained smile. "Thank you, Vardak."

Maryn returned not long after their conversation faded. He sat down between Vardak and Janna and stared into the fire.

"It's as I suspected," he said after a moment. "We're not far from the Fringe Zone. It's expanded since last I was here."

Vardak studied the Felene's face carefully, noted the tightness at the corner of his almond-shaped eyes, the rigid tilt of his pointed ears. Maryn was agitated, though his tone remained forthright.

"Expanded?" Janna echoed, her eyes growing wide.

"Yes." Maryn shifted his position to draw his knees toward his chest. "I said earlier the Living Forest is dangerous because of the plant life, yes? When plants feed, they grow."

Janna's face drained of color as the meaning behind his words became clear. "You said the plants are predatory. That the first sign of danger is the lack of birdsong." She stared at Maryn, and Vardak feared she would become sick.

"Janna…"

She glanced toward Vardak and shook her head. "I'm fine. I suppose I never realized a *plant* could…" She drew a breath and focused on Maryn. "They eat the wildlife, don't they? These plants?"

Reluctantly, Maryn nodded. "People, too. It is why we don't travel this way, why our host believed Danness would perish."

"Danness won't," Coreyaless replied, "nor will I, unless…" She shook her head. "It doesn't matter. The temple we seek lies within the ruins beyond this area, and that is where we must go."

"Are you all set on this course?" Maryn asked, resigned.

"The relic my mother seeks is in the temple," Janna said hollowly.

Maryn glanced toward Vardak. "And you?" Unspoken fear shone in his eyes.

He wished he could tell Maryn they were clear to turn back, if only to spare them all from the horrors he was certain lay ahead. He was oath-bound by Blademon to protect Janna, and in spite of his smoldering anger with the Immortals, he knew it was a promise he couldn't risk breaking. If Janna meant to continue, then he must follow.

"If I am to have any chance of returning home, I must escort Janna."

Maryn nodded slowly. "Your position, I understand, Vardak." He released a sigh. "So be it. Tomorrow will be an unpleasant day."

Less than an hour after breaking camp the next day, Vardak began to detect an unpleasant odor in the air. At first it was almost imperceptible, but the farther they traveled, the stronger the stench became. It smelled of decay and was laced with a cloying sweetness, faintly reminiscent of melons left too long in the sun.

Coreyaless produced several handkerchiefs from her satchel and doused them with clear liquid from one of her many vials. She distributed them amongst the group and tied one across her face. The others followed her example. The Airess' solution filtered much of the foul smell, though not all. Vardak silently nodded his thanks.

They continued, and gradually Vardak became aware of the silence that had fallen across the jungle. He paused to draw his axe, and glanced warily at the nearby trees. The flora appeared no different here than it had elsewhere, but the unyielding stench and the sudden lack of birds in the trees gave him pause.

Ahead of him, Janna slapped at several flies that had alighted on her arms. "Gods! I think these have grown worse!"

"Not so loud," Maryn hissed over his shoulder. "Biting insects are drawn to this place."

"Why?" she demanded in a surly tone as she swatted another fly.

Maryn only shook his head and motioned they continue.

Vardak believed he understood the Felene's hesitation. The stench, coupled with the increased number of blood-seeking insects indicated the presence of carrion. He recalled Maryn's warning from the night before and wondered how they were to avoid the same fate as the unfortunate wildlife. When he'd asked Maryn for specifics, the Felene had admitted he'd never ventured far enough into the Fringe Zone to see the creatures for himself. Few of his people had.

Vardak understood two important facts about plants, and it would not matter their size. Plants fared poorly against hewing weapons, like his battle axe, and they burned easily. In the damp climate of the jungle, he doubted fire would be an option.

Ahead, Maryn held up one furred mitt, indicating they should stop. He sought Vardak with his gaze and gestured for him to come forward. The path bent sharply just beyond the Felene's location, disappearing into the dense vegetation.

"What is it?" Janna whispered as he passed.

He shook his head. He didn't know, but he was certain that he would learn soon enough. He stopped alongside Maryn and took in the sight that had been shielded by the trees.

The trees abruptly stopped only steps away, the path opening into a broad basin. Thousands of thin, spear-shaped leaves reached upwards toward the open sky overhead, coated with what appeared to be large water droplets. Another glance told him the drops were not merely water. Dozens of animals, some nearly as large as he was, lay trapped amongst the leaves in varying stages of decomposition. He'd been right about the source of the smell, he thought grimly.

As they watched, one of the long leaves shot skyward in a blur of green. It retracted more slowly, wrapped in a tight coil around a struggling orange bird. The more the bird fought its botanical captor, the more entangled in the droplets it became. Vardak noted the liquid appeared sticky and adhered to the bird's feathers more strongly than he would have believed. The bird opened its beak several times, as though it attempted to cry out, but no sound issued from its throat.

He tore his gaze from the spectacle and studied the path more closely. It was free of the plants, but after what he'd just witnessed, he could not guarantee it was safe to tread. A fine, black sediment lined the edges of the path, but Vardak was too distant to make out what the substance was. The path wound through a maze of the sticky leaves and entered another dense stand of trees less than a quarter-mile away.

He faced Maryn. "Do you have a plan?"

Maryn met his gaze, green eyes fearful. "Until we reached this place, I didn't truly know what we would be facing. The stories I'd heard were vague, Vardak. They spoke of great danger, but nothing specific. Seeing this place…" He shook his head and looked down, his expression troubled. "I do not know what can be done."

Vardak glanced away at the sound of footsteps approaching. Coreyaless and Janna appeared around the bend, and Janna released a low moan as she took in the sight before them. Coreyaless' eyes narrowed as she assessed the danger, her expression calculating.

Vardak suspected she was formulating a plan, and he hoped whatever the Airess concocted would help see them through the glade. After witnessing the lightning-fast strike the plant had made upon the bird, he doubted his reflexes were swift enough to defend against an attack. He would do everything in his power to defend the group, even if his odds of successfully doing so were miniscule. It was what he'd been trained for, what was expected of him.

"I need to have a look at that black substance," Coreyaless stated abruptly. "I believe I know what it is, and if I'm right, it will help us."

Maryn shook his head. "It's too dangerous to—"

"I'll be fine," she replied firmly, then glanced at Vardak. "Do you have any objections?"

He shook his head. Coreyaless could be condescending and selfish at times, but he knew when it came to plants and herbs, her knowledge was unparalleled. He also understood she was in little danger, due to her "curse". It was Janna he was most concerned for.

"Good. I won't be long." Coreyaless pushed past them and strode into the clearing while Maryn gaped after her.

"She's out of her gods-damned mind," he muttered with a shake of his head.

Vardak chuckled dryly. "I've thought the same a few times, but I believe we ought to trust her."

He watched as Coreyaless moved carefully along the path, keeping to the center of the space. She was only a few paces away from the nearest of the deadly plant's leaves when she knelt down to examine the dark residue that lined the route's edge. The leaf shuddered, as though sensing her presence, but it did not strike out as its neighbor had with the bird. The glistening droplets on its surface remained firmly in place, despite its movement.

Coreyaless took a pinch of the residue between thumb and forefinger. With her free hand, she pulled the handkerchief away from her face, then held the substance up to her nose. She sniffed it, then nodded to herself and rose to her feet. She brushed her hands clean and made her way back to the group, readjusting the handkerchief as she did so.

"It's as I suspected," she said. "It's a mixture of ash and several other herbal compounds. We used to prepare the substance long ago, to keep the forest from encroaching on Vidune City. This plant, like all others, does not like the mixture. I have the necessary ingredients to replicate it in my satchel. It will not take long."

Vardak studied her. "Was this Danness' work?"

"I would assume so. Few others would know how to make it."

"What do you plan?" Maryn asked of her.

"As I said, I will make another batch. It lines the path already, but I believe we must go one step further to be safe." She eyed Vardak pointedly. "How easily does your armor rust?"

171

He frowned. "It's steel, though Travin crafted it using a new method he devised. I'm not certain. If it were our standard make, water would cause it to rust easily enough, but this is…untested."

She nodded. "I suppose we'll learn how your brother's craftsmanship withstands my draught. We must coat ourselves with it before passing through this area."

He nodded reluctantly. Travin was likely the only smith who could repair his armor properly. Even if he succeeded in returning home after they secured the Moon's Eye, Travin was held captive in the Murkor caverns—if he still lived. He was loath to knowingly inflict damage on his armor, but the alternative in this scenario was far worse. He hoped Travin's skill would prevent any lasting effects and Coreyaless' proposed solution would work to see them through the glade.

Coreyaless quickly set to work while Janna assisted her. Vardak continued to watch the glade warily, but the plants made no movement toward them. Several more birds were ensnared, and a large animal reminiscent of a boar that charged blindly into the glade. The boar-like beast attempted to halt its progress once it realized where it was, but the long, bladed leaves from several stalks shot toward it in an eye-blink. The creature squealed with terror and strained against the viscous liquid bonds the plant used to hold it in place, but to no avail. More leaves stretched toward the animal once it was subdued and coiled around its struggling form.

Vardak prayed to any god listening that Coreyaless' draught would protect them. She seemed certain it would, but he would not be convinced until they were safely across the glade. Knowing what fate lie in store for them if she failed terrified him, yet he knew they must try. The recovery of the Moon's Eye was paramount in the fight against the Soulless if Blademon was to be believed.

He sighed and forced himself to look away from the death-filled spectacle.

"Do you believe this will work?" Maryn asked him quietly, his eyes on Coreyaless.

"I don't know. I want to believe her, but…" He glanced over his shoulder toward the bulge within the leaves that held the still-struggling creature.

"I understand there is much at stake, but are you certain there is no other way?"

Vardak wished he could tell the Felene otherwise, but he knew in his heart, they must go on. "I don't believe there is, Maryn. I'm sorry. You do not have to accompany us any further. You can return to your people—"

Maryn snorted. "I gave my word to guide you through the jungle, Vardak. I won't back down now, even knowing what may happen. Besides, I was growing bored in Cynda Village, and I'm finding I rather like this adventuring business." He grinned. "Perhaps I'll continue to travel with you, even after your task here is complete."

Vardak arched an eyebrow. "You would willingly leave your homeland behind?"

"As I said, I've been enjoying the adventure so far, with the exception of today's events." Maryn shrugged. "If we survive, I plan to have quite the story to tell when I return. *If* I return."

Vardak couldn't find it within himself to agree with Maryn's position, but if the Felene chose to accompany them further, he wouldn't object. Vardak had felt distinctly out of place since his abrupt departure from the Stronghold, and he longed to see his home again. He had not said as much to the others; it wasn't relevant to their current business. He missed his people and worried over the welfare of his brothers. If given the opportunity, he would return home without hesitation. He wondered if all Felene were so cavalier about their homeland or if it was only Maryn's stance.

"That should be sufficient," he heard Coreyaless say. He looked up to find her appraising Janna, who was coated in a layer of charcoal-gray paste and was working more into her reddish hair.

"Good," Janna mumbled. "I feel ridiculous."

"It's for your protection," the Airess snapped. "Without this, I don't believe we'd make it far." Coreyaless turned to face the men. "Who's next?"

A few minutes later, Vardak was covered head to tail in the gray paste. It was thicker than he'd realized, and adhered to his exposed skin uncomfortably. He was certain he would be forced to spend the next day cleaning the gunk from his armor and from between the chitinous plates on his lower body, but if it spared them the same fate as the countless creatures trapped in the glade, he could withstand the inconvenience.

Coreyaless led the way into the glade, advising they remain in the center of the path as a precaution. Maryn followed quickly behind her, then Janna. As he'd become accustomed to, Vardak drew up the rear. He held his axe ready, even though he felt it would do little good if they were attacked. Their lives depended on Coreyaless' concoction.

They made their way carefully through the glade. Some of the leaves shuddered in anticipation as they passed, but none lashed out. As they neared the center of the clearing, he realized the leaves were much taller than he'd realized, some easily double his height. It was little wonder that even birds fell prey to them.

They did not speak until they reached the trees on the other side of the glade, and then, only after the terrible plants had disappeared from sight.

"Praise the Lady, we've made it," Maryn said, breaking into giddy laughter.

Coreyaless shot him a dark look but said nothing. Vardak wondered at her reaction; they'd just survived a passage that few of Maryn's people had dared attempt. It was natural that he'd be thankful.

"I hope to never encounter a place like that again," Janna replied with a shudder.

"How much further is it to the temple?" Coreyaless asked of Maryn.

"We should be near the ruins called Spanda," he replied. "We can shelter there for the night, but it is still another day, perhaps two, before we reach the temple. There may be more of those plants along the route ahead, but I cannot be certain."

"I will make another batch of the draught while we camp."

Maryn nodded and resumed his position at the head of the group. "It should only be a few miles to Spanda. We'll be there well before nightfall."

CHAPTER TWENTY

MURKOR TREASURES

"It's gone, Alyra. It's fucking *gone!*" Jannyn's desperation was clear in his tone, and Dranamir wondered what was missing that had the man so distraught.

Eavesdropping was not a skill she wished to hone further. With a smirk, she shoved the ornate door open with more force than was necessary. It banged loudly against the adjacent wall to announce her entrance. Jannyn looked up from the glass case to her right, startled at the intrusion. Behind him Alyra frowned in disapproval. Dranamir noted her burns had been healed but ignored her unspoken objection.

"What's gone wrong?" she asked, feigning interest. She walked toward the pair slowly, trailing one finger along the top of the case.

Jannyn shrunk backward from her gaze. "I…" He glanced at Alyra, who shook her head in warning.

Dranamir laughed. "Do I frighten you so much, Jannyn? As I recall, the master himself ordered me to cooperate with the rest of you, much as I'd wish it otherwise."

Jannyn steeled himself and stepped away from Alyra. "Perhaps you're aware that I…lack the ability to enter the Aethereum without a relic to aid me."

Dranamir nodded once. She had suspected Jannyn's weakness previously; he rarely entered the Aethereum alone, and when he did, he spent little time within.

"I used a relic. A star-shaped box, with a hinged lid. There was nothing held within, but opening the box—"

"I know how it works," she replied, cutting him off. "I assume your panic is due to this relic's disappearance?"

He nodded and would not meet her eyes.

"And you've gone to Alyra for help," Dranamir continued. "Alyra, who schemes and plays at making nice with you. It's the same story she's spun out with every man she takes an interest in. And like the rest, she will be your downfall."

Alyra's eyes narrowed with sudden fury. "I am under the same orders as you, Dranamir."

Dranamir smirked. "You've never accounted for the stupidity your very presence seems to bring out in men. And Jannyn is no different than the rest, in that respect."

"Enough, Dranamir. Have you seen the box?" Alyra seethed.

"No." She shrugged. "The last I saw anyone here was yesterday, but I don't recall seeing your relic. Are you certain you left it here?"

"Fucking gods, you're impossible," Jannyn growled. "Yes, I'm certain. Who was here?"

"I've been called worse." Dranamir smirked. "Garin came."

"Garin has no need for my relic." Jannyn scowled and began pacing.

"Unless the master ordered him to use it," Alyra pointed out. "He often comes here to receive orders through that mirror. You know that, Jannyn."

"I suppose I'd best find him." Jannyn glanced beyond Dranamir toward the door and frowned. "Would either of you be kind enough to shorten my trip?"

Dranamir laughed. "No one applies the word 'kind' to me, Jannyn. I'm certain Alyra can assist. My time is better spent elsewhere."

Alyra rolled her eyes and opened a portal in response. "I'll take you to Garin." She shot Dranamir an icy glare. "Nearly a thousand years dead, and you've not changed a whit."

"I have no reason to change, Alyra." Dranamir smiled darkly.

"Let's go, Jannyn." Alyra's venomous gaze lingered on Dranamir's until the pair stepped through the portal. Dranamir returned her look with a knowing smirk.

Alone, Dranamir crossed the room to stand before the other glass case. She peered down at the two orbs housed within its center, gazing raptly at their shifting, oily light. The orbs were her most prized possessions, stolen from the Shining Tower during what she now understood was the first Great War. *Her* war. The orbs were two members of a five-piece set, but she did not know where the others were held. With this pair, she had turned the tide of the war, transforming mere prisoners into deadly warriors, each compelled to do as she instructed.

Since her reawakening, she'd learned those warriors had spawned numerous descendants, though the compulsion spell that once bound them had shattered with her death. They had turned against the Enlightened, joined the battle against her successor, and Alyra had fallen only a handful of years later. After the war, they'd fled southwards and built themselves a home. Kama had confirmed the stories for her when he returned from the army's recent skirmish; the Stronghold, and the desert around it, had been magically sealed. Her power was useless there, the progeny of her greatest achievement protected from further coercion.

She scowled. The orbs were capable of great magical feats, and few with the Ability had managed to unlock their potential. She was among that small number, and she yearned to use them again. The Scorpion Men were safe from her clutches, but perhaps, with Kama's assistance, new prisoners could be acquired. Perhaps, she thought with a grim smile, she could recreate her previous accomplishment. It would make a fitting gift for their master upon his return.

"Dranamir."

She did not turn at the sound of her name, though she relished the longing she heard in the speaker's voice. He had come, as he'd promised. Interesting.

"Kama." She continued to gaze down at the pair of orbs within the glass, her back to him.

"You wished to speak." His voice was nearer.

"Yes."

She turned around slowly to find him a hand's breadth away. Unconcealed desire flickered through his crimson eyes, and it brought a cold smile to her lips. It would take very little to convince him to do her bidding. She wished Alyra were there to see her triumph. Dranamir had secured the attention of the only man Alyra had failed to charm into her bed.

177

"When you move the army into Balotica, I wish to take part in the fighting."

A faint smile appeared on his lips. "I suppose I can arrange that." His smile darkened and grew more pronounced. "For a price."

Perhaps he wouldn't be as easy to sway as she'd hoped. "What do you have in mind?"

"It seems the Murkor have a collection of relics in their possession," Kama informed her, his eyes locked upon hers. "Sal'zar, the...*anomaly,* told me of their location. Their Matriarch keeps them, and as you know, that portion of the caverns is sealed."

"You will grant my request if I retrieve the relics?" she asked thoughtfully. Perhaps in securing them, she would no longer be forced to search the mines. It would solve her predicament with their master and confer the bloodshed she craved.

"Yes. I cannot risk going there, at present. I am in the Matriarch's disfavor." He chuckled darkly. "Her guards do not know your face, Dranamir. A favor, for a favor."

She would be weaponless, at the mercy of the Murkor, if she agreed. Her infamous cruelty aside, she was vulnerable as a newborn without access to her magic. Kama knew it, and she suspected this was his way of testing her convictions. But if she succeeded, the master would once again smile upon her, and she would be another step ahead of Alyra. The prospect was tantalizing.

"Very well."

"I knew you wouldn't disappoint." His eyes gleamed hungrily.

She smirked up at him. "I never do, Kama."

It was mid-afternoon when she arrived unannounced at the entrance to the Underground Caverns. Several armored, black-hooded Murkor stood just inside, shielded from the unrelenting sun by the limestone columns and stalactites that dangled from the ceiling. The cavern entrance had formed at the base of a broad plateau, and Dranamir knew from previous visits that the cave system extended far beyond that particular feature of the barren landscape. The caverns were vast, and the Murkor people knew every inch of them intimately. Once she stepped inside the gaping entrance, she would be cut off from her Ability and at the mercy of her Murkor hosts.

She steeled herself. Venturing into a sealed area always set her on edge.

She'd come undisguised, and even from a distance, she knew the Murkor soldiers had recognized her for what she was. They spoke rapidly in their own tongue, and one of their number disappeared into the gloom as she approached.

She stepped beneath the overhang; immediately, she felt a buzzing sensation at the base of her skull that replaced the ever-present sense of power her magic granted her. The buzzing was an irritant, her magic inaccessible. She scowled at the remaining Murkor as they studied her silently.

"I wish to speak with your Matriarch."

They spoke between themselves as she continued to glower. Kama knew the Murkor tongue, but she did not. The sentries she faced seemed to intuit this and ignored her for several moments. They were unafraid of her presence in their home. It infuriated her, but there was nothing to be done.

Presently, another soldier appeared from the gloom, though she was uncertain if it was the same who had disappeared down the tunnel previously. He spoke to the others briefly, then turned to address her.

"The Kal asks why you choose to visit our home."

"I have no desire to speak with your Kal. I seek an audience with your Matriarch."

She could not conceal the anger in her words. She was certain the others had told this soldier the reason for her visit, yet he forced her to reiterate her previous statement. If these Murkor had been anywhere else, she would have slaughtered them all for their insubordination. The buzzing at the base of her skull was a constant reminder that these soldiers were untouchable, and her fury intensified.

"I must take you to the Kal," he replied. "He will grant your request, or he will not."

Dranamir scowled but nodded a grudging assent.

She was led down the tunnel quickly, but as the daylight faded behind her, she became aware of faint light adorning the walls ahead. Pale crystals were placed at intervals along the walls, providing muted illumination. Her eyes strained to see in the gloom, but it was better than traveling in absolute darkness.

The tunnel led gently downward to end in a large ovoid cavern. Countless stalactites hung from the ceiling high above, disappearing into shadow. Stalagmites served as vessels for the softly glowing crystals that illuminated their path. Among the natural formations, the Murkor had constructed a marketplace. She watched as hooded figures in a dazzling array of color went about their transactions, unaware of the Soulless in their midst. Each color represented a different station in the Murkor society; black for soldiers, vibrant green for alchemists, pale blue for those assigned to draw water, brown for craftsmen. There were many others, but she did not know their significance, nor did she care.

As the soldier led her through the marketplace, she drew numerous stares. A hush fell among the Murkor she passed, and though she could not see the pale eyes beneath their hoods, she could sense their wary interest in her visit. Cut off from her power, she knew she must act judiciously. The thought further soured her mood.

On the far side of the market, she was led up a short ramp and around a bend in the cave wall to a small, quiet chamber. A Murkor garbed in shimmering copper stood within, flanked by several soldiers and a pair of alchemists. A curved, black saber was sheathed at his hip, and a heavy gold chain hung about his neck, both markers of his station.

Her escort bowed low to the copper-clad Murkor, and stepped quickly aside. Dranamir stood erect; she reserved her obeisance for the Nameless god alone.

"Soulless." The voice that issued from beneath the hood was aged yet strong.

"Kal."

"Why have you come?"

She bit back her irritation with the repetition. "I seek an audience with the Matriarch."

"I'm certain you're aware such requests are rarely granted." The Kal folded his arms across his chest. "Especially to your kind."

Dranamir narrowed her eyes in fury. He would never speak to her so outside of the caverns, and she'd ensure he remembered his place, given the opportunity. She silently cursed Kama for placing her in this demeaning position.

"I am aware of several items she possesses," Dranamir stated in an even tone that belied her simmering anger. "The items are critical to our success in the coming months. Our future victories will ensure your soldiers stationed near the tower—and your gifted alchemist—remain well."

Several of the Kal's entourage whispered amongst themselves, outraged. She ignored them, her gaze focused on their leader. The Murkor must be reminded of their place, and she would not hesitate to carry out her threat if they failed to assist her.

The Kal lifted one of his midnight-blue hands in a gesture for silence. "I will take you to the Matriarch." He motioned to the others, who quickly dispersed. "Come."

She followed him through a narrow passage with low-hanging stalactites.

"Forgive my underlings," he said to her. "They do not understand all that is in play."

"So long as they remember their place, I will quickly forget this incident."

He chuckled darkly. "I have heard stories of you. I do not doubt your words."

He paused to duck through an opening that led them to another vast chamber. Hundreds of small tunnels branched away from it, and at its center was the largest crystal she had ever seen, suspended by thin filaments from the ceiling. It glowed softly, a warm, pale yellow, like a watered-down version of the sun's brilliant light.

"How did you come to know of the items you mentioned?" The Kal's voice had taken on a suspicious tone.

"Your alchemist within the tower," she replied.

She did not know the details of how Kama had extracted the information, and she didn't care. Perhaps Sal'zar had given the information freely, but she doubted it. Kama had a penchant for torture rumored to rival her own.

The Kal was silent for several minutes as he led her deeper into the caverns. Finally, he stopped before a series of natural steps formed by layers of limestone. At the top was a wide doorway framed by a trio of stone columns.

"I will announce your visit to the Matriarch. Please, wait here."

She nodded and watched as he disappeared through the door. She had been unable to read his reactions while they traveled, another irritation of this afternoon's business. He had seemed unafraid of her, unperturbed by her visit, and her words had failed to faze him. She didn't like it.

She turned to study the cavern around her. It was quiet in this portion of the Murkor domain, some distance away from the marketplace and the personal dwellings. There was another tunnel across from the one they'd exited; it spiraled gently downward and out of sight. Pale crystals adorned the walls at intervals, but there was little else to see. She was alone, aside from the Murkor within the Matriarch's dwelling.

"Soulless."

She turned to face the Kal as he descended the stairs.

"The Matriarch will see you, but I must act as your escort. She...does not trust your intentions."

Dranamir smirked. "She is wise."

She followed him up the steps and past the columns into the chamber beyond. It was adorned lavishly. Woven tapestries hung from the stone walls, and Dranamir recognized craftsmanship from the Five Kingdoms among the pieces. The carpets that blanketed the floor were plush and formed intricate designs, while the crystals that illuminated the space were suspended in delicate glass sconces. The Matriarch sat upon a cushioned bench made of a dark gray wood that Dranamir knew must have been acquired from a visiting merchant. Trees were scarce in the Wasted Land, and wood of that variety was rare.

The Matriarch wore shimmering silver robes, with dark blue trimming the sleeves and hood. She rose stiffly as they approached, and when she spoke, her voice quavered with advanced age.

"Welcome to our home, Soulless One. The Kal has told me the reason for your visit."

"Good. I've grown tired of repeating myself." She crossed her arms. "Do you have the items?"

"Yes. I've sent my maids to retrieve them for you. They are merely heirlooms, or so we had believed."

"I will be the judge of that."

Beside her, the Kal grunted his disapproval. The Matriarch was the leader of the Murkor, her words seen as law. Dranamir's lack of deference displeased him, but she ignored him. When they succeeded in restoring the Nameless god to his previous post, the Murkor would face his wrath for testing her patience and questioning his orders. She would make certain of it.

A sound drew her attention to an opening hidden between two columns of rock that she hadn't noticed previously. A trio of white-hooded Murkor entered, carrying an array of objects. The first held a dagger carved of ivory and a lacquered, red box. The second carried a long, crystalline rod that Dranamir recognized as one of Alyra's creations; it was imbued with the power of the storm and could be used to manipulate certain aspects of the weather. The last Murkor's item nearly stole her breath as her eyes settled upon it. An orb, much like those stored in the tower, was cradled in her arms, its flickering surface a rich, buttery yellow.

She forced herself to remain still as the objects were laid on the carpet before her. Though she was cut off from her power, she could sense the magic trapped within the orb and the rod. Both would prove beneficial to their designs—the orb, in particular, to her own. She forced her gaze away from the captivating orb. She could not allow the Murkor to see how strongly she coveted it.

The dagger held no magical properties. It was nothing more than a finely crafted, ceremonial piece. The lacquered box drew her attention, for it did possess magic within. She smiled wickedly and nodded in satisfaction.

"The dagger is of no use to me," she stated. "The rest would be of great benefit to the Enlightened."

One of the maids took up the dagger and laid it aside.

"If by taking these things, it will ensure the continued safety of my people, then I will not stop you," the Matriarch said. Dranamir heard a faint tremor in her tone that had nothing to do with the woman's age.

"Your alchemist was wise to inform us of these things. He will be rewarded accordingly."

Dranamir smiled cruelly. She knew the type of reward she would bestow upon him, though the honor would not belong to her. Kama would do as he chose with Sal'zar. The young alchemist would survive the ordeal, but he would emerge from it forever changed.

CHAPTER TWENTY-ONE

FREEDOM REGAINED

He'd been floating in darkness for centuries. Trapped, at the mercy of the winds, his soul tethered by tenuous threads to the magic he once wielded, to the magic he prayed would liberate him. He'd intended for the suspended state to be temporary, but years had passed, then decades. Century upon century.

His awareness was not limited to the passage of time. His cage was dark, filled with gusts that buffeted him at times, and at others, left him in relative peace. He could not escape his prison, his salvation. After all, it was of his own design. The only means to escape a life of enslavement at the hands of a cruel god was to cage himself and allow his body to die.

Death had come swiftly for him once the prison had been erected. He'd known it would, known she would not wait another moment to secure her misguided glory. He could have stopped her, could have fought and overthrown her, even in his weakened state, but he had believed it wasn't the proper time. He would face her again one day, and only then would she understand the true scope of his power.

He wondered when the time would arrive, if another would find his prison before that date. As centuries drew into millennia, he began to worry that he'd miscalculated. Someone should have discovered his prison before now. He should have been freed.

The winds tossed him violently aside, only to cease moments later. The magic that tied his soul to the world of the living refused to dissipate, and he suffered with each gale that passed through. He had defied the gods, defied Aeon, in order to rectify his mistake. He would live again, one day, his soul freed from the monster that once bound him. But it had been so damned long…

He was weary. Exhausted. Unable to seek peace, unable to find rest. The magic he'd woven was unyielding. If he had miscalculated, he was doomed to an eternity of this dark nothingness, battered by invisible forces. He could not escape. He'd designed his cage too efficiently. His thoughts circled, much as the shadowy maelstrom did as it howled around him.

He despaired, his hope extinguished with the passage of time. There would be no respite from the tumultuous storm. His dreams eroded, growing fainter with each year. The cage had been another mistake, one he could not save himself from. But the alternative…

He didn't like to dwell on what he might have become. The brand had been impressed into his flesh while he slept, and upon awakening, he'd been tethered to a fate he would wish for no one. Not even *her*. He suspected she'd taken his place willingly, however. She desired power. He desired freedom. They were fundamentally different in that respect.

In a moment of brief calm, he struggled against his cage. The magic hadn't weakened over the years, as he'd designed. He wanted to sigh but could not. He had no breath, no air, in which to do so. Which of his mistakes was the more dire? He wondered.

When at long last the presence of another enveloped him, he was stunned. He'd yearned to feel again, longed for the touch of another, but centuries had passed. He'd grown used to his solitary struggle, the endless dark, the relentless winds. The other surrounded him, held him close, uttered the words…

Air filled his lungs. Light seared his eyes. He held up one brown hand to shield them, blinking at the sudden brightness. A silhouette moved beyond his splayed fingers, and slowly, the form came into focus.

A small-framed man, his features gray and mottled with what appeared to be decay, knelt at his side. Fine blond hair clung to his skull as he peered at Ravin with eyes red as garnets. Ravin recognized the creature for what he was and seized his power without hesitation. He blocked the creature from his Ability and pinned him to the nearest wall.

The creature gaped at him as he struggled futilely in his invisible bonds. Ravin took a few moments to take in his surroundings and understood what had taken so long. The stone walls were carved with intricate designs; the light that had nearly blinded him shone from within them. His cage had found its way into Stonewall Hall. He wondered at that but knew it was unsafe to remain where he was. The Undead were indiscriminate, and unlike the creature he'd pinned to the wall, Ravin had a soul. The Undead would feast upon it if he lingered.

"The master…was right…" the man gasped.

Ravin raised his eyebrows. "Your master was a fool, and you doubly so. Do not underestimate me."

Ravin created a portal and stepped into the Aethereum. He released his magic once he was alone. He'd missed this realm, this creation of his mother's, her greatest gift to him. It had been meant as a means of escape, but once the brand had been placed upon his skin, he'd been forced to divulge his secret. *She* had made certain the Nameless knew every detail of the Aethereum. His refuge had quickly become her hunting ground. Even now, he refused to acknowledge her by name.

He twisted to look at the back of his left shoulder, the place where the brand had once marred his flesh. Smooth, unblemished, brown skin greeted his eyes. He smiled, relieved that his desperate ploy had worked. He was free. No longer tied to the council that had fallen so far from its original purpose, no longer a slave to the cruel death god that ruled its ranks. *He was free.*

He conjured a set of clothing and began to dress. Dark trousers, a white, collared shirt with laces at the neck. He chose white because it contrasted nicely with his caramel skin, his curly, black hair, and accentuated his unusual, golden eyes. He created a set of sturdy, dark boots and a thick cloak, black, lined with deep blue. He had lost track of the seasons during his long imprisonment; it was best to be prepared for the weather in the physical realm.

He thought himself away from Stonewall Hall and to the place he'd once called home, before the first of his many mistakes. A grove of trees greeted him, standing silently where the town's houses had once been. Grass and small bushes filled the spaces between. Tarren Haven was no more.

He sighed. He should have expected this inevitability. It had been centuries since his last visit, after all. He looked around the space a second time and noted with dismay that not even the stone foundations could be seen beneath the vegetation. There was nothing left for him here.

He willed himself away from the forest that had reclaimed Tarren Haven to seek the other great haunt of his youth: Delucha. When he arrived, he was pleased to find a vast city sprawled across the landscape, an ancient stone castle at its heart. Many of the buildings were visibly different than those of his memory, but that came as no surprise. The city was much larger than it had been in his day, its houses spilling into the rolling plains beyond the outer wall.

He spent a few minutes strolling through the empty streets of the Aethereum, before he selected a small alley in which to make his exit. After the comfortable silence of the magical realm, his senses were assaulted by the sounds of the city around him. Had Delucha always been so damned loud?

He winced and realized the cacophony only seemed deafening. He'd been caged for centuries, devoid of any sensation aside from the incessant wind, alone with only his thoughts for company. He would require time to readjust to living, to become used to the presence of others around him. He shook his head and made his way down the alley to the street beyond.

He did not immediately enter the throngs in the street but paused to observe them instead. He was aware that much time had passed since his last visit to the city, but he was amazed to find so much remained the same. The sight of merchant wagons, drawn by teams of horses and laden with goods, was no different than it had been in his day. Street urchins, ragged and smudged with dirt and soot, sat along the curb or darted between groups of those better off. A few noble ladies went by in enclosed carriages, waving lacy fans, though the day was mild. The fashions of the nobility had changed; their clothing was more colorful, more extravagant, than any he could remember, but little else drew his attention.

He looked down at his own chosen garb and nodded. He could pass as a businessman of sorts if he wished to. No longer overwhelmed by the cacophony, he entered the stream of people on the street. His first priority was to secure lodgings. An inn would do; he could conjure up coin enough to bribe an innkeeper for years if it suited him. The dishonesty made his skin crawl, but unless he wanted to join the urchins on the street, he had little choice.

The first inn he came to looked respectable and clean from the outside, and the interior was pleasant and smelled of baking bread. He nodded to himself and found his way to a table in the common room. It was not yet evening and the space was quiet, occupied only by a handful of locals. They paid him no mind as he sat down.

A teenaged boy approached him moments later and he made his intention clear. He sought to purchase a room for at least a week, followed by a meal. He would pay in advance. The boy nodded quickly and darted away, presumably to find the innkeeper. Ravin placed his hands under the table and conjured an appropriate sum; when the innkeeper arrived, he took the coin without question and gave Ravin a key to his finest room. The boy returned moments later with his meal.

Ravin considered his position while he ate. His desperate bid for freedom had worked as intended, though it had taken far longer for someone to seek his soul-stone than he'd originally planned. That it had been discovered by one of the Nameless' twisted lackeys was disappointing, but typical. His innate power had drawn the death god's attention, and it seemed time had not diminished his desire to claim Ravin's soul. He'd regained his freedom through an act of self-sacrifice and the sheer power of his magic; he had no intention of relinquishing it again.

He'd been certain *she* had killed him in order to take his place as the Nameless god's chosen pawn. Of course, she'd never seen herself as such. But the man who had restored him after countless centuries was clearly under the god's thrall. Had something gone awry in her plans, he wondered? Or were there more than one of her kind lurking in the world?

"Ravin." He snapped his head up at the interruption, golden eyes narrowed fiercely. The innkeeper did not know his name.

It was the same man he'd encountered in Stonewall Hall, though he'd hidden himself within the folds of an oversized, hooded cloak. He sat down across from Ravin, uninvited. Ravin stared a challenge at him, daring him to act. He could sense the man's power, and it paled compared to his own.

"Ravin," he said again, "you did not give me the opportunity to explain—"

He seized his power, held the man rigid, and blocked him from the source of his power. To a casual observer, there would appear to be nothing amiss, but to another magic wielder, it would be clear. Ravin was unafraid of this man and doubted there would be any of his associates nearby to assist him. It was not their way.

"I know what he wants with me, and he will not have it." His voice was a low, ominous purr.

"You were marked—"

He threw his head back and laughed. "Yes, I was. No longer." He peered into the crimson eyes beneath the hood, a wicked smile splayed across his features. "I am free to do as *I* choose. I could kill you right now, and no one would be the wiser."

The eyes narrowed in frustration. "I'm aware of your power."

Ravin sat back and toyed with the fork in his hand. "Why have you followed me here?"

"The master ordered me to reinstate you to the order." The man sighed. "I was not prepared when I awakened you. He spoke of your power, but I couldn't believe what he said was true. You should still be weakened, and yet…"

"And yet, you're no match for me," Ravin finished with a smirk. "I've heard this story far too many times over the course of my life. Regale me with something else before I grow bored of your company."

"Why do you resist?" the man asked, exasperated. "The master said you were once part of the Council, that you were betrayed to your death…"

Ravin laughed again, softer this time. "I was once part of the Council before your 'master' took control. The wizards' new regime had too much bureaucracy for my taste. I was free to do as I wished, to study what I desired. When your misguided 'master' began to convince others to do his bidding, I sought a way out. They bound me for a time but I've thwarted that trap." He grinned, the expression

190

feral. "I'm free again, and there is nothing and no one that will take it away from me a second time."

The man was silent as he contemplated Ravin's words. "You knew Dranamir planned to kill you?"

Ravin's grin dissolved into a glower at the mention of her name. "She is not as deceptive as she believes. I knew of her plans and allowed her to act as she did. Like you, she is no match for me." He decided it was time to put an end to their meeting. "There are two things you will do once I release you. First, you will leave this place and never return. Understood?"

"I cannot—"

"You *will*, or I'll kill you where you sit. It's nothing less than you deserve."

The man sighed, resigned. "Very well. And the second?"

"Make certain Dranamir knows what you've done today. Tell her I'm hungry for revenge. I don't believe I need to elaborate—she'll understand." He released his unseen grip on the man, who slumped suddenly in his chair. "Now, go, before I change my mind."

CHAPTER TWENTY-TWO

MURKOR STRATEGY

Aran'daj reread the message in his hand before he crumpled it in his fist and tossed it unceremoniously into the fire. The Kal had understood Sal'zar's message and indicated he had a plan of sorts. Aran'daj wished *he* understood the exchange while he pondered his options. It would be no easy task to get word into the tower without the Soulless learning of it. The Kal's instructions had been implicit; the Soulless could not learn of the Murkor scheme, and Aran'daj was to act the willing, subservient subject. That the Kal and Sal'zar had something planned was mildly comforting but frustrated him all the same. He could not decipher the full meaning behind the pair's words.

He turned from the fire, his eyes wearied from the bright flames. The soldiers were performing drills tonight, and he had wasted too much time in his futile attempt to discern the Kal's message. His presence was required to direct and oversee the drills, and he was certain Jal'den would be eager to begin. There was a small chance Kama would appear to assess the army, as well. He'd escaped the Soulless' disfavor so far but was uncertain how long his luck would continue.

He gathered himself and hurried through the camp. The drills were to be staged on the barren landscape to the west, away from the black tower and the gaping chasm at its feet. The camp was almost entirely empty, and those he did encounter raced in the same direction as their commander. Only the brown-hooded craftsman, at work in their designated space, seemed unconcerned by the time.

To his relief, he saw no sign of Kama—or of the other Soulless—as he approached the area he'd designated as his command post. Jal'den was there ahead of him, as he'd suspected, and the young

Arms Master paced in anticipation. He stopped to salute when Aran'daj drew near.

"All is ready, Commander. Shall I give the signal?" Jal'den was tensed with excitement, coiled like a spring. Aran'daj imagined he grinned beneath his hood; these were the moments Jal'den longed for.

Aran'daj studied the two battalions that had been gathered for the night's work. They were arrayed across the dry plain from one another in standard battle formation. He noted each soldier carried a practice weapon with blunted edges, as had been agreed upon. Jal'den and the captains had followed his orders precisely.

He smiled wearily beneath his hood. "Yes."

Jal'den gave the signal, and the wargames began. Drummers at the rear of each formation pounded a rhythmic beat as the two forces marched toward one another. Within moments, Murkor soldiers shouted and taunted one another as they engaged.

"I wish I could join them, Commander." Jal'den's voice held a note of longing.

"None are equal to you," Aran'daj replied. "Half would flee, knowing what lay in store for them, mock battle or not. The other half would leave the fight with broken limbs. We are ordered to keep them in form but avoid injuries, Arms Master."

Jal'den laughed uneasily. "Sal'zar said much the same thing when last we spoke." His tone was wistful.

Aran'daj studied the dark hood beside him, wishing he could see the expression on the young soldier's face. "I wasn't aware you knew Sal'zar more than in passing."

Jal'den stiffened at his words. "I...We have been acquainted for some time, Commander. Have you heard from him since he was taken?"

An idea began to form in Aran'daj's mind, and if his suspicions were true, Jal'den might prove instrumental in relaying information to their alchemist in the tower. He considered the risk inherent in sharing his last encounter with Sal'zar, the message to the Kal, and the response he'd received only minutes ago. Before he drew Jal'den into their secretive machinations, he must be certain of the Arms Master's loyalty.

"I have," he replied slowly.

193

"Then he's well?" Hope swelled in his tone.

"He is…surviving, Jal'den." He recalled Sal'zar had asked he inform Jal'den he was well, but the truth had been apparent to Aran'daj. He did not believe in promoting a falsehood that may only lead to further sorrow.

Jal'den seemed to deflate at his words and fell silent. Aran'daj considered his next words carefully, but before he could speak, a pale blue oval opened steps away from the pair. Kama's tall, angular form emerged, followed by a shorter, stockier man who also bore the tell-tale features of the Soulless. Aran'daj suppressed a sigh; he would speak with Jal'den later.

The Soulless observed the mock battle for several seconds before Kama spoke. "The army is prepared, it seems."

"We await your orders, sir." Aran'daj would trust the Kal's instructions, even if he longed to defy the creature that stood before him.

"Good. I've left some maps in your private quarters, Commander. When the time comes, we will attack the city of Jennavere." Kama gestured to the other Soulless, whose attention remained fixed upon the sparring soldiers. "Jannyn has agreed to assist me in the rapid transport of the army, much as we did before. Garin and Dranamir will be present as well."

Aran'daj nodded in acknowledgment. Garin had assisted Kama previously, when his select unit was taken to the Stronghold. Though he was Soulless, he had seemed reasonable. He inferred that Dranamir was the woman responsible for Shan'tar's death and was silently grateful Kama had kept her separate from the army's business.

Kama stared down his long nose at Aran'daj. "I suggest you do all in your power to impress Dranamir, Commander. She will suffer no failure on your part. Mercy is not in her nature."

Without turning around Jannyn growled several choice curses under his breath, which caused Kama to chuckle humorlessly. His stare hardened into a leer.

"Jannyn has been on the receiving end of Dranamir's wrath. He survived only because we are the master's chosen. Displease Dranamir, and *you* will not survive. Am I clear, Commander?"

"Yes, sir." Aran'daj was weary of the threats, but he forced his tone to remain even. He would trust his grandfather's words and pray the Kal and Sal'zar would be successful in their mysterious scheme.

Kama turned his attention to Jal'den. "Arms Master, I assume you are in agreement, as well?"

Jal'den nodded once, stiffly. "Of course, sir."

"Excellent. I expect the pair of you to study the new maps I've left in the commander's tent. I require your strategy before the week is out. The master is...eager to assert his dominance."

The Soulless lingered for several more hours. It was after midnight before the pair left, and not long afterward, Aran'daj departed for his tent. Jal'den remained behind to oversee the conclusion of the wargames, but promised to join him before the dawn. Jal'den was the greatest warrior the Murkor possessed, but he had little interest in strategy. Aran'daj would perform the bulk of the planning while seeking Jal'den's expertise only in matters of combat specifics.

Kama had left the maps in a neat stack in the center of his table, but Aran'daj immediately noted several items were out of place. The Soulless had rifled through his notes, sifted through his personal belongings. He was immensely relieved that he had chosen to burn the Kal's message; there was nothing in his tent to rouse the suspicions of their overlords. He was certain Kama would have murdered him without warning if he'd discovered anything of question amongst the commander's possessions.

His hands shook as he spread the new maps across the table. It was clear the Soulless suspected something was afoot, but they would find no proof through him. Perhaps it was best he leave Jal'den out of their schemes, no matter his ties to Sal'zar.

Aran'daj lost himself in his work. He pored over the maps, made notes of the terrain, studied the intricacies of Jennavere's layout. The city was enclosed on three sides by a high stone wall. There were two gates, one facing southeast, the other northeast. The western side adjoined one of Balotica's many lakes, and according to Kama's maps, there were an array of docks along the shore. The Murkor had no skill with sailing; he would focus his attacks along the walls. Perhaps the

Soulless and their followers could find a means to attack from the lake...

He heard the scuffing of boots outside and looked up from the table to see Jal'den enter. His demeanor seemed downcast; his shoulders were slumped, and his hood hung toward the floor. Their earlier conversation had left its mark on the young Arms Master. Aran'daj regretted that they'd been interrupted by the arrival of the Soulless.

"Arms Master."

Jal'den straightened and trudged forward to lean over the maps, though Aran'daj knew his heart was not in the work. Jal'den made no reply, but after several long moments, he released a despairing sigh.

"Jal'den," Aran'daj said firmly.

"Commander, I..." He shook his head, clearly frustrated, but seemed to brace himself as though preparing for a fight. "Commander, when Sal'zar spoke to you, was he hurt? I must know."

"I don't believe so." Aran'daj recognized the pain in the other's tone and believed his previous suspicions were correct. The two were not merely acquaintances. "Sal'zar asked me to deliver a message to the Kal. It made little sense to me, but I did as he asked. He asked that I tell you he was well, but I don't believe it was the truth."

Jal'den nodded thoughtfully. "I think I understand, Commander. He...If he returns, will you send for me? I would like to speak with him."

Aran'daj smiled, though he knew Jal'den was unable to see it. "I will, Jal'den, though on his last visit, he was unable to linger. If he cannot stay, I will tell him you've asked after his welfare."

"Thank you, Commander." Jal'den shifted uncomfortably. "I ask that you keep this between us. For Sal'zar's safety."

Aran'daj was certain there was far more at stake than the alchemist's safety, but he would not pry; such matters were kept strictly private amongst the Murkor people. Aran'daj needed the young Arms Master to remain focused if they were to succeed in the days to come, and this business with Sal'zar was an unfortunate distraction. The army would need Jal'den's battle prowess if they were to successfully storm Jennavere. And yet...

If Aran'daj was correct, he and Jal'den were more alike than the Arms Master knew. He would ensure he met Jal'den's request out of empathy alone. Aran'daj's own situation had been met with such animosity he'd given in to societal demands and given up on the true desires of his heart. If he was right, he would do everything in his power to make certain Sal'zar's communications were delivered, for Jal'den's sake. It was the least he could do for the pair.

"Our words tonight are between us alone," he promised. "I will pray for his safety—and for yours, Jal'den."

Jal'den straightened and appeared to be relieved. "Thank you, Commander," he said again. "What plans have you devised so far?"

Aran'daj smiled to himself, pleased Jal'den was on task once more. He would keep his promise if he was able. There was too little hope for the Murkor people of late, and Aran'daj would do his part to ensure what remained would endure.

CHAPTER TWENTY-THREE

SCHEROK

Dranamir unleashed her rage on the room around her. Furniture splintered and tapestries were rent with her power; the debris whirled in a cyclone of sizzling energy that threatened to obliterate anything in its path. Garin stood his ground, meeting her strike for strike, his crimson eyes ablaze with fury. She was the stronger of the two, but only by a nose.

"I was under our master's orders, Dranamir!" he roared. Flames leapt from the walls to join the whirlwind of destruction and pressed toward her in spite of her shields.

"You do not understand what you've done," she seethed.

"I don't fear you, Dranamir. I will summon our master to intervene if you cannot come to your gods-damned senses."

The flames edged nearer with his words. Realization crept through her and overrode her anger. Garin was utilizing a relic, and without one of her own, she would be forced to concede to him, one way or another. She fixed him with her most malicious glare and allowed the cyclone to wither and fade. Scraps of fabric and splinters of wood fell to the floor in a haphazard circle around them. A moment later, the flames dissolved. Garin eyed her warily.

"I did our master a favor when I removed *him* from the tower," Dranamir snarled. "He is powerful, certainly, but he has no loyalty to our cause. He serves only himself. He would have betrayed us, betrayed our master! And—"

"Our master demanded I find the soul-stone, Dranamir," Garin cut her off. "When he exerts his will, even *you* cannot resist him. I did as I was compelled to do."

198

"You've released that half-breed abomination!"

She clung to her anger, using its heat to mask her fear. *He* was the only one who had ever bested her, and he'd done in it in moments without any indication of a struggle. When she'd killed him, she had been unaware of the precautions he'd set in place. If she had known of his soul-stone, she would have destroyed it to ensure he could never return, regardless of their master's wishes.

Garin folded his thin arms and studied her with a frown. "Why do you call him such?"

Dranamir snorted. "Half-breed? Or abomination?"

"Both, I suppose."

"I assume you've experienced some of his power."

Her anger began to cool, despite her best efforts to maintain it. In its wake, she began to feel the toll her rapid expenditure of power had taken. She was unused to being challenged, and Garin had come prepared.

Garin nodded. "He is unnaturally strong."

"Only his father was human," she replied. "His power comes from his mother and is the reason why our master has become fixated on him. He is Solsticia's son."

A flicker of understanding passed through Garin's eyes. "I see." His frown deepened. "It seems he did speak the truth."

Dranamir narrowed her eyes in suspicion. "What truth, Garin?"

"Ravin stated he *allowed* you to kill him."

The last of her ire melted away at his words. It was a matter she'd kept secret from the Enlightened, a fact she hoped would never come to light once Ravin was dead. She'd been careful to keep the truth from Alyra, who claimed she'd been in love with Ravin. Alyra, whose looks could have enticed any man into her bed, had given her heart to the only one who took no interest in her.

"Alyra cannot know of his return, Garin. It will further complicate matters."

Garin raised his pale eyebrows, nonplussed. "The master seeks his return to the tower, Dranamir. He means to properly bind Ravin, as should have been done long ago. If I fail to bring him in, he is unquestionably the greatest threat we face. And if he truly is Solsticia's son—"

"He is," she interrupted firmly.

"—then he possesses magic of a scale the world has never encountered. He must join us, or we must destroy him, and quickly." Garin sighed. "I have no choice but to tell the others, Dranamir. Alyra, included. Ravin is dangerous unless he can be controlled."

"As I stated previously, Garin, you did not understand what you set in motion." She narrowed her eyes, her voice a low hiss. "The master covets Ravin's power, but I don't believe he fully realizes the scope of the problem he's created for us. Ravin will not join us, Garin, and I don't believe he can be 'controlled'."

"You sound frightened, Dranamir."

She glowered at him. "He would have taken my place if I hadn't ended his life. There is a very great chance none of us would be here now if that had happened. Ravin is nearly unstoppable. If the master had gained control over him—as he almost did—he would not have needed *us*. There are very few things I fear, Garin, but Ravin is one of them."

"Will he join with the wizards, if given the chance?" Garin mused.

Dranamir laughed bitterly. "No. Ravin desires freedom above all else. You have unleashed a being who has loyalty to no one but himself. He will not join us, nor will he join the wizards. I wish I could believe that with five of us, we might withstand a concentrated assault, but Ravin is clever, and he was fully trained in magic two decades before I was aware of my own power." She shook her head in disapproval. "No, Garin, Ravin will act of his own volition, and there is no one who can sway his path. The master may very well have sabotaged his own plans, but I suppose that is yet to be seen."

"Shall I inform the master you doubt him, Dranamir?" Garin asked in a bored tone. She was acutely aware of the implied threat in his words, and her resentment toward him deepened.

"That won't be necessary."

"Good. I'd hate to sour his mood after I've told him you recovered the third orb. Perhaps we'll let this matter with Ravin fall to the wayside for a time."

Dranamir scowled at him. She itched to lash out a second time but knew it would only infuriate him, and by proxy, their master. Garin was better left an ally than made an adversary.

After Garin left, she was faced with the prospect of clearing away the aftermath of their disagreement. His news had left her feeling vulnerable, a sensation that she hadn't experienced since the night Ravin had been killed. Or rather, the night she *thought* he'd been killed. His magic had saved him, Garin had resurrected him, and now he was free to pursue his revenge. Ravin was the only wielder of magic Dranamir had ever feared. That he was alive incensed her.

She resisted the urge to further dismantle the room around her and instead used her remaining energy to reconstruct the splintered and shattered furniture. Once her quarters were back in their proper arrangement, she sat down on the end of her bed and scowled at the floor. For all her power, she was helpless in this matter. She hated the notion, hated Garin for his role, hated their master for his clandestine schemes.

She required a release, but until she rested, her options were limited. She flung herself upon the mattress and shrieked wordlessly at the ceiling. If anyone dared open her door to learn the source of the sudden noise, she would kill them without hesitation. A grim smile quirked upon her lips. Perhaps Alyra would check in on her. She would endure the master's punishment if Alyra happened upon her unchecked wrath.

After several moments, she closed her eyes. No one had come. It was likely no one had heard her, with the exception of Garin, and he would not have cared. She imagined him in the corridor, shaking his head in disapproval as she screamed on the other side of the door. It was a shame Garin was so powerful, that he seemed to be their master's favored conduit. She would have relished his death, too.

When she opened her eyes again, the daylight had faded from her window, replaced with the starry expanse of the night sky. She glared at the stars, a reminder of the celestial goddess whose domain encompassed magic. *His* mother. Perhaps if she acquired a fourth orb, she would have the strength to combat him.

The thought energized her, and she rose quickly to her feet. The master had ordered her to scour the mines, and perhaps the relic she sought would be found within. There were five orbs in total, created by a long-dead wizard, each harboring immense power. The gray, green, and yellow were in her possession, which left the blue and white.

She created a portal into the Aethereum but hesitated before entering. The Aethereum was *his* realm. Her knowledge of the place had come from hours spent torturing him for the information. Only after he'd been branded in his sleep, when he could no longer fight the master's will, had she dared to interrogate him. He'd told her everything. She would forever remember the unadulterated hatred that burned in his golden eyes.

She would not allow thoughts of him to deter her, not when she was so near to her goal. Another orb, and she would have the power to topple Ravin from his pedestal and serve him with the true death he deserved. If she moved quickly through the Aethereum, it was unlikely he would detect her presence. She stepped through the portal.

There was no one nearby. She transported herself to the eastern entrance of the mines and hastily exited. This entrance looked down upon the flat, harsh plains of the Wasted Land. There were no merchants camping outside to provide her with bloody entertainment this night. It was a disappointment, but she knew it was best not to become distracted. She must uncover the last of Oldara's Orbs...

She prowled the winding maze of passages for hours, with only a dim magical light to guide her steps. Straying ever further from the main path, she found herself descending deeper beneath the mountains. She sensed a pressure in the dank air surrounding her, as though the weight of the rocky formations above threatened to crush the narrow tunnel she wandered. The air grew cooler as she continued, thick with the odors of damp earth, stagnant water, and centuries of dust. Condensation began to gather on the stone around her, while the rough path beneath her feet grew slick. She found herself in a portion of the mines she'd never explored before.

The tunnel opened abruptly into a large chamber. Steps away from the exit, the rocky floor disappeared beneath a lake of dark, oily water. An unpleasant odor wafted from its still surface, and the shore was littered with the half-eaten carcasses of pale, bloated fish, some of which were longer than she was tall. She examined the nearest carefully in the dim light, noting the ragged appearance of the bite marks. A large predator lurked somewhere in the mines. That the fish had been left to rot, only partially consumed, told her whatever was responsible hunted for the thrill alone.

She studied the water's still surface for further signs of the hunter. More dead fish littered the shore on the far side of the lake, and a few bobbed along in the shallows between. The cavern was silent, the lake deceptively calm. Dranamir was not renowned for her patience; waiting for the predator to show itself would not do.

She increased the illumination around herself tenfold while she simultaneously cast a vicious blast of energy toward the water. The surface roiled and bubbled at the impact, and steam rose in thick curls toward the ceiling high above. Moments later, she detected rapid motion rising from the depths, a flash of silver-green scales. With a violent splash, a serpentine head erupted from the surface with a high-pitched screech that set her nerves afire. Eyes like liquid ebony fixed upon her, and the great serpent lunged toward the shoreline. Razor-sharp teeth bared in preparation for attack, the creature found itself suddenly frozen in mid-strike as Dranamir halted its motion.

She sauntered toward it, eyeing the creature as she lifted it from the depths. It was a sea serpent, easily sixty feet in length. Silver scales covered its body, intermingled with green that formed a pattern of interlaced diamonds across its back. She'd never encountered one of the great serpents away from the ocean and wondered how it had come to reside within the Moraine Mines. The serpents were intelligent and capable of telepathic speech, if they deigned to communicate with those not of their own kind.

She crossed her arms and frowned up at the serpent, her gaze a wordless challenge. It would speak with her, or it would die.

"Your name, beast."

Its ebony eyes narrowed with contempt. *Release me.*

She laughed mirthlessly. "You are in no position to make demands, beast, and it's unwise to test my temper. I will not ask again."

I am Scherok.

"That wasn't difficult, was it?"

Scherok's eyes narrowed further, becoming little more than slits. She could sense the malice radiating from the serpent, and reveled in the knowledge that it was helpless, trapped within the web of her magic. It would be a simple matter to kill the creature, but she pushed aside the delicious temptation. Perhaps Scherok could serve a greater purpose than simply sating her appetite for blood.

"I am not without reason," she continued as her lips twisted into a smirk. "You might be of use to me."

I'm listening. The serpent's mentally projected voice dripped with venom.

"One of my associates leads a great army." She began to pace before the serpent and could feel its dark eyes upon her as she moved. "We plan to attack a human city that backs up against a lake." She ceased pacing and turned to peer up at Scherok, her face impassive. "You will attack the docks."

And if I do not agree? Scherok hissed.

She tilted her head to one side and glared at the serpent while she yanked one of its large dorsal scales free. Scherok howled in sudden pain as blood spurted from the wound. When the serpent failed to reestablish communication with her, she ripped a second scale free, this one from its underbelly. An ear-splitting shriek echoed through the cavern, and she imagined Scherok would have writhed and thrashed wildly if it hadn't been magically held in place.

I will obey. The voice was raw, agonized.

She nodded once. "As I knew you would."

She lowered the serpent into the water once more but held it firmly in place, certain it would attempt to strike if given the opportunity.

"I will heal your wounds, then I will leave you. Be prepared for my return, Scherok, and do not attempt to cross me." She frowned at the glaring serpent. "If you displease me, I will make certain your agony knows no bounds before I consign you to Aeon's shadowed realm."

CHAPTER TWENTY-FOUR

MEETING THE DRAKKON

"Where are we, Taven?"

Tavesin blushed furiously at the wonder he heard in Arra's tone. They had met on the banks of the river near Rican Mer, but she'd asked him to take her somewhere "interesting". In his limited experience, the most fantastic place he could think of on a moment's notice was the Shining Tower. They stood in the foyer, just beyond the broad, arching double doors. Staircases spiraled upwards from several different locations, and the Council's five-pointed star symbol was inlaid into the floor. Each segment of the star was colored to represent a Sect within the Council in the physical realm, but in the Aethereum, the whole symbol shone with a vibrant, multi-hued light that dazzled the eyes.

"This is the Shining Tower, Arra."

She stood at the center of the star, slowly rotating as she strove to take in every detail. The tower's foyer was impressive, Tavesin admitted to himself. Particularly within the Aethereum.

"One day soon, I'll be here in person." She flashed a broad grin in his direction. "A pair of wizards came to Bannon's Ford today. They were seeking me."

"I kept my promise," Tavesin assured her.

"Somehow, I knew you would." She spun around again, unable to tear her eyes away from the tower's impressive interior. "Do all wizards live here?"

He smiled; he'd been awestruck by the sight when he first set foot inside the Shining Tower as well. "Most do, but not all."

Arra huffed. "Why would anyone choose to live away from such splendor?"

"I'm sure they have their reasons, Arra."

He felt a tug at his subconscious and realized someone was attempting to awaken him. He sighed as a wave of regret washed through him. He found he rather enjoyed Arra's company, and he was loath to leave the Aethereum.

"Taven?" she asked, concern in her tone. He glanced toward her to find she was gazing at him intently.

"I'm sorry, Arra, but I must go."

"But we've only just met tonight," she complained.

He nodded. "I know. Someone's—" Again, he felt the tug, and his smile faltered. "Someone is trying to wake me, Arra. We'll see one another again."

"I'll hold you to that, Tavesin Drondes," she stated, placing her hands on her hips.

He smiled faintly, amused. "I kept my other promise, didn't I?"

He exited the Aethereum without waiting for her reply and opened his eyes to find Hasnin looming over him. The aged wizard's eyes were narrowed in concern. Rostin stood a few paces behind him, a stricken expression on his face. Both appeared visibly relieved when Tavesin's eyes met theirs.

Tavesin glanced toward the tiny window at the far end of the room he shared with Rostin to note the sky was still quite dark. It was far too early—or late—for an impromptu lesson of any kind. He frowned in confusion.

"Sir? What's—"

"Aziarah has come," Hasnin interrupted his query. "Dawn is still a few hours off, but she insisted upon meeting you without delay." Hasnin studied him, a shrewd frown further creasing his face. "Do you always sleep so deeply, boy?"

Tavesin flushed, recalling his meeting with Arra. "I was in the Aethereum, sir."

Hasnin nodded. "Perhaps it's fortunate Aziarah has arrived. You need a proper teacher, and the Council is helpless to protect you from that realm's dangers." He stepped back. "Make yourself presentable, Taven. I'll await you in the hall."

Tavesin waited until Hasnin had exited and closed the door before he climbed out of bed. Rostin continued to stare at him, concern etched into his young features. Tavesin shrugged and began to dress, uncertain why his friend was so worried.

"When Hasnin first came I tried to wake you," Rostin told him after a time. "When I couldn't, I didn't know what to do. I told Hasnin you wouldn't awaken..."

"I knew someone was trying to reach me," Tavesin replied, "but I was..." He trailed off, blushing furiously. He hoped the dim light provided by the candle near the door was insufficient for Rostin to take note of his reaction. He wasn't certain why he reacted as he did to the mere mention of Arra.

"You saw *her* again, didn't you?" Rostin teased. "Now, I understand. First the Drakkon, and now a girl!"

"Rostin..."

"Don't mind me," Rostin continued in mock sadness. "I'll just be in my blankets, recalling the days when I called Taven my friend. Soon, he'll be too important to bother speaking with me."

Tavesin sighed in exasperation. When Rostin took it upon himself to tease him, there was nothing he could do to stop it. Rostin's antics embarrassed him further, and his friend knew it, which served to fuel his good-natured ribbing. Tavesin imagined his face must appear nearly purple from the prolonged flush.

Rostin laughed; he'd provoked the desired reaction from Tavesin. "I hope you'll introduce me," he said, more seriously.

"To whom?"

Rostin snickered. "The Drakkon. Or the girl, I suppose. If you manage to get over your infernal shyness, that is," he added.

Tavesin shot him a dark look. "Her name is Arra. I'll introduce you when she arrives, but she won't tolerate your jibes."

Tavesin had learned from his brief encounters with Arra that she, like Rostin, had a quick mind and a sharp wit. The two would inevitably spar, and he would stand by to enjoy the show. Rostin would be put in his place before he knew what had happened.

"That remains to be seen." Rostin snickered again. "You will tell me what the Drakkon are like, won't you?"

Tavesin nodded impatiently and scurried from the room. Hasnin stood in the corridor beyond, arms crossed, until his apprentice emerged. He beckoned for Tavesin to follow him and turned on his heel without awaiting a response. Tavesin found himself scrambling to keep up with his mentor's quick strides. When they reached the stairs, Hasnin led him upward.

"Sir?" he asked, uncertain why they would venture toward the restricted area of the tower.

"The Drakkon have set up camp on the tower's roof," Hasnin replied. "They prefer the high places of the world, and the tower is the highest point in many leagues."

As they neared the first landing, Tavesin could see a faint shimmering in the air between the final step and the space beyond. He understood from his lessons the top two floors of the Shining Tower housed many magical artifacts and relics of great power; some were dangerous, some well-documented, and others not fully understood. As a precaution, the Council had placed wards over every conceivable entrance to both floors, and only a handful of select wizards knew the proper magical processes to enter. The visible shimmering was a result of the warding.

Hasnin stopped on the top step and turned to look pointedly at Tavesin. "As a member of the White Sect, I have been granted access to the restricted spaces. You will follow me closely, and you will not touch *anything* along our route. It is for your own safety. Do you understand, Taven?"

Tavesin swallowed hard and nodded. "Yes, sir."

He stood back while Hasnin summoned the proper magic to unravel the ward over the stairs. Tavesin followed quickly when his mentor indicated it was safe and kept his eyes fixed on the path ahead, resisting the urge to gape in wonder at what lay around him. Relics were crammed haphazardly onto countless shelves, heaped into crates, and perched precariously on numerous tables. There were more magical artifacts in the space than he could count, and Hasnin ushered him swiftly along. He could sense their energy, a pulsating thrum that seemed to vibrate the air around them.

When they reached the steps leading to the tower's roof, Tavesin was at once relieved to be away from the unknown dangers of the restricted levels, and terrified that he was mere moments from meeting Aziarah and the other Drakkon. He was certain the Radiant would be present; the Council's leader would not miss such an opportunity.

Tavesin clenched his fists in order to still his hands and refrain from fidgeting while Hasnin unraveled the ward between the restricted levels and the rooftop. During his brief encounter with Aziarah in the Aethereum, he'd believed she was friendly, and she'd saved him from the Soulless' pursuit. Now that he knew she was the leader of the Drakkon magi, the idea of meeting her left him reeling. He had little experience with the other races of the world, and he knew almost nothing of the Drakkon. He wondered again what he'd done to wind up in his current situation.

"Tavesin." Hasnin's voice cut through the swarm of his anxious thoughts.

He snapped his head up to meet Hasnin's gaze, eyes wide with fear. "Sir?"

"Come along, boy. The others are waiting."

He followed Hasnin up the final steps and emerged on the tower's shimmering white rooftop. The sky was beginning to lighten toward dawn, but the brighter stars still shone in the darker portions of the sky. A few paces away, the five Sect Masters and the Radiant were gathered in a cluster, facing a contingent of Drakkon. Each of the Drakkon wore leather armor, and a few carried weapons sheathed at their hips. They towered over their human counterparts, and as Tavesin approached, he noted that three of them stood taller than the rest. The tallest Drakkon were also more muscular and sported tiny spikes of bone along the crowns of their heads. He wasn't certain, but he believed they were male.

He recognized Aziarah from his encounter. She stood slightly apart from the others, at the head of their group. When she heard their approaching footsteps, she turned and offered Tavesin an enigmatic smile.

"The child we've been waiting for," she stated, her reptilian eyes fixed upon his. "You are the first of your kind in several generations to breach the Aethereum without guidance, Tavesin. Your skill is rare, and—"

She grasped his wrist suddenly in her scaly hand, and he startled at the act and the surprising strength her fingers possessed. He gasped, unable to stop himself, which elicited a laugh from the group of Drakkon.

"You are quite powerful," she said slowly and released her grip. "Do your superiors realize your true potential?" Her eyes swept across the faces of the wizards to settle upon the Radiant. "This boy has more raw talent than any human I've encountered in more than three centuries. It is no wonder the Soulless was entranced."

Tavesin's mouth went dry. He glanced at Hasnin, then at the Sect Masters, but none deigned to reply. If Aziarah's statement was true, he held more power than any of the aged wizards around him.

"We are quite aware of his potential, Aziarah," the Radiant stated, mercifully breaking the silence. "Tavesin himself does not yet understand what he may be capable of."

"A shame." Aziarah shifted her focus to peer down at Tavesin once more. "I have a proposition for you, young one. You will remain with the wizards and learn all you can from them, while I will teach you the ways of the Aethereum after your daytime lessons have concluded. There is much you can learn from my people that your own cannot teach you." She smiled. "What do you say, Tavesin? Do we have an agreement?"

His heart skipped a beat as his greatest desire—and fear—was realized. He swallowed hard and nodded. "I would...I would be honored."

CHAPTER TWENTY-FIVE

THE ADVISOR

Ravin sensed the Soulless' departure from the Aethereum long before the small, hooded figure entered the inn's common room. He cut Garin from the Ability as soon as he spied him. Ravin was angered by the intrusion and meant to make good upon his previous threats. He wished to be left alone.

Ravin watched as Garin cast a glance through the dimly lit room, his gaze finally settling upon Ravin where he was seated in the corner farthest from the entrance. Over the past week, the staff had become used to his presence, and with his conjured coin to supplement their usual income, they asked him few questions. It suited him. He wished the Soulless would learn to do the same.

As the man wended his way through the crowded common room, he drew curious stares. It was late summer, and the heavy, hooded cloak he wore was distinctly out of place. Ravin caught a faint crimson glimmer within the hood as the Soulless sat down across from him and placed his empty hands upon the scarred tabletop.

"Your precautions are unnecessary, Ravin."

Ravin smirked and folded his arms across his broad chest. "I did not block you because I fear you," he replied. "I blocked you because I wished to see you squirm."

The Soulless faced him silently, and Ravin longed to see the expression on the man's corrupted features. He'd hoped to strike a nerve.

"I have tidings from our master that concern you." The Soulless' tone was tight with anger. Progress, he thought.

"And what does that hypocritical bastard want with me?" Ravin asked in a bored tone. "I am freed of his mark, or has he forgotten?"

"How dare you call him that?" The Soulless demanded, his voice loud enough to draw further stares from the inn's other patrons.

Ravin laughed, enjoying the effect he elicited from the smaller man. "Now, now. You might want to keep your voice down. We're not alone."

The Soulless glanced over his shoulder and seemed to deflate. "I'm aware of our current surroundings," he replied bitterly. "You ought to be grateful to our master. He is the sole reason you live again."

Ravin snorted in contempt. "How carefully did you inspect my soul-stone before using it? The words to the resurrection spell were etched onto its surface. Anyone with the presence of mind to speak them aloud could have accomplished the feat your fallen deity seeks to take credit for."

The Soulless was silent for a time, his head tilted downward as though he were examining the tabletop between them. Ravin sensed the other man was livid, that he wished to harness his power and lash out. Blocked as he was, he could not. Ravin grinned wickedly and wondered how long the deluded creature before him would remain at the inn, vulnerable and miserable in the face of his magical prowess.

Finally, the Soulless lifted his hooded head and peered at Ravin from within the shadows. "The master has offered you the opportunity for revenge, should you rejoin our council."

Ravin's grin faltered as his mood quickly soured. His next words came out in a low growl. "Does he truly believe my loyalty would come so easily? I will have my revenge, and I do not need his 'help' in order to exact it. Mark my words, Dranamir *will* die by my hand. I do not need him, or his council of misguided fools for assistance."

"How dare——?" the Soulless began, outraged.

Ravin could tolerate no more of the man's indignation. He seized more of his power, applying significant pressure upon every inch of the Soulless' corrupted body. The Soulless contorted in his seat, but to Ravin's dismay, he uttered no sound of anguish.

"You know who I am," Ravin stated in a low tone. "You ought to understand what I am capable of. If you do not, I'll be more than happy to oblige you. It will be the last thing you experience, and I'll make you regret your decision to follow the Nameless and his fetid delusions."

Ravin released the man, who slumped forward in his chair and gasped for breath. "On our last meeting, I believe I told you never to return here. I will repeat myself only once. Leave now. Do not return. I will kill you on sight if you venture here again."

The Soulless stood on wobbling legs and darted from the inn. Ravin tracked his progress to an alley a short distance away before he removed the block he'd placed on the man. He scowled at the tabletop, incensed by the interruption. The inactivity of the past few days had left him restless, and his anger toward the Soulless drove him to his feet.

He crossed the busy common room and paused to speak with one of the inn's staff before he ventured outside. "I have business in the city, but I'll return before midnight."

She nodded absently, her attention upon the patrons and the trayful of used dishes in her hands. "I'll tell Gellan you'll return. You're good for coin—he'll be pleased."

Ravin strode outside into the busy street. He had no business to attend; it had simply been an excuse to leave the confines of the inn. He cast his senses across the area and nodded once in satisfaction. The Soulless was gone. He joined the throngs in the street and allowed the current of the crowd to push him where it would. He took the opportunity to assess more of the city, to note the myriad differences between its present state and that of his memory. Much had changed in the intervening centuries, but strangely, much remained familiar. He found it at once both comforting and unnerving.

Gradually he became aware of magical workings nearby, but the sensation was altogether different than what he would have expected from the Soulless. He stepped to the roadside and closed his eyes briefly in order to pinpoint the location of the energy. He turned in place to follow the flow, and when he opened his eyes once more, he looked toward the Deluchan royal palace.

He frowned; he had not anticipated the wielders were within the palace. There were two distinct entities, one floundering as though in the early stages of learning to harness their power, while the other was…

He scowled. The second wielder was shrouded from his inner sight, a sign they had either attempted to hide their workings from others, or they were under the influence of a stronger mage. A wizard would have been open with their magic, which left only a member of the Shadow Council. The wielder was not Soulless, but he could at the very least make an example of them. Perhaps then the Soulless would steer clear of him in the future.

With a grim smile, he made his way toward the palace looming at the city's heart. The stout iron gates were drawn closed in preparation for the evening, and he could see numerous guards upon the ramparts. Entering his realm would provide him a means to breach the walls, but he would be unable to trace the magic's path while there. Perhaps a compromise was in order.

He turned into the nearest alley and opened a portal into the Aethereum while concealed behind a stack of worn crates. He smiled after he stepped into the other realm and paused to quickly assess its state. He alone was capable of the feat; the Aethereum had been created for his use alone, though Dranamir had tortured much information from him. His mood soured at the memory, and temptation to draw her into a battle nearly overrode his present curiosity. She would pay for her treachery.

He shook his head, frustrated at his momentary lapse. It was best to bide his time, learn what he could of the Soulless, and engage Dranamir when he was certain she would fall in defeat. The wielder within the palace must be dealt with first, and in the most gruesome fashion. There was no other way to impress upon the Soulless the caliber of mage they were dealing with in Ravin.

He thought himself beyond the palace walls, beyond the guards and their show of strength, and into a wine cellar. Kegs and barrels lined the ancient stone walls; their appearance was solid in the Aethereum, an indication they had not been touched in many years. Their physical imprint had bled into the magical realm over time, making them appear almost as they would have in the cellar of reality.

214

He smiled faintly at the realization that no one would be present to witness his reentry into the world.

He created another portal and exited the Aethereum, then immediately cast his senses through the area. The pair of mages were almost directly above his present location and continued to channel their power. His brief foray into the Aethereum had not caused him to lose their trail.

The wine cellar was dark and smelled of dry earth. He navigated the space toward the rickety wooden steps he'd spied while in the Aethereum without creating a magical light. He wanted nothing more than to surprise the unwitting mage above, and harnessing his power now would reveal his presence. He smiled grimly as his mind conjured numerous bloody ends to the mage's existence, a clear sign to the Soulless he had no intention of rejoining their misguided cause.

The steps led him into a root cellar, filled with crates and strung with bunches of hanging onions and garlic. The space was lit by a pair of torches near another short stair. It was clearly used more frequently than the wine cellar below, and the aroma of cooking meat wafted toward him from the stairwell. The palace kitchens would be directly above. He hoped his sudden appearance would not draw unwanted attention, but passing through the area could not be helped.

He entered the kitchen and strode purposefully toward the exit. A few members of the kitchen staff glanced at him in passing but none seemed overly concerned by his presence. Only one man openly stared after he noticed Ravin's unusual eyes. Ravin shot him an imperious frown, summoning his best impression of an entitled nobleman. The man paled and quickly looked away.

Ravin continued to follow the trail of magical energy out of the kitchens, across the great hall, and down a long, quiet corridor lined with tapestries. His path took him to an iron-bound wooden door. When he tried the handle, he found the door was locked. The magic was flowing strongly on the other side; he was certain his quarry was within.

He scowled but made the decision to force the lock with his magic. It would take a miniscule amount to open the door, and perhaps the wielder beyond wouldn't take notice of his brief use of power, consumed as they were with their own workings. It was a risk he was willing to take.

He steeled himself, harnessed his power for a brief moment, and sprung the door's lock. The magic continued to flow on the other side of the door, the wielders oblivious of his proximity. He smiled grimly. It was time to make an example of the shielded mage and announce his dominance—and freedom—to the Soulless.

He pushed the door open to find himself in a neatly manicured courtyard. Trees and shrubs alike had been shaped and sculpted into fanciful forms, while bright flowers swayed in the gentle breeze along a gravel pathway. He glanced at the surroundings momentarily while he pinpointed the source of the energy he'd been following. His gaze drifted upward to a stone balcony, where a teenaged woman of obvious noble rank stood facing an equally young man. The woman was clearly the wielder attempting to learn her power, while the man was her teacher.

Ravin studied the pair momentarily, and his desire for revenge dissolved, to be replaced by a weary anger. The young man moved erratically, his movements jerky and uncoordinated, while his eyes rolled skyward. He was clearly under the influence of a powerful magic wielder, his mind and body no longer under his own control.

Ravin shook his head; the man's fate was not so different from the one he had nearly suffered himself at the hands of the Nameless god's followers. The example he'd intended to make would have to wait. Ravin was not heartless, and he had the power within himself to remedy the man's plight.

He drew a breath and channeled a burst of energy, severing the man's tie to his master. Immediately the man slumped forward and fell to his knees. As his eyes came into focus, a panicked expression crossed his pale features. Ravin was certain he was unaware of what had transpired while he'd been under the other mage's power.

"You!" The woman shouted from above. "How did you come to be here?"

He shifted his gaze away from the man to find the dark-haired noblewoman's eyes were fixed firmly upon his. He channeled more of his power and lifted himself through the air and onto the balcony before he made his reply.

216

"I followed the scent of magic here." He turned away from her to kneel at the man's side; his concern for the man outweighed the trouble his presence may have caused with the woman. "Can you stand?"

The man lifted his gray eyes and nodded, though his hands trembled. "Where are we?"

"What do you mean, 'where are we'?" the woman demanded, incensed. "You've come here every night for nearly a week to teach me the ways of magic."

Ravin shot an irritated glance in her direction. "He was under mind-controlling magic. He cannot remember what he has done while under the influence of the other." He turned back to the man. "Since she cannot find the manners to answer your question, we are in the Deluchan royal palace."

"How dare you speak of manners to me?" the woman demanded. "I rule here. I could see you hang."

Ravin frowned at her, unimpressed. "You will not. Don't threaten me unless you fully intend to make good on your words. Even then, it would be unwise."

Something in his tone caused her to reconsider. "Who *are* you?"

"The pair of you might consider me your savior," he replied while studying the man for any sign of residual effects from the mind-control. "I believe one of the Soulless controlled your friend here. I severed the tie rather permanently. A wizard would not dare use such magic upon another. It is against their vows."

The man blanched. "The…Soulless? They're real?"

Ravin suppressed a sigh. The poor sot wasn't even aware of his own ability, and he'd been duped into acting the puppet for the Shadow Council.

"Yes." Ravin turned his attention to the woman, recalling her earlier words. "You mentioned you rule here. Are you the queen?"

The look she gave him could have curdled milk. "After the many parades and celebrations, I'd expected the whole of the Five Kingdoms to recognize me."

"I don't care for parades or parties. It is senseless frivolity."

She snorted. "You come here dressed as a Santinian nobleman and expect me to believe you don't care for such things?"

"I am no nobleman." He returned his attention to the man. "Do you feel ill?"

He shook his head. "No. I'm…fine, other than my memory. I can't seem to recall anything about this place—or her. How did I come to be here?" His voice rose, taking on a note of hysteria.

"The mind-control magic erased all memories you may have had while under its influence." Ravin sighed helplessly. There was nothing he could do to restore the man's memory, though a part of him believed it was better that way. There was no end to the atrocities he may have committed while under the Soulless' control.

"He truly can't remember…anything?" the queen asked from behind them.

Ravin nodded. "I may be the most powerful mage on this earth, but I never took the time to study the arts of healing. A gifted healer might be able to restore his lost time, but given who his master was, it may be best if he remains ignorant of his deeds."

She eyed him suspiciously. "I don't believe you are boasting…"

"I'm not."

"I suppose that explains how you came to be here." She crossed her arms. "You seem to hate the Soulless, but you're no wizard, either."

"I am my own man," he replied evenly.

"I am in need of a teacher," she said slowly, "and I rather like the idea of having a mage unaffiliated with either Council in my employ."

Ravin arched an eyebrow, intrigued in spite of himself. "What would this arrangement entail?"

"I will name you advisor to the queen regarding all matters magical," she replied. "I would require time for lessons, of course, but much of your time will be your own. And I ask that you keep the matter of *his* involvement quiet." She looked pointedly at the young man.

"What will become of me?" the man lamented. "I am a farmer's son, from Balotica. I've never been to Delucha, and now I've found myself in the presence of the queen. I have no useful skills…"

"You will remain here," the queen replied promptly. "I'll ensure your safety and welfare. Now, if you'll excuse me—" she eyed Ravin. "I'm afraid I don't know your names."

"Jasom Riversend," the young man replied. "And I thank you, Your Highness. You show great kindness to me."

"It is nothing," she stated and offered him a coy smile. She looked to Ravin once more. "And you?"

"Ravin."

"Very good. If you'll excuse me, Ravin, I have a private matter to discuss with Jasom. Go to the great hall and take a meal. I will find you and discuss your arrangement in more detail later."

Ravin smiled to himself as he made his way toward the hall. Gellan, the innkeeper, would be sorely disappointed to find Ravin's coin would no longer be spent under his roof, but he sensed his new position might prove beneficial. It would relieve the tedium of his days, if nothing else, and the queen was an intriguing, albeit difficult, woman. Perhaps her unwitting ties to the Soulless would provide him the means of revenge, given time.

CHAPTER TWENTY-SIX

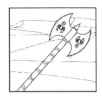

SOLSTICIA'S TEMPLE

"According to the maps I've studied, we are nearly there." Maryn paced the length of their latest campsite while he spoke. His long tail lashed erratically, a sign he was agitated.

Vardak paused in his work to watch the Felene guardsman in the morning light. He'd been checking his equipment while they waited for the women to awaken; his axe blade was honed to a keen edge, his armor polished and rust-free. He understood Maryn's frustration. The maps Maryn possessed indicated the ruins of Spanda lay only a day's journey north of the temple they sought, yet they had traveled for two days with no sign of their destination. Their provisions would run dangerously low if they persisted much longer, making a return to Veran appear bleak.

"If we do not find the temple by nightfall, we will return to Veran."

Vardak would not risk the lives of the others on Flariel's foolish errand. He would endure her fury if he must, but Janna was innocent, thrown into a situation she was wholly unprepared for. He would protect her, as he'd been tasked to do.

Maryn scowled at the ground as it passed between his boots, his ears twitching. "It is the only hope of surviving this journey, if the temple remains elusive. But, by the gods, the thought of wending our way through that death-filled glade a second time makes my skin crawl."

Vardak nodded in agreement and resumed his task. While they'd made it through safely once, he wasn't certain Coreyaless had enough herbs to prepare another batch of the strange salve that had protected them. He'd overheard her grumbling about low quantities

220

the previous evening as she sifted through her satchel. A return trip would likely be their last.

His heart sank at the thought. Patak was injured, Travin imprisoned, and he was an immeasurable distance away, helpless to remedy his brothers' plight. The odds of death if he failed to escort Janna to the Star Keeper's temple were high. He bottled his anger and silently cursed the gods once more for driving him away from his family and his people in their time of need.

"We will reach the temple before mid-afternoon," Coreyaless stated as she exited her tent. "I've taken another look at your maps, Maryn, and I believe there was a mistake made by the cartographer on the scale." She ducked back into the tent briefly and returned with one of the maps in question. "Look here."

She unfolded it as she strode toward Maryn and pointed at two locations. "We traveled this distance in the span of two days' time. This distance—" she pointed at another pair of locations, "—is supposedly the same. The scale indicates we should have traveled between Cynda and Veran in a third of the time it actually required, which means our delay in reaching the temple is due to a mistake on this map. If my calculations are correct, we will find the temple today."

Maryn frowned, consternation painted across his feline features as he studied the map in her hands. "I'll be damned," he muttered after a moment. "I can't believe I failed to notice this before."

Vardak, relieved their plight might not be as dire as he'd come to suspect, set his axe and whetstone aside. "The sooner we reach the temple, the sooner we can be done with Flariel and her relic."

Coreyaless arched one pale eyebrow in his direction. "Do not count on the gods' meddling to end simply because you've done as they've asked, Vardak. Proving yourself capable is of use to them, and they'll not forget it."

He knew she was right, but he was loath to admit it. He needed to return to the Stronghold, and completing Flariel's task seemed his only means of leveraging favor enough with the goddess that she would grant his request. He would agree to another mission if she required it, so long as he was given the opportunity to wrest Travin from the Murkors' grasp. He would do all in his limited power to spare his brother further indignity at their hands.

"Even so," he replied, "I'll do what I must in order to return home."

"Be wary in your dealings with the Immortals, Vardak," she cautioned. "They will exploit your every strength and capitalize on each perceived weakness in order to achieve their own ends."

He nodded his understanding. She would know better than most what dealings with the gods might lead to, and he had no intention of becoming their unwitting pawn for millennia.

They spent another long morning sweltering beneath the canopy of the jungle as they forced their way onward. Vardak began to lose the tenuous hope Coreyaless' discovery had elicited as time wore on. They must reach the temple today or their mission would end in failure, a prospect he could not afford. He kept his thoughts to himself as he brought up the rear of their party; he did not wish to sour the others' morning.

Several paces ahead, Janna and Coreyaless were deep in discussion. Janna was effervescent as always, happily oblivious to the desperation of the day's march. Coreyaless was pensive, and Vardak spied her glancing behind them longingly several times. He had no doubt her mind was on Danness and his whereabouts, though they'd encountered no sign of his passage beyond the deadly glade. Maryn led their group, slashing at the occasional vine or branch that threatened to obstruct their passage. The guardsman brooded; his mood was darker than Vardak's own.

It was just past noon when Vardak noticed Maryn had stopped mid-stride, his gaze riveted on something beyond the foliage that obscured Vardak's sight. Slowly, Maryn turned to face the others, his face breaking into a grin.

"We've found the temple grounds!"

Silent relief flooded Vardak at the words and Janna began to chatter excitedly ahead of him. Coreyaless managed a tight smile, but he understood her strange melancholy. They'd located the temple, but Danness had continued to prove elusive. Would she return to the northern lands with them, given the chance, he wondered? Or would she remain behind in the jungle seeking her lost love? In spite of her terseness, she'd proven invaluable to their journey. If she chose to stay

222

in the southern lands, he would miss her, but he would not dissuade her from her course. She'd waited too long and come too close simply to give up.

When the temple grounds came into view, Vardak was astonished at the sight. The jungle had not encroached upon the space, as though an invisible force, some magic, perhaps, held it at bay. Carefully plotted gardens filled areas between buildings and tiled walkways, filled with exotic blooms the like of which Vardak had never encountered. Fruit-bearing trees towered above the other flora; he recognized only a handful of varieties, but most were wholly unfamiliar.

The tiled paths were clear of debris, as though they'd recently been swept. There were no people in sight, and Vardak suspected the same power that held the jungle's unruly flora at a distance was likewise responsible for the cleanliness of the space. The paths led to a central structure that was built to resemble the rising or setting sun. The domed roof sported thin, golden beams that glimmered in the noon light as they stretched upward and outward. Beneath the dome were a series of thirteen silver columns adorned with an array of strange symbols. Some he recognized from the common tongue, some were Murkor, yet there were many others unfamiliar to him.

"It's beautiful," Janna breathed as she gazed up at the columns they passed.

"The stories fail to impart the true splendor of this place," Maryn agreed. His green eyes were wide with wonder.

Vardak conceded that Solsticia's temple outshone the ruins of Flariel's in Stonewall Hall. He appreciated the craftsmanship that had been employed in its construction, though he found he preferred the simplicity of Blademon's temple near the Stronghold. He frowned at the thought; perhaps he was merely pining for his homeland, concern for his brothers overshadowing the wonder he ought to be experiencing.

Vardak followed the others through a wide door that led into the temple proper. The room they found themselves in sloped gently downward toward a broad, stone altar with an ovoid, obsidian mirror affixed above it. He glanced up and stopped mid-stride to stare, awestruck, at the ceiling. It followed the contours of the outer dome

223

and was painted with intricate designs of the night sky. He recognized some of the constellations depicted, though many others were unfamiliar. Each star emitted a soft glow, mimicking an unobstructed view of the true sky beyond the temple's walls. Interspersed between the stars were other shapes and objects that glowed more faintly; some were spiraling whorls, others amorphous clouds. A few glowed with vibrant colors in blue, red, or green, twisting into fanciful shapes that he could not name. He began to agree with Maryn's assessment.

"We ought to join Janna below," Coreyaless said quietly from beside him.

He tore his gaze away from the celestial sight above and nodded. Janna had made her way to the altar along with Maryn, and she turned to face them expectantly. It was clear she intended to call forth one of the gods, though whether it was Solsticia or her mother, Vardak didn't know. It was not a matter they'd discussed previously.

"Do you know what she plans?" Vardak asked as they descended toward the altar.

Coreyaless shook her head, her expression resigned. "She hasn't mentioned her intention to me, though I suspect she means to summon her mother."

"I was taught calling a god in another's temple would be considered an affront to the presiding god," he replied uneasily. It was one matter to have been chastised by Blademon as he had in Cynda Village, but another entirely to call forth the wrath of Solsticia while visiting her altar.

Coreyaless shrugged. "The gods do as they please with no regard for the likes of us. Why should we fear to reciprocate?"

She strode ahead of him as he wrestled with her impropriety. He understood her anger with Karmada but was stunned that it extended to the other gods as well. He shook his head in disbelief before traversing the remainder of the distance to the altar.

Janna glanced at each of them in turn, her eyes settling on Vardak's last. "If the Moon's Eye is truly within this temple, as Coreyaless has said, Solsticia will know its location. My mother may reprimand me for choosing to summon Solsticia first, but we are standing in the celestial temple. I do not wish to offend its goddess."

Vardak nodded, relieved at her decision.

Beside him, Coreyaless crossed her arms and leveled a flat stare in Janna's direction. "Solsticia is no more likely to help us than your mother."

Janna's eyes narrowed in momentary irritation. "I must try, Coreyaless. It is the only way we might negotiate a return to the Five Kingdoms. My mother may have sent me on this mission, but Vardak had no say in the matter, and his people need him. I may not possess the skills required to make the journey alone, but I mean to help him in return for his assistance to me." She offered him an uncertain smile.

Vardak was silent for a time, surprised and grateful for her gesture. He had not anticipated that Janna would wish to repay him, and he would not have demanded she do so. "Thank you, Janna."

Coreyaless' expression was sorrowful, but she nodded before turning away. "I will wait outside while you conduct your business. I've no desire to entangle myself further with the Immortals."

Vardak watched her leave, unable to conceal his frown. He suspected her sudden change in demeanor had more to do with their failure to reach Danness than it did with Janna's proposal. He was not angry with the Airess, merely disappointed. A part of him hoped she would choose to remain behind so that she might reunite with the man she loved.

"She'll return, Vardak," Janna said quietly after a moment. "Perhaps it's best she's not here while I call Solsticia. She blames the gods for matters that she should not, but it is not my place to reprimand her."

"She is a damned complicated woman," Maryn added with a shake of his head.

Janna shrugged uncomfortably and turned her attention to the altar and the mirror suspended above it. The obsidian glittered darkly in the starlit dome, its polished surface reflecting Janna's pale face as she placed her palms upon the altar. She closed her eyes in concentration.

Vardak stared intently at the mirror's surface while Janna silently called out to the temple's mistress. There was no visible change for several moments, then a burst of light illuminated the glass from within to reveal Solsticia's countenance. She was the patron goddess of the human race. She appeared as a strikingly beautiful woman with raven-dark hair and smoky skin. Her eyes, alight with the glow possessed by all gods, were golden; the color reminded Vardak of the newly-risen sun shining in a dawn sky. She smiled serenely at the trio before her.

"I've been expecting you," she said in a musical voice. "Flariel said you would come."

"We seek the Moon's Eye," Janna replied. "My mother—"

"Your mother was foolish to send you on such an errand," Solsticia cut her off. "She does not understand human nature as I do, and she has risked your life needlessly in the process. I must concede she had sense enough to send you with one of Blademon's chosen, though her actions were reckless."

Vardak narrowed his eyes at her words. He recalled his previous encounter with Blademon and the war god's allusion that he had trained another warrior. The notion continued to unsettle him.

Solsticia focused upon him, noting his reaction. "In order to maintain our neutrality in mortal conflicts, Blademon cannot favor one side over another. There are always *two*."

Vardak nodded stiffly. Solsticia's words reiterated Blademon's, but with her mention of taking sides, his unease intensified. That the Soulless might secure a warrior with skills to match his own was troubling. He began to better understand Coreyaless' mistrust of the Immortals; why had Blademon failed to mention the other would fight for his opposition?

"I do not have time to speak with you properly at present," Solsticia continued, "but I shall return on the morrow." She gestured toward the altar, and a fantastic spread fit for royalty appeared upon its surface. "Eat, drink, and refresh yourselves while you wait."

"Thank you—" Janna began, but the celestial goddess had already gone.

Maryn picked up a skewer of roasted meat and flashed a grin. "At least we have no concern for our rations tonight."

Vardak nodded again, though he was unable to muster a smile for the guardsman. Solsticia's words would continue to plague him until he found the opportunity to confront Blademon.

Would the other possess the same advanced knowledge of tactics that Vardak had been imparted with? Or would they simply be an elite warrior, nearly unstoppable on the field? How much blood would be spilled when the two found themselves at odds, and was there any means of preventing such devastation?

He scowled at the food, his appetite vanquished by the turmoil within his mind. Blademon had much to answer for.

CHAPTER TWENTY-SEVEN

THE QUEEN'S REVELATION

"She's within, sir."

Ravin nodded to the wiry servant responsible for leading him to the palace's solar. The queen had announced his new position as advisor the previous day, then promptly disappeared into her private quarters. He'd expected she would wish to begin her lessons in magic immediately, but instead, she'd summoned Jasom to her side.

He quickly learned the palace's servants were a wellspring of information. They did not speak with the nobility unless spoken to, but they observed everyone within the palace and spoke with one another frequently. Ravin made it his first priority to befriend as many of the palace's staff as he was able. He learned Jasom had remained with the queen until well after dark, and the servants were eager to learn more about the awkward farmer from the northern kingdom. The implications of his prolonged visit with their monarch was the topic of every conversation.

Now that she'd decided to summon him, he meant to learn the source of her interest in Jasom. Speculation amongst the servants was informative, but he wasn't certain he could trust what he'd learned implicitly. Gossip was often rife with inaccuracies.

Ravin stepped through the wide door and entered a long room lined with windows. The queen was perched on a cushioned divan, her skirts arranged carefully to display the intricate embroidery that decorated their velvet panels. A trio of noblewomen sat on cushions at her feet, chatting and sewing to pass the time.

At his entrance, the queen motioned to the nearby women, who collectively rose to their feet, curtsied, and departed her company.

They eyed him with unconcealed interest as they passed him on their way to the door. Ravin nodded politely to each of the women in turn, and he heard them begin to speak excitedly amongst themselves before the door closed behind them. His experience with women had always been much the same.

"The Duchess of the Mers thinks you quite alluring," the queen informed him as he stopped to stand before her. "She was the one wearing blue. Her words, Ravin, not mine."

He resisted the urge to scowl; he had no interest in romantic entanglements, least of all with a noblewoman who was likely married. He opted to steer the subject away from himself and to the matter at hand. "You sent for me?"

Her smile was bemused. "Yes. There are several matters that I would like you to attend to. As my advisor on all things magical, I believe they will be of interest to you." She gestured to the recently vacated cushions near her feet. "Please, sit."

"I'd rather stand." He'd agreed to the post in order to assist her and potentially secure the resources required to bring Dranamir to her knees. He would not kneel to this queen, nor any other. His days of obedience to another power were long past.

"Very well." She shrugged as though his response was of no consequence, but he noted the flash of annoyance in her green eyes.

"What matters would you have me look into?" he asked, ignoring her obvious displeasure with his conduct.

"Foremost, our defenses," she replied curtly. "The Soulless know of me, and of...Jasom. I've offered protection to him, and he plans to remain here, which pleases me greatly." She looked down and smiled wistfully for a moment. "I must be certain they cannot return to the palace, Ravin. Do whatever you deem necessary to ensure it is so."

"To make such a demand of any mage shows your ignorance when it comes to matters of magic," he replied slowly. "Luckily for you, I'm not an average mage, nor am I bound to the oaths of suppression the wizards cling to. I will do as you ask."

The task suited him. Already, he had formulated several schemes that would ensnare one of his enemies if they were shortsighted enough to stumble across them. His recent experiences

229

with the frail man told him it was a likely scenario. He smiled grimly, thrilled at the prospect of turning the Soulless' plans on their heads. If Karmada's fortune smiled upon him, perhaps his first victim would be Dranamir.

"Secondly," she continued, pulling him from his daydream of Dranamir meeting a horrific end, "I would like to begin my lessons on the morrow, as would Jasom. We shall be learning the magical arts from you, together."

"That was not part of our original agreement."

He stared a challenge at the young queen, but she held his gaze unflinchingly. He had no desire to act as mentor to the *pair* of them; both were young, both touched by the Soulless, and he was certain there was more going on between them than the mind-control that had unwittingly brought them together. He didn't like the idea of teaching magic to anyone, but he'd agreed to train the queen due to the opportunity her offer presented. There was nothing more driving his decision. The addition of teaching Jasom, who he was certain knew nothing of his power beyond the events that had landed him in the palace, was a burden he was loath to accept.

"If you wish to retain your position as advisor, then you must learn to adapt, Ravin." She folded her arms carefully, her expression cool.

He narrowed his golden eyes in momentary anger, then nodded tersely. He needed the post in order to secure the proper information and gather the necessary relics to exact his revenge. He could not bring Dranamir to her knees without those resources.

"Very well."

She smiled knowingly, though the expression did not touch her eyes. The effect was unsettling; with her dark hair and green eyes, she could have passed for a younger version of the Soulless herself, long before she'd sworn her soul to the Nameless god. He pushed aside his sudden discomfort as she made her final demand.

"There is one final matter, Ravin." She stood from the divan and paused to straighten her heavy skirts. "You made it quite clear that you are no healer, but I must know one thing before you depart. Do you have the power to determine if someone in your presence is ill? Or, perhaps, afflicted with…something?"

Her last question came as a surprise, and he raised his eyebrows. "If I know what sort of affliction I am searching for, perhaps. I am not attuned well to such magics."

She nodded, a troubled frown creasing her brow. "Very well. I must think on this matter for a time. Perhaps we will speak of it again on the morrow when I send for you. Until then, please go about your other duties."

As he turned to leave, she called out to him. "And, Ravin? Be sure all matters we speak of in private remain that way. I'd hate to exile you for spilling the royal secrets to a maidservant...or a wily duchess."

He glowered but did not turn to acknowledge the comment. No matter what the Duchess of the Mers might think of him, he had no interest in her or her kind. The queen would learn quickly he had little tolerance for meddling, and possessed a long, sharp memory. He hoped he would not be forced to display his power and reveal his location to the Soulless simply to avoid unwanted political intrigues.

As he passed into the corridor, the trio of noblewomen came into view, accompanied by a fourth. Each smiled and batted their eyelashes at him as though their flirtations alone would interest him. He suppressed a growl, nodded to each in turn, and went on his way. He silently cursed the queen and her transparent manipulations. When they returned to the solar in his wake, he had no doubts she'd been responsible for their behavior. By the gods, what had she told them?

He returned to the chambers he'd been assigned, a spacious room on the palace's second floor with a large window that overlooked the main gates. The bed had been tidied since he'd departed earlier in the day, and the enormous wardrobe on the opposite wall had been closed and polished. He had little in the way of personal possessions and did not mind the servants' intrusions to clean the room. He made his way toward the window, but before he reached it, his door opened.

A harried man with a trio of younger assistants burst inside, their arms filled with various garments. Ravin sighed; he'd forgotten the queen had ordered new clothing for him the night of his arrival.

"My lord?" the leader asked. "We have the items Her Majesty requested for you. Do you have time for a fitting?"

Ravin stilled his rising temper. The tailors were merely doing their jobs, and his anger was better utilized in preparing the palace defenses. He cursed himself for failing to enter the Aethereum promptly when he returned, for now he was obligated to endure their ministrations. The queen's advisor on magical affairs must look the part, she'd told him, and reluctantly, he'd agreed.

"Let's get on with it," he growled, only to receive an amused chuckle from the tailor in response.

"I promise you, sir, this will not take long."

Two hours later, the royal tailor and his assistants left Ravin's chambers with his measurements and a list of alterations required on the existing garments. Ravin's mood continued to sour the longer the men delayed him, and by the time they'd finished, he was unable to erase the scowl from his face.

"A damned waste of my time," he muttered as they departed.

He stared balefully at the door for several seconds, giving silent challenge to anyone unfortunate enough to open it. When it remained closed, he turned his attention upon the matter of the palace's defense. He had numerous traps to employ, both in the physical realm and the Aethereum. He required solitude in order to work, and further disruptions by the palace staff would not be tolerated. He opened a portal into the Aethereum to begin his preparations there.

If the queen saw fit to summon him again, she'd be forced to await his return. The thought brought a brief smile to his face. She believed she was entitled to his obedience; he meant to show her he would bow to no one, that she was nothing more than a means to an end.

It was nearing midnight when Ravin returned to his chambers, exhausted from the expenditure of his magical energy. The palace was warded on all fronts, and he would be immediately alerted to the presence of any Soulless foolish enough to cross the invisible boundaries he'd erected. The wards were complicated and would take hours for even a powerful mage like Dranamir to unravel. One misstep would land the offender trapped within the Aethereum, cut from the source of their power, and left to rot until Ravin determined it was time to pay them a visit. He prayed that Dranamir would fall victim to his devices; it was no less than the Soulless bitch deserved.

He stumbled into his room and collapsed upon the bed, fully clothed. Sleep enveloped him readily, and he succumbed to its blissful darkness without delay.

Pounding on his door awakened him. He snarled awake, only to find bright daylight streamed through the window. He'd slept for hours, though it felt mere minutes. He stifled his temper and stood to straighten his rumpled clothing.

"A moment," he called, no trace of his ire detectable in his tone.

The pounding ceased. He determined his appearance would suffice after quickly running his fingers through his dark hair. After all, the tailor had not completed his new wardrobe, and he could use it as an excuse for the current state of his attire. He doubted anyone would remark upon it, save the queen herself, and he cared little for her opinion.

He pulled the door open to reveal a palace messenger awaited him in the corridor. "Her Majesty wishes to meet with you at once, sir."

"Of course, she does." He smirked at the man's startled expression. "Lead on, man. You ought to know better than I that Her Majesty doesn't like to be delayed."

The messenger muttered an oath under his breath and shook his head in disbelief. Ravin, unable to hide his amusement, wore a grin as he followed behind. He knew without his magical prowess, his irreverence toward authority would have landed him in someone's dungeon ages ago.

He was brought to the inner courtyard garden, the same area where he'd first encountered the queen and her mind-controlled compatriot. She was seated on a low, stone bench amidst a cluster of rosebushes; the fragrance of the blooms scented the surrounding air with their sweet perfume. Standing behind her was the young Balotican farmer, dressed in attire fit for a prince, though he appeared decidedly uncomfortable. Once the messenger departed, the three were left alone in the courtyard.

"Ravin, I'm pleased you've come." The queen offered him a deceptively serene smile.

"I'm sure you are," he replied dryly. Jasom's presence indicated she wished to begin her lessons. He'd been awakened by her messenger, and he hadn't eaten since the previous morning; he was in no mindset to teach a pair of bumbling novices.

She folded her arms carefully and eyed him coolly. "I did not summon you for training, as it is still early in the day. I have much to attend to before supper. No, this matter is something entirely different."

He relented, marginally placated by her words. "Very well."

"Do you recall the third matter I mentioned to you yesterday? The matter I said I wished to think upon further?"

"I rarely forget. As I stated previously, I'm no healer."

He glanced toward Jasom, who looked as though he wished to disappear. The subject she was on the precipice of broaching made the boy uncomfortable to the point of avoidance. Interesting.

The queen closed her eyes briefly and drew a breath as she steeled herself for her next words. "You mentioned you must know the nature of one's condition in order to detect it."

He shifted his gaze to her once more. Curiosity compelled him further down the path he knew he should not trod. "I did."

Her green eyes bored into his. "I must know if I am carrying a child, Ravin."

In the span of an instant, the fragments of her story melded, and he understood the magnitude of what had transpired between the pair.

"He was under mind-control when he—"

"Yes," she snapped. "He remembers none of it, which is why I needed to speak with him privately. If I am pregnant, we will marry, so the child will know both of its parents. I cannot blame Jasom for what he did to me during that time, but I hope to one day meet the man ultimately responsible for the act. I will ensure he suffers for the violation he caused."

She quivered with rage, her jaw set in furious determination. Ravin had no doubt she would make good upon her words, given the opportunity. With her revelation, he began to see the young monarch in a new light, and he regretted his former impudence.

"I have warded the palace," he informed her, "and if any of the Soulless attempts to trouble you, they will be forced to answer to me, within the bounds of *my* realm. I assure you the past will not repeat itself, so long as I draw breath."

Her expression softened and she blinked away unshed tears. In that moment, she looked far younger than her sixteen years, and Ravin found himself feeling inexplicably protective of her.

"Thank you, Ravin. Now, can you answer my question? The deed was done perhaps a week ago. It is too soon for me to know for certain without your help, and I'd rather not bring an apothecary or a wizard into the mix. I cannot trust them, though strangely, I feel I *can* trust you."

"It will take but a moment," he replied quietly.

He closed his eyes and drew on his power. He stretched one hand toward her, though he would not make physical contact. He'd honed his power over decades into a formidable weapon but rarely had he used it on a matter so delicate as this. He allowed a mere trickle of energy to escape his fingertips and sent it through the air toward the young queen as he sought an answer.

She gasped as the magic entered her body and shuddered as he directed it to her womb. He was only dimly aware of her reactions, his focus trained upon the tiny cluster of cells growing rapidly within. He knew the answer to her query, yet was repulsed that he must give her such news. With a heavy sigh, he released his magic and opened his eyes.

She studied him for a moment before her eyes welled with tears. He could not hide what he'd learned from his expression.

"I'm sorry, Your Majesty," he said quietly before he turned away.

CHAPTER TWENTY-EIGHT

ARRA'S ARRIVAL

"Young Master Drondes."

The sharp tone brought Tavesin's attention back to the lesson at hand and to the elderly wizard whose steely glare was now fixed upon him. He met Andola's expression with a terrified one of his own. Andola Trentehk's temper was legendary amongst the tower's apprentices, and it seemed he'd garnered her wrath.

"Repeat for the others what I've just told them," she instructed.

He gulped and cringed in his seat. His thoughts and been miles away from the lesson. The previous evening, he'd met with Arra in the Aethereum, aided by Aziarah's guidance. The Drakkon believed he had significant talent in Aethereal magic and had praised his efforts at the conclusion of their time together. It wasn't Aziarah's praise or his knack with the Aethereum that caused Tavesin's mind to wander, however. Arra would be arriving in the tower later that day, and he planned to meet her in person as soon as he was able.

"I'm sorry, Andola," he muttered uncomfortably. "I do not know what was said."

Behind him, Rostin snickered. His embarrassment intensified.

Her expression hardened as her thin lips compressed into a tight line. "I know you've been chosen by the Drakkon, but I expect you to perform in your other lessons just as well as you would for those scaly brutes."

He gaped at her blatant disdain for the Drakkon. In his limited experience, he'd found they were adept with magic, and Aziarah had proven an excellent mentor.

She crossed her arms, oblivious to his shock. "You will remain afterward and copy lines for me until I am satisfied you've learned it's best to keep your mind on the matters at hand." Andola fixed her gaze on Rostin. "And you, Master Ver'an, will remain afterward to clean my ink wells as punishment for your antics in my study this afternoon."

Tavesin sullenly listened to Andola drone on about ancient Kamshati history for another half-hour. He didn't understand the purpose of learning non-magical history about the Five Kingdoms, unless he intended to enter the White Sect and become an historian himself. He had no intention of following that path, and he found the long history lessons tedious. When Andola mercifully ended the lesson, Tavesin and Rostin remained behind as the others filed into the corridor beyond.

"What am I to do with the pair of you?" Andola asked with a shake of her head. "You'll never pass your trials if you continue to daydream and provoke unrest in your fellow students during lessons." She shot Rostin a pointed look with the last part of her statement.

"I'm sorry," Tavesin said again, as Rostin stated, "I didn't mean to disrupt the others."

"Nevertheless," Andola replied, "the pair of you need to learn focus. Particularly *you*, Tavesin. The Drakkon will not tolerate any lapses on your part, young man."

Tavesin nodded his agreement. Aziarah had shown great patience with him as he began, but she expected mastery of his newfound skills within hours of his learning them. Coupled with his daytime lessons and the covert meetings he'd shared with Arra, Tavesin had managed little sleep in the past weeks. His fatigue and the excitement he harbored at meeting Arra in person for the first time had shattered any focus he'd mustered earlier in the day. Andola was right to be frustrated by his performance.

He was tasked to copy a lengthy passage from a scroll that detailed the succession of Santinian Kings, while Rostin was given a half dozen dried inkwells for cleaning. Tavesin struggled with his penmanship; prior to his journey to the Shining Tower, he had never learned to read or write. It was a skill deemed unnecessary by most of the adults in Rican Mer but was one of the first he'd been made to learn upon arrival.

Rostin finished his task first and sat down across the table from Tavesin with a grin. "It's going to take ages for me to clean the ink from my fingers."

"What did I tell you about disruptions, Master Ver'an?" Andola scolded from across the room.

Rostin sighed and fell silent while Tavesin finished the last of his copy. Tavesin shrugged and offered his friend a knowing smile. He was accustomed to Rostin's interruptions, but rather than contradict Andola and secure more chores for both of them, he said nothing. They would talk at length once they were freed from the wizard's spacious study.

Tavesin forced himself to ignore his friend in order to complete his assigned task as quickly as he was able. His fingers were clumsy with quill and ink, his penmanship only marginally legible, and he struggled not to smudge the completed lines with each stroke. Writing was best left to trained scribes, he thought, not to a former farmhand from rural Delucha.

Andola studied his finished copy with pursed lips for a time, her expression rife with disappointment. "Your writing is atrocious, but you've completed the task as I assigned it." She sighed and shook her head. "You may go."

The pair scurried from the room and nearly collided with Badolo in the corridor outside. The younger boy grinned, unperturbed by the near-miss. "I've been waiting for you," he told them. "She's here!"

Tavesin knew immediately he referred to Arra, but Rostin blurted, "Who?"

Badolo rolled his eyes. "Arra Shannin. Taven's friend from that dream realm he visits."

"The Aethereum," Tavesin corrected him. "Where is she?"

"They took her to the kitchens for a meal. If we hurry, she may still be there." Badolo flashed another grin. "She *asked* for you, Taven."

Rostin snickered, and Tavesin felt his face flush. He wasn't certain what he felt for Arra, but the others clearly believed there was more between them than mere friendship. Arra was opinionated, brazen, and commanding at times, but she had a ready smile and an openness about her that drew him. The result left him flustered and often tongue-tied. Perhaps his friends would better understand his current predicament once they met her.

The trio dashed through corridors and sprinted headlong down the stairs. They darted around those who chose to move more slowly, drawing curses and irritated glances. Tavesin was giddy with the knowledge of Arra's arrival, while his friends were eager to satisfy their own curiosity. Every moment spent wandering the tower were moments lost to their first true conversation, and this thought pushed Tavesin to ever greater speeds. Rostin and Badolo careened through the halls behind him, laughing while they received sharp looks and scowls from the older denizens of the tower.

They reached the kitchens to find many of the tables occupied. Tavesin ignored the growing queue for supper and scanned the premises eagerly, seeking the familiar red hair that would indicate Arra's presence. He spied her at a table near the center of the room, surrounded by a trio of adults. They spoke while she picked at her plate of food, her eyes downcast, her expression one of discomfort.

Tavesin bounded away from his friends and wound his way toward her. Rostin and Badolo were quick to follow his lead.

"Arra!" he called loudly as they neared, unable to keep the grin from his face.

She looked up, startled, but quickly found him in the crowd. Her face lit up with a beaming smile, and she brushed her long hair away from her eyes. The wizards that accompanied her glanced at him briefly before they continued their conversation.

"Arra," he said again as they stopped alongside her table. "Um, I'm Taven. Tavesin. But you know that..." He trailed off, flustered, his cheeks inflamed. He could not understand why it became so difficult for him to speak when she was near.

She laughed, bemused. "Yes, I know who you are, but your friends...?"

Tavesin's flush deepened as Rostin nudged him with an elbow. "This is Rostin. He came to the tower the same time I did. And Badolo is new, like you. We met a few days past."

Rostin extended his hand in greeting, and Arra shook it. "Taven can't keep quiet about you," he informed her with a smirk.

A light blush arose on her cheeks at Rostin's jibe, and she shook her head. "I suppose not, given how we met. The wizards have told me the talent for Aethereal magic is rare." She turned her attention upon Tavesin and offered him a smile. "I must thank you for keeping your end of the bargain. If not for you, I'd be wasting away in the Marshwood until my mother deemed it time for me to marry. Now, perhaps, I'll have a bit of adventure instead."

Rostin snorted. "You'll have to pass your trials first. The tower makes certain we have our fill of lessons long before we're allowed to taste adventure." He eyed Tavesin pointedly. "Unless, of course, you happen to be Tavesin Drondes. First, he wanders into the Aethereum untrained, then he meets a Drakkon mage, and now he's found you!"

"I didn't find her," Tavesin mumbled, his words nearly inaudible as he struggled with his embarrassment.

"That's true," Arra replied with a quick grin. "He didn't find me. *I* found *him*."

Beside her, the wizards began to rise from their seats, and one motioned to Arra impatiently. Her smile faltered and she sighed.

"I'm to meet with the Radiant this evening," she explained. "It's to do with my training in Aethereal magic."

"The Drakkon are teaching me," Tavesin blurted.

"I know. They may be teaching me, as well." She beamed at him. "Perhaps we'll be learning together?"

He bobbed his head and grinned foolishly in spite of himself. "I hope so."

"I'm certain we'll see each other again, Taven," she said, then glanced at the wizards. "I'd best go."

He watched her leave, following her progress through the crowded kitchens with his eyes until she disappeared into the corridor.

"Badolo, my friend, it seems Tavesin has been stricken by love," Rostin said with a dramatic flair. "He may be lost to us."

Badolo cackled in response. "He may be content to moon after her, but I am famished. We should take servings before the staff closes the line."

"I'm not in love," Tavesin replied defensively, "and I'd like supper, too. Arra's my friend, nothing more."

He followed the others toward the dwindling queue but could not tear his thoughts away from Arra Shannin. He was only fourteen; he knew little of romance and even less about women. He believed Rostin's teasing was unfounded, but each time he spoke to her, he became flustered. His reaction to her mere presence was a thing of mystery to him, but love? His father would have told him he was too young to fall in love, while his mother would have said he would understand once he was older. Neither were present to guide him, however, and he must learn to tread his own path.

"I'm not in love," he repeated stubbornly, which elicited another snicker from Rostin in response.

CHAPTER TWENTY-NINE

FINAL PREPARATIONS

Dranamir scanned the note a second time before she tossed it carelessly into the hearth near her bedside. Kama wished to speak with her privately. She was surprised it had taken him this long to make the request; he'd made his intentions toward her clear from the start. She wondered how long she could draw out his desires before he attempted to force himself upon her. The attempt would be futile, of course, for there was no man alive who could pose a challenge to her power.

Except for *him*. She scowled and shoved all thoughts of Ravin from her mind. His was a problem for another day.

Kama suggested she meet him in his command tent at the center of the Murkor encampment at midday, when the army would be inactive. She smirked; Kama did not fully understand what he was playing at. No one met willingly with Dranamir in private.

Fortunately for him, torture was not on her mind at present. Perhaps she could twist his unconcealed lust into something useful to her own ends, but toying with a man's emotions was not part of her skillset. That was Alyra's tactic of choice, but one Dranamir strove to avoid. Inflicting pain yielded better results, with fewer complications.

She went about her morning as planned and set aside the implications within Kama's note. She would deal with him once the time of the proposed rendezvous arrived. She spent several hours with a handful of new recruits who possessed an aptitude for combat magic. They must learn all they were able, and as quickly as possible, in order to satisfy her Master's needs.

Among those she'd chosen to train was the Murkor anomaly. She continued to be astounded by his magical prowess and knew that given time, he would grow to rival the Soulless in power. She was especially hard on him for that reason alone. He was the first of his people to show the spark of Ability, and he must be prepared to face the severe odds stacked against him. If he managed to survive his training and subsequent initiation into the Council, he would become a formidable opponent.

The others in her lesson were human and seemed relieved her attention was fixed upon the unfortunate Murkor. Before she departed, however, she made it clear that none were exempt from her wrath if they failed to accomplish their tasks. All left battered and bloodied, though she'd restrained herself. In times past, she would have eliminated the weakest of their number without a second thought, but the Master had impressed upon them that no unnecessary casualties must be taken. She would obey, so long as the recruits remembered their place and continued to cower before her.

As the sun neared its zenith, she entered her private quarters and opened a portal into the Aethereum. She transported herself to the center of the Murkor encampment and spied a pair of large tents nearby. One belonged to Kama, the other to the Murkors' sullen commander.

She scanned her surroundings briefly to ensure she had not been followed—and that the telltale signature of Ravin's presence was not in the vicinity. Garin had provided no updates on his progress with the man, and she would not be caught unaware while traversing his realm. Unlike other wielders of magic, Ravin's power was amplified within the Aethereum. It made him an even greater threat to those who lingered, particularly those he despised. She exited to the physical world quickly, relieved to emerge undetected.

Her fear of Ravin ignited her fury. Her previous indecision regarding Kama vanished; she would unleash her rage upon him if he attempted anything more than mere discussion. It would be to his benefit if he sensed her current mood, but if he did not, he would learn to prepare himself better in the future. She was not a woman to be trifled with.

She focused her senses and detected Kama within the further large tent. The Murkor camp was quiet, though she spied a few hooded sentries on patrol near the perimeter. Most of the soldiers would be asleep at this time, given theirs was a nocturnal people who struggled with the heat and brightness of the sun. Had she been one of the others, perhaps she would have felt pity for those tasked with patrol, but she was not and felt little more than cold detachment.

She strode into Kama's tent unannounced to find him standing over a wide table littered with documents. A map was spread out before him, marked with several pins. He looked up at her entrance, crimson eyes gleaming with curiosity, though his expression remained neutral. She'd been hoping for a smile, a leer, anything to justify lashing out to assuage her anger, but he yielded nothing. Perhaps he was more intelligent than she'd given him credit for.

"Dranamir," he said by way of greeting.

"Kama. Why have you asked to meet with me?"

"I have a proposition, of sorts."

He gestured to the map and she made her way to the table in order to see it properly. It depicted Balotica Kingdom. She noted a cluster of pins had been placed around one of the vast lakes, Jennavere, and the city of the same name.

"I assume this is the location you plan to attack first," she said. She tapped a fingernail against the city's location.

"Yes. I've asked Jannyn and Garin here, as well. They should be arriving soon." He glanced toward the tent's flap briefly. "I've come to understand that you rarely help others willingly, even amongst our own kind. I require your help to move the army."

He pointed to an unmarked valley some miles south and east of Jennavere.

"And in return?" she pressed.

"I have spoken with Aran'daj, and he has agreed to signal you when the time is right for true devastation to begin," Kama replied. A knowing smile crept across his angular features. "I am granting you the opportunity to unleash your particular brand of destruction upon the city."

She grinned savagely. Perhaps Kama understood her needs better than she'd anticipated. "The Baloticans will rue this decision, Kama. I approve."

"Then you will help transport the army?"

"Yes. But know this: If you rescind our agreement, you will curse the day you first drew breath. The Master may have forbidden me to kill any of you, but he said nothing of torture."

He chuckled mirthlessly. "You will find I am a man of my word, so long as you uphold your end of our bargain, Dranamir. Like you, I do not tolerate betrayal." He crossed his arms and studied her. "I am aware you spoke with the Murkor leaders and secured the relics. I would like to believe I can trust you, but given your history…"

"You're not up to the challenge of opposing me," she replied with a smirk, "but I have agreed to your terms."

Kama's expression was impassive. "I have resources you are unaware of, but think what you will, Dranamir."

She folded her arms, exuding skepticism. She doubted Kama had the means to carry out his threat, and his refusal to be intimidated by her was strangely titillating. She was unused to harboring such thoughts about any man, but Kama intrigued her. He was different from the others, unafraid, ruthless.

Behind her, the tent flap opened to reveal Garin's diminutive frame while Jannyn's stout figure loomed behind him. Garin's face was twisted with irritation, while Jannyn wore a glower.

"I will not apologize for the delay, though we would have been here sooner had my counterpart not spent a quarter-hour mooning over Alyra." Garin shot a venomous glare in Jannyn's direction.

"She promised she'd make another Aethereal relic for my use," Jannyn explained with an exasperated sigh. "The other is lost, and without it, I'm fucking useless."

Dranamir smirked. "You were useless before it vanished."

"Heartless bitch," he growled.

She sensed him seize his power, but before she was able to react, Kama struck. Jannyn staggered as a wave of energy slammed into him. Kama stormed across the tent, his face a mask of raw hatred. He stopped to loom over the shorter man, his crimson eyes ablaze as he began to rend gashes across Jannyn's torso. Jannyn's grasp on his power faltered under the severity of the assault. He moaned and fell to his knees. Blood seeped through his clothing and began to spatter the tent's canvas floor.

Dranamir watched with interest as the scene unfolded. She admired Kama's deft use of power. He was not as strong as Garin, but Jannyn was no match for him.

Garin appeared bored, and after several moments he stepped between the two. "Enough, both of you." He peered up at Kama with obvious distaste. "I brought Jannyn here since you requested our presence. If this was yet another scheme of *hers*—" he stared daggers at Dranamir, "—our master will hear of it."

Dranamir laughed. "I'm flattered you believe I'd lure the pair of you here simply to remove Jannyn from our ranks. He may be useless, but I have no quarrel with him."

"I asked you here because I must move the army," Kama replied. His smoldering gaze was fixed on Jannyn's cowering form. "I require assistance. I will not allow his foul temper to further hinder our progress."

Garin studied the two men, then nodded once as though satisfied. "Very well. You will have my aid, but I cannot speak for Jannyn."

Jannyn glowered at him. "You stand aside while this bastard assaults me, then simply go along with his demands?"

"You drew on your power first," Garin pointed out. "If you cannot learn to ignore Dranamir's words, however barbed they may be, your fate is of your own making." Abruptly, he knelt at Jannyn's side. "I will heal your injuries, and then, perhaps, we can get on with this business."

Jannyn swallowed his outrage and allowed Garin to tend his wounds. His baleful eyes found their way to Dranamir's, and she knew the matter was not finished. If the fool believed himself capable of catching her unawares, let him. She hadn't gained her position by being careless or merciful.

"As recompense for assisting me, I offer you the chance to join the battle," Kama declared to the others.

Jannyn tore his eyes away from Dranamir to leer up at Kama. "And I suppose *she* has already accepted your offer."

"Yes."

"I'll not be left behind, and I mean to prove I am capable," Jannyn replied, his voice a low growl. "I will prove you wrong,

Dranamir. The master has chosen me for a reason. Wreaking havoc is in my blood. There is a reason I was once named The Butcher."

"Very well. Prove me wrong," she challenged. "I doubt your body count can compare to my own."

Garin stood, finished with his ministrations, and looked about the tent with disgust. "I will help move the army, Kama, but I've no interest in the battle. It seems it has already devolved into a competition of egos, and it hasn't yet begun."

Kama shrugged. "I will inform the commander to break camp and prepare to march."

As he turned to leave, Dranamir decided it was time to unveil her own secret to the men. "I have acquired an ally of my own to assist with the attack."

Kama paused mid-stride and turned to peer at her suspiciously. "Why did you not inform me sooner?"

"It wasn't important, previously," she replied with a smile that failed to reach her eyes. "During my exploration of the mines, I encountered a powerful sea serpent in the depths. I have convinced him to assist us."

Jannyn snorted in contempt. "I'm certain you did."

Kama ignored the other man and nodded thoughtfully. "I will inform the commander. After the army has been relocated, we shall discuss our new ally's role further." His gaze lingered on her, his interest renewed. "You continue to surprise me, Dranamir."

Jannyn snickered. "Some of the histories refer to her as The Man-Flayer, you know. She killed most of her male rivals and numerous commanders who failed to live up to her standards."

"Your point?" Kama asked.

"You're better off attempting to woo our master than her," Jannyn replied. "But if you insist on traversing this path, don't say no one warned you of the consequences."

Dranamir did not contradict his words; he spoke the truth. She met Kama's heated gaze with a cool one of her own. "As I said, Jannyn's body count cannot rival my own."

"Then I'll be certain I won't displease you."

He smiled wolfishly before exiting the tent. It was a rarity that Dranamir could think of nothing to say in response. She despised the awkward heat that settled over her body and once more, wished she could find a reason to unleash her anger upon Kama. Rage was a simple emotion, pure, without the subtle undercurrents of desire. The feeling did not suit her, and something must be done to quash it before it grew into something far more distasteful.

She was impressed by the speed in which the Murkor disbanded the encampment. The black hooded commander had issued the order only moments after his conversation with Kama concluded, and by late afternoon, the Murkor were ready to depart. Dranamir took her place on the western edge of the gathered army and prepared to link her power with the others'.

Kama had taken a position on the northern edge, while Garin went to the south, the side nearest to the chasm's edge. That left Jannyn to take up the eastern point, far enough across the sea of black hoods that she could not make out his stout form. It was just as well; he'd already chosen to side with Alyra, and she found him tiresome. Likewise, Garin's small form was concealed beyond the press of bodies, though she could sense his distinct energy signature clearly enough. His was entwined more closely with their master's than anyone else could boast. It gave him an air of foreboding that unnerved her when she focused upon it. She was reminded once more that Garin was not a man to be dismissed lightly.

Kama was to initiate the linkage, and she sensed his tentative probing moments after she was in position. When she accepted it, she was immediately inundated by his essence. He hadn't linked with the others yet, but had sought her out first. She was unsurprised, given their previous encounters, though she hadn't anticipated the raw lust she glimpsed in his mind. He'd done well to conceal its magnitude thus far, but the linkage revealed its every perverse facet as he struggled to adjust. It was clear he'd never attempted to link with another previously, or he would have learned to shield his thoughts.

I need a moment. His thought came to her through the link, and she laughed aloud. The sound drew the attention of several nearby Murkor, but she ignored their stares.

I'd say you require more than that, Kama, she sent back, amused, before she mentally issued him the proper instructions on shielding.

The effect was immediate; she was relieved when his lascivious mind was once more clouded from her inner sight.

I must apologize, Dranamir. That was not what I'd intended.

She smirked. *Don't allow it to happen again. Link with the others before Garin grows impatient.*

Momentarily, she sensed Garin's malignant presence join theirs. He was adept at shielding his thoughts. It was disappointing; she'd been particularly interested in learning more about the small, dour man's past.

I don't appreciate your attempted invasion of my thoughts, Dranamir. He sent in a tone laced with venom. *Pry elsewhere.*

Her attention was diverted as Jannyn joined the linkage. He, too, failed to shield himself properly, and she was momentarily consumed by his fantasy of dismembering her splayed corpse. Rather than instruct him as she had Kama, she waited for one of the others to take pity on the fool.

Given the opportunity, I will do far worse to you, Jannyn, she sent, injecting venom into her words. *Learn to conceal yourself, or I'll end your pathetic existence now.*

The images stopped, and Jannyn sent a wave of dark laughter through their linkage. *I know how to shield myself, Dranamir; I'm not a gods-damned novice. I thought you'd enjoy my musings.*

She scowled, and the nearest Murkor soldier stepped back, startled. She ignored him and closed her eyes. *Your musings are the work of an amateur. Perhaps when we arrive in Jennavere, I'll have the opportunity to show you the artistry employed by a master.*

Enough, Garin growled. A foul undercurrent vibrated through the link with his word. *We have a task to complete.*

Kama sent a mental image of the location he wished to transport the army to; together they summoned the necessary energy. She sensed a whirlwind whip around them while the sunlight overhead flickered and grew pale. The Murkor shouted in surprise and some attempted to back away from the magical maelstrom that enveloped them. Moments later, she sensed their surroundings had changed, and the energy quickly dissipated.

When she opened her eyes, the sky above was overcast, and thick mats of grass grew beneath her feet. Steep mountains rose to the northeast and southwest, their sides adorned with dark boulders and tall pines. They were nestled at the heart of a broad valley with a clear stream burbling along to the south.

It has been many years since I last set foot in Balotica, Garin sent, his tone strangely wistful.

I hope you're not homesick, Jannyn sent maliciously.

We are finished here, Kama cut in before he severed the link with all three of them at once.

Dranamir stepped aside as the Murkor began to form ranks at the behest of their commander. He was taller than most of his brethren and sported a curved saber at his hip, the only indication of his rank. Another joined him, and she recalled mention of the Arms Master's role in the Murkor army. She could remember the name of neither, but deemed it unimportant.

After a time, the others joined her. Garin led Jannyn away after a brief statement of his intentions. They would return to the tower, and await further word from Kama, or their master. Dranamir lingered after the pair departed, eager to discuss Kama's plans for Scherok.

"You're certain this serpent will obey?" he asked of her.

"I made it very clear what it risks if it does not. I do not mince words."

"Transport him to the lake, but order him to remain hidden until he is signaled," Kama instructed. "I can assist you. The linkage did not drain me as much as I feared it would."

"And moving the army took little of my own reserves," she countered. "I will take him myself."

He nodded reluctantly, unable to hide the longing in his eyes. She smirked in response.

"Jannyn spoke true, you know. I've killed hundreds of men, and I have no reason to change. You will not be exempt from my tally should you cross me."

CHAPTER THIRTY

THE SKY PALACE

"Apparently 'on the morrow' means anytime between dawn and midnight," Maryn grumbled as he paced.

Vardak had taken the opportunity to clean and polish his armor yet again while they awaited Solsticia's return. He sat just beyond the temple's broad dome while Maryn paced across the stone path not far away. The Felene's tail lashed in agitation. The afternoon was drawing toward evening, and there had been no further sign from the celestial goddess other than the replenishment of the food and drink she'd provided them with the previous day.

"The gods do not operate on the same schedule as we mortals," Vardak replied, focused on his task.

"I suppose you would know better than I."

Maryn paused mid-stride and grew suddenly still. Vardak looked up, sensing the change in his demeanor. The Felene's ears were pricked forward, his body tensed as though ready to spring.

"Maryn?" he asked in a low tone.

Maryn's tail twitched in response, but he remained still for several moments before making his reply. "Someone is coming," he hissed over his shoulder. "The women are still inside, yes?"

"Yes."

Vardak set the armor aside carefully, hoping to avoid making unnecessary noise. He rose silently and moved to the nearest column where he'd left his axe propped, then quickly removed its leather sheath. If the newcomer proved hostile, he did not have time to don his armor, but he would face them armed at the very least.

He joined Maryn on the path, and the pair effectively blocked the entrance to the temple's dome. Maryn had drawn a pair of long knives, though where the guardsman kept them on his person, Vardak wasn't certain.

"The steps sound bipedal," Maryn whispered. "None of my people venture here."

Vardak frowned and focused his attention on the path before them. Maryn had mentioned there were humans beyond the jungle's perimeter, but to encounter one here, in its treacherous heart, was unlikely. It left them with the prospect of an unwanted encounter with one of the gods, or the equally unlikely chance the intruder was the other Airess. Coreyaless believed the concoction they'd seen along the path through the Living Forest could not have been made by anyone but him, yet Vardak harbored doubts. There had been centuries in which Danness could have taught the recipe to the Felene people, and he felt her yearning to reunite with him clouded her perceptions.

Presently, the steps grew near enough that Vardak heard their approach. He entered a defensive stance and held his axe at the ready. They would not be taken unawares.

"Whoever it is must not know we're here." Maryn aimed one of his daggers at the bend in the path as he prepared to throw. "Shall I warn them off?"

Vardak shook his head. "Not yet." He wanted to be certain of the intruder's identity before they acted.

Maryn nodded in agreement but remained poised to strike, balanced gracefully on the balls of his feet. The footsteps continued their steady approach while the pair waited for the owner to appear. Insects continued to buzz around them and birds called overhead; the newcomer was not seen as a threat to the denizens of the jungle. Vardak resisted the urge to relax and instead held his ground.

"Identify yourself," Maryn called as a figure appeared around the bend in the path.

Vardak heard movement behind them but did not turn to see which of his companions had exited the temple. His focus was upon their visitor—a tall, bipedal person swathed in shades of green that blended in with the surrounding foliage. He could make out few other details from a distance, though he believed it was a man.

There was a sharp intake of breath from the edge of the dome. "By the gods, it cannot be!"

Coreyaless' words reverberated through the air, and in an instant, Vardak understood who the newcomer must be. He lowered his axe and glanced over his shoulder. The Airess' gray eyes were wide and brimmed with tears. She had lifted one slender hand to cover her mouth in an attempt to hide her shock. Beside him, Maryn sheathed his knives. He tucked them deftly beneath the sleeves of his leather armor. The visitor continued his approach, eyes riveted on Coreyaless.

As he drew near, Vardak noted with some surprise that he stood at eye-level with the man. Outside of his own people, he'd learned few stood as tall as he. Their visitor sported a sturdy frame, honed from years of trekking through the jungle and cutting away the dense undergrowth. Like Coreyaless, his hair was ash-blond, though he kept it cropped short. His eyes were dark brown, his wings a lustrous green that matched his clothing and the flora around them, a natural camouflage.

He glanced at Maryn briefly as he passed and studied Vardak for scarcely longer before his eyes returned to the woman standing beneath the lip of the dome. "Coreyaless?" His voice trembled.

Coreyaless remained motionless for several long seconds, her eyes wide with disbelief. Slowly, as though awakening from a deep slumber, she dropped her hand and broke into a sprint. She covered the distance between the dome and her partner in an eye-blink and came to an abrupt halt a hair's breadth away from him. She stared up at him, as though unable to comprehend his presence before her.

Gently, he touched the side of her face. "Please tell me I am not dreaming, that the gods have finally decided to put an end to our curse."

"I'm here," she replied in a choked whisper.

Vardak glanced toward Maryn. "We ought to give them a moment alone."

Maryn grinned knowingly. "Agreed."

They made their way past the pair of Airess and toward the temple's dome. Before they entered, however, another voice spoke up behind him.

"Ah, such a blissful reunion."

He spun around, alerted by the ice he heard in the other's tone. An impossibly tall woman stood not far from the Airess, her dark hair bound in a multitude of braids. Her eyes glinted silver in the afternoon light, illuminated from within. She wore a form-fitting gown of crimson silk, and when she gestured toward the pair, she did so with three right arms. Her dark lips formed a smile, but the remainder of her face was expressionless.

Vardak gaped at the newcomer. He'd seen artist's renderings of the goddess Karmada, and a small statue in her likeness adorned the foyer to Blademon's temple in his desert homeland, but to behold her compassionless countenance left him with a distinct sense of unease. Karmada was the goddess of luck, chance, and risk-takers; revered by some, feared by many. It was said that each gift she granted a mortal was accompanied by a dire price. Most were unwilling to pay for her favors. In rare cases, she was known to bestow gifts without consulting the affected mortals first, as was the case for the Airess, yet she remained merciless when it came to obtaining her desired payment.

Coreyaless straightened and pulled away from Danness' embrace. Her eyes narrowed as they landed upon the goddess. "Karmada," she seethed.

"When Flariel informed me of your travels southward, I deemed it time," Karmada replied, unperturbed by Coreyaless' hostility. "With your reunion comes true life once more. A thousand years apart was sufficient payment for my role in your survival."

"We did not ask for your blighted interference!" Coreyaless shouted while Danness growled something that Vardak was unable to hear.

"You would rather have died with the rest of your people?" Karmada asked coolly. "The Airess would have been lost to history, much as those you call the builders were. I saved your people."

"There are but two of us," Danness replied. "If you meant to save the Airess, you would have spared others from the plague as well."

Karmada crossed her many arms and looked down her nose at him. "You are a male and a female in love. Nothing more is required to save a species, and I could do no more at the time. The one you call Nameless was too dangerous, and even I could not afford the risk."

She lifted her otherworldly gaze to study Vardak and Maryn before she returned it to the Airess before her. "I know of your errand. I suggest the pair of you lend what aid you can to the coming fight, for war is coming and Blademon's protégé cannot stem the tide alone." She smirked at Vardak. "Or shall I say, protégés? Perhaps I will smile upon one of you when the time comes."

Karmada faded from sight, her laughter ringing in their ears.

Vardak scowled and moved to retrieve his armor from where he'd left it, oblivious to the strange looks he received from the others. Coreyaless hadn't been present to overhear Solsticia the previous day, Danness was unaware of their objective, and Maryn simply appeared discomfited by the encounter. Given what he knew of the Airess' dealings with Karmada, he prayed she kept her unwarranted smiles to herself.

Vardak found himself dozing not far from the altar several hours later. Maryn had taken over the watch just before midnight, though neither man was certain of its necessity. The temple grounds had proven safe, a veritable sanctuary from the jungle beyond. Janna slept fitfully on the ground several paces from his location while the Airess huddled near the entrance, talking quietly amongst themselves. Vardak nodded off to the sound of their distant murmurs, the knowledge that Solsticia had failed to make good on her promise forefront in his mind.

It was sometime later when he was awakened by Maryn. The Felene had the sense to speak his name rather than attempt to shake him from slumber; Vardak often reacted defensively when startled from his dreams. He blinked, his eyes bleary for several moments before they focused.

"She's come," Maryn whispered. He nodded toward the altar with an irritated frown.

Vardak turned to look in the direction indicated. Solsticia's peered at him from within the obsidian mirror, unconcealed interest in her golden eyes. Janna remained asleep, curled in her cloak at the base of the altar. He did not immediately locate the Airess.

"We should wake the others."

Maryn shook his head. "She asked to speak with you first. I'm not certain what you did to garner the attention of so many gods, but I don't envy you. I'll be at the door until you've finished."

Vardak nodded as Maryn strode away. He wasn't certain of what he'd done either, and he was growing weary of the Immortals' interference. First Blademon and Flariel, now Solsticia and Karmada. He grimaced and rose to his feet, then made his way silently toward the celestial goddess within the mirror.

Vardak made no attempt to hide his scowl as he faced her. "You wished to speak with me?" He kept his voice low with the hope he would not disturb Janna.

"Yes. Blademon asked that I provide you with an update regarding your brothers."

"Travin, is he——?"

A slow smile crept across her face. "Travin is resilient, Vardak. He and the others have been treated well enough, though none are pleased with their situation. The Murkor have not harmed them, but they are prisoners. I'm certain you understand what that entails."

Vardak looked away and nodded tersely. The Murkor alchemists coveted his people's natural venom; it was a key ingredient in the production of the black metal they used to forge their weapons. He imagined his burly brother chained in the depths of the caverns, forced to endure the shame of daily milking at the hands of his enemies.

"We need to acquire this damned relic so that I can return to my people." He crossed his arms and refused to make eye-contact. The gods had toyed with him long enough and he no longer wished to be a party to their games.

"I will return you to the Stronghold once your journey is complete, Vardak."

He looked up, his expression unyielding. "I will hold you to your word."

She chuckled, amused. "You may try, but you are only mortal." She waved her hand dismissively as though his words were irrelevant. "Nevertheless, I will keep my promise to you, Vardak. I do not believe our interference in your lives is as necessary as some of my siblings deem it to be."

"And Patak?" he pressed.

"Patak is recovering," she replied. "Now, I believe it is time for you to rouse the others. We have much to discuss, and this setting is less than ideal."

His frown deepened. "What do you mean?"

256

"Exactly what I said. We will speak once the others have awakened."

He swallowed his rising anger and bent over Janna. She appeared younger than her twenty years, her face at peace as she slept. He was loath to interrupt her respite from the world, but with Solsticia eyeing him only paces away, he reluctantly reached down to gently shake her shoulder. Janna made a face and sat up, stifling a yawn.

"Vardak, what's wrong?"

He shook his head and pointed toward the goddess framed in the mirror. It was best he keep his misgivings to himself while within earshot of Solsticia.

"Oh! She's returned." Janna smiled brightly. "Perhaps now we can be done with this business of my mother's."

As he turned to seek Maryn, he noted the Felene had roused the Airess and the trio were walking toward him. He nodded a silent thanks to Maryn and moved to stand alongside Janna.

Solsticia observed them impassively for several seconds before she spoke again. "I will give you a few moments to gather your belongings. I must speak with you, but not here."

"But the Moon's Eye—" Janna began.

"The relic you seek does not reside within my temple, but I am its keeper. We shall travel to my home, and its whereabouts will be revealed to you." Solsticia studied them each in turn as her golden eyes scrutinized their every move.

Vardak met her gaze with a steely one of his own. It was typical of the gods to send them on a fool's errand, only to learn another of their member kept the prize safely hidden. He was over and done with their meddling.

"Flariel has much to answer for."

Solsticia smiled knowingly. "Flariel does not concern herself with such matters, Vardak. She believes this errand will strengthen her daughter's character. Who am I to argue with her? I have catered to the needs of my own mortal child when necessary."

Vardak shook his head in irritation and stalked away to retrieve his armor and battle axe. The gods would never understand the root of his frustration.

When he returned to the altar, Janna was sobbing while Coreyaless attempted to console her. Vardak shot another disapproving frown at Solsticia, certain she was the cause of Janna's distress. Once again, the gods failed to realize the impact of their actions upon those they deemed lesser. It required every ounce of his resolve to refrain from striking at Solsticia's mirror in his rage. She was his means of returning home, he reminded himself. Angering her further would only complicate matters.

"I will transport you to the Sky Palace now," Solsticia informed them, and without waiting for a response, a blinding white light enveloped them.

Vardak experienced the same falling sensation he had when Flariel transported them to the jungle. He grimaced and braced himself for the impact he was certain was in store. After several long moments he realized he stood upright and unscathed. Slowly, he opened his eyes.

He and the others stood in a vast, open-air courtyard ringed by tall, stone arches. Above was a vast expanse of dark sky, sparkling with thousands upon thousands of stars that glittered more brightly than any he'd encountered before. The courtyard itself was bare stone, smooth and polished to a reflective sheen.

Solsticia stood at the center of the courtyard upon an oval of obsidian much like the one hanging above the altar in her temple. Though she was human in form, she stood much taller than her mortal counterparts. She wore a gown of midnight blue, embellished with embroidered golden stars the same shade as her incandescent eyes.

"Welcome to the Sky Palace. Few mortals have been granted the pleasure of visiting here." Solsticia beckoned for them to follow her as she led them toward the nearest stone arch.

"I'd rather not be granted any 'pleasure' by the gods," Maryn muttered darkly as he fell in beside Vardak. "This damned business sets my fur to itching."

Vardak raised his eyebrows, unable to imagine such a sensation. "I'm not pleased by this turn, either."

Solsticia led them through a series of stone corridors and abruptly stopped before a closed door.

"Beyond this door lies the relic you seek, but before you rush inside to remove it from its ages-long resting place, know this: Only a mortal may take hold of the Moon's Eye, but in so doing, their life will be forfeit." Solsticia's gaze raked across each of them in turn.

Vardak looked down, unable to hide his dismay. Flariel had insisted he accompany her daughter on the pretense that Janna must be protected. Had the Fire Maiden orchestrated his coming here to take the relic for Janna, and end his life in the process? He could not believe Blademon would wish him dead, but the Master of War had sent him along at Flariel's behest. His thoughts reeled, and it took him several moments to refocus on Solsticia's next words.

"The relic's maker believed it too powerful and cursed its very creation. I have been its keeper since the time when the Thirteenth retained his name. If your need is great enough, the Moon's Eye will be yours—if you are willing to make the required sacrifice."

CHAPTER THIRTY-ONE

A MIDNIGHT MARCH

At one hour past midnight, Aran'daj signaled the Murkor army to begin their march. He moved at the head of the column with Jal'den on his right and the tall, angular Soulless known as Kama on his left. He prayed to the gods for forgiveness of his future acts, but he could see no way around his present course. The Soulless had made it clear that insubordination on his part would result in the massacre of his people left behind in the caverns. The deaths of human strangers would weigh less upon his conscience than the slaughter of the Murkor people.

The soldiers marched soundlessly through the night, the drummers silent until called upon. For his plan to work as intended, their initial strike must take the humans by surprise. The Soulless had informed him the city of Jennavere was heavily defended; it was the easternmost city in the kingdom, and the monarch had wasted no time in deploying soldiers to his borders once word arrived of Shan'tar's threat. Aran'daj did not know if the Baloticans knew the Soulless were now in command, but he'd prepared his strategy on the assumption they did.

Beyond the army, the world was quiet, the air cool and crisp. A thin crescent moon hung overhead, shrouded in an iridescent halo of thin cloud. The silence was broken only by the occasional hooting call of an owl overhead. The darkened landscape slid by unchanging for some time; tall pines stood sentinel along their path, interspersed with boulders and the rare grove of white aspen. They encountered none of the locals, but he had chosen their path carefully for that reason. He meant to save the army's might for the true fight at Jennavere.

After two hours, he spied pinpricks of torchlight in the distance. By his calculation, they had another hour before the army would reach the outskirts of the city. He sent a pair of scouts ahead to confirm his supposition that the lights belonged to a rural farmstead.

"You will leave no survivors, Commander."

Kama's tone was unyielding, but mercifully he spoke in the common tongue. Most of the nearby soldiers would not understand their exchange, save for Jal'den, whom Aran'daj trusted would keep matters to himself.

"In the past, we were granted the right to take the able-bodied prisoners to bolster our workforce," Aran'daj replied evenly. He hoped the Soulless would see reason; he did not wish to kill innocents, particularly those unable to defend themselves. Laboring in the caverns was difficult work, but their lives would be spared if the Soulless consented.

"Hmm." Kama crossed his arms and frowned thoughtfully. "Your people have cooperated thus far. You may take only those who do not attempt to oppose us. All others must be killed."

Aran'daj nodded his thanks and focused on the path ahead. It was a minor victory, but one he would silently relish. He believed his people would treat prisoners fairly in exchange for their servitude. If he was allowed to return to the caverns, he would speak with the Kal and ensure it was so.

The scouts returned promptly and confirmed his suspicion. A large farmstead lay directly in their path, and several others beyond it. The scouts reported the farmhands were soundly asleep, and many of the animals, as well.

Aran'daj glanced warily at Kama. "We will take them prisoner before they awaken and keep the livestock to feed the men as we journey."

Kama's hard, crimson eyes met his with unspoken challenge. "If they resist, your men will dispatch them without question. If they fail to carry out my order—my *master's* order—they will share the humans' fate."

Aran'daj bobbed his hooded head once in acknowledgment. He feared his voice would betray his displeasure or reveal his intentions, and he said nothing in response. To his relief, Kama appeared content with his nonverbal assent and focused his attention elsewhere.

Aran'daj signaled the army to resume its march while Jal'den issued Kama's heartless orders in a rapid-fire manner. Aran'daj sensed the young Arms Master's displeasure but could do nothing to alleviate it. The Murkor would obey to save themselves from the Soulless' wrath.

As they neared the first farmstead, Aran'daj detected movement within the main house. He drew his saber and stood alongside Kama as a select group of soldiers burst into the structure. Shouts and screams accompanied their intrusion, but within moments seven humans were dragged from within, their hands bound securely behind them. They were marched before Aran'daj and Kama for inspection.

Kama stepped forward to leer at the captives. Wisely, they remained silent as they cowered; Aran'daj suspected if they had spoken, the Soulless would have killed them instantly. Aran'daj studied each in turn and wished he could spare them all from Kama's bloodlust. There were two who were clearly unsuited to the proposed labor that would save the others. One was an elderly man, his body frail and spotted with age. The other was a small child. He prayed the gods would intervene to spare one or both from Kama's cruelty, but he feared his plea would remain unanswered. The gods were unlikely to interfere in what they deemed mortal affairs.

Kama focused on the elder first. "I have granted the commander leave to send worthwhile prisoners to his people's homeland. You do not appear fit for the task."

One of his companions, a woman, released a terrified sob and fell to her knees. The man glanced toward her and shook his head sadly, an exchange Aran'daj understood was meant to quiet her. "Perhaps not, but I am—"

Kama made a sweeping motion with his arm, and the man fell over, blood spurting from his nose and ears. "You are useless," Kama spat at the corpse. "Take the others to the alchemists."

Aran'daj managed a weak smile beneath his hood. The Soulless seemed to have missed the child amongst the others; perhaps one of the gods had heard his anguished prayer after all.

They marched on, taking several other farms along the way. At one, they were met with a trio of burly farmhands who bore scythes and pitchforks in a futile attempt to defend their home. The soldiers carried out their orders without question while Kama set fire to the structures around them. Several screams issued into the pre-dawn air as unnatural flame engulfed the home. Aran'daj hardened his heart and looked on while Kama chuckled grimly nearby.

As the screams reached a fever-pitch, a blue-white oval appeared only paces away from Kama's location. Aran'daj watched with dismay as two more Soulless joined them; a stocky man and the cruel-eyed woman responsible for Shan'tar's death.

"It seems you've begun without us," she said with a frown.

"There will be plenty of destruction awaiting you in Jennavere, Dranamir," Kama replied. "The commander will signal us when it is time."

Aran'daj suppressed a shudder as her cold eyes scrutinized him.

"The commander had best keep his word, Kama. I have no tolerance for those who would thwart me." She crossed her arms and smirked. She seemed to enjoy Aran'daj's obvious discomfort.

"He has proven himself thus far, Dranamir." Kama chuckled mirthlessly. "Your threats only serve as a reminder of his loyalties."

The Murkor arrived on the outskirts of Jennavere as the sky began lightening toward dawn. Aran'daj surveyed the walled city for a time, comparing the reality to the hand-drawn maps he'd studied. All seemed as anticipated, and he began to issue commands. The trio of Soulless stood some distance away, talking amongst themselves. It provided him with a brief window in which to speak with Jal'den.

"Lead the elite unit as we planned, Jal'den, but when it comes time—" he glanced toward the Soulless furtively and noted their attention was elsewhere, "—to signal their serpent, order it to attack an incorrect location. Confuse it, if you can."

"Sir?" Jal'den's tone was baffled.

"The woman will not abide failure, nor will she tolerate disobedience. They are unaware of our signals, Jal'den. If the serpent strikes incorrectly, she will kill it."

"One less weapon in their arsenal, sir? Very well." He drew his steel broadsword from the scabbard on his back and motioned for his unit to follow. "Good luck, sir," Jal'den added before he strode quickly away.

"You as well, Jal'den."

Aran'daj drew his curved, black saber and signaled to the drummers to begin the attack cadence. He doubted he would need his weapon; his role was no longer in the midst of the fray but to orchestrate the army's maneuvers from a distance. Nevertheless, its solid weight in his hand gave him a measure of comfort as the Soulless looked on.

The first wave of Murkor soldiers marched upon the walls. Those in the front line bore large shields to protect themselves and those behind them from Balotican arrows. Behind the shield-bearers were small clusters of soldiers, tasked with the deployment of siege ladders. Between them were green-robed alchemists, armed with the more destructive tools of their trade; explosive sand-blasts, vials that would erupt in toxic fumes when broken, fire-sticks, and bottles of molten tar.

A few arrows rained down from the city's high walls accompanied by frantic shouts, but it seemed Aran'daj's ploy to strike with the dawn had borne fruit. There were few defenders, and the Murkor quickly scaled the walls. The iron-bound gates of the city swung open to allow the second wave of the attackers inside while much of the city continued to slumber.

An orange flare shot into the sky from beyond the city's walls and veered north. It was Jal'den's signal to the serpent hidden in the lake. A few minutes later, a blue flare burst forth and detonated with a brilliant flash of light near the city center. His lieutenants within were prepared for the third wave—and the entrance of the Soulless into the fight.

Aran'daj swallowed his distaste for his next task and motioned to the drummers. As their rhythm changed and the third wave of soldiers began to charge forward, Aran'daj made his way to the trio of Soulless.

"Commander?" Kama asked, a hungry light in his eyes.

"It is time, sir."

Dranamir's savage smile sent a shiver through his core. "You have done well, Commander."

CHAPTER THIRTY-TWO

SAVAGE DESTRUCTION

Dranamir watched eagerly as the first of the flares burst into life above the beleaguered city, then scowled in disappointment. Orange was the signal for Scherok. She was too distant to know for certain if the beast had deigned to uphold its end of their bargain, but she believed it would. Her threats of torture and death would bind the creature to her will, and the promise of raining terror upon the shores of Lake Jennavere for months to come was further incentive.

She tapped her foot impatiently. The second wave of the Murkor army had been within the walls for some time, and the next signal should have been sent by now. She longed to seize her power and rend the commander's head from his shoulders for the act of forcing her to wait. Kama believed the commander performed well, but his assessment meant nothing to her. She'd killed others in his position for lesser crimes.

"Patience, Dranamir." Kama's tone was amused.

She shot him a glare. "Patience is for those with no ambition."

"There," Jannyn interjected, pointing to another flare, this one blue. As it reached the apex of its arcing flight, it exploded with a bright flash.

She turned to face the hooded commander as the chorus of her bloodlust sang through her veins. He strode toward them steadily, one tattooed, blue hand gripping the hilt of his black saber. He stopped several paces away from them, keeping his distance. She swallowed the urge to laugh; so long as he remained within eyesight, she could end his life in an instant. His pretense was foolish.

"Commander?" Kama asked.

266

"It is time, sir."

Dranamir grinned wickedly, eager to begin her part of Jennavere's fall. "You have done well, Commander."

The Murkor made a half-bow to them and returned to his post more quickly than he'd walked toward him. Dranamir laughed, gleeful to find she was the source of his fear.

"What do you plan, Dranamir?" Jannyn asked.

"Destruction. Mayhem. Panic." She grinned. "Do as you will. I'll seek you out when the city is reduced to rubble and ash."

She opened a portal and stepped through. Jannyn called out to her, a growled plea that she must wait. She ignored him; she was not his keeper, and he would suffer the setback of having lost his Aethereal relic. The man was inept, a burden to her progress.

She closed the portal behind her before he managed to break through. A brief scan of the surroundings told her *he* was not present. Good. She transported herself to the city's center and exited to the physical realm once more.

A broad square adorned with the statue of an armored knight on the back of his rearing steed occupied the heart of Jennavere. Four wide cobblestone streets branched away from the square to lead in each cardinal direction. Murkor soldiers battled humans in the streets, but it was apparent the Murkor had the upper hand. Though the city had been defended, most of its guardians had been awakened at the onset of the attack, and many failed to arm themselves properly before stumbling into the streets.

She followed the eastern street toward the docks and the lakeshore beyond, casting gouts of flame at human passerby attempting to thwart her progress or flee. Their intent was of no concern; she was indiscriminate in her murderous spree. If her target failed to wear Murkor garb, they were dispatched without hesitation.

As she neared the docks, she encountered a cluster of wealthy merchants and their families, trapped between the onrushing Murkor and the docks. Scherok's silvery head crested the waves to fall with a crash upon the nearest vessel. She smiled grimly. The creature seemed to be doing its part.

She focused on the merchants huddled in the street, unable to extricate themselves from the devastation of their city. It was time she had a bit of fun.

She swept toward them like a wind-whipped inferno as she sent shockwaves of powerful energy toward the buildings that lined the street. The structures crumbled and faltered, roofs collapsed, screams erupted. It was an overture to her power, a symphony of devastation laced with the acrid tang of the merchants' fear.

The merchants attempted to flee toward the docks, foolishly believing they were safer risking the sea serpent's wrath than hers. She smiled grimly. They weren't wrong in their assessment, but running wouldn't save them. She was Enlightened; blessed by the Nameless and made Soulless, nearly unrivaled in her power. She would crush them. Unlike the Murkor, she had no need for prisoners and would leave no survivors.

She bore down on them. Energy sparked in the air around her while the earth trembled at her passage. It had been too long since she'd last felt such release; her blood sang the aria of chaos to the accompaniment of Murkor drums in the distance.

One of the merchants, a middle-aged man with a potbelly, was foolish enough to interrupt her rapture. "Who...Who are you?" he stammered.

She ignited his entrails from within. The magical fire seared his innards and caused his blood to boil while she looked on impassively. He doubled over with an agonized scream moments before the flames burst forth to consume him. He was dead before she deigned to answer his question.

"I am Soulless." She fixed her gaze on the others, a sweating, terrified waste of humanity. She raised one hand, preparing to strike the group down with a single blow.

"Have you no mercy?" A woman cried from their midst. "We have children amongst us!"

Dranamir tipped her head back and laughed. "Then let them blame their foolhardy parents for their current predicament. I mean to ensure Aeon has an eventful day. The god of the underworld admits all ages into his realm."

268

She unleashed an explosive wave of energy and watched with glee as the merchants tumbled and fell in the street. Bones shattered with the impact, veins ruptured, organs were reduced to a bloody pulp. Most died instantly, though a few unfortunate souls clung to life for a handful of tortured seconds. She ignored their dying moans and continued her swath of destruction toward the lakeshore.

The serpent continued its assault along the docks, and she nodded in satisfaction. The cold gray waters, choppy from the stiff breeze that had sprung up, were filled with flotsam. The broken masts of ships jutted from the surface haphazardly while their tattered sails fluttered useless in the wind. A few smaller vessels were attempting to disembark as she approached, but Scherok took note of them and dove beneath the surface to reappear moments later in their midst. The horrified cries of those aboard drifted to her as the serpent demolished the crafts.

The creature was proving more efficient than she'd anticipated. It would survive this battle, and her attention, until the army struck its next target. Its life would not be forfeit so long as it continued to serve her adequately. Scherok had demonstrated its worth this day.

She joined the serpent for a time and disintegrated portions of the docks it was unable to reach from the water. Ash and wood particles choked the air. The odor pleased her; it was an indication of the havoc she'd sown. This was her element, her outlet, her passion.

It was only when she began to stagger that she became aware of the toll her energy expenditure had taken. Jennavere lay in ruins around her, its docks a mass of splintered wood and broken ships, its buildings ablaze in the wake of her destruction. Her reserves were nearly depleted, but she was euphoric. The day had been glorious.

She stood on unsteady feet to peer up at the silver serpent as it continued its assault along the shoreline. It was a monster after her own heart, it seemed. She smiled coldly in its direction, though it paid her no heed.

"Dranamir." Kama's voice caused her to turn away from the serpent, and she nearly stumbled from exhaustion. He was at her side in an instant, wary curiosity mingled with yearning in his crimson eyes.

"I've done all that I can today," she informed him. She shirked the supportive arm he offered her. "I am weary, but I am not an invalid."

A shadow crossed his face, and he dropped the arm to his side. "It was invigorating to watch you at work."

She smirked; he was persistent, but his efforts were futile. "Destruction is my specialty. It is why the Nameless chose me."

"You are truly a master."

"Flattery is unbecoming." She crossed her arms, irritated by the banter. "Why are you here?"

He chuckled dryly. "Jennavere is in shambles, Dranamir. Those who weren't killed have been taken by the Murkor as laborers. You leveled half the city yourself." He gestured to the devastation around them. "There is nothing more to be done."

"Then allow me to speak with the serpent before we depart." She turned away and began to stumble toward the shoreline and Scherok's scaly form.

"Fucking gods, Dranamir, you need to rest." He caught up with her in two long strides, relentless in his pursuit.

"I'll rest once I've finished here." Again, he offered her his arm, and again, she shunned it.

A growl of frustration issued from his throat, but he kept any further thoughts to himself. She wished she'd saved a scrap of her energy; she would have sent him careening into the nearest smoldering structure for his tenacity.

Scherok reared its head out of the water and silently watched their approach. *The humans in this place are gone. Their ships are destroyed. I have done as you commanded.*

"You have," she agreed. "Would it please you to continue terrorizing the lake?"

Kama muttered darkly under his breath, but she ignored him, her focus on Scherok.

Yes.

"Then you may do so."

"Wait," Kama interjected with a snarl. "I will have need of you again. Already, the commander plots the razing of another Balotican city."

I am listening.

"Our next target is a city to the south. Stone Hill." Kama paused to glower at Dranamir. "The army will rest here, tonight and tomorrow, then resume its march. It will take another night of marching to reach the city."

I will arrive before you. Scherok flicked its gaze to meet Dranamir's. *I take orders only from her.*

"Of course, you do." Kama released an exasperated sigh and gestured for Dranamir to continue the conversation.

She smirked, amused by his obvious frustration. "Terrorize the lake while you make your way to Stone Hill. The Murkor will signal you as they did today. I don't believe I need remind you the price of failure, Scherok."

You do not. I will obey. The serpent dove beneath the muddied waters and vanished from sight.

"It is my role to dictate military matters, Dranamir." Kama's voice betrayed his growing rage.

"And it was mine to uncover assets," she reminded him. "I found Scherok, I broke its will, and it answers to me."

"You are encroaching on *my* territory, Dranamir. I will not fucking back down, and I don't fear your gods-damned power."

He seized his magic, and in her weakened state, she could produce only a partial shield. She glared at him, furious he'd pounced upon the opportunity to overwhelm her.

"No more pretenses," he growled.

Her eyes narrowed as she realized he'd been operating beneath a veil since the day they'd been resurrected. He dropped it to reveal the full extent of his Ability. His power surpassed Garin's, and was equal to her own.

"Why, Kama?"

"I do not trust the others." He sighed and restored the veil before he relinquished his hold on his magic. "Let it be a surprise to them if they attempt to cross me. Or you," he added with a frown.

"At least I finally know where you stand," she replied, "but your pursuits are wasted on me, Kama."

He shrugged. "It doesn't matter. Let us return to camp. You need to rest if you mean to seek vengeance upon me."

She snorted. "I allowed myself to be outplayed. It won't happen again."

CHAPTER THIRTY-THREE

WHISPERS OF TROUBLE

Emra tossed her braid over her shoulder in a gesture of impatience. The queue to board the ferry was interminably long this morning; it was unusual to encounter delays before winter, but clearly something was amiss. Whether it was an issue at the docks in Ridgewater or something in the lake beyond, no one seemed to know.

Beside her, Fyrmane, her tall bay, stamped his hooves in frustration. The war horse was eager to move on, as well. She patted his shoulder affectionately. "Easy. The line ought to be moving soon."

"I doubt that," a voice said from behind her.

She turned to find her long-time friend, Lucas, grinning in a roguish manner. His dapple gray was taking the delay with more grace than Fyrmane had shown.

"Do you know something I don't, Luke?"

He shook his dark head, amused. "Of course not, Em. Or shall I call you *Ser* now that you've been knighted?"

She rolled her eyes. "I don't mind if the puffed-up nobles at court call me Ser, but you, my friend, should not. It's…awkward."

Lucas snickered. "Yet you've been charged with the task of leading us to Jennavere. I'll be forced to scrape and bow to you, *Ser.* You are the knight in command." He grinned, but his expression quickly became serious. "Do you truly believe the threat's as bad as they say?"

She shrugged. "We'll know once we arrive. Word travels slowly this far from the capitol, as you well know."

Emra Castledowns and Lucas Silverthorn had grown up in the small city of Pine, on the southeastern shore of the vast Lake

Jennavere. Both had aspired to knighthood and at age fifteen traveled to the capitol, Balotica City to become squires. Nearly two decades later, they'd trained, sparred, and jousted their way to their current positions. Her recent knighting had been celebrated, though she suspected Lucas was disappointed he'd failed in his own aspirations. He was the better swordsman, but he'd never mastered the art of jousting. It had cost him the title and the prestige that accompanied it.

She lifted her gaze to the line behind them. Another ten armored soldiers waited restlessly with their steeds, eager for the ferry to begin boarding. She began to wonder if she'd made a mistake in choosing to cross the lake by ferry rather than have her unit ride around the lakeshore. Riding would have taken more time, but if they were forced to wait much longer, the time savings would be negligible.

She released a sigh; she was in command of Lucas and the ten others, but she wasn't certain which path was best. Fyrmane, sensing her frustration, stamped his hooves again and snorted.

"I'm in agreement with your mount, Em," Lucas said. "I'd rather be moving. It's nearly midday, after all. If the ferry hasn't arrived by now, something's happened."

"With the wind we've had lately, the sails were likely damaged again," the man in front of Emra replied. "Happened twice last week, and the ferryman wasn't able to repair them until nightfall."

As she was considering her reply and their next course of action, a commotion erupted at the head of the line. Emra rose to her toes and attempted to peer over the heads of those in front of her but could not see what the trouble was. She handed Fyrmane's reins to Lucas.

"Watch him for me, Luke."

Lucas snorted and eyed the horse warily. "More like, he'll be watching me. I assure you I'll behave, but I can't speak for him."

With a laugh, she broke from the line and strode ahead, determined to uncover the source of the excitement. A pair of dockworkers blocked the line and attempted to explain the situation while a dozen citizens shouted angrily. It seemed Lucas had been right; the ferry wouldn't be arriving this day.

She placed one hand on her sword hilt and pushed her way between the workers and the citizens. "What seems to be the trouble here?"

Her armor, the blue cloak she wore, emblazoned with the sigil of the royal house, marked her as a knight of the realm. The shouts quickly died away, and several of the citizens had the grace to appear ashamed. The dock workers were grateful.

"I was trying to explain that the ferry won't be coming," one of the workers stated in a huff. "This lot seemed to think I've been keeping it a secret when we've only just learned ourselves. A runner came from the south with news you may be interested in, Ser."

She nodded. Their path was decided then; they would ride along the lakeshore to Jennavere. First, she wanted to learn what she could from the runner.

"I'd like to speak with the runner."

The other worker pointed a thick finger in the direction of the dock master's hut. "He's there, Ser. Speaking with the master. He's mighty frightened, too. Poor sod."

"Thank you. When you reach my unit, tell them where I've gone. They, at least, will understand your trouble with the ferry." She frowned in the direction of the trouble-makers as they began to disperse.

"Will do, Ser. You have our thanks."

Emra made her way past the harried dock workers to the low, wooden building at the edge of the docks that was the master's hut. The door was ajar as she approached, and she could hear voices within; two men and a woman. She rapped her knuckles against the doorframe to announce her presence, then entered as the voices died away.

The dock master, garbed in a leather jerkin and roughly woven trousers, nodded in greeting. A woman of approximately the same age stood at his side; his wife, she suspected. The wiry man facing them wore the light leathers and sturdy boots that marked him as a career runner. His tanned face was ashen, however, and his eyes bloodshot from distress.

"Your men outside informed me there was news to be had regarding the ferry."

275

The runner nodded and drew a shuddering breath. "It won't be coming, Ser. Not today, nor any other." He shook his head and stared at the polished, wood-plank floor, his eyes distant and unseeing.

Emra shifted her attention to the dock master. "What's happened? My unit was dispatched to Jennavere by the king. We were to bolster its defenses but only arrived here this morning."

"The city was besieged when I fled," the runner said, his voice cracking. "It was the hooded ones. As they began to attack, a monster rose from the depths of the lake and started smashing the harbor. The ferry…The ferry was destroyed." He paused to sniffle. "I was sent to warn Ridgewater, and another was sent to Pine. I came as quickly as I was able, Ser."

She looked away, stunned by the news. Jennavere besieged, and by a people of myth, no less? She'd long believed the stories told to children about the hooded ones were mere legend, meant to scare them into behaving. And a monster in the lake? It made little sense.

"I'm from Pine," she said evenly. "If there were monsters in the lake, I'd have known about them long ago."

"Ser, the timing was no coincidence. That monster works with the hooded ones!"

"Easy," she said in the same soothing tone she adopted with Fyrmane. "My unit will travel to Jennavere. We'll sort out this business."

The prospect of facing the strange people depicted in childhood fairy stories made her uneasy. She knew nothing about them, nor what their intent must be, but she kept her manner optimistic for the sake of the citizens. Inciting a panic over rumors would help no one.

The runner shook his head adamantly. "Ser, you'll be riding into a death trap. The city was *besieged*. How many soldiers accompany you? How many fellow knights ride with you?"

"We'll do all we can," she assured him.

She didn't have the heart to tell him they numbered a dozen, or that she was the sole knight in the party. If the situation was as dire as the man described, at least Warren had his trio of messenger pigeons along. Warning could be sent quickly to the capitol, while she determined the best course of action for their meager group of reinforcements.

She made her way back to Lucas and the others. The dock workers had dispersed the remainder of the line, but the king's soldiers had stayed to await her return. Fyrmane whickered at her approach and pulled at his reins, though Lucas' grip kept him in line.

"It sounds as if we're riding," he said to her, "but I sense there's more going on than torn sails on the ferry."

Emra nodded uncertainly. She doubted the soldiers would believe the runner's tale; she didn't believe it herself. After a moment's hesitation, she divulged what she'd learned.

"Hooded ones?" Cora asked incredulously.

"A monster in the lake?" Warren added, baffled.

"That's what he said," Emra replied with a shrug. "Regardless of the truth, we were ordered to Jennavere by His Majesty. The ferry isn't coming, so we must ride."

Lucas shifted uncomfortably. "Em…Ah, Ser. If there is any truth to the city being under siege, we haven't the numbers to oppose them."

"I know, Luke." She sighed. "Warren has three pigeons, and I don't want to waste them on baseless rumor. We'll travel to Jennavere, then send a message once we know more."

She knew even if they rode hard for the remainder of the day, they wouldn't reach Jennavere before nightfall. They would be forced to make camp for the night somewhere between Ridgewater and Jennavere. The paths were rocky and treacherous, and it would be unsafe to push the horses after dark.

She studied the faces around her, grim with the knowledge that something was amiss in their lands, staunch in their resolve to defend their kingdom. They gave her the confidence to continue.

"Mount up," she ordered. "We've a long way to go."

CHAPTER THIRTY-FOUR

THE MOON'S EYE

The Sky Palace had proven to be far larger than Vardak imagined when they'd first arrived. Solsticia had led them away from the fateful door that housed the Moon's Eye and down several more corridors lined with tall, arching windows. He hadn't paid any heed to the wondrous sights beyond the crystalline panes of glass; his mind had been preoccupied with the goddess' dire revelation. They had each been shown to a private room, where Solsticia encouraged them to rest and reflect.

He'd done neither. He sat before the window his room sported, his legs folded beneath him as he silently contemplated his options. He could not shake the feeling that Flariel had planned for this moment since the start, had counted on his obedience to Blademon that would inevitably lead him here.

Concern for his brothers clouded his thoughts. He would not forfeit his life when theirs were in danger. Solsticia had promised she would return him home when their errand was complete, and he meant to return *alive*. His corpse would save no one from the Soulless' army. He would not become a victim of Flariel's twisted machinations.

The two Airess would not sacrifice themselves, not after their recent reunion. He doubted Maryn would offer himself, and Janna… He shook his head in frustration. Janna was Flariel's daughter; it was foolish to believe she would take the relic in direct defiance of her mother's plan.

His sense of obligation told him the act was for the greater good, that he would save more lives by acquiring the relic than he would in refusing it. But the truth was, he wasn't ready for death, no matter the purported celebrations that awaited the departed upon

278

entrance to Aeon's realm. He meant to see his brothers again. He longed to feel the hot sands of his desert home beneath his feet once more, to feel the dry breeze blowing through his hair. Surely, his life's journey was not meant to end here.

In the early hours of the morning, exhaustion claimed him. Troubled dreams infected his sleep. In some, he was forced to take the relic against his will, while Flariel cackled in the background. In others, he watched as his homeland was overrun by Murkor, the remainder of his people forced to submit to their will.

He awakened to the somber tolling of bells, disoriented. He rubbed his temples as his eyes adjusted to the light beyond the window. The first foul traces of a headache were building beneath his skull. He took in the view, truly seeing it for the first time, while he came to his senses.

In the distance, a bright blue sphere, swirled with white and mottled in places with green and brown loomed large. He recognized the shapes of the continents from the countless maps he'd studied, sprawled across the face of the sphere. He realized belatedly that he was looking down upon the world he'd called home from the vantage point of the Sky Palace. The white swirls were cloudbanks, the blue, the vast oceans.

It was a stunning scene and one he wished he could better appreciate. Solsticia's revelation continued to hang over him, its pall casting a shadow over the wonders beyond the glass. A decision must be made, yet he was unprepared to give his answer.

The bells began to toll again, and he pulled his attention away from the window. Three slow peals reverberated through the Sky Palace before it fell silent once more. He could recall nothing from Solsticia's words during the night regarding bells, nor could he decipher their meaning. He frowned and stood up, pausing to stretch his legs before he sought the small pile of his belongings. He'd removed his armor after entering the room and left it stacked beside his untouched satchel. He sifted through the contents, located a clean shirt, and exchanged it for the sweat-soaked one he'd spent the night in.

He wasn't certain where he meant to go, but he needed to understand the meaning behind the bells. A part of him feared to learn the truth, convinced it was tied to the Moon's Eye in some manner. He pushed the thoughts aside and chided himself for entertaining the irrational. There would be another reason for the sound, and when he located Solsticia, he believed she would tell him. He told himself all would be well, though he could not ignore the nagging voice that suggested otherwise.

Maryn was in the corridor as Vardak exited his room. The guardsman was on edge; his fur bristled outwards in alarm. "Coreyaless was just here," he said. "She hasn't been able to locate Janna. Then this infernal noise began…" He trailed off and began to mutter curses beneath his breath.

"Where is she now?" Vardak asked. He was forced to raise his voice as another trio of tolls echoed through the hall.

Maryn grimaced and pulled at his ears in discomfort. "Gods, this noise! Follow me."

Maryn led him to the courtyard where they'd first entered the palace. He spied the two Airess near its center, but there was no sign of Janna or Solsticia. His sense of unease continued to grow as he greeted the pair.

"Have you seen her?" Coreyaless asked of Maryn, her face drawn with worry.

He shook his head. "She's likely still asleep, Coreyaless. We both know she's not an early-riser unless prompted."

"Maryn's right," Vardak agreed as he continued to ignore the warnings of his subconscious.

Coreyaless looked away, her expression distraught. "I'm not certain. She said something to me before Solsticia left us last night, and it has me concerned."

"What did she say, Coreyaless? It's not like you to withhold information," Maryn said before his feline features twisted into a grimace. The bells began their somber tolling once more.

She waited for the noise to subside before forming her response. "She said she knew what must be done, that her mother would understand." She glanced skyward and her eyes brimmed with unshed tears.

"Surely she would have told us her plan," Danness added quietly. He wrapped one arm about Coreyaless and drew her to his side in an attempt to comfort her. "I do not know her well, but she doesn't seem the type to harbor secrets."

Vardak wanted to agree with Danness' assessment, but the part of his mind that growled its warning would not subside. Janna was open with her feelings, cheerful, her personality little short of effervescent. Yet, he'd watched her seemingly fold into herself when under duress, falling uncharacteristically silent rather than voice her fears. Her absence, coupled with Coreyaless' concerns, set him on edge. Had Janna made the fateful decision he'd grappled with through the night?

He shook his head and turned away from the others, the rumblings of his headache beginning to intensify as his thoughts continued to spiral. In spite of his initial misgivings, he'd grown to consider Janna a friend. Surely, she would have told him of her plan, if indeed she had sought out the Moon's Eye? No, he countered; she was closer to Coreyaless than she was to him. The Airess would know her mind best.

Vardak was the first to note Solsticia's reappearance. The goddess' expression was somber as she beckoned to him. He glanced over his shoulder toward the others to find they were still deep in conversation, unaware of their hostess' return. Silently, he crossed the courtyard to stand before her.

"I have a message for you, Vardak."

Inexplicably, he knew it was from Janna, yet he refused to accept the fact. "My brothers, are they—?"

She smiled sadly. "I'm afraid I have no update on their conditions, Vardak, but I believe you know what this is truly about." She reached into the pocket of her gown and withdrew a carefully folded sheet of parchment. "Janna asked that I give this to you."

Before he reached for the message, he said, "She took the relic. Gods, why did she choose such a path?"

He was stunned, wracked with guilt, ashamed he'd allowed her—the one he had sworn to protect—to make the ultimate sacrifice. He'd failed in his mission, too consumed with his own selfish desire to return home to stop her. He was certain Blademon would reprimand him, and Flariel would likely be furious. Her daughter had perished.

"Perhaps her final words to you will explain her motive." Solsticia's voice broke through his dark thoughts.

He nodded and accepted the parchment, unfolding it to reveal Janna's message, written in a neat, flowing script.

Vardak,

Out of all of us, I have known you the longest. You are dour at times, gruff, and stubborn, but you have a good heart and have led me through terrifying places I would never have dared to venture alone. I will confess I've grown fond of you, despite your rough exterior.

When Solsticia informed us of the curse laid upon the Moon's Eye, I knew then what I must do. I don't believe my choice was part of mother's plan. She has done little but antagonize me since we met, and perhaps this is my way of asserting my independence. This choice is my own.

Coreyaless and Danness have only just reunited, and it would be cruelly unfair to ask one of them to take up the relic. Maryn has been helpful, though he is brash and irritable more often than not. He joined us only to guide us through the jungle, and I hope you will pass my gratitude on to him. He is not meant to forfeit his life for a cause that is not his own. And you, Vardak, will be needed in the days to come. Blademon chose you for a reason, and I'm certain your skills will bolster those fighting against the oppression of the Soulless. Which leaves only me.

If you are reading this, it means the deed is complete. I have asked Solsticia to give you this message, as well as the relic we have chased for so many weeks. Take care of yourself, Vardak.

Please tell the others it has been a pleasure coming to know them. We will meet again one day, in Aeon's realm. —Janna

He stared at the message for some time after he'd finished reading, oblivious to the approach of Coreyaless and the others. Janna was gone, his fears realized.

"I wish she would have spoken to me last night." He was surprised by the tightness in his throat as he spoke. His voice sounded strained.

"She feared you would stop her," Solsticia replied. "The choice was hers to make, Vardak. Do not blame yourself."

"Vardak?" Coreyaless asked uncertainly from behind.

He didn't trust his voice any longer. He simply handed her the note instead.

"There is the matter of the relic itself," Solsticia said quietly after a moment. "Janna wished it be passed to you, now that its curse has been broken. The enemy will be seeking it. Guard it well."

He nodded as she withdrew the Moon's Eye from her pocket. It was carefully fashioned from a pale, green-white stone, and it glowed softly in the goddess' hands. Shaped like a teardrop, its pointed end had been hollowed out, and a thick leather cord threaded through it. Solsticia placed the cord around his neck and stepped back. The relic was the size of his thumb, but it was heavy for its size.

Coreyaless began to sob. "It should not have been her. She had so much life left ahead of her..."

Danness handed Janna's message to Vardak. "I suspect you'd like to keep this," he said quietly before he turned his attention upon his grieving partner.

Vardak accepted it with a nod, his heart heavy. He was now the relic's keeper, but without a wizard to use it properly, it was little more than a weighty reminder of his failure. He vowed he would guard it with his life, in honor of Janna and the sacrifice she'd made.

"You were sent to retrieve the Moon's Eye in order to counter the Shalin Stone," Solsticia said, "but as Blademon has already informed you, it is too late. There is another use for the relic, however." She studied him with her golden eyes as though scrutinizing his reaction. "The Moon's Eye may be used to destroy the Tower of Obsidian. In fact, the tower cannot be razed without it."

He shrugged. "None of my people harbor the Ability for magic. As I understand it, magical relics can only be used by those who do."

"That is true," she conceded. "I suggest you find a trustworthy mage to use it properly. The tower is not merely the home of the Soulless, Vardak; its existence is vitally important to the Nameless god himself. Its destruction may prove a setback from which he cannot recover. I won't order you to follow such a path, but I hope you will heed my suggestion."

"The welfare of my brothers comes first," he replied stubbornly. Once Travin was rescued, he would consider a journey to the Shining Tower.

"I understand. I will return you to the Stronghold once our business is concluded. As the child of an Immortal, it is custom we hold a memorial in her honor. It is set for tomorrow." She paused to eye him carefully, her gaze unreadable. "I suspect you wish to take part."

"Yes." He looked down at the relic where it glowed softly on its cord. "I will honor her last act before I am forced to go."

CHAPTER THIRTY-FIVE

JENNAVERE'S END

As darkness fell, Aran'daj watched as lightning split the threatening sky overhead. Wind whipped through the camp, and he knew they would be in for a restless night. He tugged at his hood to keep it firmly in place. Storms of this caliber were rare east of the Gray Mountains, but his army was equipped for the difficult weather. He'd made certain of that before they departed the Wasted Land.

The Soulless had granted them a brief reprieve. They would remain on the outskirts of Jennavere this night and rest the following day before marching south toward Stone Hill. There was still much to do, even though the city had been reduced to timber and ash.

Another jagged fork of lightning careened through the sky to momentarily blind him as he moved toward the perimeter of the camp. He muttered a curse under his breath and blinked away the afterimages. He wondered if the storm was a natural event or the result of Maelstrom's displeasure with the Murkor's recent actions. The storm god was fickle and prone to fits of rage, or so the stories told.

He met with several of his lieutenants and Jal'den at the perimeter. Raising his voice to be heard over the wind, he stated, "I would like patrols to continue within the razed city. Collect anything that may be of use to the army. Food, weapons, tools. Each patrol is to take an alchemist along. There are likely items to be found that will be of use to their order. If you encounter any survivors, they are to be captured if fit for labor. Follow the Soulless' orders for the rest."

He managed to keep the distaste from his tone, though he loathed giving voice to his final words. He would make certain his soldiers knew the true source of the heartless command.

"But the storm, sir?" one asked uncertainly.

"We have only tonight in which to loot the city," he replied. "We must make the most of our limited time to gather supplies, storm be damned. We march south at nightfall tomorrow."

A chorus of acknowledgements greeted his statement. The lieutenants saluted and went about their assigned duties, but Jal'den remained behind.

"Sir, might I have a word?"

He nodded to the Arms Master and motioned that he should accompany him back into the camp. Aran'daj detected nothing amiss in the other's tone, but Jal'den hesitated a few moments before he next spoke.

"Sir, I've spoken with Blademon."

Aran'daj turned to peer at Jal'den, startled yet curious. "What did the god of war have to say?"

"Foremost, he brought word to me of Sal'zar. It seems he is coping well enough in the tower." Jal'den sighed. "I don't like to think overly long on his current predicament. He's capable. I must remember he can look after himself."

Aran'daj suppressed the urge to pry into Jal'den's relationship with Sal'zar. It would be considered an insult to inquire about Jal'den's personal life, and he feared the Arms Master would react adversely to such an intrusion.

The first cold drops of rain began to fall. He wished to conclude their conversation and return to the relative shelter of his command tent. He had maps to study, terrain notes from the scouts to look over, and another potential siege to plot. He doubted Stone Hill would prove as unprepared as Jennavere; their presence on Balotican soil was no longer secret.

"I sense there was more, Jal'den."

"Yes." He sighed again, and this time, Aran'daj detected a note of despair in the sound. "Blademon indicated there is another, sir. I was not his only pupil in recent times."

"Shit."

Jal'den chuckled. "I believe I said the same to him."

"Did he give you any further information, Jal'den?"

His mind raced. He'd counted on Jal'den's specialized training to give them an edge against their human adversaries. Now, it seemed, he must factor in the presence of another, equally skilled in arms.

"He said only that we were destined to meet on the battlefield, one day." Jal'den fell silent for a time. "I believe Blademon is eager to watch our fight, sir. The prospect troubles me."

Aran'daj glowered beneath his hood. "As much as I don't like the news, I should have anticipated this. The Immortals do not take sides. If Blademon has chosen you, it is only reasonable that he would choose another. He is evening the odds."

"Sir, I'd like this kept between us. If *they* were to learn…"

"I understand." They'd arrived outside the command tent, and the rain had begun to fall in a steady stream. "If he returns with any further information, I hope you will confide in me again."

"Of course, sir." Jal'den saluted before he strode quickly away.

Aran'daj remained outside for a few more seconds to watch the other disappear into the night. Jal'den had proven himself time and again, but he remained something of an enigma. He hoped the obsession with Sal'zar would not cloud Jal'den's judgment. Several of his plans hinged on the young Arms Master's unique and formidable skill in battle, and he could not afford to make mistakes. The Soulless would not abide them, no matter their origin.

The storm continued to rage outside through the night, to escalate into what Aran'daj could only describe as a tempest. The Murkor were unused to weather of such dark intensity; most of the army huddled within their tents, praying that Maelstrom's unmitigated fury would abate with the dawn. It did not, and the Murkor spent the daylight hours in fitful sleep broken by the relentless howling of the wind.

Aran'daj studied his maps and plotted through the night. His ploy to confuse the sea serpent had been unsuccessful at Jennavere, but he would not fail a second time. He hadn't divulged to Kama his reason for striking at Stone Hill next, and to his benefit, the Soulless never asked.

The lakeshore was uneven, and half the city was perched atop a high cliff. The serpent would have only a small area in which to inflict damage. He would speak with Jal'den as they marched. Together, they would ensure the Arms Master's signals to the serpent would be mixed and that he must send them from a location nearer the shore.

There was a significant risk that the creature would attack some of his own men during the maneuver, but Aran'daj felt it was worth taking. The sea serpent could not be allowed to continue. Jal'den would likely protest this course of action, but he could see no other way to achieve his objective.

The wind began to diminish during the afternoon hours the next day, and soon after, the sun burst forth from the dense cloud to sear Murkor eyes with its brilliance. The ground was muddied and the air cool, but the army would be able to move on as scheduled. He was certain the Soulless would not tolerate a delay, no matter how vile the weather had been. With the emergence of the sun, he issued the order to break camp; they would resume the march at nightfall.

The Soulless had not yet returned after the razing of Jennavere and had left him to scheme unhindered. He summoned Jal'den to the command tent that afternoon to discuss his plans in Stone Hill and what must be done about the serpent.

Jal'den crossed his arms at the news and was silent for some time. Finally, he said, "I don't like it, sir, but I understand. If the Soulless' anger is diverted to the serpent, our people will remain safe for a time. That gods-damned beast is a terror, and I agree with you that it must be stopped. I'll do what I can."

Relieved, Aran'daj nodded his thanks. "Keep our people out of harm's way, if you are able, Jal'den. I cannot guarantee what the serpent will do once we've confounded it."

"My sword is always ready to defend our own, sir. No matter the source of the threat."

"Be cautious where you make such statements," Aran'daj reminded him. "There are those who would choose the Soulless over our people, seeking the promise of power and glory. You are one of my greatest assets, and it would be a shame to lose you due to misplaced bravado."

Jal'den chuckled. "I speak freely only with three people, sir. You, the Kal, and Sal'zar. There is nothing to fear."

"And Blademon?"

Jal'den hesitated. "I tell him only what I deem pertinent. He knows nothing of our schemes beyond what he may observe from afar. He chose me, yet I'm not certain we can trust any of the gods to help us, sir. As you said last night, they strive for neutrality."

"Very good. I will not keep you from your duties. We can speak again while we travel."

CHAPTER THIRTY-SIX

THE AFTERMATH

Fyrmane stamped his hooves and snorted indignantly at Emra's approach. The big bay seemed determined to make his displeasure known. He and the other horses had been forced to shelter under a hastily-erected canopy during the storm while she and the humans were cozy in their tents. She shook her head, amused at his antics.

"You know as well as I that you simply won't fit in my tent."

He huffed in response as she began the task of saddling him. He stamped again and succeeded in splashing mud onto her greaves.

Their campsite was still drenched, even the morning after the storm had cleared. She'd planned to be in Jennavere by now, yet they had several hours of riding left ahead of them. The deluge had cost them a full day's journey and more. Maelstrom had chosen a poor time in which to unleash his fury upon the land.

Finished with her task, she turned to survey the others riding with her. Seven men, four women, many seeking the renown required to achieve knighthood, all career soldiers. Most tended to their mounts, though a few had finished their task and were awaiting her command to depart. All were armored, various weapons sheathed at their hips, or in Dalton's case, across his broad back. Warren was feeding scraps to the messenger pigeons mounted precariously behind his horse's saddle.

"We ought to reach Jennavere around noontime," Lucas said as he sidled up to her. "I'm still uncertain what we'll find there. Hooded ones? A monster? It seems a load of shit."

She shrugged, as she had so many times during the past two days. The runner's news was difficult to swallow, she conceded, but she feared discounting it outright. A part of her wondered if there was truth in his tale. He hadn't seemed the sort to spout nonsense simply to gain attention.

"We'll learn in a few hours, I suppose."

Lucas grunted in response and crossed his arms.

"Luke, I can't simply dismiss that poor man's fear," she continued. "He was terrified. No matter what occurred, it wasn't good. I'm trying to keep an open mind."

"The king sent us to bolster the defenses for a reason," he replied grudgingly. "I won't believe this business about hooded ones unless I see them for myself. If anything, it's a rogue human army sent by the Shadow Council. I trust the king's judgment on that matter."

"And if it is the Shadow Council at work, we've more problems ahead," she replied with a frown. "We were sent afield without a wizard in the company. Unless you've been concealing your magical talent all these years, we're at a hard disadvantage."

"I was merely trying to point out that the Shadow Council is far more likely than a contingent of mythical soldiers or a monster in the lake."

Behind him, Fyrmane whickered as if in agreement. She sighed. "It seems I'm outnumbered in this matter."

Lucas chuckled. "I knew your steed had good sense."

She shook her head, bemused. Her eyes drifted over Lucas' shoulder to where the others were gathered. She noted they seemed to be waiting on her.

"We'll find out whose 'good sense' prevails in a few hours, Luke. It's time we go."

As they neared Jennavere, Emra realized they'd passed no one on the road for miles. With the ferry out, she'd expected to encounter traffic as those seeking to flee the rumored destruction took to the road. She could see no smoke wafting into the sky, but given the recent storm, it came as no surprise. Her senses clamored with warnings; she was certain something dire had befallen the city long before its walls came into view.

"Em, you can feel it, can't you?"

Lucas rode abreast of her where he'd been silently studying her reactions for some time. He'd learned when they were children to trust in Emra's instincts; they were often inexplicably correct, even if she could not explain why or how she'd come to understand a given scenario.

She nodded and tossed her blond braid over her shoulder in frustration. "Whatever happened in Jennavere is finished, but I suspect we'll find no survivors." She suppressed a shudder. "The whole of the universe screams to me that something is very wrong."

Another quarter-hour passed in silence before they began to see muddy boot prints on either side of the road. Countless prints marked the passage of a sizeable force. The soldiers began to murmur and speculate amongst themselves.

The city came into view not long afterward. Its walls stood erect, though the gate was thrown wide, as if in welcome. The road remained empty, the city walls unoccupied by the requisite scouts. Jennavere was devoid of its populace.

She halted their progress and turned to face the others. "I want you to pair up. Search the city for any sign of what occurred here. Return here in one hour, and report what you've found."

"Em, I'm with you." She'd expected Lucas to insist on riding at her side, and she nodded in thanks.

As the others made their way toward the abandoned city, she turned Fyrmane southward. "The tracks we've seen led from this direction. I mean to see if we can locate their source."

Lucas sighed. "Is this wise? If we're seen…"

"I don't think they're here any longer, Luke. It's too quiet." She shook her head, unable to explain her blind certainty. She simply *knew*. "It looked to be a large force. They would have set camp. Perhaps they've left further clues behind."

"I suppose if you're leading us into a trap, I can take consolation in the fact that we'll be captured together," he joked.

"We won't be captured, Luke."

He pulled slightly ahead, which provided her the opportunity to study him as they rode. She could not recall a time when they hadn't been friends, and only a handful of occasions in which they'd not been together. She'd long been in love with him, but she didn't believe he felt the same. He seemed content with his role as friend and confidante. Asking for more would upset their balance, and she feared the repercussions.

The muddy impressions led them into the mouth of a broad valley. A wide swath of ground had been trampled, and she noted scores of round holes punched into the earth, indicative of tent poles. At intervals, they found the charred remains of cookfires.

"They must number in the thousands, Em." Lucas shook his head, stunned. "Where do you suppose they've gone?"

She pointed to the southern horizon. "If they'd traveled north, we would have encountered them on our way here. Let's return to the others. We need to send word to the king."

"We ought to warn the outpost, too," he suggested. "If they send their garrison, perhaps Pine and Stone Hill will have a fighting chance."

It was a solid plan, but she feared their plea would arrive too late. They had lost too much time weathering the storm, and the enemy was well ahead of them. She kept her concerns to herself and guided Fyrmane toward Jennavere.

"This news will keep Warren and his birds occupied for a time," she said.

"Will you follow standard protocol, Em?" Lucas asked pointedly.

She sighed heavily. "I have no choice but to do so, Luke. You know that."

When she'd been knighted, she'd sworn to uphold the laws of the kingdom, follow the chivalric code, and follow military protocol on all matters of security. Protocol dictated they send word to the king and his generals, then remain in place until new orders were received. It was her first military outing as a knight, and she was not about to jeopardize her position by ignoring the rules she'd vowed to follow.

Lucas nodded in approval. "Good. We are only twelve, against a force of what looks to be a thousand or more. I don't plan to find myself entering Aeon's gate any time soon."

"Nor do I." She offered him a weary smile. "Perhaps the others will learn more from within the city itself. I'm not certain what I should tell our superiors about the enemy. Rumors won't suffice."

She and Lucas were the last to return to the designated rendezvous point. At their approach, Dalton began to beckon frantically. She glanced at Lucas, who merely shrugged and spurred his gray into a canter. She followed suit, and they covered the distance rapidly. She dismounted a few paces away from Dalton, then strode to his location.

"Ser, you need to see this." Dalton's expression was grim as he pointed to a body that lay on the road behind him.

At first glance, she would have believed the body human, though it wore unusually crafted black leather armor beneath a suit of bright ring-mail. The face was obscured by a black hood.

"Bandits?" she asked of Dalton, who shook his head.

"Take a look at his face, Ser."

As she and Lucas neared the body, she noted the others remained at a distance. She knelt beside it but shot a disapproving frown at her unit. "Was this person diseased? Should I be concerned?"

"No, Ser," Cora replied uneasily. "We've all had a look at him, but…"

"He's not human, Ser," Warren added.

"Perhaps there was truth to the rumor," Lucas said quietly as he crouched along the corpse's other side. He drew his belt knife and used its tip to pull the hood from the face.

She gaped as it was revealed. A young man, she supposed, hairless, with skin blue as the midnight sky. His forehead and jawline were adorned with an array of silvery tattoos, none of which held any meaning to her. A trickle of dark blood had dried along one corner of his mouth. She examined his torso and found a puncture wound near his abdomen. An arrow, she surmised. He might have lived if he'd left the missile in place, but his wound had turned deadly when it was pulled free.

"Gods, he resembles Ukase." Lucas sat back on his heels, his face ashen with shock.

She nodded absently while her mind raced. "I wasn't aware Ukase was the patron of a people."

"I was wrong, Em. He wore a hood…"

"We were wrong, Luke. The hooded ones are real, and they've brought war to Balotica."

CHAPTER THIRTY-SEVEN

A STUDY IN PAIN

Tavesin surveyed his surroundings and cast his senses through the Aethereum as Aziarah had taught him. He'd promised her he wouldn't venture into the realm alone, but he wanted to see Arra. The opportunities to speak with her since she'd arrived at the tower had been few. Between Hasnin, Aziarah, and her assigned mentor, Lyrra, the pair had been kept apart. Tavesin resented the interference; Arra was his friend and the only other human mage born in a generation who shared his gift for Aethereal magic. He must know how she fared.

Besides, when Arra arrived, he would no longer be alone. His promise to Aziarah would remain unbroken.

That evening, Badolo had arrived at their usual table in the kitchens, bearing a note for him. Arra harbored the same sentiments as he did, it seemed. Her message had been brief, but he'd understood.

Midnight, at the place we first met.

He was early, but he'd been unable to wait any longer. He sensed nothing amiss in his surroundings and began to pace along the riverbank outside Rican Mer. The water was frozen in place, the harsh light of the Aethereum reflecting from its surface in a bright glare. He averted his gaze, unable to withstand the brilliance for more than a few seconds.

He sat down in the tall grass to await her arrival. A thrill cascaded through him; he rarely disobeyed his elders, and tonight he was doing just that. If Hasnin learned of their unauthorized liaison, Tavesin would be faced with a months' worth of menial chores as punishment at the very least. If Aziarah found out...

He snickered in spite of himself. The Drakkon believed the tower's policy regarding disobedience was lenient. He wasn't certain *what* she'd have in store for him, but he felt he could endure any punishment so long as he could speak with Arra. Their forced separation was unjustified, unfair.

Midnight arrived, and still he waited. He began to worry Lyrra had learned of their plan to meet, and Arra would not be coming. He stood and began to pace, then kicked irritably at the unnaturally still grasses underfoot.

"It seems I've found our thief."

Tavesin's blood became an ice floe within his veins. He recognized the voice, the malice it contained, the danger inherent in its words. He swallowed hard, afraid to turn around, to look into the distorted features of the Soulless. He was frozen in place, rooted by the sudden terror that gripped him. Aziarah was not present to send the creature away this time; he was utterly alone.

The world tilted abruptly, and Tavesin found himself gasping for air as his body slammed roughly against the earth. He attempted to cry out, but no sound would issue from his throat. He tried to push himself upright, but his limbs refused to move. He attempted to flee, to return to the waking world and his bed, safe within the Shining Tower, but found he was blocked from the source of his magic. Too late, he realized he was bound, subdued in an instant. Panic welled within him.

"A pity you aren't here physically, thief." The Soulless suddenly loomed over him and bent to peer into his terrified eyes. "Yes, I know about the box you stole. And I know it was *you* that stole it. I've been tracking it and was quite disappointed to learn it resides within the shielded portion of your tower."

He stood swiftly, and the sharp toe of his boot collided with Tavesin's ribcage. The air was forced from his lungs with the impact. Tavesin gasped but found himself unable to make any further sound, nor could he brace himself for the next blow. Another kick found its mark near his groin. Pain radiated from both sites. Silent tears began to leak from his eyes.

The Soulless' mirthless laughter filled his ears. "Since your physical body lies within your tower, I cannot end your life, but I certainly can make you wish that I had."

Tavesin squeezed his eyes closed, sickened with the knowledge that he'd become the Soulless' prisoner. Unable to flee, unable to resist, he resigned himself to the inevitability of the next painful strike. He was helpless to stop it.

More blows rained down on him, some from the pointed toes of the Soulless' boots, others from his fists. Bruises blossomed beneath his skin, bones cracked, blood welled from lacerations. All the while, Tavesin could think only of Arra, his reason for entering the Aethereum that night. It was fortunate she'd been unable to join him, for she, too, would have become a victim of the Soulless' wrath.

His consciousness began to fade toward black, but the beating continued relentlessly. He could no longer discern one injury from another; his whole body screamed in agony, though his voice remained mute.

He'd been reprimanded for stealing the star-shaped box, then lauded hours later when one of the Yellows discovered it was an Aethereal relic. He was informed it was stowed in the restricted area of the tower for further study. At the time, he'd felt pride. The wizards had recognized his discovery, claimed it was a wondrous gift he'd brought to them. Now, he wished he'd never set foot in the black tower, or at least had resisted the urge to handle the box and unwittingly pilfer it from the tower's stores.

His world became a study in pain, and the Soulless seemed tireless in his pursuit of inflicting it. Each time he felt himself drift toward the darkness, he was brought back to his senses by a sharp jolt of energy, white-hot as it arced along his spine. He would have screamed if he'd been allowed the use of his voice.

"Garin, that's quite enough."

Abruptly the beating ceased, and Tavesin opened his swollen eyes a sliver. The Soulless was dangling in the air in front of him, his body bound by the magic of another. Belatedly, he realized he could move, but he no longer wished to. Every joint in his body protested, every muscle writhed in anguish. No, he would remain where he was and observe what he could of the Soulless and the newcomer.

Tavesin could see nothing but the newcomer's boots. They were finely-crafted, made of blackened leather, and polished to a shine. His rescuer was either quite wealthy, or had spent a significant amount of time creating them with magic. Tavesin assumed it was the former.

The boots strode nearer to the suspended Soulless, and Tavesin caught the first true glimpse of his savior. A middle-aged man with sharp features, browned skin, dark hair, and strangely golden eyes. His features were distinct; he was not one of the Soulless, but it was clear he was familiar with them.

"I knew your order was without heart, but I'd hoped torturing children was beneath even you." The golden eyes narrowed menacingly. "I also believed I'd made it very clear you were not to return here."

The Soulless spat but said nothing in response.

"Ah, Garin, so predictable." The man chuckled mirthlessly. "You will leave us now."

He motioned dismissively with one hand, and the Soulless vanished with a sudden, anguished scream. The man knelt before him, and Tavesin was relieved to find compassion in his strange eyes.

"I'm afraid I cannot heal your injuries, but since you aren't here physically, you'll awaken unharmed." He frowned as though troubled. "I don't know what you've done to incur Garin's ire, but I hope you'll take this as a warning. My realm is not safe at present, and I cannot always be here to monitor it."

"Your...realm?" Tavesin's words were slurred through his swollen lips.

"Yes, this realm was supposed to be mine." A wistful smile crossed his fierce features, momentarily softening them. "That is ancient history, I'm afraid. Do you know how to return home?"

Tavesin nodded. "Thank you."

"I am no friend to the Soulless, but I will accept your thanks." He rocked back on his heels. "I hope you heed my warning, friend. Go now, and find peace in the physical world. I'm certain we will meet again."

Tavesin gasped and attempted to sit, his forehead colliding with a hard object as he did so. Hands gripped his shoulders, and an uttered curse filled his ears. It took him several moments to take in his surroundings and to realize the only pain he now felt was from the knock he'd just taken to his skull.

Hasnin stood over him, his aged features drawn with worry, fear clear in his dark eyes. Rostin was at the foot of his bed, the source of the curses; he massaged his own forehead with both hands. On the other side of his bed stood Aziarah, her reptilian features tense while her long tail lashed behind her.

"Praise the gods, you're awake," Hasnin rasped.

"You were not to enter the Aethereum unsupervised," Aziarah added in a growl. "You have learned enough to keep yourself out of the realm. I know this was no accident, Tavesin."

"It was—" he began, wilting before her heated gaze.

"It was Arra. Yes, we have been informed," Aziarah replied acidly. "You are a foolish child, unworthy of such magic if you cannot listen to reason."

"You were cut off from the source," Hasnin said, more gently. "Tavesin, you must tell us what occurred."

He began to speak, his words punctuated by sniffles while he struggled to rein in his sobs. He told them of his plan to meet Arra, her failure to appear, and the subsequent encounter with the Soulless named Garin. Something held him back from telling them about the golden-eyed man, and he concocted a story that Garin became distracted and he'd managed to flee. It seemed Hasnin and Aziarah believed his tale plausible, and they did not question him further. By the time he'd finished speaking, his voice raw with the remembrance of agony, even Aziarah's sour expression had softened.

"It is my belief you have learned your lesson," Hasnin informed him, "but this matter must be brought before the Radiant. He will determine what punishment you must endure."

"You will not enter the Aethereum again unless I accompany you. My previous edict was meant for your safety, you foolish boy," Aziarah added, though he detected a note of fondness in her tone. "I expect to see you this evening, Tavesin."

After the Drakkon had departed, Hasnin said, "I pray you will be more careful in the future, Taven. The Soulless are not to be trifled with."

He nodded somberly. "I know, sir. Is Arra well?"

"It seems Lyrra learned of her plans and quickly put a stop to them. I hope your experience is also a lesson to her." Hasnin patted his shoulder. "Rest, Taven. I will have you excused from your other studies today."

Grateful, Tavesin nodded again and looked down. He was exhausted, though he'd been sleeping much of the night. He would not enter the Aethereum alone again.

CHAPTER THIRTY-EIGHT

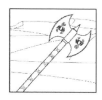

THE MEMORIAL

Vardak followed the others as Solsticia led them to a vast chamber within the Sky Palace. She'd asked them to wear their finest attire for the occasion; in his case, it was the armor Travin had painstakingly crafted for him. He'd left his axe and other belongings behind in his borrowed quarters, though the Moon's Eye, that cursed relic, hung on its cord beneath his breastplate.

The chamber was carved with detailed images of the twelve Immortals performing acts according to their roles. An array of ten massive thrones had been placed facing a stone slab, each decorated in ornate symbols. Another handful of smaller, plainer chairs were positioned behind them. The room was empty at present, save for the pale figure lying motionless atop the slab.

Vardak looked upon her face, once so full of life, curious, always ready with a smile. Janna had been dressed in a white gown with red embroidery tracing its way up the skirt and along the sleeves. The stitching appeared to resemble flames, in honor of her mother. Her eyes were closed, her expression peaceful, but in death, she did not smile.

He looked away as guilt wracked him. This fate should not have been hers.

"My siblings will begin arriving soon," Solsticia said quietly after a time. "We conduct ceremonies of this caliber only rarely, and never have we shared it with living mortals." She gestured to the smaller chairs near the rear. "You have been permitted to observe, but do not interrupt. Flariel will not abide it."

As the others seated themselves in the provided chairs, Vardak folded his legs beneath him to sit directly upon the floor. Chairs were

301

not designed to accommodate his species. Solsticia lingered beside him to speak in a low tone the others could not hear.

"Flariel did not wish for you to attend, Vardak. She blames you for Janna's choice, though we both know you are not at fault. I spoke on your behalf. You deserve closure, just as the others do." She placed one hand on his armored shoulder. "Keep your distance from her, Vardak. In her rage, she may lash out."

He nodded wearily. He'd expected to incur Flariel's wrath. He'd wallowed in indecision, and his failure to act had prompted Janna's sacrifice. He deserved to become the target of the Fire Maiden's anger, in his own mind.

Solsticia dropped her hand and peered at him shrewdly with her luminous golden eyes. "Janna's act was not of your doing, Vardak. You cannot continue to walk the dark path you now tread."

He averted his gaze but made no reply. She continued to study him for a moment; he could sense her eyes boring into his very soul. He made no attempt to explain himself or to divulge his innermost thoughts. He was weary of being the target of the gods' interest. He simply wished to be left alone in order to wrangle with his grief. Finally, Solsticia released a disapproving sigh and departed, giving in to his stubborn desire.

Several minutes later, a bell tolled. The sound reverberated through the air and rumbled through the foundations of the Sky Palace. As it faded to the accompaniment of Maryn's muttered curses, the first of the gods entered the chamber. Maryn quickly fell silent, his attention riveted upon the Immortals.

Dus'tanne, the Earth's Keeper, walked arm-in-arm with Solsticia. Dus'tanne, like most Immortals, was humanoid in form. Her skin was the color of damp soil, her hair a lustrous green; the color reminded him of the dense foliage they'd traipsed through as they ventured into the Felene jungles. An array of flowering vines covered much of her torso, and several trailed behind her as she walked toward the stone slab at the front of the room. Her eyes were a luminous shade of vibrant green, reminiscent of new growth at the onset of spring.

The pair paused to bow before Janna's still form. Dus'tanne removed a delicate, ivory bloom from her shoulder and placed it upon the slab, while Solsticia created a glowing, yellow star between her hands. The star was placed beside the flower, and the pair turned to seat themselves in the center-most of the carved thrones.

The bell tolled again, and a second pair of gods made their way inside. Cirrus, the Wind-Maker, accompanied Hydralene, Keeper of the Seas. Cirrus was the patron of the Drakkon and sported their winged, reptilian form. His scales were the vibrant blue of the noon-day sky, his eyes, a pearlescent gray. Beside him, Hydralene moved forward on the crest of a wave. Like Cirrus, she was nearly covered in scales, though her body below the waist was in the form of a large fish. Her scales sparkled and glittered in the light in myriad shades of aquamarine, violet, and gold.

The pair bowed to Janna, as Dus'tanne and Solsticia had. Cirrus produced a large gray eagle's feather to place with the other items, while Hydralene left a delicate pink conch shell. Vardak wondered at the significance of each item, but he kept his question to himself. Solsticia had cautioned them to remain silent, and he needed no further reason to incur Flariel's ire.

With the next bell came Flariel and Ukase. The Fire Maiden's molten gaze sought his, and she narrowed her eyes in a withering glare. The flames that swirled around her intensified. Vardak was certain she would have struck him down had Ukase not murmured something in her ear. With a snarl, she tore her gaze away from his and focused on her daughter's body at the front of the room.

Ukase was the patron of the Murkor people, though unlike his mortal counterparts, he shirked the dark hoods they used to conceal their features. He sported midnight blue skin adorned with a complex swirl of silvery tattoos. His garments were dark, billowing robes, indicative of his position as the Judge of Mortal Affairs. His pale eyes shone with a piercing light. Ukase presented Janna with a golden scale, while Flariel did not leave a parting gift.

Vardak was puzzled by her action. Did the fire goddess deem her daughter unworthy, or was it simply not her place to leave an item for her kin?

As the pair turned away from the slab, Flariel caught his eyes once more. There was far more than mere anger in her gaze, and he was certain there would be trouble in his future. He looked down, unable to maintain eye contact with the irate goddess. Solsticia believed he was not at fault for Janna's decision, but he continued to blame himself for his inaction. He'd been sent to protect her, and he'd failed.

The next pair to enter were Karmada and Minora, the goddesses of luck and time. Minora's features appeared to be carved of white marble; her face was smooth and unlined, expressionless and unyielding. Her garments appeared to be chiseled from the same stone as her body, and it seemed not to shift nor wrinkle with her passage. Karmada wore the same crimson gown she had when she visited the Airess in Solsticia's temple. One of her six arms was linked with Minora's as they strode to the front of the room.

Minora presented Janna with an intricate clockwork mechanism, with dials to indicate the time of day, the season, the position of the moon, and the years passed since the end of the Time of Chaos. Karmada left a pair of large, ebony dice. She rolled them gently along the length of the slab before she turned to take up her seat.

Vardak forced himself to straighten his posture as the next pair entered. Blademon, clad in his black armor, weapons crossed behind his back, strode alongside his twin and polar opposite, Armistral, the Keeper of Peace. Blademon nodded to Vardak in greeting as he passed, while his brother's attention was drawn to the Airess. Armistral was their patron god and sported a pair of moth-like wings that shimmered gold, then silver, as he moved.

Legends stated the pair rarely cooperated, but it seemed Janna's death was cause enough to mend their present rifts, at least for a time. Blademon placed a silver dagger bearing his scorpion sigil on its haft alongside the other gifts, while Armistral left a crystalline gem, colored and shaped to resemble a rainbow. The pair moved to sit at the opposite ends of the thrones; Armistral occupied one of the seats, while Blademon folded his legs beneath him to sit directly on the tiled floor in the same manner Vardak employed.

The final pair of Immortals entered the room to a resounding peal of the bells. Maelstrom, the storm god, walked alongside Aeon, the Underworld's Keeper. Aeon had assumed the form of the Felene people, though his shape was somewhat indistinct and ethereal in nature. His feline eyes glowed with an eerie blue-white light, and his fur was black as coal. He nodded at Maryn, who shrank into his chair and shuddered at the acknowledgment. It was believed Aeon's attention upon a mortal soul indicated that soul's imminent demise. Vardak hoped it was merely superstition; he held Maryn in high regard.

Maelstrom maintained a humanoid form. He appeared to be constructed of storm clouds that whirled around his person. Tiny forks of lightning erupted from his joints as he moved, and his eyes were a baleful, incandescent orange-red, much like the sunrise that acted as a harbinger of foul weather to come. Maelstrom offered Janna a pristine flake of snow as large as Vardak's hand before he took up the final vacant seat.

Aeon remained standing before the stone slab, eyes trained on the motionless form laid before him. Slowly, he raised his arms, and with the motion the gifts began to hover in the air. The objects disappeared in turn, and with each departure, Janna's body emanated a faint glow.

Vardak watched the proceedings uneasily, uncertain of their outcome. It was unlike any funeral procession he'd attended previously, though amongst his own people there was little fanfare. The deceased was taken into the desert, where a funeral pyre was prepared. The Warleader would speak briefly, then the family of the departed would host a feast in celebration of a life well-lived. The symbolism involved with the Immortals' ceremony was utterly foreign to him.

Aeon turned to face the others, a faint smile upon his face. "Janna has accepted the offered gifts and thanks you all for your kindness." To Flariel, he said, "She asks that you blame no one, Flariel. Janna insists she made the choice alone, so the others would not be burdened with unfinished business in the afterlife."

Vardak watched as the fire goddess began to tremble in her throne, her thin fingers digging into the carved arms of the seat. Her face was a mask of rage and flames burst into life across her body. She rose to her feet and turned her smoldering gaze upon Vardak.

"*He* was tasked with ensuring her safety." She pointed an accusatory finger in his direction. "*He* should have been the one to take up the relic. It was his duty."

Vardak met her stare, his jaw clenched in frustration. There was nothing he could say that would alter Flariel's perception of him, and his own guilt continued to gnaw at his gut. He said nothing in his own defense.

"Flariel, *enough*," Blademon growled. He came to his feet and swiftly stood between Vardak and the angry fire goddess. "Our agreement was that Vardak would ensure your daughter arrived here safely. What transpired after their arrival was no fault of his, nor any of the others'. He upheld the mission, as I understood it."

Fire roared toward Blademon, who braced himself and held it at bay. Vardak felt the searing heat, but he and the others remained unscathed.

"It was meant to be *him*," Flariel seethed.

"Then you are a greater fool than I'd believed, sister," Solsticia interjected. Her words caused Flariel to falter momentarily. "The Master of War always trains *two*. You would have eliminated one to satisfy your selfish desires and allow the balance to be shattered?"

"Such an act is not without precedent," Minora replied in a neutral tone. Vardak found it unsettling to hear her speak when her marble-sculpted features remained motionless.

Dus'tanne tossed her mane of leaf-colored hair. "The perpetrator of the act was stripped of his name, and sealed away in the planet's heart. Tell me, Flariel: Do you wish to join him?"

Deflated, the Fire Maiden sighed heavily. The flames she'd ignited extinguished seemingly of their own accord to leave behind only a thin layer of ash. "I wasn't considering your precious balance. Janna was mine. I wished glory and fame for my daughter, not meaningless death."

Aeon appeared at her side. "Death is rarely meaningless, Flariel, and Janna's was an act of selflessness the world rarely bears witness to. I have given her a place of honor."

Flariel's face crumpled in anguish as tears began to leak from her eyes. They quickly evaporated with an audible sizzle. After a moment, she gathered herself. When she met Vardak's eyes again, he no longer saw a goddess possessed by rage but a grieving mother consumed by anguish.

"We are not finished, Vardak," she vowed. "Before your life ends, you *will* serve me."

She vanished in a plume of smoke, leaving Vardak and the others to wonder at the meaning behind her words.

CHAPTER THIRTY-NINE

DESPERATE ORDERS

They'd made camp within the charred ruins that had once been the great city of Jennavere. Emra was astounded at the devastation that had been wrought in the span of a few short hours. Rubble littered the broken streets, sundered walls jutted skyward like jagged teeth poking up from the shattered rooftops and splintered windows. The harbor had been obliterated. Wreckage from dozens of sailing vessels choked the waterfront, while what little remained of the docks was smashed beyond repair. Jennavere could be rebuilt, but it would be years before the city would rival its former grandeur.

She and the others had spent two days pulling bodies from the wreckage and lighting funeral pyres for the dead. There were far more human casualties in the ruins than there were hooded ones, and they'd yet to find a single survivor. It sickened her.

On the morning of the third day, a messenger bird arrived from the outpost, requesting a more thorough report. While Warren handled the bird, she scrawled a reply, furious that the knight in charge refused to send aid. She detailed the devastation of Jennavere, explained a second time that the enemy appeared to have moved south, and requested again that soldiers be deployed in the direction of Stone Hill and Pine.

She scowled at the signature on the bottom of the message they'd received. Michael Hightower. He was a stickler for protocol, which was well and good when their borders were secure and they weren't under attack by a force of creatures straight out of legend. She handed Warren her reply and resigned herself to await orders from the capitol. Perhaps the king or the knight-commander would provide

308

instruction that didn't leave her with the sour taste of inaction. Perhaps they would perceive the true magnitude of the threat and send forces to aid the cities to the south.

They continued to scour the once-proud city for survivors into the afternoon. More bodies were discovered, and evidence that at least some of the residents may have escaped alive, but perhaps not of their own accord. They had uncovered lengths of rope, cut precisely and knotted, abandoned in what remained of the city's square. To Emra's eye, they looked ready-made to bind wrists or ankles.

"Do you believe the hooded ones take prisoners?" Lucas asked in an echo of her thoughts.

"It certainly appears that way," she replied. "We know so little about them. Will the prisoners be treated fairly? Will they wish for death before the week is out?" She kicked at a loose stone and paused to watch it bounce haphazardly across the square. "Gods, Luke, I don't know what to do."

"You're following protocol," he reminded her. "Await new orders, render aid to the current location until told otherwise, care for the bodies of the fallen. There's nothing more we can do, Em. We're twelve, against what appears to be a thousand or more."

"I wish there was something more we could do."

Weary and sore by the end of the day, Emra was silently thankful Callan had drawn supper duty for the evening. Not only was he possibly the best cook of their meager band, he rarely complained about the task. She took the opportunity to check on Fyrmane, where he was hobbled a short distance away with the other horses. He snorted at her approach and turned away, making his displeasure known.

"Gods, Fyrmane, if we were given leave to ride from this place, I wouldn't hesitate," she muttered as she began rubbing him down. The big bay snorted again, but she detected less derision in the sound this time.

"For a horse bred for his loyalty, you're certainly opinionated."

"Ser!" Warren called from the campfire. When she looked up, he waved at her frantically.

She sighed. "We'll continue this later," she promised Fyrmane, patting him on the snout before she went to see what Warren so urgently needed.

"Ser, we've received a pigeon from the capitol."

Warren handed her a tiny roll of parchment, sealed with blue wax. The royal sigil, a rearing snow leopard, was impressed upon it. She brought her eyes up to meet his. "This did not come from the knight-commander."

"No, Ser. Our message comes from the king, himself." He gestured to the kestrel perched near their remaining carrier pigeon. "His Majesty prefers swifter birds."

She nodded and broke open the wax seal. The others remained silent as she read her next orders, then reread them to ensure she understood. The situation was more dire than she'd believed.

"Cora, you are to take Warren and one other with you into Delucha. The king asks that you present yourselves as emissaries to the young queen and request her aid." She turned to Callan. "You are to take the rest of our group, with the exception of Lucas, to the outpost. The king is sending further reinforcements there as we speak. You will assist Ser Hightower as needed."

"And what of me?" Lucas asked, one dark eyebrow cocked in suspicion.

"You and I are to travel across the mountains and seek the aid of the Scorpion Men," she informed him. "We'll return to Ridgewater first in order to acquire provisions for the journey. The king believes the Scorpion Men may know more about the hooded ones' threat and may be willing to help us."

Lucas swallowed hard but nodded in understanding. "The journey across the Wasted Land is no easy feat."

"I realize that, but as the only knight in the region, I've been chosen for the task." She glanced at the soldiers around her, keenly aware she may not see some of them again. "We must depart at first light. The gods be with you all."

They returned to Ridgewater as the sun was setting the next day. Emra was keen to secure the necessary provisions before the dwindling merchant stalls finished closing up shop for the night; she insisted they wait to approach the inn until their shopping was done. Lucas had been unusually quiet for much of their journey, but she chalked it up to his preoccupation with what they'd encountered in Jennavere.

He followed her through the city, assisting when needed, but it was only after they'd stabled their horses at the inn that he finally broke his silence. "Em, I wasn't ordered to accompany you, was I?"

The question caught her off guard. The king had decreed she ride into the Wasted Land, but he'd not specifically stated she must do so alone. The journey would be grueling if the stories were true. It was unwise to attempt the trek solo, and not simply because the hooded ones might have a presence there.

"I wasn't forbidden from asking one of you to accompany me," she replied evasively.

Lucas groaned. "Em, if he finds out..."

"I am fully aware of the consequences, Luke."

Her act could be interpreted as disobedience. As a newly-ranked knight, she risked losing her hard-won title, but the alternative... She would rather be stripped of her title than dead in the barren landscape beyond the Gray Mountains because she'd been too vain to seek another's assistance.

"It was likely meant as your first great trial," Lucas continued, concern knotting his brow.

She frowned and tossed her braid over her shoulder in irritation. "And it would do the kingdom no favors if I attempted the journey alone and succumbed to the weather, the wildlife, or the lack of water. With two of us, there is a greater chance we will reach the Stronghold with the king's request, and the wildlife will be a lesser threat."

"There is no arguing with your logic, Em," he replied. "I'm in agreement, but I wanted to make certain you'd thought things through."

"I have." She crossed her arms. "Now, if you don't mind, I'd like to go inside for some supper. Arguing in the stable yard will not fill my belly."

He managed a tired smile and gestured that she should lead the way. Of all the soldiers who had accompanied her to Jennavere, Lucas Silverthorn was the only one who would fully understand her decision.

311

He might grouse or poke fun at her, but he was her oldest friend and the only person she fully trusted.

There was no one else she would undertake a perilous journey with and remain confident of their eventual success.

CHAPTER FORTY

A BLOODY EXAMPLE

The trio of orbs shed their oily light across the other nearby relics, arranged neatly in the glass case. Dranamir yearned to take hold of one of them, to draw upon the nearly limitless power once more. Now was not the time to utilize them, however; the orbs were not designed for destruction, but rather creation. She was still formulating her plans for them, and the glorious gift she would one day present to her Master.

She tore her gaze from the orbs, though her hand lingered upon the glass above them. She required a relic to aid her in the next battle, and the orbs were simply unsuited to the task. It was a shame, truly, that such vast power could not be harnessed to kill or destroy. The orbs' maker had abhorred violence, had wished his legacy be used only to better the world.

Her lips quirked at the thought. She'd corrupted two of them, forced them to create beings that were never meant to exist. Abominations, they'd been called in her day. Now, it seemed, they'd become a respected race unto themselves. Creation was not an ability limited to the gods, and she meant to repeat her earlier feat.

"Dranamir?"

She scowled as Jannyn's voice broke through her reverie. "What do you want?"

"It's nearly time, Dranamir. I've asked Alyra to transport me to the field today, seeing as you left me on the gods-damned outskirts the last time." His tone was bitter.

She shrugged but did not turn to face him. His loss of the Aethereal relic was not of her concern, and if Alyra hadn't bothered to make him a replacement yet, that was his problem to untangle. She was aware that Garin had traced the relic's whereabouts to the Shining Tower. Garin seemed to believe one of the young wizards had stolen it, but the scenario was unlikely. His last foray into the Aethereum had resulted in a confrontation with Ravin, and Garin was still abed two days later, nursing his injuries.

Her eyes locked on the thin, crystalline rod near the far end of the case that she'd recently acquired from the Murkor. The relic harbored the power of the storm, a perversion of Maelstrom's godly fury. It had always been one of Alyra's chosen relics. It allowed one to cast lightning, even when they lacked the power to do so on their own. A few powerful bolts would sow chaos amongst the Balotican defenders. It would do quite nicely.

As she removed the rod from within the glass, Alyra arrived. Dranamir frowned. She'd wasted too much time reminiscing over the orbs and now must endure the other woman's bothersome presence. Not for the first time, she wished their master had failed to intervene that night in the Deluchan palace. Alyra was useless, weak, an embarrassment to the Soulless.

"That's *mine*, Dranamir."

Dranamir turned slowly to face the other woman. Alyra was outraged; her nostrils flared and her full lips were compressed into a thin line.

"I was under the impression the relics kept here were for our collective use." She smiled grimly, enjoying the other's displeasure. "I'll return it after the battle is done. I doubt you'll have any use for it, holed up in the tower like the coward you are."

Incensed, Alyra clenched her fists at her side. Dranamir expected her to grasp at her miniscule magical power, but wisely, Alyra refrained. With the crystalline relic in Dranamir's hand, Alyra would not stand a chance, even if Jannyn leapt to her aid.

"There is a difference between cowardice and not wishing to be party to blatant cruelty, Dranamir." Alyra's voice quivered with rage.

"It continues to astound me that our master believed you fit for your current position." She waved one hand in the air and opened a portal to the Aethereum. "At least your current partner makes up for some of your shortcomings," she added with a pointed glance in Jannyn's direction.

314

She heard Alyra's cry of disgust as she departed the tower. The days were few when she could both antagonize Alyra and destroy half a city, and she meant to capitalize on this one.

She met Kama at the center of the army's temporary camp. It was immediately clear he was in a foul temper, that all was not going as planned. She surveyed their surroundings in a matter of moments. The Murkor battled atop Stone Hill's walls; they were taking heavier casualties than they had at Jennavere, though they appeared to be making headway. Their commander had entered the fray alongside his second. She couldn't recall the ridiculous title the man held, but she knew he was incredibly skilled with his blade. The curved, black sabers each carried marked the pair as distinct from the rest of the dark-hooded masses.

At the base of the rocky hilltop that gave the city its name, Scherok assaulted the lakeshore. There were Murkor soldiers near the creature, engaged with human defenders. Bodies from both sides lay broken and battered upon the splintered docks, and even from her distance, she noted a distinct lack of blood. As she watched, the serpent reared its head and struck a devastating blow at the epicenter of the combatants. Murkor and human alike fell to its strike.

Smoldering rage gripped her, and she rounded on Kama. "What does that gods-damned beast mean to accomplish with this act?"

Kama's eyes held none of the desire she'd become accustomed to seeing. The angular planes of his features were hard as he snarled his reply. "I was about to ask the same of you, Dranamir. You brought the creature along, and it is your responsibility. We cannot fucking afford these unnecessary casualties."

She crossed her arms and met his iron gaze with a cool one of her own. "Its orders were clear, and I did not believe it would attempt to betray us."

"Put an end to it, Dranamir."

She smiled wickedly; she'd been awaiting those words. "Gladly. Tell your commander the serpent will no longer feature in his future plans."

A portal appeared nearby and Jannyn exited. She ignored him as she made her way toward the docks, hoping he'd speak with Kama and leave her to the serpent. Instead, he fell into step alongside her. She gripped the crystalline rod so tightly it would have shattered if it hadn't been crafted of magic. The man was a nuisance.

"I'll not be left behind again, Dranamir."

"Then speak with Kama. I'm not going into the city."

Jannyn continued to pursue her, dogged in his persistence. She was certain Alyra had put him up to it, if for no other reason than to satisfy her petty revenge. Her mood darkened.

"Whatever your plans are, Dranamir, I mean to be a part of them."

She rounded on him faster than he managed to react. She seized her power, felt it thrum through her veins and connect with the relic clenched in her fist. She jabbed its translucent point at his throat and sent an arc of lightning into his body. He shrieked, though from pain or surprise, she wasn't certain, nor did she care.

She intensified the bolt until the odors of burnt flesh and ozone overpowered the stench of sweat, blood, and churned earth from the surrounding field. Jannyn's stout face became a rictus of agony in the moment before she released him. He staggered and fell to his knees, panting.

"I've business with the serpent. *Go speak with Kama.* I will not repeat myself again."

"Watch your back, Dranamir," he growled. "There will come a day when you'll find yourself begging for mercy."

She bent to stare down at him until their foreheads were nearly touching, her eyes ablaze with fury. "I do not beg, Jannyn, and I guarantee you will regret making threats against me. The master said only that I mustn't kill you. But torture? That remains a possibility."

He snarled and backed away before regaining his feet. He reminded her of a cornered animal. She smirked as he left to seek Kama. Perhaps the man could see reason after all, but it was a pity she had to beat it into his dense skull.

She refocused her attention on the silvery serpent at the lake's edge, rage like molten metal coursing through her veins. Scherok lashed its massive tail toward the docks and struck down another pair of Murkor. The creature's wanton destruction must come to an end. She would tolerate its betrayal no longer.

316

She encountered little resistance as she stormed across the battlefield. The Murkor held the humans at bay, and those witless enough to challenge her were quickly dispatched. She'd begun to understand why Alyra loved the crystal rod as she did; it was deadly and efficient. Her only lament was that it spilled too little blood.

Scherok noticed her approach moments before she reached the shoreline. It ceased its attack, eyes wide with uncertainty and fear. She suspected it knew why she'd come. She tucked the rod into her belt and drew on her magic. She would tear this creature apart, and she would do so by the goriest means possible. The relic would not assist her in spilling the serpent's blood, and she meant for it to suffer before it was dispatched to Aeon's dark realm.

She struck the creature with a blow meant to daze before she lifted it above the water. She watched as it writhed, its discomfort evident in its every sinuous movement.

"I thought I'd made it clear what would occur should you defy me." Her voice was low, menacing, her words scarcely heard over the clamor of battle.

I did not—

"Do you think me a fool, Scherok?"

She began to pull its silvery scales out by their roots, one by one. She started the process near its sensitive underbelly while the serpent hissed in agony. She allowed each scale to fall with a papery crunch onto the rocky shore, watched as rivulets of dark blood streamed from each new wound she inflicted. Scherok thrashed in its invisible bonds, helpless to stave off Dranamir's magic.

She paused to allow the creature to regain its breath. "You will tell me why you attack our forces, Scherok."

A mistake. A mistake!

She snorted. "Unlikely." She used a bit of magic to amplify her voice so it would be heard over the battlefield. "Allow the Murkor and our other allies to observe what happens when you fail the Soulless."

Panic blossomed in the serpent's inky eyes as the sounds of combat faded around them. Dranamir did not turn to acknowledge their audience, but she could sense countless pairs of eyes upon her. She withdrew the relic and aimed it at the creature's broad throat. Blood continued to stream from its previous wounds to stain its underbelly in a garnet hue. She channeled power into the relic, and its pointed tip began to spark and flicker. Scherok roared, but no amount of vocal protest or writhing would save its scaly hide.

She summoned a bolt of blue-white lightning and arced it in a jagged line toward the terrified serpent. The air crackled and hissed. Her long hair reacted to the vast quantity of energy, billowing outward in a dark halo as she maintained the outpouring of magic. Scherok's body contorted painfully, and she was certain she heard the snapping of vertebrae over its anguished roars.

An acrid stench filled the air as the serpent's remaining scales began to char. She continued her onslaught even as it fell silent. Blue flames erupted from within Scherok's body as its life faded, and moments later its body exploded outward in a barrage of bloody tissue, bone fragments, and singed scales. The lakeshore—and those near it—were spattered with gore.

She turned to face the nearest Murkor, who quickly resumed their fight. She could not see their expressions, but she could sense their fear. She laughed mirthlessly as she began her trek toward the camp.

Human and Murkor alike steered clear of her. Her demonstration not only served to reinforce the Soulless' dominance, but it asserted her power as well. They did not need to know the toll it had taken, that even with the use of the relic, her energy waned. Her corrupted features, spattered with the serpent's blood, must have appeared horrific.

Let them all fear her. It was best this way.

CHAPTER FORTY-ONE

HOMECOMING

Vardak gazed across the balcony, taking in the incredible sight of his home, far below, surrounded by an ocean of stars. Solsticia had promised to return them home once evening fell, and though he suspected twilight was near at hand, there was no true way of knowing the time in the perpetual light and ever-present darkness of the Sky Palace. His belongings were packed, his armor donned, his axe sheathed across his back. He was eager to return home but had come to the balcony for a final glimpse at the wonders of Solsticia's celestial abode. It was unlikely he would be granted a return to this place during his lifetime.

Since Janna's memorial and the confrontation that had ensued between himself, Flariel, and Blademon, Vardak had taken time to reflect on the situation. The words of the gods, with the exception of the Fire Maiden's, forced him to realize his guilt was misplaced. In its wake he found himself weary; since the day Blademon had selected him, he'd been nothing more than a pawn of the Immortals. Janna's fate was much the same, but it had taken her untimely death before he realized the truth.

Flariel's parting words continued to haunt him. She sought reparation for her daughter's decision, and Vardak was meant to pay. He doubted Blademon would intervene further in the matter. He resigned himself to the fact his destiny was intertwined with the will of both gods, and there was little he could do to extricate himself from them. At least Solsticia seemed to understand his desire to protect his family; he wasn't certain the other gods harbored such empathy for the plights of their mortal counterparts.

319

An echo of footsteps behind him forced him to turn away from the celestial view. It was Coreyaless, her satchel of herbs slung over one shoulder. He supposed she'd sought him out to say her farewell. Now that she and Danness were reunited, there was no longer any reason for her to remain in his company.

"It's beautiful, isn't it?" she asked as she came to lean on the railing beside him. Her gaze swept across the myriad stars to focus on a single point upon the planet's vast surface.

"Yes."

"More than a thousand years, and this is a sight I never believed I'd see." She smiled wistfully then peered up at him. "I never properly thanked you, Vardak. When we left Vidune Forest, I knew I was chasing the fragment of a dream, but I never truly believed it would become reality. Danness and I… We've decided we will help you free your brother."

"I believed you'd come to say goodbye." He smiled then, overwhelmed by gratitude. "Your aid is welcome, Coreyaless. The Murkor aren't a mean-spirited people, but I cannot believe my people will be released unscathed. Not with the Soulless involved."

"That is my assessment, as well. We have already spoken to Solsticia about our intention, and she has agreed to take us to the Stronghold with you." She shifted her gaze to the starry expanse beyond the balcony. "Janna would have wanted it this way."

"Yes…Thank you, Coreyaless."

The simple statement felt inadequate to convey the depth of his gratitude, but he hoped she understood. Janna had been thrust into his life, helpless yet bound by the gods from the moment of her birth. He had resented her presence at first, had been confused why the gods would entrust such a mission to a young woman with few worldly skills. Over time, he'd grown to appreciate her optimism, her ready smiles, and her offer of friendship. Her decision to take the Moon's Eye continued to gnaw at him. He would not allow her sacrifice to be made in vain.

Sometime later, Danness joined them, followed by Maryn. Vardak glanced curiously at the Felene guardsman, uncertain of his plans.

"I've spoken to Aeon," Maryn confided in a low tone. "This war in the north is larger than I'd realized. His realm is flooded with new souls..." He looked down, his furred countenance troubled.

"What do you mean to do?"

"What I must," Maryn replied. "My people may be sheltered from the coming storm for a time, but they are unaware it's on the horizon. I will represent them in this fight. Aeon has agreed to inform my siblings of my decision since I will not be returning to the jungle."

"Where will you go?" Vardak asked, though he suspected he knew the other's answer.

Maryn chuckled. "With you, of course. You're Blademon's chosen. If I plan to fight—and I do—the best place to seek action is at your side."

The two clasped forearms. "I'll be glad to have you watching my back," Vardak told him.

"Likewise. Perhaps one day I'll finally see that beastly axe of yours serve its purpose." Maryn grinned, a mischievous glint in his eyes. "I'm not convinced it's anything more than a deadly decoration at this juncture in time."

A brief laugh escaped him, the first he'd managed in what seemed to be days. He was glad Maryn planned to continue the journey with him; the guardsman had become a friend during their foray through the jungle.

"I think you'll get on well with Patak," he replied.

He hoped his eldest brother's injury was mending as well as Blademon had insinuated. He harbored no doubts that Patak would join him once he learned Vardak meant to free Travin and the others. He would learn soon enough how Patak fared.

Solsticia arrived before Maryn could respond. She commanded their attention with her mere presence. "It seems everyone is here. Shall I transport you now?"

Vardak glanced at the others, and as each nodded, he said, "Yes."

He anticipated the disorientation that accompanied the goddess' method of transportation, but it still left him reeling for several seconds. When he opened his eyes, he found it was early evening; the pale glow of the sun's dying rays rimmed the distant

321

mountains in gold. The air was blissfully dry and warm, though he knew it would become much cooler before long. White sand carpeted the earth for as far as he could see in every direction and crested into vast dunes to the east. The sky was clear and speckled with faint stars.

Before him rose the metallic, domed roof of the Stronghold. The small portion visible from the outside belied the structure's vast size, buried deep beneath the desert sands. Four armed sentries guarded the entrance, which he noted was barred for the night.

Vardak smiled to himself. He was finally home.

"I think it wise for us to follow you, Vardak." Coreyaless' tone held a note of concern. "Your people are at war, after all, and the guards don't appear friendly."

"They won't harm you," he assured her. "Follow my lead, and I'll introduce you when we are nearer. There is a good chance I'll know some of the soldiers on duty."

As they closed the distance to the Stronghold, Vardak not only recognized two of the four on duty, but one dropped his vigil and broke into a grin at his approach. Vardak increased his pace, eager to speak with Patak once more. The others fell behind Vardak, while Patak broke away from the other sentries, a joyous whoop issuing from his lungs. The two embraced in a clamor of armor plates.

"You chose a fine time to run off adventuring," Patak stated as they stepped away from one another. "We could have sorely used your skills a few weeks past." His grin faltered and he hung his head. "Vardak, Travin's been—"

"I know. It's why I've returned."

Patak brightened. "Then you have a plan?"

"Not yet. I know where they've been taken, and I will have them freed."

He glanced over his shoulder as the others caught up with him. Patak stared at each in turn and paused to eye Maryn with unconcealed interest.

"By Aeon's hairy ass, I didn't believe your people were real."

Maryn smirked. "It was Aeon's hairy ass that prompted me to come here." He glanced at Vardak. "I suppose this is the brother you've spoken of?"

Vardak chuckled. "Yes. He's the uncivilized one."

Patak feigned hurt. "Oh, that stings worse than a gods-damned sunburn, little brother."

Vardak suppressed a laugh and managed to ignore Patak's antics long enough to make proper introductions.

"We may as well go inside," Patak said once they'd been acquainted. "Mother will be pleased to see you. She's been a right wreck since the battle, as has Dakna. She learned two days afterward that she's with child."

Vardak's eyebrows rose with the news. Travin would be a father in a few months' time. "All the more reason to see him released."

Patak nodded in approval. "Now that you're home, we can form a plan. Word will undoubtedly reach Sevic before long…" Patak suddenly broke into an amused grin. "Look at me, Vardak. I'm relying on *you* to get us out of this bind. My little brother, the hero."

"I wouldn't call myself that," he muttered, embarrassed.

One glance at the others told him there would be no end to Patak's teasing. Coreyaless wore a bemused smile while Maryn smirked, ready to pounce on the next opportunity to poke fun at one or both of them. Patak would capitalize on their attention and make a show of his provocation for the sake of his own entertainment. Patak rarely poked fun at strangers, but his brothers were always fair game.

They wound their way through empty corridors toward the living quarters. The occasional sentry skittered by on their way to patrol or watch duties. Most saluted Vardak as they passed, and though he failed to recognize many of the faces, he returned the gesture. Patak was right in that assessment at least; the Warleader, Sevic, would soon learn of his return. His many sparring sessions with Blademon had cemented his features in the minds of the masses.

He heard his mother's voice in the corridor ahead well before they'd rounded the final bend to her quarters. He recognized the gruff tones of Sevic, as well, and suppressed a sigh. His hope for a quiet homecoming was quickly coming unraveled.

Patak snickered as he registered the conversation ahead. "I told you he'd find out."

"And I'd hoped for a peaceful night at home." Vardak frowned at his brother.

"I'm beginning to believe peace doesn't follow in your wake, Vardak," Maryn replied, which only served to make Patak laugh aloud.

"My brother certainly did not train with Armistral," Patak quipped.

They rounded the bend to find Zaria had ceased her conversation with Sevic. The pair were awaiting their arrival; Zaria with a proud smile, and Sevic with a stoic expression.

Sevic nodded in greeting, then eyed Patak critically. "I trust you've told him the news?"

Patak's mischievous grin faded. "Yes, sir."

Sevic clapped Vardak on the shoulder. "We'll speak in the morning. Your mother and brother will wish to have this evening with you."

Zaria offered Maryn and the Airess sleeping mats for the night once she'd ushered them inside. The family's quarters were no longer as cramped as they once had been; Patak had acquired his own space some time ago, as had Travin when he married. Vardak still maintained a room within his mother's home, though he'd scarcely been present during the past five years. His training with Blademon had kept him away from home for much of that time. When he was in the Stronghold, he'd often been scheduled for patrol duty.

Once the others were settled in the rooms that had previously belonged to his older brothers, Zaria led her sons into the tiny kitchen. She prompted Patak to recall the recent battle with the Murkor while she began fussing about the hearth.

Vardak listened carefully, frustrated once more that he'd been leagues away and unable to bolster their defenses. The Murkor had arrived unexpectedly, and unbeknownst to the patrol. Patak described a strange man who seemed to oversee the battle from afar and who later issued orders to the Murkor attackers. Patak claimed the Murkor seemed fearful of the man, and Vardak began to wonder if what his brother had seen was one of the Soulless. Neither side had sustained many casualties, though the Murkor had fared better simply due to the surprising nature of their attack.

"It was damned strange what they did at the end, Vardak," Patak told him with a shake of his head. "The dozen or so of our soldiers that were captured were led away while they sounded a retreat. I was wounded near the front line, and I overheard the Murkor commander as they pulled back. I don't believe the Murkor truly wanted the fight but were forced into it."

"If that's true," he said slowly, "then perhaps we can negotiate the release of our people."

Patak shrugged. "Sevic doesn't seem to believe it, but I'll leave that discussion for the two of you."

Vardak studied his brother for a time. "Blademon told me you were injured. How are you healing?"

Patak shrugged, the hint of a grin crossing his face. "I still must bandage it daily, and the apothecary believes it'll leave an ugly scar. I'm mending."

"Coreyaless is a skilled healer."

Patak laughed. "I'm surprised you'd subject one of your new companions to me so easily."

Vardak shook his head. "She knows you were hurt, Patak. It wouldn't surprise me if she demanded to have a look at your wound as soon as she wakes in the morning."

"Do you believe she's better than our own people?" Zaria broke in as she set a kettle on the hook within the hearth.

"I do, mother. Coreyaless is far older than she appears, and she tended my own hurts a few times."

Zaria faced him them, concern blossoming in her dark eyes. "You were hurt, Vardak?"

"I think it's time my younger brother tells of his own adventures," Patak added with a smirk. He crossed his arms and settled into a more comfortable position.

Vardak sighed, but knew it was best to oblige them. He told them of all that had transpired since Blademon whisked him away from the Stronghold; his meeting with Janna and Flariel, their journey to seek Coreyaless, the eerie trek through Stonewall Hall. He spoke of the Felene jungles and Maryn, the flesh-eating plants they'd narrowly avoided with the use of Coreyaless' strange herbal compound, the discovery of Solsticia's temple, and the Airess' reunion. When he began to recall the recent events within the Sky Palace and Janna's unfortunate role, his mother departed the hearth to gather him into her arms.

"Grieve, Vardak. You'll feel better afterward," she whispered gently. "At times, you remind me very much of your father."

He allowed himself a few moments in which to shed tears, wrapped in his mother's embrace. Patak observed them wordlessly; even he understood Vardak's emotional turmoil. Only amongst his family was he comfortable enough to allow his stoic façade to vanish.

After a time, Zaria moved away and began to prepare three cups of a golden liquor, brewed from the fruits of a desert cactus, and laced with a variety of spices. She pressed one mug into his hands with a knowing expression. "Drink," she ordered as she passed another to Patak.

"Gods, Vardak," his brother managed after a time. "I can't imagine being forced to make such a choice. And Flariel wanted *you* to take this relic?"

Vardak nodded, his expression souring at the goddess' name. He pulled on the leather cord around his neck to draw the Moon's Eye into the open. "I'm to find a wizard capable of using it, but I told them Travin's rescue comes first."

Patak's eyebrows rose in disbelief. "You told the gods...?"

"I've grown weary of acting the damned pawn," he replied in a growl. "I will do as they ask—*after* I know our brother is safe."

For all his resolve the previous evening, his plans were left in tatters after meeting with Sevic. The Warleader would not allocate forces to attempt a rescue mission. Vardak's mood careened between fury and despair with each word that spilled from Sevic's lips.

"If the Soulless have truly returned, as you claim, your proposed mission is simply too dangerous, Vardak. All paths between the desert and the caverns lead past the black tower. I'm sorry, but we cannot risk losing so many in order to retrieve so few."

"A small unit can slip past unnoticed." Vardak was determined to persevere.

Sevic crossed his arms, his expression steely. "You will take that cursed relic to Dar Daelad. Locate a wizard willing to aid our people, and deliver it to them. Then, you will return here."

"Sir—"

"That's an order, Vardak. Do not discuss the relic or your mission with anyone who is not already apprised of the situation. Dismissed."

He swallowed his anger, forced himself to salute the Warleader, and stalked into the corridor. He'd never considered insubordination against Sevic, but he contemplated it now. Sevic was wrong to leave their people in the hands of the Murkor. If he could not find a way to change Sevic's mind, he would risk the Warleader's inevitable reprisal and disobey the direct command.

Travin and the others would not remain imprisoned within the enemy's lair. He would ensure their release, and consequences be damned.

CHAPTER FORTY-TWO

A DISAPPEARANCE

Since the night he'd suffered at the hands of the Soulless—Garin, he reminded himself—Tavesin had been kept under close watch by the wizards. Arra, too, though they'd finally been allowed some time to speak each evening in the kitchens. His days were filled with history lessons and the fundamentals of magic, his evenings with studies of the Aethereum under the Drakkon mages. Aziarah continued to teach him directly, but Arra had been paired with another. It was for their safety, he'd been told.

The evening began no differently than the others. They finished their supper, met Hasnin in his study, and were escorted to the tower's rooftop. A brisk wind blew in from the north, bringing with it the promise of autumn. Several of the Drakkon circled in the sky overhead, relishing the sensation of the wind beneath their scaly wings. Aziarah and Trozyen were grounded and had been awaiting their arrival as usual. Trozyen was taller than Aziarah and considerably younger in appearance. In spite of his youth, the other Drakkon often deferred to him, but Tavesin had not yet unraveled the intricacies of their society enough to understand the reason for it.

Aziarah drew him aside. "Tonight, you will both learn how to enter the Aethererum directly from this realm. It is dangerous to perform such magic alone, Tavesin. Your last encounter with the Soulless is proof of that. He was there physically. If you'd been as well, he could easily have killed you."

"I know."

Tavesin hugged his arms to his chest as a chill coursed through his body. He'd secretly been hoping Aziarah would push this bit of his training back. He wasn't ready to face Garin another time, and he knew he could not count upon his mysterious savior's arrival if he found himself in danger again.

"When we enter, you must remain with me at all times, Tavesin. The rules of the Aethereum are no different if you visit while dreaming or there physically. You must guard your thoughts carefully." She studied him, her reptilian eyes seeming to pierce into his very soul. "Do you understand?"

"Yes."

He wondered if there were some way to change her proposed lesson for the evening without making himself look the coward. When nothing came to him, he looked down at his hands while his chest tightened in fear. He did not wish to go through with this. If Garin were there, or one of the others...

"Tavesin?" Aziarah asked sharply.

"I don't want to go, Aziarah," he blurted. His face flushed at the admission. Certain she would be angry, he refused to meet her eye.

To his surprise, she said, "I understand. Perhaps we shall review last night's teachings, then. There is no reason to forge ahead if you aren't ready. In fact, I am pleased that you have spoken up. Our people believe one must be prepared, mind and body, to perform such potentially dangerous magics, and with good reason. Those who push themselves beyond their limits often fail to return from the celestial realm."

A surge of relief passed through him. He knew Arra would tease him relentlessly the next day once she learned she'd pulled ahead of him in their lessons. He would take the ribbing. He could not face the prospect of meeting Garin again, not so soon.

"Thank you."

Aziarah began to quiz him while he did his best to focus on her words. She seemed pleased with his answers, though he couldn't help but watch as Arra opened a pale, luminous portal across the rooftop. Moments later, she and Trozyen disappeared through it and were gone.

His heart despaired at the notion that he would not be joining her. He simply could not muster the stomach for such adventure this night. He may have awakened from his last encounter physically unscathed, but the fear of another run-in with the Soulless terrified him. If the golden-eyed man hadn't appeared when he did, Tavesin was certain Garin would have held him captive indefinitely. It was not a notion he wished to dwell on.

He refocused on Aziarah, determined not to disappoint her further. Arra might tease him, but he could endure her jibes. He could not endure another prolonged and merciless beating.

"We each must learn at our own pace, Tavesin. Do not concern yourself with Arra's progress overtaking your own. She has much yet to learn from your Council of Auras that you have already taken to heart."

"I know." He was unable to keep the despondency from his tone.

"When you tell me you're prepared to progress, we will do so," she promised, "but *you* must determine when that time is. I cannot read your mind."

Tavesin nodded but was never given the opportunity to respond. Another pale portal opened several paces away, and Trozyen darted through. Tavesin knew immediately something was wrong; Trozyen's eyes darted wildly, and his expression appeared panicked. He shifted his gaze back to Aziarah, who had stiffened as she awaited the younger Drakkon's news.

Tavesin's concern grew as Trozyen closed the portal before Arra emerged behind him. Why wasn't she with him?

"Aziarah, has she returned?" Trozyen asked as he scanned the rooftop.

"She has not. Were you separated?"

Trozyen bobbed his head anxiously. "I was explaining to her the dangers inherent in visiting the Aethereum physically. She was at my side, and then suddenly, she was not. I have no doubt her thoughts strayed, but when I attempted to trace her location, I found her essence gone. *Gone,* Aziarah! How can this be?"

Tavesin bit his lower lip to keep it from trembling. His emotions roiled between terror and blind optimism, fear she'd been taken by the Soulless and hope that she would emerge from another portal at any moment.

"Tavesin, return to your mentor and inform him that Arra is missing."

His heart sank, and for several long moments he merely stared at the pair of Drakkon, unable to speak, unable to move. Arra was missing. What if Garin had taken her? What if she'd been discovered by one of the others?

"Tavesin," Aziarah said in a gentler tone, "you must tell Hasnin."

Her words spurred him into action. He raced across the dark rooftop toward the stairs and prayed that Hasnin would be awaiting him. Tavesin had never bothered to ask his mentor if he remained near the magical shield throughout the duration of his lessons with the Drakkon, or if he returned to the lower levels of the tower while his apprentice was otherwise engaged.

He burst through the door and flew down the steps at a reckless pace, only to find the landing nearest the shield empty. Tears of frustration stung his eyes. He brushed them away angrily and returned to the rooftop at a slower speed, despair weighting his steps like lead.

Aziarah noted his return and immediately motioned to one of the nearby Drakkon. Tavesin watched as he leapt from the rooftop in a graceful dive toward the ground, far below.

"Hasnin wasn't there," he informed her in a quavering tone.

"I know," she replied in a soothing tone. "We'll find her, Tavesin. I promise you this."

"What if it was *him?*" The question tumbled from his lips unbidden, his fear exposed to the nearby Drakkon. He no longer cared what they must think of him; his only concern was Arra's safety.

"I've dealt with him before," she reminded him, "and if he is the cause of this trouble, I will deal with him again."

It was some time before Hasnin reappeared on the rooftop. Aziarah had departed, leaving Tavesin under Trozyen's charge. The younger Drakkon spoke little, but in spite of his relatively strange features, Tavesin sensed he was plagued with guilt. The silence suited Tavesin's own mood well enough; he wasn't certain he could speak without losing the tenuous hold on his roiling emotions.

When Hasnin knelt beside his apprentice, Tavesin told him all that had occurred. He blinked away unwanted tears and refused to allow them to fall. Instead, he stared into the darkness beyond the rooftop's edge.

"Aziarah's gone to search for her," Trozyen said at the end of Tavesin's retelling. "I tried to locate her myself, but it was as if…" He looked away with a shake of his head and would not meet Tavesin's eye. "It was as if she'd left the Aethereum altogether. We hadn't yet discussed how to perform the exit magic."

Tavesin's heart wrenched at the news, more certain than ever that Arra hadn't disappeared of her own volition.

Hasnin perceived a change in Tavesin's demeanor. "Aziarah is the greatest Aethereal mage of the Drakkon people," he said gently. "She will find Arra."

"And if she doesn't?"

Hasnin released a heavy sigh. "Then gods help us, Taven. Pray for Arra's swift return."

CHAPTER FORTY-THREE

DRAJAK'VEN

"He's granted me leave to return to the caverns, sir." Jal'den paced the length of the commander's tent. His buoyant mood propelled him into near-constant motion. "I don't believe he suspects anything."

Aran'daj straightened from his position, bent over a map of the Lake Jennavere area. He was in agreement with Jal'den; if the Soulless had suspected the pair were responsible for the serpent's "mistake", they would have been mercilessly killed as soon as the city had fallen. The Murkor had lost several dozen soldiers to the serpent's might, but the creature was no longer a threat. The casualties were unfortunate, the deaths a blight on his conscience, yet they'd been unavoidable.

"We must ensure it remains that way, Jal'den."

"Of course, sir." Jal'den paused mid-stride to peer at him, and Aran'daj suspected he grinned beneath his dark hood. "I volunteered to assist the alchemists with the transportation of our prisoners. It will provide a brief opportunity to speak with the Kal."

Aran'daj nodded, pleased at the prospect. "I will prepare a message for him." He had much to tell his grandfather and little of it good.

"Kama stated he will magic us away from here at dawn," Jal'den continued. "We don't have much time."

Aran'daj shoved the map and several missives away from the center of the table, then took up a small scrap of blank parchment and a quill. He began to write in the code he'd been taught by his father as a child. The code was known only to the Kal and his descendants for use in situations much like this one. He could not risk the Soulless learning the true meaning behind his words, and it was best that Jal'den remained ignorant of them, as well. If his ploy failed, Aran'daj understood his life would be forfeit, and command of the army would fall to Jal'den. The less the young Arms Master knew, the safer he would be.

Kal Aran'jandah —

Jennavere and Stone Hill have fallen. Our overlords are pleased. The aquatic threat has been vanquished. I will provide details once I am allowed to return home. They seek to further their dominance of Balotica, and have their sights set on a city called Pine.

Jal'den has been granted only a brief stay in the caverns. There are many human prisoners accompanying him. I have done all I can to avoid bloodshed, but the humans have suffered greatly at the hands of the Soulless. I fear some may be unsuited to labor, yet I pray you will find a place for them. The alternative is unspeakable. These creatures of magic possess no heart.

Aran'daj scanned the message quickly before he folded it and passed it to Jal'den. It had been many years since he'd last written in the Kal's coded script. He prayed he hadn't forgotten any crucial elements and that the Kal would understand. Even with the cryptic script to mask his words, he feared its discovery by the Soulless. Magic was a curious and unpredictable variable, one he wasn't certain could be foiled by a written cipher.

The note disappeared into one of Jal'den's pockets. "Is there anything else, Commander?"

Aran'daj shook his head. "Gods be with you, Jal'den."

"You as well, sir."

Aran'daj returned the map to its previous position as Jal'den exited his tent. Kama, pleased with his successes at Jennavere and Stone Hill, already had his sights set upon the city of Pine. Pine was located at the southernmost tip of the vast lake, and unlike the other two cities, was within a days' ride of the nearest Balotican military outpost. He was certain their arrival was no longer a secret to the kingdom's residents and knew they must prepare for much heavier resistance. The Murkor would be in for a true fight.

His plans must be flawless. He'd known since the Soulless' arrival, that night at the chasm's edge, that they were without mercy, conscienceless as the void. The sea serpent's brutal demise had served to cement this fact in the commander's mind; he must achieve victory, or his fate would be the same. He could do nothing to save his people from their plight if he were dead.

It was daylight before he realized he'd been staring at the map for hours but had managed to formulate nothing of a plan. His head ached from the mental strain, compounded by the diffuse light that filtered through the canvas overhead. He would never devise a cohesive plan in his current state. Resigned, he turned away from the maps, charts, and missives strewn across the table to seek an elusive day's rest.

Aran'daj was awakened by an uncertain whisper. "Sir?"

He sat up swiftly. He was unused to sleeping so soundly that he failed to notice the arrival of another in his tent. He scrambled to fix his hood in place before seeking the voice's owner. The sun had set again, and his tent was blissfully dark. A tall shadow stood near the exit, a curved saber at its hip. Relief flooded his veins; Jal'den had returned.

He pulled on his sturdy boots and rose to his feet. "Arms Master."

"Commander. I would have come sooner, but I didn't wish to arouse suspicion. The Kal has sent word."

He nodded. "His message?"

Rather than retrieve a note, Jal'den hesitated. "Sir, I hope you understand its meaning. It made little sense to me."

"Jal'den?"

"He read your note, then said I must tell you this: He will do all he can but makes no promises. The others watch endlessly. We must recede into the depths." Jal'den shook his head, clearly baffled. "He would not write a reply. He claimed it is no longer safe."

The others referred to the Soulless, he believed, but he was comforted to know the Kal would attempt to treat the prisoners kindly. The final statement held no meaning for Aran'daj, and his concern was intensified with the implication the Kal believed his cipher was no longer secret.

"Was there anything more, Jal'den?"

"No, sir. Nothing from the Kal." Jal'den paused for effect, then said, "Sal'zar was in the caverns when I returned. He will do what he can from within the tower to help us, sir."

Aran'daj frowned. He did not know Sal'zar well, though he trusted Jal'den. Bringing a fourth person into their schemes amplified their risk of discovery and increased the likelihood their plans would end in failure. The idea of including Sal'zar in their plans had occurred to him previously, but he hadn't acted upon the notion despite the Kal's dealings with the alchemist. There were too many unknowns, too many opportunities for failure, given the alchemist's proximity to the Soulless. He'd suspected Jal'den's connection to Sal'zar for some time. Propriety demanded he not pry, but for the sake of his people's future, he was compelled to seek the truth.

"What is your connection to Sal'zar? I do not know him well, Jal'den."

Jal'den was silent for several moments, and Aran'daj felt certain he'd crossed a line. Jal'den had good reason to be angry; such questions were seen as crude and insulting. If Aran'daj were correct in his assumption, Jal'den would be furious, and rightly so.

Jal'den crossed his arms, and when he spoke, his voice was steely. "You can trust him, Commander. I will swear my life upon it."

"And you don't believe the Soulless will corrupt his mind? He's been taken to the tower to train in the ways of magic, a thing none of our people have done in the entirety of our history. I cannot merely take your word when it comes to his character, Jal'den."

Aran'daj kept his tone even. He did not wish to enflame Jal'den's temper any further. He needed the truth, and Jal'den's assurances were not sufficient any longer.

Jal'den released a snarl of frustration. "Fucking gods, Commander! It's none of your damned business!"

"Under usual circumstances, I would agree," he countered, "but our times are far from usual, Jal'den. If you mean to include the alchemist in our plot, I need to know if he can be trusted. *Implicitly.*"

Jal'den began to pace, his movements akin to the panthers that were known to stalk the northern reaches of the Wasted Land. He was deadly, dangerous, and primed for attack. Aran'daj knew he'd pressed Jal'den too far.

"If the Kal didn't speak so highly of you, I'd end your life now," Jal'den growled, his hand straying to the hilt of his saber. "It would be within my rights to do so, Commander. You pry into matters that are not your concern." The heat had dissipated from his voice, leaving in its wake cold malice.

Aran'daj was keenly aware of Jal'den's position within the tent. He continued to pace, but his path blocked the only exit. If the Arms Master drew his blade with intent to kill, Aran'daj might hold his own for a short time, but the fight would inevitably end in his defeat. He'd witnessed Jal'den's skill on the battlefield, knew how ruthlessly efficient the Arms Master was with his blades.

"The Kal indicated he cannot trust his own cipher," Aran'daj stated quietly. "Is there any chance that Sal'zar will falter, Jal'den? Of the four of us, he is at the greatest risk. He is—"

"Don't you think I know that, Commander?" Jal'den roared. "Every gods-damned day, I worry what they'll force upon him. I am helpless to interfere! Never in my life have I been unable to assist those who mean the most to me, and yet I can do nothing to ease his suffering."

It wasn't a direct confirmation of his suspicions, but Jal'den's admission sufficed to affirm them. "I believe I understand," he replied.

"Know this," Jal'den continued to seethe. "If *anything* happens to Sal'zar, I will tear the world asunder with my bare hands to avenge him. He would do the same for me."

"I will take you at your word, Arms Master. If you trust him, then so will I."

Jal'den dropped his hand to his side and continued to pace. "Do not attempt to pry again, Commander. I won't hesitate to bring our disagreement up with the Kal."

"As you say," Aran'daj said uneasily.

The Kal might understand his reasoning, but he would be forced to endure the humiliation of a direct reprimand. Such a blight on his public persona could very well land him amongst the gray-robed casteless. Jal'den was young, but he was astute and understood the workings of the Murkor society as well as any elder. His threat was far from baseless.

337

Jal'den stopped abruptly and turned to face him. "Might we discuss Sal'zar's offer, now that the question of his loyalty is moot?"

When Aran'daj nodded, Jal'den said, "Sal'zar has agreed to feed us what information he can. He overhears things in the tower that may be of great value to our people. He has also learned a means to communicate directly with me."

"And only you, Jal'den?"

"Yes. Perhaps over time, he may learn to contact others, but he hasn't mastered that talent yet." Jal'den hung his head, seeming to deflate. "Commander, I... Perhaps I must answer your intrusive question, after all. I've already implied enough."

"You are *ujar'havel*." A bonded pair, recognized by the matriarchs of both families, united by the words of the Kal.

The words brought with it poignant memories of his own past, of a time when Aran'daj had hoped for the approval of his own *ujar'havel*. Rej'amin's mother had refused to accept the proposed union, and Aran'daj had refused the offer of bonding to another. He'd become known as *drajak'ven*, an adult Murkor who'd chosen to pass his life without a mate. He did not regret his decision; his heart would always belong to Rej'amin.

Reluctantly, Jal'den nodded. "We don't often share this with others, Commander. A bond such as ours isn't readily accepted by many."

"I understand far better than you know, Jal'den." He smiled sadly beneath his hood. His brief time with Rej'amin had left him with many cherished memories. "You and I are not so different. Sal'zar's help will prove invaluable, if I haven't angered you into abandoning this cause."

Jal'den chuckled hollowly. "You haven't, Commander, though it was a very near thing."

"I had to be certain, Jal'den."

Jal'den folded his arms and tilted his head to one side. "I see that now. I thank you for understanding *us*. My father disowned me when we made our request. Thankfully, mother's word was the only one that carried any weight. There are few times I have been as grateful the women rule our people as I was on that day." He sighed. "I pray with each dawn we will both survive this war, Commander. Fate seems determined to drive us apart at every turn. If we live to see the end, we will make a life together, those like my father be damned."

CHAPTER FORTY-FOUR

INTO THE DESERT

"It's little wonder why they call this place the Wasted Land," Lucas said wryly from his saddle.

Emra nodded in silent agreement as her thoughts drifted to their dwindling supply of water, the unrelenting sun that beat down from the cloudless sky above, and her fear they'd strayed from their intended path. There was nothing in the way of landmarks to guide them save for the position of the sun. She knew the general direction they must take in order to reach the Stronghold, but until the landscape began to change into sandy desert, she could not be certain they were on the right track.

It had taken three days to cross the mountains, following the trek commonly referred to as the Wizard's Path. It passed beneath the feet of Nuarno Peak, and she'd shuddered upon glimpsing the dark entrance to Stonewall Hall. An unfamiliar sensation had crawled along her spine as they rode by, as though she'd been to the place before. She'd shaken it off, and by the time the mountain disappeared from sight, the sensation had fled. It was preposterous at its heart; she'd never traveled farther east than Stone Hill prior to the king's latest missive.

They'd traveled another two days through the Wasted Land, taking a southeasterly route that she believed would lead them to the Desert of Snow and the Stronghold. Lucas did not question her decision, though he'd quickly become surly from the heat. They both sported sunburns, hers more severe than his; Lucas had been graced with slightly darker features.

"Em, I'm not blind—in spite of the gods-damned sun's attempt at making me so," Lucas stated after a moment. "Something's on your mind. Speak."

She opened her mouth, thought better of burdening him with her uncertainties, then shook her head stubbornly. She fixed her gaze on the horizon line and the seemingly endless expanse of cracked, arid soil that spread before them. The landscape was broken only by the occasional scrubby bush or gnarled tree that clung desperately to life in spite of the harsh environment's best efforts to eradicate them.

"Fine, I'll make a guess as to why you've fallen silent and taken to brooding." He flashed a grin. "First, we're low on water. I know as well as you what that implies. Second, there's no true means of navigating this gods-forsaken wasteland, and you're worried we're off track. Am I nearing the mark yet?"

"How can you be so cavalier about this, Luke?" Her voice cracked to reveal the depth of her fear.

He chuckled. "I share your concerns, Em, but there's little we can do now that we've come so far. We'll continue on this path and find the Stronghold, or we won't. Turning back will only make our situation worse."

"And pushing forward if we've gone the wrong way isn't any better, Luke." She sighed, her despair and sense of helplessness captured in the exhalation.

"Em," he said seriously, "I was with you during navigational exercises. You came out on top of every trial—even dour old Ser Kaplan was impressed. If anyone can lead us through this barren landscape, it is you. I suspect it's why His Majesty sent *you* on this mission. It wasn't because you were the knight nearest to the mountains."

She shrugged, unconvinced. "Navigational training was twelve years ago, Luke. I've had little need of it since."

"And I don't believe you've forgotten it," he replied as his grin resurfaced.

Fyrmane huffed in agreement. She rolled her eyes. Her bay always seemed to side with Lucas. Whether or not he understood their conversation, the horse's timing did not seem to be mere coincidence.

She drew a breath and resigned herself to another long day, withering in the saddle beneath the sun's intense glare. "We'll continue as we are. I hope you're not mistaken, Luke."

"It appears as though I was right," Lucas stated smugly several hours later.

The scorched earth that marked the Wasted Land had begun to disappear beneath a layer of pristine, white sand that glimmered in the afternoon light much like freshly fallen snow. If the temperature hadn't been so infernally hot, she might have believed they were indeed traveling across a winter plain in the northern reaches of Balotica. Strange, thorny plants grew up from the sands, some adorned inexplicably with delicate yellow flowers, at odds with the flora's prickly nature. Beetles and small lizards darted across their path at remarkable speed. After three days of traversing the Wasted Land, Emra found it heartening to see signs of life once more.

"If the maps I studied are correct, the Stronghold won't be far," she replied. She ignored Lucas' knowing smirk.

"Then I'll plan to be sleeping in a proper bed tonight." Lucas grinned. "That is…Do you suppose they sleep on beds, Em? They're not built like us."

"As I understand it, they have accommodations for humans," she replied with a laugh. "Merchants travel to the Stronghold often enough, after all."

"What's that?" Lucas pointed suddenly ahead.

She shielded her gaze from the sun but was still forced to squint her eyes due to the glare from the sand below. After a moment, the object Lucas indicated swam into focus through the heat shimmer. It appeared to be a large rock, but on closer inspection, she realized it was pyramidal in shape, an unnatural form. She grinned; she recognized it from her days spent studying the navigational markers of other races. Perhaps twelve years wasn't so long ago, after all.

"It's a marker. We're on the right path."

"I won't say I've told you so, but…" Lucas trailed off with a snicker.

She swatted at his shoulder playfully, and he nudged his dapple gray out of striking range, laughing heartily.

342

"Em, I knew you'd see us through safely," he said through his laughter.

As they neared the marker, Emra discerned writing etched into its surface. The top half of the pyramid was written in the common tongue, while the lower half was in a flowing script she did not recognize. The message was brief and directed the weary traveler to continue southeast for another mile.

Elated, she flashed another grin at Lucas. Somehow, she'd seen them across the Gray Mountains, through the Wasted Land, and into the Desert of Snow unerringly. She'd always believed she had a solid sense of direction, but it had never been put to a real test. That she had succeeded was surreal, an unbelievable feat she struggled to comprehend. Her navigation had little to do with her military training, but she feared Lucas' reaction if she confided that she'd been guided strongly by intuition. It was best to leave that detail out of their conversation.

"We're nearly there!" Lucas exclaimed. "What's one more mile after the scores we've already traveled?" He shot her a sidelong glance, mischief in his eyes. "Fancy a race, Em?"

She dug her heels into Fyrmane's flank without a word. Her bay lunged forward with a whinny and passed Lucas on his gray. He reacted swiftly; within moments, the two horses were galloping through the sand, neck-to-neck. Emra laughed gleefully, even as Lucas pulled ahead. She'd known Fyrmane couldn't keep up with the gray for long, though his own competitive streak drove him onward at a pace that surprised even her. For a few moments as she sped across the desert, her cares fled and she reveled in the joy of the race, the thrill of the wind as it whipped through her hair.

A glimmer appeared in the distance not long after they'd begun. It grew larger and brighter as they neared its source, but only when they were close enough to see individuals on patrol did she realize it was sunlight reflecting from a low, domed surface, half-buried in the sand. She reined in Fyrmane as several armored Scorpion Men began to move in their direction. Lucas, a short distance ahead of her, did the same. She nudged Fyrmane forward until he was abreast of Lucas' gray.

"They're more intimidating than I'd anticipated," Lucas whispered, though the sentries were too far away to overhear.

"They're Blademon's people, Luke. What were you expecting?"

She'd meant it as a jest, but her voice wavered to betray her nerves. She knew little of the people she'd been sent to negotiate with, and they were an imposing force. The men stood nearly as tall as Fyrmane, the women slightly less so. All wore plate mail or boiled leather, and each carried a weapon. Those with bows stood back from the others, arrows nocked with the anticipation of trouble.

"Em, I hope the king hasn't made a grave mistake by sending us here."

She nodded stiffly in agreement as her heart fluttered rapidly in her chest. The Scorpion Men weren't known to be hostile, but they certainly did not appear friendly. They came to a halt a dozen paces from the Baloticans, and a pair near the center began to confer in low tones. She watched them, fearful they would be taken prisoner or turned away. Neither scenario appealed to her.

"Gods, Em…" Lucas looked down, and she realized his hands were shaking.

"Luke, I'll speak with them when the time comes." The prospect filled her with dread, but it was her duty as the knight in command.

It seemed an eternity before the shorter of the two began to make his way toward them alone. A two-handed battle axe was slung across his back, and to her relief he did not reach for the weapon as he approached. Deep blue eyes set in an attractive face met hers, and he nodded in greeting to each of them. His expression was unreadable, and she found herself watching his hands carefully for any sign he meant to attack. They remained at his sides, though she realized the scorpion's tail coiled behind him would prove just as deadly a weapon.

"Forgive my people for appearing mistrustful, but the Murkor have grown hostile. Why have you come here?"

She swallowed her confusion. She did not know who or what he referred to as Murkor, but decided it wasn't important. She introduced herself and Lucas, then proceeded to inform him of the king's request. While she spoke, she noticed the other Scorpion Men began to relax their stances, and the archers released their draw.

Their host remained silent for some time after she finished, his expression troubled. Finally, he said, "This matter must be brought before the Warleader. Follow me." He glanced over his shoulder to ensure they complied and said, "My name is Vardak. The blond lout making his way toward us is my brother."

As the brother approached, Emra noted their similarities. Vardak was slightly shorter but carried himself with an aura of self-assurance his brother seemed to lack.

"I'm Patak," the other told them with a ready smile. His eyes were the same deep blue as Vardak's, though they sparked with mischief. Emra was put immediately at ease by his demeanor.

"I'm afraid we don't have stables for your mounts," Patak continued. "The merchants usually hobble their horses in the shade of their wagons, but after the attack, they decided to return home."

"You were attacked?" she asked.

"A few weeks past," Patak replied. He received a warning look from his brother, but he either ignored it or was oblivious. "It was the Murkor, as Vardak said."

"What are Murkor?" Lucas asked.

Patak laughed good-naturedly. "The people you call 'hooded ones'. They are Murkor."

"There is some shade to the north side of the entrance," Vardak cut in. "You can leave the horses there."

She nodded her thanks and eased Fyrmane in the indicated direction. The king had been wise enough to understand the Scorpion Men knew of their foe, but Patak's admission of an attack on the Stronghold concerned her. The Scorpion Men would not leave their home vulnerable to the enemy and travel leagues across the wasteland simply to help a human kingdom. She began to doubt her return to Balotica would be lauded as a success.

"They didn't kill us outright, so I'll consider that a minor victory," Lucas said as he dismounted. "Gods, I didn't realize they'd be so *tall*. Do you think the stories are true, Em? That they were once…human?"

She shrugged and began to untie her saddlebags. "The stories claim it's true. Regardless of how they came about, it was nearly a thousand years ago."

"And I still wouldn't wish to be on the wrong side of one of their blades." Lucas shook his head. "Or their stingers. Come on, Em. I don't want to keep them waiting."

She slung the bags over her shoulder and patted Fyrmane's nose. "Behave yourself," she ordered, only to receive an indignant snort in return.

"Vardak mentioned speaking to a Warleader," Lucas continued nervously as they made their way toward the Stronghold's entrance. "Who do you suppose that is?"

"We're about to find out, Luke. Let's hope he's as reasonable as this pair seems to be."

CHAPTER FORTY-FIVE

THE NEXT JOURNEY

Vardak left Patak at the entrance to wait for the humans while he went inside to inform Sevic of their arrival. He was troubled by their news but relieved that they knew where the Murkor army had gone. It was an opportunity he meant to seize; with the army away from the caverns, they had a greater chance of freeing Travin and the others without further bloodshed.

He located Sevic in his public quarters near the training hall. Vardak was forced to wait near the door until Sevic finished his conversation with one of their patrol leaders, a woman whom Vardak recognized but could not recall her name. She nodded to him as she departed, and Sevic waved him inside.

"Vardak, I wasn't expecting you until later."

"I know, sir, but this is important."

Sevic listened thoughtfully as Vardak described the new arrivals and their king's request for aid. He'd nearly finished by the time Patak arrived with the humans and paused to introduce the pair to the Warleader. Sevic glanced at Lucas briefly, but his attention was fixed upon Emra.

"A knight, by the look of that shield on your back."

"Yes, sir."

She was nervous, but Vardak supposed her reaction was natural. It was rare for Baloticans of any sort to undertake the long journey to the Stronghold from their homeland, and she'd been dispatched out of sheer desperation. He sympathized with her plight but knew Sevic's stance on the situation. The defense of the Stronghold was priority, followed by the rescue of the Murkor

347

prisoners. He doubted Sevic would lend Emra's people the aid they sought.

"Vardak has apprised me of your situation," Sevic continued. "We've had our own dealings with the Murkor of late, and I'm afraid I cannot spare the forces your king seeks. I am sorry, Emra, but my people must come first."

She was crestfallen, though she made a valiant attempt to hide it. "I understand."

"Gods, there must be something you can do!" Lucas interrupted, his tone heated. "We risked our lives in coming here—"

Sevic held up one hand for silence. "I'm well aware of the toll such a journey takes. I said only I cannot spare the forces your king seeks. I did not say I would sit idly by and do nothing." He gestured at Vardak. "Tell them of your plan to save our prisoners. If they are willing to assist in this endeavor, I will allow you to accompany them into Balotica *after* your mission is complete."

Vardak bristled at the notion of being used as a bargaining chip between his people and the humans, but he kept his misgivings to himself. He'd failed to obtain the Warleader's approval for his rescue mission the previous evening. Now Sevic seemed to be considering it in exchange for Vardak's unspoken obedience. He'd managed to free himself of the Immortals' grasp, only to find himself in a similar situation with Sevic. It was infuriating, but there was little he could do.

"The news of the Murkor attack in Balotica provides us with a short window of opportunity in which to negotiate the release of our prisoners," Vardak informed them. "The Murkor aren't typically hostile. I believe I can negotiate with them and have our people returned without further bloodshed. Sevic has allowed Patak to accompany myself and three others—they are visitors, like yourselves."

"I believe I understand," Emra replied slowly. "We help you with this matter, and then you will accompany us."

"I don't see how two Scorpion Men will turn the tide of battle," Lucas muttered darkly.

Behind them, Patak chuckled from his position in the doorway. "You know little of our people and less of my brother."

"That I am willing to allow Vardak to accompany you is a boon in itself." Sevic's impassive stare met Lucas', and the human quickly looked away. "Vardak was trained by Blademon. He is a greater asset to your cause than you realize. I am willing to allow Patak to accompany you as well, though he requires more time to heal from his recent injury. I cannot spare anyone else."

Vardak refused to meet the others' gazes. He would have preferred to keep his training a secret from the humans, to tell them of it in his own time, as he'd done with Coreyaless.

"Thank you," Emra said. "Lucas may not agree, but you have done us a great honor. I doubt my own king would send his greatest champion along with a pair of strangers."

"If not for Vardak's insistence on this matter with our prisoners, I would not send him at all," Sevic replied. "Be certain to thank the gods for his innate stubbornness, or you'd be leaving here alone."

Vardak resisted the urge to contradict Sevic. It was not his place to do so, not when in the presence of human strangers, but he could not keep his frustration from seeping into his expression. He was weary of being played and deployed as one would a piece on a chessboard.

"We'll gather our supplies this afternoon and depart in the morning," Vardak told him icily. "If you have further need of me, I'll be…somewhere."

He pushed past the humans and made his way into the corridor beyond, unable to contain his anger any longer. Patak scurried away from the door and caught up to him as he reached the wide entrance to the training hall.

"Vardak—"

He shook his head and turned away. He didn't want to discuss Sevic's treatment of him, didn't want to hear his brother's sympathy. He simply wished to be left alone, to work out his rage in the only way he knew how: sparring.

"Fucking gods, Vardak, I understand why you're angry. Vent your rage on me. I'm at least prepared for it." Patak grinned. "I'd feel sorry for any of the poor bastards in here who'd agree to a sparring match with you today."

349

"No, you're—"

"Listen, brother," Patak cut him off in a warning tone. "I may taunt you and tease you to no end, but that's part of my role. I'm not jesting with you now. My injury is healing—better than I'd expected, since your Airess friend had a look at, I might add. You'll annihilate anyone who challenges you today without mercy, and I'd be lying if I said I didn't need the practice."

Patak drew him into the room and selected a heavy practice sword for himself from the array of blunted weapons that hung upon the wall. Vardak scowled but reluctantly chose a two-handed sword for himself. He was as deadly with the sword as he was with his axe. Patak knew it, yet he wouldn't be persuaded to back down. Vardak was keenly aware of the determination in his brother's eyes.

"You're certain of this, Patak?"

"I would not have suggested it otherwise." Patak hefted a shield from the wall and quickly strapped it to his arm. "I don't believe I've had the honor of a match with you since Blademon's announcement."

"I won't hold back."

"I wouldn't expect you to."

Patak grinned and led him to an open space across the room. There were several dozen other pairs scattered throughout the training hall, and most paid them little notice. Vardak hoped it would remain that way. He was in no temper for an audience, and he meant to best Patak handily at least once before they were through. His elder brother had done the same to him countless times before he'd been chosen by Blademon. It was past time to turn the tide.

Patak took up an offensive stance, and Vardak knew immediately what his brother intended. It was the same maneuver Blademon had drilled him on weeks ago, during the same fateful afternoon the gods had decided to intervene in his life. It was little wonder Patak had opted for a sword and shield; he meant to strike Vardak's only perceived weakness. Vardak braced himself. He would prove his brother wrong and show him the error of comparing his own skill to that of the war god's. Patak was not Blademon.

He waited until the last moment, then sidestepped as Patak swung his sword. He brought his own blade up at the same moment, and the clang of metal reverberated through the hall as the strike was blocked. Vardak slid his blade free as Patak swung the shield toward him, intent on hitting his mark. Vardak's sword crashed into the shield with a loud crack, and he shoved Patak backward with his full strength. That he'd successfully performed the maneuver didn't register in his mind as he prepared for the next attack.

Patak stumbled, one eyebrow lifted in surprise. He quickly regained his footing and charged once more. Vardak was ready. This time, he did not wait for his brother's strike but instead rushed forward to meet him head-on.

As their blades met a second time, Patak let out a growl. "You've grown stronger."

Vardak parried, once, twice. In spite of his injury, Patak continued his onslaught, but it would not be enough to grant him the victory he craved. Unlike his brother, Vardak was patient. He continued to parry Patak's blows, a grim smile slowly spreading across his face. It was only a matter of time before his brother grew weary of the seemingly even match and attempted something reckless. It was Patak's way.

"Enjoying yourself, brother?" Patak asked breathlessly as their blades collided again.

"It's not every day I have the opportunity to best you." Vardak shoved Patak backward and bore down on him when Patak faltered.

"I'm not done yet."

Patak blocked the blow with his shield but failed to protect his sword arm. Vardak pounced on the opportunity. He shifted and hit Patak's arm hard enough to cause his brother to yelp in pain. Patak dropped his sword and backed away, his breathing heavy.

"I yield."

Vardak eyed him for a moment, concern replacing his previous ire. He'd anticipated Patak would attempt a reckless maneuver, but it had never come. Perhaps he'd finally learned the importance of patience, or perhaps Vardak had pushed him too hard. A twinge of guilt twisted his gut as he realized it was likely Patak's injury had decided the battle and not his own skill.

"By the gods, that was impressive to watch."

351

Vardak looked away from his brother to find the humans were standing nearby. Lucas' face was split by a grin, while Emra's expression was pensive. Lucas strode forward, his eyes alight with enthusiasm.

"Vardak could have ended that battle much sooner had he wanted to," Patak groused. "I'm aware you were merely toying with me, little brother."

"Perhaps you'd give me the honor of a sparring match during our travels," Lucas continued. "I've never witnessed a match like that. You're both incredibly skilled."

"We train at arms from the time we can walk," Vardak replied with a shrug.

"That is Vardak's attempt at humility." Patak smirked. "I'd say you're in better spirits, too, little brother. We ought to find our way to the market before the vendors close shop for the night, to supply ourselves as you told Sevic we'd do."

They returned the practice arms and made their way into the corridor, the two humans following in their wake. Patak began to roll his left shoulder while he muttered under his breath. It confirmed Vardak's suspicion; he'd pushed Patak too far and aggravated his injury.

"Patak, I'm—"

Patak snorted. "I'm fine. If you'd paid any attention to me the past few days, you'd know the injury I took from the Murkor attack was on my *right* side. The shoulder was entirely of your doing."

Vardak sighed; Patak's words failed to assuage his guilt. "I should not have taken my frustration with Sevic out on you."

Behind him, Emra released a heavy sigh. When he glanced over his shoulder, her gaze was fixed firmly on the floor. Lucas appeared uncomfortable. He hadn't considered how his words might be taken by the humans and shook his head in dismay.

"To be clear," he said slowly, "I am not angry with your arrival here. In fact, it was the only reason Sevic has granted us leave to negotiate with the Murkor for our prisoners."

"Vardak's right," Patak agreed. "Sevic meant to send us directly to Dar Daelad—"

Vardak elbowed his brother and shot him a glare. Their trip to Dar Daelad was meant to be secret, as was the reason behind it. The fewer who knew the Moon's Eye was in Vardak's possession, the safer the relic would remain.

"Gods-fucking-damn it, Vardak. *That's* where the real injury lies," Patak growled through clenched teeth. "*Shit.*"

"Learn to watch your tongue," he snapped in a low tone.

"Why Dar Daelad?" Emra asked, as though she hadn't witnessed their exchange.

"It's not important," Patak replied hastily.

"If we're to believe you're going to help us, I'd rather not be lied to." Emra's voice was like steel.

Vardak glowered at his brother and said, "We'll discuss this after we're away from the Stronghold. Sevic's orders."

It wasn't strictly true, but the humans did not need to know that. It was simpler to blame the need for secrecy on the Warleader, particularly after his refusal to assist Travin and the others. It would remain a sore spot with Vardak for some time.

"I suppose that's the best we can ask for," Emra replied wearily. "While the three of you procure supplies, I'll look after the horses."

She strode away, her movements stiff with unconcealed anger.

Lucas waited until she was out of earshot before he said, "You certainly know how to get under Em's skin."

"I don't break my word," Vardak replied evenly. "I'll explain on the morrow."

"You'll meet the others, as well," Patak added. "I have to say, we'll be an odd lot."

Vardak managed a faint smile at his brother's words. An odd lot, indeed. Tomorrow they'd embark on the next leg of his journey; two Scorpion men, a pair of Airess, two humans, and a Felene. He hoped to wash his hands of the gods-forsaken relic that hung from his neck, to be done with foul memory of the sacrifice required in order to obtain it. First, however, there was the matter of Travin and the other Murkor prisoners.

He would pray for their success and hope none of the gods decided to further interfere with his plans. He was certain his hope was futile; Blademon would no doubt make another appearance, and Flariel's threat continued to loom over him. Perhaps if he survived the war, they'd finally allow him to forge his own destiny.

The story continues in The Talisman of Delucha.

THANK YOU FOR READING THE MOON'S EYE!

If you enjoyed reading this book, please consider leaving a review. I hope you will continue the saga in book two of the series, The Talisman of Delucha.

Information about release dates will be posted on my website (www.ajcalvin.net), as well as shared via my newsletter. If interested, you can subscribe by visiting my website and clicking on the "Newsletter" tab.

ACKNOWLEDGMENTS

This project was a long time in the making. I want to thank my family for their support and understanding as I launch my writing career—and my husband, especially. I spent countless hours reworking this manuscript and I'll admit I was often scarce while immersed in this project. I'm grateful they understood my need for time to myself in order to complete it.

I'd like to mention the incredible Jamie Noble, whose artwork is featured on the cover. Working with him was a pleasure and I'm not sure anyone else could have captured my vision as well as he has. He's also created the cover art for books two and three in this series.

And a very big thank you to Sheena Sampsel, who despite a heavy workload otherwise, took the time to edit the manuscript. If you're reading this, you'll understand how long and complex this book is, and what an undertaking it would have been.

And last but not least, thank you to all of my readers. Without you, none of this would be worthwhile.

COMING SUMMER/FALL 2022:

THE TALISMAN OF DELUCHA
The Relics of War: Book Two

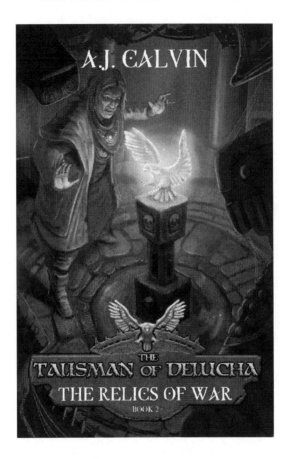

Ravin is an anomaly amongst those who use magic. He refuses to join the Council of Auras and tie his fate to the wizards, and long ago escaped a terrible fate amongst the Enlightened, called the Shadow Council by some. His escape gave him freedom few others with his power enjoy, and he means to keep it, no matter the cost.

Serving as an advisor to the Deluchan queen, Ravin learns a powerful relic is kept deep within the catacombs below the palace. War is on Delucha's doorstep, brought about by none other than the council he fled from and their Soulless leaders. He resolves to retrieve the relic in order to combat the imminent threat, but collecting the talisman of Delucha is not without its own danger.

As the Soulless' army prepares to besiege the Deluchan capitol, Ravin makes one final, desperate attempt to secure the talisman. The kingdom's survival depends on his success, but time is not on his side.

ABOUT THE AUTHOR

A.J. Calvin is a science fiction/fantasy novelist hailing from Loveland, Colorado. By day, she works as a microbiologist, but in her free time she writes. She lives with her husband, their cat, Magic, and a fairly large salt water aquarium.

When she is not working or writing, she enjoys scuba diving, hiking, and playing video games.

For more information on the author and news about her writing, please visit her website at www.ajcalvin.net.

Made in the USA
Middletown, DE
11 January 2022

58329252R00220